G. B. S

(1890-1973) was christened Gla[...] [...]
wyn' as her second name), th[...] [...]
Elizabeth Stern. The family liv[...] [...]
River diamond smash in which [...] [...]
of fourteen to twenty five, G. B. Stern lived in a se[...]
boarding houses and furnished flats. She attended Notting Hill High
School until at sixteen, she travelled with her parents to Germany
and Switzerland and attended schools there. She then spent two
years at the Academy of Dramatic Art. G. B. Stern wrote her first
play at the age of seven and her first novel *Pantomime* was published
in 1914. Five years later she married a New Zealander, Geoffrey
Lisle Holdsworth, but they soon divorced.

The appearance of *Twos and Threes* in 1916 brought G. B. Stern
critical attention, but her most substantial and popular achievement
was the series of novels based on her own family circle. The first of
these, *Tents of Israel* (1924, published by Virago as *The Matriarch*),
was followed by *A Deputy Was King* (1926), *Mosaic* (1930), *Shining
and Free* (1935) and *The Young Matriarch* (1942). In 1929 Mrs
Patrick Campbell starred as 'the Matriarch' in the stage version,
co-written with Frank Vosper, and in 1932 the first three volumes
were published as *The Rakonitz Chronicles*.

G. B. Stern's friends – who called her 'Peter' – included Noel
Coward (with whom she selected the songs for *Cavalcade*), John van
Druten, Rebecca West, Somerset Maugham and Sheila Kaye-Smith
(with whom she wrote two books about Jane Austen). She continued
to travel throughout her life: she spent five years in Italy and lived in
New York, Hollywood, France, as well as Cornwall and London
(where her home was bombed during the Second World War). In
1947 G. B. Stern converted to Catholicism, and wrote of this in *All in
Good Time* (1954). She died at the age of eight-three.

G. B. Stern's other work includes over forty novels, several plays,
volumes of short stories, and a book about Robert Louis Stevenson,
in addition to five discursive and semi-autobiographical works.

Virago's publication of *Mosaic* is forthcoming.

VIRAGO
MODERN
CLASSIC

NUMBER
301

G. B STERN

A DEPUTY
WAS KING

WITH A NEW INTRODUCTION BY
JULIA NEUBERGER

Published by VIRAGO PRESS Limited 1988
20-23 Mandela Street, Camden Town, London NW1 0HQ

First published in Great Britain by Chapman & Hall 1926
Copyright G. B. Stern 1926
Introduction Copyright © Julia Neuberger 1988

British Library Cataloguing in Publication Data

Stern, G.B. (Gladys Bronwyn), 1890-1973
A deputy was kind.—(Virago modern classic)
I. Title II. Series
823'.912[F]
ISBN   0-86068-523-3

Printed in Finland by Werner Södersrtröm Oy

INTRODUCTION

G.B. Stern dictated all her novels. She wrote of that activity: "I dictate all my books, normally lying back in a chair and watching the pictures evolve before me. If I wrote them myself, I know I should always be stopping to draw patterns. As it is, when I get the manuscript from my secretary I go to work on it and cover it with the most beautiful signs and symbols. Baroque, I should call them. I really ought to have been a wallpaper designer."

Her secretaries partly adored her and were partly driven mad by her. One, Freda Bromhead, having worked for her in the twenties, was called back in extremis when G.B. Stern was in a nursing home where the cure for her acute septicaemia was total starvation. The regime nearly reduced her to death and friends, Rebecca West amongst them, devised a plot to rescue her from this strange place at midnight. But Freda refused to be drawn in and her role as secretary ended again.

The vividness of the "Rakonitz Chronicles" comes in part from G.B. Stern's own life and that of her family, the clan of the Rakonitzes, Czelovars and Bettelheims. She knew as a child the incredible intensity, the constant talk, the insistence on the proprieties, the thick accents. And she knew the food—the crème-düten, the goulasch, the apfelstrudel, that made an occasion festive.

The first novel was called *Tents of Israel* when originally published in England, and retitled *The Matriarch* for American publication and for the later play. That title illustrates most clearly the content of the novel, but it loses some of G.B. Stern's feelings about her Jewishness, which the original title and that of the second volume, maintain. The inscriptions in the frontispiece of *A Deputy Was King*, taken from the First Book of Kings, reveal all:

I saw all Israel scattered upon the hills, as sheep that have not a shepherd: and the Lord said, These have no master: let them return every man to his house in peace. (I Kings 22:17)

Nothing could be more appropriate as a pointer to the first novel where the men are pale, shadowy figures, where, come the collapse of the gem industry, they die or fall into disarray. The women keep things going; women are the support of the family. They have no master, and they return home. But then the original Matriarch, Anastasia, has a stroke. No longer able to control the family, she must needs—unwillingly—surrender control to her granddaugher Toni, herself the eldest child of the eldest child, of the eldest child. And so the new Matriarch takes control, but much less lightly. It is all a far greater struggle. It comes less naturally, though with equal love. But there is poverty and responsibility, the gritting of teeth and few crême-düten. This is the serious life, and hence the even more appropriate title of the second volume of the "Chronicles": "There was then no king in Edom: a deputy was king." (I Kings 22-47) Toni is indeed a deputy, without the easy charm and unquestionable and unquestioning authority of the original Matriarch.

But the novels also convey G.B. Stern's ambivalence about her ancestry. She hated the term Jew and described herself as having friends who were all "goyem" (it should be Goyim, meaning "nations", or in this precise usage, non-Jews). She regarded the term Israelite as nobler, and described herself as having "no anti-Israelite prejudices". But in her mind, there was a world of difference between the two: "A Jew can cringe, an Israelite never." Hence the title *Tents of Israel*, for there was pride involved, pride in her own family, pride in their Jewishness (which she would no doubt have described as their Israelitishness), and pride in their cosmopolitan, exotic, flamboyant richness which she conveys so well.

This pride, though, was juxtaposed with her ambivalence about being Jewish, which manifests itself in the contrast G.B.

Stern draws between Anastasia and her gentile daughters-in-law and grandchildren but is most apparent in this second volume of the trilogy. For Toni marries Giles Goddard, a county farmer's son with independent means. They marry in a registry office, without any ceremony. Much of that is in order to defeat the family. Toni is marrying to get away from them—and from the tribe too. Her cousin Val is surprised, almost disapproves, and then reflects:

theirs was actually the first unorthodox generation. The first generation, totally irreligious, hardly knowing what the inside of a synagogue looked like, nor even, alternatively, the inside of a church. The first generation which was the result of intermarriage between Israelite and Gentile; the first generation to throw away as valueless the traditions of the tribe and the obligations of the family.

So the family is carefully screened from Giles. Toni doesn't imagine that he could want "a family like the first eight chapters from Chronicles, who would expect to be asked to the wedding, and to the house-warming, and to the Baronit-zutahs [sic.] of many sons".

Much more surprising on the theme of race is the character of cousin Helen Czelovar who reappears from volume one. A stylish but still very Jewish looking young woman, her appearance has always been a family joke because her father Raoul married the Dean's daughter, and their other children look extraordinarily un-Jewish. Helen is the throwback. "However, as I was born the most blatant type of Whitechapel Yidd, I have to confine myself to sober blacks and whites . . ." That same Helen remarks about another cousin, Eileen Moss, that she has started an atelier:

"Not common photographs, but portrait studies; rather impressionistic! She started off on Basil Courtland—you know, little Benny Kohlbach that was, before the war! And by a sort of happy accident, she got him looming out of a fog, looking like a Christian! She was bothered about it, at first; but Benny was simply delighted; sent all his friends there. Now Eileen's made a big thing out of subduing—subjewing her clients!"

So much for one ambivalence. The other, well demonstrated

in the first volume too, concerns men. G.B. Stern had herself been disappointed by men, including—perhaps especially—Geoffrey Holdsworth whom she married and divorced. Toni has no doubts on the subject: "Men let you down! All the Rakonitz men, the men of the family, had been weak and charming, and had let their women down." This is so clearly stated at various points throughout the trilogy, that Toni's impetuous flight into an all-male environment is all the more surprising. At the beginning of this book, she sees a group of men walking towards her, having dreamed of such an event a few minutes earlier. One of them turns out to be rich, young, attractive and unattached, and she marries him. There are no women in this family. The mother is dead, and there is the father, the engaging Jimmy, and two brothers, one of whom has a wife who has run away, leaving him—of course—with two sons. No women! What that conveys about Toni's own experience of all the dependent women, dependent upon her business acumen, is revealing. But even more startling is what it apparently reveals about the author, who always lurks, more or less comfortably, in the background. Certainly, all G.B. Stern's friends, relations and acquaintances who have been kind enough to provide me with information recall her as someone whose friends were almost entirely women, with the exception of some gay men. They also recall that after her disastrous marriage she did not allow her ex-husband to be spoken of in her presence. This may, however, betray another complication in her own background. For before she married "her beautiful Geoffrey Holdsworth" (as described by Rebecca West in a postcard to Sylvia Lynd), her mother had tried to push her into marriage with a suitable Jewish young man. Rebecca West once more: "Miss Stern was silent because she is being worried into marriage with a corpulent and moneyed Jew by her mother." Was he one of the clan? Was this the source of the story later in this volume, held over from the last, of Richard Moss and Jeanne-Marie, with roles reversed? Or does that story with its ring of truth, come from some other family event? Whatever, G.B. Stern's opinion of men was low, although Giles Goddard, unlike most of her male characters, has a likeable presence.

Once Giles and Toni are married, their lives become paradies of those bright young things of the twenties. But first comes their honeymoon in Venice (where else?) and the trip in the gondola with Toni pretending to be the little wife. At last she has got away, from family, Jews, business, financial worries, the female sphere. In her new world of the masculine and unemotional English, the little woman doesn't have her head bothered with horrible bills. Toni hands them over to Giles, though not entirely seriously, or entirely easily. Understanding men proves all too difficult. She is shocked to discover that Giles has been kissing her employee Aimée (Amy in real life as we are told with revealing snobbishness), and cannot accept it. Nor can Giles come to terms with the fuss she makes. There is a language barrier. He would not, of course he would not, kiss her friends. But shop girls are somehow different, and they expect it and find it fun. Toni cannot understand.

Nevertheless Toni has an urge to become a mother. The Matriarch in her will out. And so they have children, in rapid succession. But Toni is less than good as a mother and still plays the little woman. In one instance Giles is allowed to create financial havoc because she must not show that she understands or can cope. If she does, the game is over, and she will have to re-enter the real grown-up world of responsibilities, which she left so very deliberately on her marriage. In a curiously sarcastic scene for G.B. Stern, Toni is depicted handing over the bills:

"My dear little girl," Giles's voice swelled and rounded, as he deliberately burlesqued the pompous city husband; for he guessed that Toni wanted her bills paid; and guessed that it might be easier for her to ask this favour of him, as a figure of exaggerated comedy, than if he remained Giles ... "My dear little girl, you'd better let your great, big, strong, bull-and-bear man know the worst; he will then go into the city and make lots of money; become a Director or a Preferential Dividend Holder" ...

"Oh! Thankyou, Giles. You *are* so good to me. I don't know what I should do without you."

Then enters long-lost cousin Loraine, a parody of Toni herself. She makes Toni aware of how she must appear in others' eyes, and Toni longs for her departure "back to Spain or to Ireland or to Lower Beckenham—wherever it was that she really came from". That is not to be, and the plot takes on an unexpected twist. Yet Loraine is never quite accepted as family, and when she asks, after the Matriarch's deaith, for two family portraits nobody else wants, she is viewed with horror by the other women of her generation. Loraine is going too far. That reaction provokes her into doing just that. She reproaches Toni for a neglected responsibility and Toni collapses, almost cowering, in one of G.B. Stern's finest scenes. In amongst it all there is a grain of her own life, the responsibility she felt, as she became rich, for her own family who fell on hard times. And she describes brilliantly the sense that Toni always has of responsibility for the whole family, at all times, whether she knows the individuals or not, whether they have any legitimate claim on her or not. This is the pan-European Jewish family without a doubt, the family where everyone feels that they have a right to stay with the others, to be supported by the others if necessary, and to be rescued by the others where appropriate, without gratitude. It was the way families were supposed to behave. When Toni escapes into Giles' non-family, his non-Jewish arms, she finds that, whilst she thinks she has been dispensing matriarchal support, she has not done so properly. Grieving, she begins to think again and reassert her personality—in her marriage, in her business and in the family.

The next series of scenes, for much of this is in the nature of an unfolding physical drama, take place in Italy. The characters are different. Giles is there, but Aunt Elsa takes the stage, the old generation is back. She comes to the fore, her accent ever present. G.B. Stern's handling of Mittel-European is little short of brilliant. Elsa does not emerge as a clown, yet her language is bizarre in the extreme, and some of her sentiments banal: "What I always say is, everyssing or nossing," or "And zen she runs about with a vase full of blooms and moch too full of water, and puts it in ze middle of the table." The accent is not consistent, but it works. It sounds plausible. It certainly reminded me constantly of my various Mittel-European great-aunts, with their mixture of strong accents and quaint phrases, followed by sophisticated concepts and an almost accentless voice.

Richard Marcus, the anglicised cousin, the one who got away and went to farm, comes to stay. He hears it all—Italy, with the chatter of Italian staff, of Aunt Elsa, Val, Loraine, Giles. It is all so noisy. Under his breath, at the back of his mind, he thinks "Foreigners!" He has married a nice English girl, with a fine seat on a horse. Yet he longs for the food, one of the classic motifs of the trilogy. "For he and Molly and his sons ate proper food, joints and roly-poly and the like." So he yearns for "those ripping things like dumplings, only in a sort of rich gravy and stuffed with eggs". But he has to listen to Elsa and Loraine exchanging memories of Viennese cake-shops. "'Those sandwich at Demmel's—you went in there? The Hof-Konditorei, ach, delicious! And especially the Lachs—the smoked salmon.'" They think of nothing but food, these foreigners, and yet Richard is one of them, tempted by the mysterious spicing, the richness, of a Rakonitz meal.

G.B. Stern uses the emotions of food expertly. Later on, the young girl Queenie is upset. She cannot take the extraordinary high emotional pitch all the time. She needs more temperate climes. "Her moral digestion, having been fed almost entirely on cold mutton and rice pudding, was not equal to all this pâté de foie gras and truffles." G.B. Stern partly saw the world in terms of greed. Her loyal secretaries rarely described her as greedy, but she was always fat because she liked such things as cream, butter and eggs . . . She wrote about food specifically, too, and not only in her "Rakonitz Chronicles". In *The Epicure's Companion* (London, 1937), she wrote about the child as epicure and described chocolate cream bars from automatic machines as having a "peculiar dreamlike flavour". She used food to evoke conditions elegantly, with few words, such as in her account of Uncle Maximilian at the siege of Paris in 1870, who awed her with his laconic statement that he had fed almost entirely on rats and Marquis chocolate! This was in marked contrast to the description of her mother as "a tiny little bit of a rip" (was this perhaps Haidée of the trilogy?) who was surrounded by charming cosmopolitan gentlemen who kissed her hand, paid her compliments, and sent her boxes of—Marquis chocolates.

No surprise then that one of her treasured possessions was a letter from Max Beerbohm comparing the "full, rich milieu" of her "Rakonitz Chronicles" to soup,

thick turtle soup—of which one doesn't merely sip one's plateful to the end. Say, rather, a great lake of thick turtle soup in which one swims warmly at one's leisure, swallowing from time to time gratefully and without indigestion one of the lumps of green fat that float so prodigally on its surface.

A treasured food remark, kept in the knife-box, of course, and utterly within the Stern tradition.

A Deputy Was King is full of such food allusions. It is also a better structured novel than *The Matriarch*, with a tighter plot. Although there are irritating features—one being the slight changes in relationships from the previous volume, which make following the family tree almost impossible—the characterisation of those people who do appear is infinitely superior and there is no doubt that these are figures with whom G.B. Stern is familiar. To some extent she *is* Toni.

The pageant goes on, the tale continues. There was a rich tapestry unfolding before her eyes as G.B. Stern lay back and dictated to her secretaries. It was, in one way, the rich brocade curtain from the Paris exhibition of 1889, which G.B. Stern's Rakonitz uncle presented to the Matriarch, and which was passed on by her to G.B. Stern's mother, and draped over the piano when she was a child. There are real possessions, real food, real people here. But they move between history and back into fiction, spending most of the time comfortably between the two, not in fact historical, but entirely believable, and utterly absorbing.

Julia Neuberger, West Cork and London, 1987

TO

PETER BENSON

IN FRIENDSHIP AND WARM GRATITUDE

FOR THE IDEA HE GAVE ME

WHICH I HAVE USED

IN THIS BOOK

". . . I saw all Israel scattered upon the hills, as sheep that have not a shepherd: and the Lord said, These have no master: let them return every man to his house in peace."

1 KINGS xxii. 17.

"There was then no king in Edom: a deputy was king."

1 KINGS xxii. 47.

CONTENTS

A DEPUTY WAS KING

PART I

THE GOOD TIME

CHAPTER I

A SLIM girl in pale yellow, sitting beside a duck-pond in the full sunshine, her eyes screwed up with gay laughter at some mischievous thought which had just occurred to her, this was Toni Rakonitz as Giles first saw her. And, indeed, Toni *was* amused; five tall men were walking towards her, across the lawn of her cousin Richard's garden. Such lavish bounty was absurd, when she had so moderately asked for only one. For this was 1921, when the world seemed strangely empty and drained of all men. They had poured away, some abroad and into the colonies, perhaps; a great many had been killed; a great many were struggling with uncongenial work, crouching low down, and out of sight. Toni herself had been working hard now for two years, establishing her own dress-making business; this was her first real holiday, and it had proved, from this same lack of men, less a holiday than a complete rest. A rest, blessed in itself, was yet so very different; silent in all the songs that hum beneath the word holiday.

To-morrow she would be going back again to Hanover Street and the show-room, without really having had a good time. Sitting out there, alone, near the duck-pond, and stewing in the slow September warmth, Toni had first felt gilded all over ; and then, as the warmth and laziness had soaked in, she enjoyed a pleasant illusion of being a grape ripening in the vineyard : dust of powdery bloom outside, and within, a bursting sweetness. It was one way of spending a holiday afternoon, to be a grape, if you could not capture a lighter, vivider, more exciting way. And next, her thoughts drifting and darting, irrelevant as dragon-flies over water, she composed a delectable fairy-tale, that if she closed her eyes for a moment, and swiftly opened them again, she might see a man, not a business man, but a perfectly complete and conventional specimen, hero of a girl's good time, walking towards her across the grass. Childishly, Toni tried it ; shut her eyes . . . opened them again——. And this was why Giles, the first time he saw Toni, saw a laughing Toni. Because it was so preposterous, you could not take it seriously ! One tall man, breaking triumphantly into her world of facts and reality, would have been an answer to prayer, too gracious to be believed ; and the story to follow it, the fairy-tale, incredibly pretty-pretty. But they had said, granting her wish : " Oh ! well, let's be generous ! Let's make it five ! Five's as easy as one ! Let's make them all tall ! She likes them tall ! "

. . . Of course, the sun was in her eyes ; presently, she knew, when it dropped behind the hedge, glinting red through the reddening tangle of nut and bramble and old-man's-beard, and she could see clear into reality again, this bountiful supply of conventional tweeded heroes would disintegrate into something like ordinary, everyday life ; one of the five, perhaps, would prove to be Richard, and one would be old, and one would be married, and one would be horrid, and one— she could not imagine, for the moment, a reason for the fifth disappointment.

They came nearer ; some wore breeches, and some, plus-fours ; four of them smoked pipes ; two of them wore Old Carthusian ties. Toni, still wishing, for she had had so little time to wish during the last eleven years, wished that the clockwork of moving events might break down, so that this moment should become fixed, and not go on and break up ; wished that the men of her whim, abundantly and even unnecessarily multiplied, might always remain in one block, a vision solid, satisfying, instead of presently scattering, as they were bound to do, into individual and probably disappointing personalities. How attractive never to have to know anything at all about them, except that a universe empty of men had suddenly become full and brimming over with an ample supply, simply because she had wished, and the spirit of burlesque had answered her, and, for once, had not been meagre, with the usual : " There, you must make that do ! "

And one was Richard, and one was old, and one was married, and one was horrid, and one—was Giles. And they were, in definite name and category, a neighbouring land-owner, Jimmy Goddard, and his three sons, who had dropped in, on their way home from the local Horse Show, to see Richard, and to have a drink, and to ask him some question about the prospects of cubbing the next morning.

" I've told them to bring drinks out here," Richard Marcus told his cousin. " Will you look after them, Toni ? Molly isn't back yet ; won't be for ages."

He went on to tell Goddard that Molly stood a very fair chance of winning a first in the hunter class, riding her mare, Mitzi. . . .

" Mitzi ? how queer ! " mused Toni. To hear that name, a favourite name for a Schnitzler midinette, for the " little pals " of Viennese students, waltz composers, and smart young cavalry officers, in pre-war times ; to hear it now and here, in this typically English scenery . . . for she counted Goddard and his three sons in with the surrounding scenery on Richard's farm in Gloucestershire ; they seemed as brown and as fawn and as dun-coloured ; mellow from old custom, yet hard in their leanness and lack of subtle adjustment. Talking without enthusiasm and, nevertheless, with total absorption ; unaware of Toni's existence, to a degree which was hardly human—except as, politely, Miss Rakonitz : a low form of pond life . . . reflected a quite happy Toni. Their talk she hardly understood, for it had never been a part of her life ; quiet talk, not very interesting, with the smell of roots in it, and the early morning mists, and tang of September ;

talk in which beasts were as important as men. One of Richard's beagles was sick, and he was asking advice on it; and then the conversation turned slowly and unemotionally, as the turning of freshly-furrowed earth on to its side, to last week's Horse Show over at Carsbury, at which Molly had shown a mare, and a mare and foal, and had been highly incensed because her mare had only been awarded a second.

" But she was a three-year-old, you see," Goddard explained, " and Taylor's was a six-year-old; they'll always award the prize to the animal that'll fetch her value. I've seen it over and over again."

And now Toni, outwardly just a pretty girl, and Marcus's cousin, stepped demurely into the picture, pouring out the whiskies and sodas that the Goddards had asked for. She wondered whether they would behave doggishly as the men of a party recently given by her book-keeper, serious and reliable Miss Wildblood. Most of them middle-aged, temperate husbands, devastatingly faithful to their wives, and to the monogamous ideal, they pleased themselves and each other mightily by uttering formulas, when raising their glasses to drink, such as : " Our sweethearts and wives, may they never meet ! " or even more waggishly suggestive of ripe philander-ings and unconfessed dare-devilries in hotel corridors : " Two pairs of shoes . . ."

But she had misjudged her men :

" —Say when—fill right up with soda, please—thanks, that's fine—cheerio !—chin-chin—— ! "

A pause in the conversation. Richard's gaze went dream-ing contentedly over his fields. Toni felt chilly and desolate ; suddenly an alien. If only they would, accidentally and by a miracle, begin to talk on *her* subject, now, for a little while. But she had learnt that directly she succeeded in noosing a man's interest in the work she did, she promptly loosened and lost it for the girl she was. Toni was not in the least proud of her talent for business organisation, which could be rated very highly indeed. It stood, not as an asset, but as a dis-advantage, when she desired to be desirable, and what bucks of the Regency period would have described as a demned attractive girl. Therefore, she buried this talent for business organisation, deeply and guiltily, with all a murderer's sensations of impatience towards a refractory and large-sized corpse.

" D'you live in London, Miss Rakonitz ? "

" Yes. . . . I like London." . . . But no more than this : " I like London " or " I like Paris," perhaps. Not Budapest, for instance ; Budapest was eccentric ; the normal man could stand very little. And indeed, Toni herself had never seen green copper domes rising on the two banks of the Danube. But it was part of her, nevertheless. Her grandmother's sister, Simone, by living and dying there had brought it into the region of family property, Rakonitz property. They were all children of the cities, this large family ; back and back for generations—London, Paris, Vienna and Budapest ; Constantinople and Madrid ; cosmopolitans, whose inside knowledge was not of cubs and beagles and three-year-olds, but of jewels, highly polished walnut wood, exquisite flavours and textures ; a family of brilliant instincts and insanely foolish lapses, in trade and barter ; and here Toni herself linked on : head of " Toni's " in Hanover Street ; the window was significant with its one exquisite evening-dress. . . . How she had worked over the creation and carrying out of that dress, subtle blend of orchid and iris tints ; only a French girl could have put in such fine embroidery, strewn as though accidentally round the bottom of the skirt. They had discovered Angèle at last, in Charlotte Street ; and she did it well and remarkably cheaply. Yes, Toni was as much child of the cities and master of her trade as any of them. But these men—she fancied she knew the type they were ; utterly conventional. A girl who could hunt, Richard's young wife, say, who had been Molly Dunne, niece of Commander Dunne, R.N., was well within their experience ; a rattling good sort, Molly ! and she had a fine seat—sure of a first in the hunter's class, if Mitzi did not let her down ; but Richard was not sure whether Mitzi had quite recovered, yet, from a lameness in her near fore.

. . . Mitzi and Toni, Liserl and Franzi—Toni was away again, dreaming herself back into this light-footed and sentimental company of minxes with hearts so brittle for any man's breaking. . . . Wiser, this generation; hearts were elastic now, not frangible. . . . And wouldn't it be funny if you knew all the nonsense I was thinking, only you never never never will ! . . . The while Toni listened, grey eyes attentive, head deferentially uplifted towards the eldest Goddard male, entertaining her with an anecdote of pig-sticking in India.

. . . Much more fun they had had, the last generation but one : aunts and great-aunts and grandmothers—sweet young girls who were really sweet young girls ; and not, as now she was, pretending ; sweet young girls of the Rakonitz family, and plenty of officers to go round, for all of them.

And, with a jump of memory, she recalled that elusive connection between then and now, which had been haunting her ever since, sun-dazzled, she had seen the five men sauntering towards her. Her great-great-grandmother—stay, was that right ? how far back was Babette ? Bertrand, Anastasia, Sigismund . . . yes, that was it, her great-great-grandmother Babette, whose portrait, painted when she was seventy, was well known to Toni and all the other Rakonitz children. Babette had been the heroine of just such another incident, when at the age of sixteen, five officers from Napoleon's Army in Pressburg had escorted her to the camp every morning, and back again every evening, because she spoke several languages, and could interpret for the troops : " It is not fitting that my daughter should go among the rude soldiers unless she is properly chaperoned," Babette's mother had most certainly said. Toni laughed aloud at her mental vision of the chaperons —ten white trouser-legs arrogantly marching. . . . The scene shifted and broke, and transported her to a hundred years later, and over a hundred years ; a farm in England ; and again ten legs, stockinged and plus-foured, carelessly sauntering—— Not so much difference, after all, between the outward Babette and the outward Toni. The fashion of the year had lengthened the skirts and ballooned them out ; and Toni's little pale oval face, so naturally demure, and Toni's soft smooth, brown hair, bobbed on either side, and curling round her cheeks, long behind and gathered up at the nape ; this, too, might have been Babette, living again, ingenuously glad of plenty of men—plenty of men in the quiet little town of Pressburg ; big, handsome men who would look after a little girl and listen to her chatter, and enlighten her ignorance about the great world, and enlighten her ignorance about the countries far away from the Hungary she knew. . . . Sweet young girls !—and then by an easy and gliding transition, directly they were married they became autocrats, with powerful wills, like Grandmère, like Aunt Elsa, like great-great-grandmother Babette. But never *before* they were married. No, no, that would have been foolish—(Toni could hear them calling *her* foolish !) Sweet young girls ! Sweet little coquettes ! Rows of them, decorous and alike, with never a sign of the embryo matriarch ; dressed as Babette had been at the time of the five officers, in wide green skirts, hats tied under the chin, dangling scarves, black sandal shoes strapped over white stockings. . . . Was it too late for Toni Rakonitz, Antoinette Rakonitz, now, in 1921, in the twenty-seventh year of her stormy existence, to become a sweet young girl ? . . .

—" And my spear stuck for half an hour in the brute's hind-quarters ; I couldn't get away, and nor could he ; if I'd pulled it out, he was so savage he would have jinked again, and you can't do much with a long spear except make your thrust. It's up to the other fellow of the heat to finish him off. So I just had to wait, trusting to luck that my man would come galloping back. I'd *told* him his pony was too fresh, but he wouldn't believe me. He'd got it for a tenner because some damn fool of a vet had said it had permanent ringworm and ought to be killed ; and after all, Bettany had six years' use of it, and had passed every other pony on the ground. I was jolly glad to see him back that evening, though."

"By the way, Marcus, I brought Jimmy a picture I would like you to see, done by a fellow who has just been axed. I've never seen a better painting of pig-sticking ; he's got that queer yellow between-times light over the nullahs—makes Jimmy homesick to look at it.—Yes, thanks, I'll have another small one ; good whisky, this ! "

" Pre-war stuff," said Richard ; " haven't much left of it."

So they accepted Richard as one of themselves, this set ? No wonder he seemed at peace. There is no more restful sensation than this one, of definitely belonging. The stories went on and on, one leading to another, all told in the same pleasant, level, gun-room and country-house voice, common to all four Goddards.

Toni inevitably did not join in. It was a well-finished lump of English country atmosphere, and she wanted to carry it back, straight to Hanover Street, where she was boss and over-lord.

Richard's home was a plain farm-house ; nothing very remarkable in the faded pinks and fawns of the bricks, the low door into the garden, and straight flagged path with Michaelmas daisies growing either side of it ; then the bank sloped up, and dipped sharply down again to the sepia-brown duck-pond, quacking with animated residents. In the angle between the gate and the low grey wall which divided the garden from the lane, was an isolated tall bush of some yellow stuff, spiky, like broom, only it would not be broom this time of year. A yellow butterfly was hovering near. Toni was surprised at the fanatically vivid effect of both the bush and the butterfly ; then it struck her that it was because they were lit brilliantly by the sun rushing from the west, against an eastern sky which was the dark and threatening hue of gun-metal. She hoped, as an artist in clothes could not forbear from hoping, that her own yellow dress gained equal magic from the accident which had placed her with a background of opaque thunder-grey, and in a stream of pure clear limelight. True, nobody was noticing, much. The ducks waddled and fussed uneasily on the quaggy water ; and the five men continued at intervals to re-fill their glasses, and to say " chin-chin " and " cheerio," and to talk of " Bobbery packs," and " grand leppers."

" Curse work ! " thought Toni, " curse the independence of the modern girl ! Why have I got to go back to-morrow ? " She wondered whether she were never to get a good time ? Perhaps no such good time existed, or had ever existed for anyone, as Toni Rakonitz had in fancy erected for very desire of it. Somewhere, so her illusion firmly stated, was a special group among whom she belonged, and who would welcome her ; and they went about enjoying things more than anyone else. They were young, but not stupidly young ; and they were lords of time and masters of space, and squandered time and overleapt space, gloriously, more than anyone else. " More than anyone else," was, indeed, the nursery-rhyme tag to this nursery-rhyme of Toni's, crude in its colourings, illimitable in possibility. They had more money to toss in their wake, than anyone else ; and no responsibilities, no family, no relations. This set—the set with whom one had a good time —were not bonded together by any links more tangible than the sense of golden well-being in each others' company, and by liking the same things : speed, for instance : sailing, ski-ing, hunting ;—and quick wits, and a peculiar enjoyment of meals eaten in little cafés that were built out over the sea. They all wore incredibly expensive but entirely casual clothes, of which Toni herself had been responsible for neither the design nor the making ; and everyone—everyone *else*—would envy her for being in that set, and for doing these things, and for talking so brilliantly. You *must* have people, outside, envying you for being inside, or how are you to appreciate fully the triumph of being inside yourself ?

It was hard to define the mysterious reason which gave her good time its clearness and lightness and shining quality ; that gift of fiery living which distinguished her group of companions, beyond all other groups, as the Elect ? Toni herself could not define it. But then, she did not believe herself to be the creator of this good time. . . . It was going on, somewhere, all day, all night, the harmony and the wit and the wine ; the laughter that was never vapid, the enjoyment neither bucolic nor precious. All she had to do was to join it . . . if she could. But up till now, it lay like enchantment, always just on the yonder side of tiresomeness ; bills and grandmothers and bronchitis and dissatisfied clients, relations who did not admire you at all ; and being tired and tired and tired. . . . " I've been cheated ! " cried Toni.

Now, certainly, financial troubles were lightening, and her name was beginning to be known : " My dear, you *ought* to get a dress at ' Toni's ' ; she is really clever, and not expensive yet, though, of course, her prices will soon go up."—Yes, but a reputation as a dressmaker, and just the negative advantage of release from financial pressure, *that* was not what she meant ; it was no good trying to put her off with that !— Showers of twinkling lights, and a sufficiency of men, the right sort of men . . . oh ! not boringly amorous, but with the true swashbuckling touch of enterprise in courtship—— So that for once Toni Rakonitz, who had *always* had to take the initiative, could be passive and yielding and let the actual work be done by another. Perhaps, for all her business abilities, Toni was old-fashioned ; she would have liked to have been the " belle of the ball " ; she would like to have been the " reigning toast " ; those girls in little French towns who were yearly elected Queen of Beauty, amid bewildering showers of flowers : cotton flowers and real blossoms, these dark-eyed girls must have tasted the climax of a good time, for a short twenty-four hours. But it ought to go on and on. . . .

Toni was astonished, at the end of her reverie, to find herself alone with one of the Goddard men. The others had apparently been taken off to see some special crops, or harness, or prize sow, she never quite knew which ; but Giles, the second son, had remained behind at the duck-pond. He had been wondering all the time what the girl in the yellow dress was really like. She was beautiful—any fool could see that— fragile and wholly feminine ; she looked as though she had been most exquisitely dressed for the country, but in town ; not in the least with the more rough and casual air of having dressed in the country for the country. " Got a good maid with her, I should think," reflected Giles—which summing-up would have appealed irresistibly to Toni's sense of humour, had she guessed. He furthermore assured himself that, judging from outward signs, she had nothing much to talk about, and was a conventional type—one of these dancing parasites, at once bold in demand and helpless in behaviour, whom his brother Fred had described to him as the girl of to-day.

He was curious to see how she would open a duologue; probably by trying to force the personal touch. Giles was good-humouredly aware that girls thought that men liked to be encouraged to talk about themselves; girls took credit for such perception. He waited. Unfortunately for him, Toni waited too, coolly, and without getting in the least flustered or discomposed by the pause. . . . You could always watch the ducks! Presently Giles said, as though answering a question which had never actually taken shape:

" I'm only just back in England, you know. I was with the Army of Occupation in Cologne; got my discharge a couple of weeks ago. Now—*now*, I mean to have a good time."

CHAPTER II

WHEN Toni returned home, late on the following afternoon, she found a telephone message from her cousin Val, telling her to come round to her studio that evening—"because I start for Italy to-morrow, with any luck."

Toni already knew that Val had meant to go South that autumn, though the date of departure had been left rather vague. This younger generation of Rakonitz met only spasmodically, not with the solid regularity of their elders; nor, when they had a plan, did they bother to lay it before a tribal council. Val Power was an artist of some reputation, and could afford to do as she liked.

Toni, having walked quickly down the shadowy lane which led off a square in Kensington, past mysterious little doors which always seemed to promise more adventure than normal front doors, because they were dwarfed by their setting in high blank walls, was admitted by Val into what looked like a blend of the Paris Exhibition of 1899, a vorticist cyclone, and the Last Day of the Sales in High Street, Kensington.

"Sorry," said Val; "don't mind the mess. I'm packing."

"Are you?" politely replied Toni, knowing full well, from experience, that Val was not packing, but had merely emptied everything she possessed on to the studio floor, in the hope that Toni was coming along and would offer to pack in her stead.

"Righto! I'll watch you." She would not be eternally ruthless; but Val might as well suffer for ten minutes longer. Val, who physically and in all practical matters had about the energy and self-reliance of a favourite Sultana, and no more, had a habit of imposing service on whoever happened to be handy, by the phrase: "I say, as you *are* up, you might just fetch——" . . . This phrase worked equally well, as she had often explained in fatal moments of confidence to Toni, whether they were " up " or not ; it created a hypnotic illusion that they *were* just crossing the room or in the neighbourhood of the door, so that without protest they rose from the arm-chair, and did not even realise that they were pandering to Val's worst quality.

" How's ' Toni's ' ? " asked Val. " Oh ! of course, you haven't been there for ten days. It's fairly flourishing, isn't it ? I shouldn't be surprised if Lucilla Danby didn't give you her new play to dress ; ' The Laplander,' I think it's called. What are Lapland fashions ? Or she might have said ' The Straphanger '—they were shifting scenery so heartily that I couldn't catch half she said. She was immensely bucked with that one kit you made for her, last year. The cigarettes are beside you. You might chuck me one."

" They are *not* beside me. They are on the other side of the studio. You can't try that game on with me, Val. Actual measurement will prove that they are about seven yards nearer to you. Yes ! that was rather a jolly frock. I adapted it from a Vionnet model. But then, anyone can dress a tall and lovely woman, with dark eyes and white hair ; and Lucilla, especially, could give an indescribable *flair* to a piece of sackcloth. I got horribly caught out, though, just before I went down to Richard's, by a terribly important county frump you sent me."

" Do you mean the Hon. Mrs. Wensley ? My dear kid, you made a wonderful hit with her. She came to me raving about you. She said you were *such* good form, and that you must have ' cut,' because of the quiet but perfect style in which you were dressed yourself."

Toni rocked with happy laughter. The honourable lady of county family, had, as it happened, appeared in Hanover Street very much earlier in the morning than clients were usually expected. Toni, having been dissatisfied, as she often was—being a very particular young woman—with the way the staff had cleared the show-room, was showing them how she wanted it done, wearing her oldest black dress, her head tied up in a handkerchief, and no powder upon her face.

There had been just time, as she now described to Val, to whip off the handkerchief, and glide elegantly forward, with much aplomb and *savoir-faire*, to welcome her first county client. . . .

"That's the way to get on, obviously."

"Is it?" said Toni, mutinously, astride of the hat-box, her hands hugging one knee. "Well, I'm fed up with work. I don't think I want to get on—not by my own unaided efforts, anyhow. I'm sick of the show-room; I'm sick of my office behind it, with my good little book-keeper looking at me reproachfully through her spectacles, because I've spent two-pence rather more recklessly than the firm's credit will allow. I'm sick of being everywhere at once, superintending the fittings and watching the cutting, dashing about the shops to match silks, because none of the girls can be trusted not to waste time, and don't know cinnamon from tabac. I'm sick of feeling completely done in and ill and tired to the bone, with a journey to Paris in front of me, scrambling for the new season's models, and coming back to all the messes made while I was away, by that ass Aimée to whom God gave the perfect mannequin figure instead of to me. I'm sick of a week's doleful slack, and then seven clients all round me at once, each one believing herself entitled to all my attention, and Aunt Elsa choosing that moment to appear with Pearl and Gisela and a beaming smile and a piece of sky-blue satin sent by Aunt Berthe, and some bead trimming for a blouse——"

Val had previously heard of that visit, from Aunt Elsa herself: "I do sometimes vonder vether Toni is so clever as all that she thinks herself in business? That blouse looks nossing now that she has sent it home. But *nossing*——" . . . Val chuckled; and then ceased to chuckle, wrestling incompetently with the folds of a brocade and feather evening cloak. Toni, melted to professional pity for the evening cloak, not for her cousin, exclaimed: "Here, Val, you'd better leave that to me! flesh and blood could just bear to see you playing a sort of Rugby football among the clothes you bought at other shops, but when it comes to things I've designed for you myself . . ."

Val, with a sigh of relief, relinquished her task, curled

herself up into a vacant corner of the divan, and purring with idle content, began to murmur flatteries to Toni, who was doing intricate and beautiful things with tissue paper.

"I can hardly bear to unpack, Toni darling, when *you* have done the packing. It's a special art, of course."

"It's a very inconvenient art, in a large family," said Toni. "Anyway, I'm only intending to fold this one cloak."

Val murmured: "C'est le premier pas qui coûte . . . ! Chuck me a cigarette now you *are* nearer them—why, you said so, yourself, when I was standing where you are; a good seven yards. . . . Is your Aimée the willowy, ethereal creature in the show-room, who dreamily puts a lorgnette up at me whenever I come in, and has a fluting voice like moonlight on Venice at Earl's Court?"

"Yes, my head sales-woman. She's too ladylike to live!"

"Why don't you sack her? Bet you her name is Amy, anyway."

"Oh! it is. I've heard her younger sister call her Amy, and then Aimée languidly complains to me of the child's too awful French accent. She has a marvellous figure, and even her taste can be trusted, more or less. I don't need her for anything else. Miss Thompson does all the principal dog-work, of course. She's one of the best cutters in London. I was in luck to get her from the Wolffs.—What's this hard round object sticking up, where I want to lay your evening dresses smoothly?"

"Don't know. Forgotten."

Toni pulled it out, and unpacked it. It proved to be a snow-storm quiescent in a glass ball, with a tiny wooden doll, debatably female, in the midst of the snow-storm.

"*Must* you have this with you?"

"I shall need it, down South," said Val, voluptuously. "Think of the heat and the palms and the hibiscus and other tropical vegetation. When I'm too hot, I shall just shake out the snow-storm, and dream about England."

Toni, from the stern point of view of costumier and modiste, disapproved of packing nobbly snow-storms among ethereal creations of ninon and *crêpe de Chine;* yet she was fascinated into shaking the toy, and was now morbidly gazing into the tiny falling flakes, imagining the winter to come ; November, December, January, February, March . . . long days of work, when the air was clear and dark, as you would imagine the air of Purgatory ; or the air was thick and sulphur-coloured and choking, like the air of Hell ; and you would have to get up by artificial light ; and switch on the electric light, grudgingly, at three in the afternoon ; and the work-girls would all have chilblains on their fingers, making them clumsy and pathetic ; and every day, some would inconveniently have stopped at their homes, in bed, because of influenza ; so that all the rest would have to do extra work and stay later. Yet for all that, work would go slowly ; and the insides of home-going buses and tubes would be crammed with bodies, and smell of damp, rusty clothes. And clients would draw up, complacently, outside the door in Hanover Street, in closed cars like glowing, little, comfortable caves ; cars that waited, motionless, until it was time for them to start up again with that easy expensive ripple so irritating to people who have not got a car. . . . Toni, in a temper, shook and shook the glass bowl till it was a whirl of criss-crossing snow-flakes. . . . It swelled and swelled, engulfing her. . . . The tiny doll-figure in the centre of the fury was herself, and she could not get away. . . . Shudder of winter was near, inescapably all around her——

" Val," she suddenly burst out, " it's the biggest fallacy going, this splendour of independence and work that we hear so much about. Haven't you been told over and over again how lucky you are to be born into an age where girls are given a chance to earn money and be on their own ? Well—we've had time to try it ! What's the verdict ? What do you think about it ? "

" Oh ! I'd like to be kept," said Val, frankly. " I'm with you all the time. Kept in idleness. . . . What does that remind me of ?—A little Western flower. . . . Yes, that's it. Shakespeare at school. . . . ' Before, milk-white, now purple with love's wound, and maidens call it—kept-in-idleness.' And in a really opulent and vulgar way, for choice. A large, luscious villa on the Riviera ; cars ; furs ; money no object ; presents every day. One never gets enough presents. . . ."

" One never gets any at all," Toni amplified the complaint.

" There are about five posts a day in London, and how many presents does one get by post ? "

" Girls of our station-in-life can't possibly accept presents. . . . *Can* they ? "

" *Can't* they ? " briefly, from Toni. " Mother and Wanda and Truda—that generation—were allowed to accept white kid gloves—long ones, for balls, not the short afternoon-visiting kind. There's a difference. And a few natural flowers to place against their rippling hair. There was no *harm* in that. Add cigarettes and silk stockings—and we come down to to-day. *I've* got a lust for presents that have to be brought by pantechnicon. In Grandmère's time, when the Uncles' business friends were still having rather unexpected pick-ups of rubies and sapphires and so forth—' Hello, you chaps, I've found a new mine !'—they used to have special stones set into ear-rings or brooches, and give them away gracefully to the Charming Ladies, for luck. That's why Grandmère and Aunt Elsa and all the generation-before-last, have got so much jewelry."

" And they *accepted* these valuable gifts ? " Val was shocked. " Well, well, well—how much more fortunate are we, with our sturdy self-respect rather than gaudy trinkets ! . . . Yes, I think decidedly one ought to be kept, and do as little as possible for it. Long live the parasite ! You just coo a bit, and then somebody or other gives you a cheque, and you've done nothing to earn it."

" Earning ! " Toni groaned ; " sweat of one's brow. Sturdy self-respect, indeed ! What'll you sell your sturdy self-respect for, Val ? One thousand pounds a year ? Five thousand pounds ? "

" No ! Damn it ! Let's do it well while we are about it. Twenty thousand pounds a year ! . . . And all in payment for nothing but simply so beautifully being ! "

If anyone had overheard this startling conversation, from two representatives of an enlightened and progressive age, the artist, famous enough in her own line, and the cool, responsible, successful business woman, he might have found it hard to realise that both knew they were talking nonsense—ignoring the stone in the peach, while babbling about the husky sheen of its outer velvet. But they were in a mood to intoxicate themselves with such deliberate, illogical nonsense . . . piling it on, recklessly ; as much an outlet as, twenty and thirty years ago, rebellious discussion had been an outlet, declarations of " the right to lead one's own life." Val's mother, Haidée Czelovar, had vented her suppressed irritability, and gained whole bouquets of admiration, by saying " shocking " things, when among her gasping, bright-eyed young cousins. Shocking—because she was so " advanced," so " fast "—the things she said to men ! Val, and especially Toni, who could hardly hope to shock even the aunts of the family, any more, by declarations of independence, found a queer relief from weariness in shocking imaginary spectators —Splendid Women, all of them !—by swaggering sentiments that were totally reactionary.

Toni went on : " I've sometimes been so badly off for want of being spoilt, that I've spoilt myself. It's a poor substitute, rather like sham eggs in puddings, but better than nothing. I take myself about in taxis, and give the man a lordly tip, and tell myself I like going around with this person who does things so well. Then I treat myself to a sensuous meal in a first-class restaurant, and tell myself that only the best is good enough for this adorable little Toni. The best, and never ask the price. There's a sort of quiet generosity in the way I do things, when I'm my own escort. D'you remember that scarlet *moiré* bag I had last year, oblong, with a jewelled clasp ? That dainty, useless, expensive trifle—Rue de Rivoli, of course—was a present. That's why I carried it so jauntily. Only—I paid for it too. Oh, it's *not* the same ! —spoiling oneself ! I, the child of the age, the privileged daughter of the twentieth century, the beneficiary of years of fighting for women's emancipation from harem slavery, I solemnly declare that there's nothing in the world I want quite as much, as to do no work, and, for no reason at all, to have tons of money to spend which is all made by somebody else."

Val, who was suffering from acute depression over an ex-hibition of her paintings which was going to be opened the following week, when she was safely out of the country, remarked that Toni's views were absolutely sound ; and that if she found two lonely millionaires instead of one, knocking about loose on the Riviera, she'd summon Toni by telegram.

" You needn't bother to do that," her cousin said, quickly ; " I'm going to get married, next week."

It was part of Val's creed to disapprove of sensational announcements. So she complained, now, that Toni had not led up to her present effect with enough subtlety or delicacy. But underneath this flippant response, Val was suddenly anxious. She was four years Toni's senior ; and however carelessly she might talk, the pendulum-swing of her actual doings was never as marked from good time to bad time, as Toni's. Toni's moods, chastened and pruned of exuberance as they had been, by conflict and poverty, were, nevertheless, a counterpart of her grandmother's. And Anastasia Rakonitz was famous among all the branching families of Rakonitz, Czelovar and Bettelheim, for her fantastic and *insouciante* treatment of everybody's destinies ; as though there were but one destiny, and that her own, to be gaily spun like a diabolo reel from the taut string. Toni had been sober and hard-working, a devotee of duty, both disciple and high priest at the altar of " Toni's," for two years ; ever since the catastrophic summer of 1919, when Anastasia had been laid powerless by a stroke ; and Danny, cuckoo in the Rakonitz nest, had gone away. He had gone away so completely that Toni, who had loved him, knew that his silence was not a deliberate silence, which he might therefore break at any moment ; but an absolute and happy forgetfulness of Rakonitz existence.

Val said, at last, in quite a different voice from the one which she had used till now in their discussion :

" Does the family know ? "

It was a strange comment ; you might have expected that at least her first involuntary question would have been about the man himself.

" The family aren't going to know," replied Toni ; and her voice, anyhow, remained off-hand and flippant as before. " Why should they ? Haven't they spoilt enough for me ?

I'll tell Mums, of course. Mums is different. And you, wel ,
you are going away to-morrow."

" I'm not sure that I am. Shall I stop, Toni ? "

" We're not having bridesmaids, darling. If we were, of
course, you should wear rose-pink *crêpe de Chine* and a leghorn
hat, a sheaf of blush roses, and a turquoise locket, present from
the bridegroom. Sorry to do you out of it, Val, but I have
about ninety-two other small cousins who couldn't be left
out once I began ; and I'm not keen on Giles realising too
soon that he's marrying half Europe ! "

" Doesn't he realise ? "

Toni's level eyebrows twisted quizzically at the corners, and the
blue eyes beneath them were not tender, but hard and mocking :
" You haven't grasped the idea one bit, Val. The old order
changeth. . . . I'm not marrying Giles to bring him into the
family. I'm marrying him to get out of it, myself. I've served
the tribe well and truly for twenty-seven years, haven't I ? "

"Hardly that. You were a spoilt brat until you were fifteen,
always tossing your curls about, and talking about your ' imperial sway ' . . ." Val broke off, realising that she had been
tactless. It was for dread of that same " imperial sway," that
Danny had finally escaped from Toni Rakonitz, two autumns
ago—" And even after you were fifteen, you had lapses."

" I'm having a lapse now ! one of my ' bad times,' you and
the others would call it, I suppose ? The queer part of it is,
that I have a good time during my ' bad times ' ; and a rotten
bad time, dull and dreary and hopeless, all work and no fun,
when you all say complacently : ' Toni is having one of her
good times.' Aren't you going to congratulate me, Val ?
Aren't you going to hope that I'll be as happy as I deserve ? "

" You're not a bit in love, Toni, and that's the trouble.
That's where I pucker my brow and shake my head."

" I'm not all stupefied and beglamoured, if that's what you
mean. What a sweet, old-fashioned girl you are, Val ! When
you were talking, just now, about being kept in idleness . . ."

" Shut up and don't be a fool ! " retorted Val, brusquely.
" Talking, what's talking ? That was all hot air. . . . Passing
the time away."

"I'm marrying for money," Toni repeated, squatting on the floor beside the trunk, and gaily tossing balls of magpie silk into the air, alternately black silk and white silk; Val's stockings, really, which were lying strewn about, ready to be packed. She tossed them faster and faster, as her statements became more challenging and provocative. "I'm marrying to escape. I'm marrying to get away from the family, and a family of women, into the bargain. I'm marrying so that I can chuck work. I'm marrying for a good time."

"Some horrible, elderly man, I suppose?" Val was thoroughly disgusted with her naughty little cousin. Reaction had produced, as out of a conjuring box, the identical Toni who, twenty years ago, had marched into the nursery, and by some sort of royal prerogative, which Val, the elder by four years, had been too indolent to check, had annexed the best paint-box and all the gold and silver paint, and all the children's books with the best illustrations, and had given all the people in the pictures gold and silver faces, and then, laughing heartily, had danced round and round the room, chanting: "I'm the eldest of the eldest of the eldest of the eldest, so I shall do just what I like, always, because nobody can stop me!" It was an unfortunate day when Toni had been given the family tree, showing her own distinguished place in it.

"He's not an old man, and he's not a bit horrible. He is exactly the same age as I am, in fact. His name is Maurice Giles Goddard, and I met him down at Richard's. He was in the Army all through the war; been at Cologne ever since; lately demobbed; got a father, whom they call Jimmy, and two brothers, and two small nephews, and no female possessions at all. *He* doesn't want to work, either; wants to play; wants to have a good time; wants to have a good time with me; thinks me a darling, frightfully attractive and irresistibly amusing; and he likes my yellow dress, thinking that God designed it, instead of 'Toni's' in odd moments; doesn't really grasp that 'Toni's' exists, except as a sort of amateur hobby. He said: 'I expect it provided you with pocket money?' . . . Wasn't it naïf of him, Val? I didn't let on, naturally, that I'd run a household of four people, entirely on my earnings, for the last ten years or so."

"The conventional young Army man! Well, it might be worse, I suppose. What does he look like?"

"He looks exactly the sort of man that, when you see him, you are sure you can't be so lucky that he doesn't already belong to somebody else."

"Bad grammar and high compliment!"

"You know what I mean," impatiently; "tall and ordinary, and decently washed and brushed, and the right way of wearing his clothes, so that you don't notice them; quite nice-looking, too; not vulgarly handsome or striking in any way. I forget, really, what Giles *does* look like. The sun was in my eyes when I saw him." . . .

"It's still in your eyes," said Val, grimly. "And what may be the income of this—sun-in-your-eyes?"

"Would you ask him that question if he were here, Val darling?"

"Come on, Toni, I'm not to be trifled with! Look on me as representing the Family! . . . *Ei*, but is he then a *parti?* I must know, isn't it?"

Toni folded her hands, and answered staidly: "He has no money of his own, dear Aunt Elsa; but, please, Aunt Henrietta, his father will ladle out about two thousand pounds a year. We can just manage on that to begin with, can't we, Aunt Gustava? Aunt Truda thinks we can, but I haven't asked Aunt Gisela yet. . . . She's dead, you see!"

"Two thousand a year. Not earned by you, and not earned by your husband, and—does your husband's father earn his income, by any chance?"

"Not he! Jimmy's bone-idle. Landed gent. in the country; bit of a rake, I fancy, when he stays in town, at his club. He inherited from his wife, whose people were awfully well off, I believe. About six thousand pounds a year."

"So that really you'll all be living, quite complacently, on a fortune drifted down from an unknown father of an unknown lady who married 'Jimmy' and died! Bit of a change for you, Toni!"

" How full you are of the dignity of honest toil, all of a sudden," cried Toni, exasperated into her wildest outburst of rhetoric, by Val's soft, ironical inflexions. " I don't care— I've struck gold, at last. As crude as that, if you like. I've wondered for years about what is so picturesquely called unearned increment. What a dream-vision, when you're tired-out, and have managed, after days of rush and disappointed anguish, to scrape together, by your personal toil, about sevenpence halfpenny ! . . . Unearned increment ! The two most lyrical words in the English language ! How *did* people stumble on it ? Whereabouts did it lie ? Or was it just some fabulous legend like on the old maps : ' Here is gold, much gold.' ' Here is gold and silver.' . . . But now I've struck it. Actually me ! What luck ! Hurrah for plunder ! "

" You're over-excited, my child. . . . ' Toni mustn't be over-excited '—I was brought up to remember that. Nanny used to din it into me. . . . ' And when she's over-excited, she ends by hurting herself ! '—So watch out ! "

Toni did not argue. She sat there, juggling with the silk-stocking balls, flinging them higher and higher, her lips curved into that elusive smile which might not have been a smile at all, for it was the crescent shape, tilted up at the corners, into which the Rakonitz mouth curved itself naturally when in repose ; and behind that tantalising bend of her lips and sparkle in her eyes, she was thinking happily how safe and immune she was from hurt, and how Val did not know it, nor anybody else except Toni herself. But her soul had found its talisman, and the talisman was this : that beyond all doubt, and established by all proof, men were no good ; men were assets, amusing sometimes, decorative sometimes, necessary to go about with ; they had, perhaps, a few muscular advantages ; but for stuff in life to support you, for decency and chivalry, you went to women. Men let you down ! All the Rakonitz men, the men of the family, had been weak and charming, and had let their women down. Then there had been Danny . . .

It was all right, now that she knew it ; she was safe ; safe as though she had been given a magic coat of mail, cap of darkness, and winged sandals, such as the mythical demi-gods used to wear to preserve them from such hurt as common mortals must risk. Perversely, she stood upon disillusion as firmly as though it were religion, and a strong rock. Giles would let her down, of course; and if she had sons, they too would let her down. None of this mattered, because she had passed, not without toll, through that silvery, fatuous stage in her life when she could believe any one man, and say: "he is different." None of them were different. She was not embittered; she was just sure and safe.

Val did not understand; yet Toni still valued her opinion.

"Look here, Val," letting all the balls of black and white fall rolling about the floor, "it's only the way, after all, that our grandmothers and great-grandmothers had their marriages arranged for them. Pretend, for a moment, that I'm split into two people—I've often had to be two people. I told you I used to take myself about, and spoil myself, and buy myself scarlet *moiré* handbags. Well, now I am Toni, the old-fashioned mother, *and* Toni, the sweet and pliable daughter. Toni-the-mother arranges a good marriage with an eligible young man, and Toni-the-daughter casts down her eyes demurely, and without flaring out in any of this new-fangled rubbish about marrying for love and so forth, just accepts her destiny. Wasn't that the way our great-grandmother Babette was married off by her mother? and the way Babette's mother had been married off by *her* mother?"

"And the way Jephthah's daughter had been sacrificed by her father?"—Val, accustomed to Toni's sophistries, took as little heed of them as though they were skittles in her path, as lightly to be brushed over. "You're not the typical Israelite maiden of the tribe, any more, Toni. What *is* the good of hoodwinking me over this reversion-to-type business? Our generation is our own generation, and not any other; and we are the likelier to make a mess of things, because . . ."

"Because why?"

"Oh! I don't know."

What Val had been thinking, only she did not wish to plunge into what might have sounded like priggish generalisations, was that theirs was actually the first unorthodox generation. The first generation, totally irreligious, hardly knowing what the inside of a synagogue looked like, nor even, alternatively, the inside of a church. The first generation which was the result of inter-marriage between Israelite and Gentile; the first generation to throw away, as valueless, the traditions of the tribe and the obligations of the family. They were going their way independently, without law or precedent or interference. . . . What was going to become of Toni?

Suddenly Val ceased to be solemn and portentous; it was no good bothering! besides, it was really rather exciting that Toni was going to get married. Such ages since there had been a wedding in the family. Sylvia had been the last, Sylvia Czelovar; and "Toni's," at the start of its career, had provided the trousseau. But Sylvia's mother was Constance, the Dean's daughter, so that it was rather a wedding in the *haute école* style; everybody stepping their paces with lofty deliberation, and dainty good form, like a carefully controlled horse round and round the circus ring; not a ripe, rich and juicy wedding in the true family tradition. The last perfect specimen of its kind that Val could remember had been in 1916, when Deb Marcus had married Samson Phillips, himself a good Jew of inflexible morality. She could remember, too, when Étienne Czelovar had wedded Camille de Yong; Paris cousins, both of them. She and Toni sat now, once more cosily in touch, in the dishevelled studio, smoking cigarettes, and recalling, as you recall features of a really first-class procession, the organised routine of an engagement and marriage as it used to be when the Burmah Ruby Company was at its height; and Anastasia's three brothers, Uncle Felix, Uncle Max and Uncle Louis were rich and powerful; and the parents of the young pair put it formally before them, the three Pashas, to decide whether this engagement were suitable and should be sanctioned as such; while the fiancés themselves, painfully aware of what was going on, painfully self-conscious, automatically fell into the postures of diffident rapture, prompted by their ancestors. The children of the family, Toni and Gerald, Val, Maxine and Derek and Iris, and the four good girls of Aunt Elsa, were expectant and on tip-toe, knowing that all this romantic upheaval would eventually express itself in terms of extra food and feasting. Next in order, came the announcement of the *fiançailles*, and correct exclamations of the shrillest surprise from everybody who had anticipated it for weeks past :

" ' And here follows a passage for the woodwind,' " Val, not being musical, burlesqued a concert programme, " repeating the *motif* of the first movement ; crescendo of dinner-parties for the aunts, all the old Viennese recipes lugged out again, Goulasch, Pflaumentorte, Crême-Düten and Apfel-strudel ; speeches in the jokeful spirit, as Uncle Otto Solomon-son used to call it ; and then Aunt Elsa going round to Aunt Anastasia, and grandmother going round to Aunt Elsa, and Aunts Hermina and Gisela writing from Paris to Aunt Henrietta, to Settle about the Presents ; they did 'em well in those days, I must say ; no duplicates. . . . And the Uncles, the Uncles, the Uncles gave a cheque !—that was the refrain ; thumping cheque, too. Anecdotes of earlier weddings were sort of mixed in with the gravy to make it rich ; and Aunt Elsa became almost *too* Viennese . . . and slapped the Only-Dean-in-the-family's face, giving as excuse that she thought it was that naughtee Rabbi . . . ! Poor Aunt Constance ! " Val, much more than Toni, was recalling these dead pageantries, echoes of the Rakonitz prosperity, with voluptuous relish.

—" Toni, you can't seriously be meaning to break away from all this richness ; to forfeit the congratulation and wedding presents ; to defy the ritual of parading your Giles round to each of the family in turn, to be inspected and approved and blessed ? "

Distinctly and emphatically, Toni said that she *was* going to forgo all this pleasure and excitement :

" I'm marrying into a family of men, and none of them care tuppence about each other. Isn't it gorgeous ? No women at all ; no aunts, no grandmothers ! it's like a fairy-tale ; just Jimmy Goddard, widower, and his three sons, Reginald, Giles and Fred. Reginald's married, and even *his* wife has had the decency to run away and leave him to divorce her, after presenting him with two little sons—not daughters, mind you—sons." She did not believe nor trust in men ; nor rely upon them for support. But long years in a family where matriarchy was the supreme rule, and where the men, ineffective to begin with, were also, for some curious reason, the first to die, leaving behind them widows and daughters, had satiated her with the actual sight and ways and voices of women; their rustle, and the touch of their hands; and had caused her to regard this new territory, on which tall men walked solitary, and forgot each other's birthdays, as indeed the Fortunate Isles and a Kingdom of Enchantment. . . .

"You see them together, accidentally, sometimes; but they don't mind if one of them happens to disappear for two or three years without leaving an address. They have no ghastly customs like meeting under one roof for Christmas. . . . It *is* considerate of Giles's mother to be dead, too. Just supposing she welcomed me as a daughter! My Mums is an angel; but a mother-in-law——! I'm getting right away out of it, Val; right out of a family of women, into a family of men. And I'm never going back, any more, to a crowd of superfluous relations who remember anniversaries!"

"Good!" said Val, "then I needn't worry about sending you a tortoiseshell hair-brush for your birthday, as I'd meant to do; or an Italian shawl; they're cheap in Italy, so I'm told. Never mind, I'll respect your desire to let all sentimentalities drop into oblivion. R.I.P. . . .! Let's be sensible: would you care to take on this studio, for instance? I've just thought of it, but it's a notion. Do nicely for you and your young man, and relieve me of a burden. I've got it for another four years, and I was going to leave it with Davidson and Davidson to let, furnished, at six guineas a week?"

"And how much would it be for me?"

"Six guineas a week," promptly.

Toni gazed at her with reproach: "To a relation?"

"Oh, we've dropped all that," said Val. "You haven't got any relations. As Christian to Jew, six guineas a week!"

"You forget," said Toni, "I'm only half a Jew!"

"And you forget," countered Val, swiftly, "that I'm only half a Christian!"

They paused, at a deadlock. . . .

CHAPTER III

MAXINE SILVER was the Matriarch's grandchild, co-responsible with Toni. And as Anastasia Rakonitz, since her first paralytic stroke, two years ago, had lived with her daughter Truda, and with Truda's children, it was Maxine's task to break to her the news that Toni had been quietly married at a registry office, that chapped and boisterous morning of early October. Maxine did not enjoy the job; but she knew that her mother would enjoy it still less; so she took a half-day off from the Bank, where she held a high position as the head partner's confidential secretary; and came home to Ealing, feeling exceedingly sorry for herself, and yet a great deal more sorry for her grandmother. If this were the sort of blow that to-morrow's Matriarch dealt to yesterday's—but Maxine saw Toni's point of view, too; Anastasia, with her fitful adoration of Toni, had yet succeeded fairly well, in her old days of despotic power, in treating Toni's slight chances of happiness very much as a splendid, dark elephant, enormous and majestic, decked out in sonorous purple, and radiantly intoxicated with an 1870 vintage of Clos de Vougeot, might have treated, with benevolent trumpetings, a flower-bed of small white violets just beginning to unfold beneath her dancing feet. . . .

Anastasia still had her good times, and her bad times; but they were now no more than enfeebled shadows of what they used to be; shadows swaying on water, when the sunshine is in its pallid winter. Truda could just distinguish still, and be relieved, when the unreasoning excitement of the bad times merged at last into a gentle, querulous, gossiping state, in which the bed-ridden old autocrat gave no trouble, and seemed grateful for what was done for her. Just now, at the period of Toni's truant wedding, she was nearing the end of one of her bad times. . . .

" You will fetch for me at once," she commanded Maxine,
on hearing the news, " Elsa and Henrietta; also Gustava,
who, Heaven knows, is not much help, but she will think she
has a right to be here. You will also fetch Susie, so that I
can hear all about it, and I do not care if Haidée comes or
not, but telephone her, so that she need not imagine nothing
is being done. Yes, and also Wanda, who should have been
married long ago herself, if she had had any sense, and if she
had listened to what I say; but first, fetch me Elsa, you
comprehend? I cannot understand why Susie is not here
already, but she has no consideration, and this would be the
time, if she had any right feeling, to bring me my Sèvres
coffee-cups back that Mr. Mendelberger gave Bertrand to
make up for a flawed ruby, but it was I, and not Susie, who
always had to entertain Mr. Mendelberger at my house to
dinner, isn't it so? And Bertrand, my son, is dead, who would
not let his wife have slighted me over this marriage of Toni's,
nor have kept the cups so that I must thank Truda, yes, my
own daughter, every time I crack one of hers that have that
ugly gold and pink pattern on them, by washing my Venetian
ear-rings in boiling water." The skin sagged in heavy folds
of suffering from the two deep lines that grooved either side
of Anastasia's mouth. . . . " And tell your Mama," finished
the Matriarch, " that she is to make Crême-Düten ! "

Maxine nodded; she was puzzled, nevertheless. Why
Crême-Düten? which, when she was a child, and up to the
time of the fall of the House of Rakonitz, but very rarely
later, had been special treats that marked some festivity, some
occasion of pomp and rejoicing in the family. There had
always been Crême-Düten for birthdays, and at silver weddings.
Only the Matriarch and Truda knew the recipe, which had
come down from old Maria, who had been their cook in Vienna.
But why did the Matriarch desire them for tea, to-day?
which, by rights, was a day of wailing in the calendar, because
the eldest granddaughter had defied law and the autocrat,
and had done as she pleased in a way that was not the fashion
for Rakonitz maidens? Then suddenly Maxine understood:
Anastasia had need, to-day, to reassure herself and to show

others, when the news smote her, that she could still give her wayward, extravagant orders, and have them obeyed.

"Elsa, Henrietta and Gustava," the Matriarch called after her, in reminder, as she turned to leave the room. "And we will decide what is to be done."

"Poor old devil," muttered Maxine. What is to be done? . . . Why, what did Anastasia imagine *could* be done, now? Nevertheless, she would not forgo the gathering at head-quarters; the calling-in of the tribe. Only it was looking-glass administration; first, Toni got married; afterwards, the family decided if it were to be permitted or not.

"I can just see myself trotting up to Hampstead to fetch Aunt Elsa," reflected Maxine; "still, with a bit of luck, she'll have sniffed the news, anyhow; they do, in a wonderful way; jungle instinct! I don't believe Toni would find it necessary for Aunt Susie to be lugged in and upset by all their jabber, just now. I can telephone Aunt Henrietta and Aunt Gustava," and she remembered to stop at the kitchen door, and inform her mother about the Crême-Düten. Truda was almost as shocked as she had been at the news of Toni's wedding!

"Crême-Düten! to-day! when the girl is out, and I have none of the right things in the house? She must be mad! *Why* Crême-Düten to-day? I am willing to do anything in reason for poor Mama; I have never forgotten to get in her rusks . . ."

Maxine smiled; if the Matriarch's turbulent emotions were expressing themselves that day in terms of food, she could realise, better than Truda, that rusks were inadequate.

"Besides," Truda went on, "what would Doctor Burton say? Crême-Düten! Poison for her, even as light as I make them; and nobody coming to tea, at least, nobody except Henrietta and Gustava, and then we are not sure, if you have not 'phoned them yet. No, Maxine, you can tell Iris to run out and buy a sponge-cake."

Maxine, whose sense of pitiful imagination was wide-awake for the moment, could not quite visualise an insignificant British sponge-cake in place of the richly spiced and decorative Gugelhupf and the Zimmtkuchen, the Crême-Düten and the

Nuss-Torte, that ought to have upheld the Matriarch's sense of dignity at this crisis.

" Oh well—make her the Crême-Düten, mother darling, as a favour to me. I'll stand the racket out of my private funds. I don't suppose she will eat them up, but Iris and you and I can walk away with the remains. I haven't had them for years, anyway, and you do make them so rippingly. I'll buzz out and buy the ingredients as soon as I've done some telephoning. Might as well be useful, as I *am* at home on a Wednesday. Hello! who's that?"

" That," an impatient ring at the front-door bell, with sundry agitated rappings, proved most fortunately to be Aunt Elsa, who had indeed, as Maxine had foretold, scented agitation and trouble and momentous news; and not only had arrived to discuss with that poor, poor Anastasia, what was to be done—and Maxine chuckled at the repetition of the exact phrase which she had heard, upstairs, a few minutes ago—but had already been out to Bedford Park to see Susie, and had gathered much information, unwillingly imparted, about Toni's marriage and Toni's husband. Aunt Elsa, quivering from head to foot, her toque rather awry, crying a little, but honouring the occasion by her best, stiff, black silk coat, a-glitter with jet trimming—commanded Maxine to stand out of the way, and let her go straight upstairs; and not to enter the room, because her elders had important matters to discuss, but to remain handy in case they wanted anything fetched, and to keep a look-out for Aunt Henrietta, to whom she herself had already telephoned, and who might be here at any moment, and to send for Gustava, and Haidée was unnecessary—but quite unnecessary; Haidée had always too much to say and no sense in it : " And then look, Maxine, be but a good girl and run home for me, to help Gisela with the supper, no? I forgot to leave word I was out, isn't it, and Emma and Eileen are invited. Zey are so looking forward to it and a little game of Bridge afterwards. . . . I must say, it is so like Toni——"

Maxine excused herself; she said she had to help her mother with the tea.

" And quite right that you should," cried Aunt Elsa.

" You don't help her enough, you and Iris. We know you
have to work, but there are other times. . . ." Aunt Elsa
disappeared into the Matriarch's bedroom. A couple of
minutes later, Aunt Henrietta turned up ; and then Aunt
Gustava in a taxi. She had called for Wanda on her way.
Truda, who longed to be at the conference, was kept downstairs by Maxine's generous plea that she should humour the
Matriarch and send up an exciting tea, baroque in its architecture, modelled on tradition, and well-flavoured with
memories. As for the frivolous Haidée, Val's mother, it was
just as well that she had not been sent for, because her habit
of dropping little amusing and bitter remarks, when they were
least wanted, always led to a quarrel with Aunt Elsa.

" I have seen Susie," Aunt Elsa declared : " I hurried down,
yes, just as I was. ' How much has he, then ? ' I asked her.
' Is it a *parti* ? For goodness sake, Susie, don't choose *now* to
be sentimental, and talk silliness about hoping she will be
happy.' "

" But that *is* Susie ! " remarked Anastasia, who was Susie's
mother-in-law ; " as if happiness did not depend, first of all,
on if a man has a sound business, and whether his parents
approve of the match. I must meet his parents at once. Has
anyone been sent for them ? Why not ? " Her glance roved
imperiously round the room ; hovered, for a moment, over
Wanda. . . .

" Goodness ! " ejaculated the latter. " I hope you don't
mean to send *me* to fetch them ? " and she tittered nervously.

" Is it not a marvel ? " the Matriarch appealed to Henrietta
—for Gustava, as usual, was on the verge of weeping, and not
of much assistance—" Is it not a marvel, how Wanda can always
laugh in that silly way ? One would suppose, isn't it, that she,
and not Gustava, could sit down, and cry, and thank Heaven
that we helped her ; yes, I, and the blessed Max and
Louis——" Aunt Elsa dabbed her eyes—" So that she isn't
married now to a bad husband, like my poor Toni."

Henrietta remarked, in her over-emphatic way, that they
could not be sure yet that Toni's choice was so utterly bad,
as none of them had seen the young man. " *Is* he young, by

the way ? I hope, at least, that. I will give her a nice wedding-present, if he is young. Come, Elsa, what is the good of your poking your nose into everything, if you have nothing fresh to tell us now. He is a Goy, of course ? and his name ? and his profession ? Does Susie like him ? and where are they going to live ? "

"And above all," interrupted Anastasia, bringing out her idiom with an air of one clinching the matter, "why—that is what I ask you—*why* has my granddaughter made this toad-in-the-hole marriage ? "

"His name is Giles Goddard," began Aunt Elsa, mysterious with the information which she alone possessed ; and pronouncing "Giles" with a hard G, and "Goddard" with a soft one.

"And his income ? "

Elsa was silent, struggling with a sneeze ; having once begun to sneeze, she did not stop for some time.

"He *is* a Goy," Gustava Czelovar put in. "That is why Constance thinks that Raoul will feel it so much that he was not consulted."

"And why, sought-out, should Raoul have been consulted ? " barked Henrietta. And Gustava subsided, murmuring vaguely, "Because of the Dean ! " . . . She was inclined to be elated that the Dean, the only Dean in the family, was her stepson's father-in-law.

Elsa, meanwhile, had recovered her speech :

"I cannot stand these English winters. For next winter I go abroad. I am all rheumatism ; my bones . . ."

"Your bones, for the moment, do not concern us. This Joddard, where did Toni meet him ? No, you need not tell me. At Richard's. Am I right ? Whatever goes wrong is from Richard's ; that boy is a curse. . . . I should not be surprised if you told me that Toni has married one of his farm workers. My delicate Toni married to a farm worker ! " wailed Anastasia, "making her hands rough with earth and cows' bludders ; she has such pretty hands, like all of the family, but especially her Aunt Simone ; my poor sister Simone ! "

Aunt Gustava, from weeping at Henrietta's snub, began to bridle and to smooth the silk dress over her knees, and to make other petty, trembling gestures, signifying that she had been directly insulted ; as she always did whenever Simone was mentioned ; for she was herself only the second wife of Karl Czelovar, who, previous to marrying her, had been married to Simone Rakonitz, the beautiful Miss Rakonitz of Vienna.

At that moment the entrance of Iris, the younger Silver girl, carrying a large tray with the best Sèvres tea-service, caused a diversion. Aunt Henrietta, in the brusque manner and repellent voice with which she covered her strong affection for all the children in the family, said at once :

" What is this we hear, Iris, that you want to bob your hair ? let's have no more talk of such nonsense, but be thankful that you have beautiful hair ; this ugly fashion of cutting may be all very well for others, but you should be proud, and not grumble."

Iris sighed, and began to clear the tea-table of its accumulation of old lace plunged in a basin of coffee, piles of faded photographs, broken jewelry, playing-cards, liniment, lamp-shade materials, and three open pots of different varieties of continental savoury pickle : " Gurken," which the Matriarch was interestedly sampling for a new firm, in defiance of the Doctor's orders : " Yes, yes, but it gives me something to wake up for, when I cannot sleep at night. And besides, it is an arrangement ; I get a commission on every pot I sell, and as this room is full of visitors always . . ." But very few people came any more to the Matriarch's room in Truda's house at Ealing. She received companies of ghosts . . . who did not purchase continental pickles.

" What ! " cried Aunt Elsa, " Iris cut her hair ? Shame yourself, Iris ! " They all glared at Iris, unwilling to make her more conceited, by informing her of a fact with which she had already been satiated, that she alone, of all the family, had inherited the famous red-gold hair of Simone ; hair which waved and rippled, in the true fairy-princess style, far below the knees ; they were shocked beyond words that she, unworthy of the privilege, should dare to talk of bobbing.

"Oh, I'm not going to bob," said Iris, gently. "Not if you really feel it would be a pity, Grandmère!"

Anastasia and Elsa and Henrietta were conscious of a quiver of uneasiness at this good-little-girl reply. It was the same with all the children, of late years: Toni, Maxine, Val, Pearl . . . they were indulgent. Almost terribly indulgent; they suppressed their own opinions, and were tolerant of the opinions of the older generation. This was as it should be, and yet—not quite as it should be. Respectful, yes; but tolerant—was it not almost an insult? Once upon a time, young girls had been afraid of their elders, and fear had kept them timid and obedient; and next-upon-a-time, they flared out into rebellion, and rebellion led to revolution, and revolution to escape. . . . All these phases were subtly flattering to despotism. But now—did Iris mean to be impertinent, with her yielding answer?

Iris, as it happened, concealed a real grievance; for even Truda, in all other things a kind and reasonable parent, was stuck fast in a bog of sentiment over this one matter; and Iris knew she would have to carry on her unwilling head, the burden of Simone's hair, with all the waste of time involved, and the heaviness of hairpins, for the remainder of her natural life. For she would not upset Truda; nor, indeed, Grandmère, and the few remaining aunts of the family: "They're pretty old and feeble nowadays; and one can see their point of view about all that ginger jam of yours!" advised Maxine.

One could. Maxine could; and Toni and Iris and Val and Pearl. They were a soft and chivalrous generation, these hard women of the twentieth century.

The natural result of the unspoken thrill of discomfort caused to the four old ladies and Wanda, by the Iris interlude, was a greater truculence than even before, when they returned to the question of Toni and Toni's husband.

"How much *has* he, then?" repeated Aunt Henrietta, "and what, I beg of you, does he do?"

"But nossing, I tell you. Nossing, nossing! He has just come out of the Army; he was at Köln; they say his father is rich, and will allow him something. Susie spoke of two thousand pounds a year. . . . That is not too much, if they have to keep Susie too."

Wanda reminded them that there was still the business in Hanover Street : "Toni's."

"Yes, well, and what is to become of that ? And just as it was beginning to do well ! Is she to go on going every day, leaving her home ? leaving her husband to look after the babies ? "

"But I *asked* Susie that, if only you would listen. I asked her, and she said, ' No, Toni is tired of business.' Toni will remain a sleeping partner, and draw a little every year and no more ; and what she draws, she will give Susie."

Aunt Henrietta said slowly, and there was more prophetic force behind her words, and less shrill denunciation than had yet been heard in that room to-day :

"Toni won't like being dependent on her husband for money, and having to ask him for every penny, now, after she has been the paying one for so long. It was different for us ; yes, it was easier for us, because we had known no other way ; and even then, not so easy," and her voice was as though marked and seamed and pocked by the many times in the past that she had had to go unwillingly to Otto Solomonson, and say, not daring to let her impatience be visible : "Otto, give me money," and Otto's invariable reply—the reply of all the Ottos in the universe : "Vot do you want it for ? I gave you some last week."

"I cannot settle anything," said Anastasia, "until I have had an interview with Mr. Joddard, the young man's father. I must know for certain what is being settled upon the young people, and if it will be enough for them to live in the style to which my Toni is accustomed." The Matriarch was speaking in the grand manner. She had forgotten many things. She forgot on the same grand scale as she had done everything else, for over eighty years. As though to materialise the momentary dreams that were drifting through her mind, Truda appeared now with the Crême-Düten, which she had made as a favour to Maxine ; and Iris followed with the coffee ; and Aunt Gustava stopped crying ; and Aunt Elsa pulled up her veil; and Anastasia was a very gracious hostess; and they were all quite sure, already, that she had only to meet Mr. Joddard senior, to vanquish him. But it was queer . . . that Toni should have married like this . . . like this . . . without permission, without any coloured display; violating tradition, upsetting her grandmother. Like this . . . without congratulation, without Crême-Düten, without anything . . .

" I do not think, mind you," pronounced Aunt Elsa, " that Toni was ever so very wonderfully clever at her business, as you always said, 'Stasia. I thought, several times, that I must help this poor, brave girl to get along; so I took her that lovely piece of blue silk brocade which Berthe had sent me from Paris—I believe die Tante Gisela bought it at the Exhibition of 1890—and some beautiful trimming—I was going to have it made up into a blouse for Pearl—but I assure you, Toni made nossing of it at all. She was not even attending when I gave her my ideas, and she had no fashion-books there that I could see from, a little bit. Perhaps she is better married than in business, but that doesn't take it away that she is very ungrateful."

Aunt Gustava agreed that Toni was highly ungrateful.

The Matriarch was exhausted, but she rallied for a final defence of her favourite Toni : " Now you need not talk so swelled, Gustava; we all have trouble with our grand-daughters; what is this I hear, by accident, from Maxine, about your Val going abroad without a chaperon? and rubbish about a house in Italy? and not even coming to say good-bye? I must say, I never thought much good would come of it to let her learn that painting, and now, you see—it is a quite mad idea; they do mad things, young girls, nowadays."

" Her pictures are terrible, terrible ! " put in Aunt Henrietta, " too terrible ! "

Quite unexpectedly, Aunt Elsa ruffled up, in her turn, defending Val. She possessed one of Val's pictures, a conciliatory present after strife !—and did not like to hear its value depreciated : " And why should she not go abroad, and see our relations at San Remo ? " . . .

"*If* she goes to see them," began Henrietta, ominously.
. . . "I know Val; she is not fond of paying calls on her
relations."

And Anastasia had just begun to say: "If anyone ever
brought up her daughter badly, and spoilt her, and gave her
no ideas of what was right, it is Haidée" . . . when Haidée
walked in, and put an end to that section of the discussion.

"Well!" she queried, impertinently. "What about
Haidée?" She had always been less afraid of the Aunts than
either Truda or Wanda, who were about her age. "Crême-
Düten! Good! Who ordered Crême-Düten? I thought
they were a relic of the Franco-Prussian War. And what's all
this about Toni and her runaway match? I suppose you are
terribly angry with her, Aunt 'Stasia? She *is* a young scamp!"

Anastasia Rakonitz said, severely: "It will no doubt
astonish you, Haidée, for you are used to your daughter, Val,
doing harry-carry things without you or Francis being told;
but Toni is not like that. She told me at the same time that
she came to ask my approval of her engagement to this Giles
Goddard"—and, accidently mispronouncing the name she
had heard from Aunt Elsa's lips, she got it right—"and she
told me, too, that for private family reasons, that it is not
likely I would tell you about, Haidée—you who are so indis-
creet, and go babbling everywhere—the wedding would have
to be a very quiet one. My granddaughter has made a good
match, and I am satisfied."

CHAPTER IV

THE scene was Venice. The October moon decorated the vague spaces between sky and lagoon, like romance's first round platitude spoken for the first time; it burnished the water which slapped at the steps of the Doges' ghost-white Palace; it fingered the sharp, black edges of the buildings on the island of San Giorgio; they lay like one building, flat against the sky's pallor. In a gondola on the Grand Canal, Toni and Giles were holding hands.

Toni was holding his hand, because this was Venice by moonlight, and she was on her honeymoon, and had a mocking sense of the fitness of things. She held his hand from the same capricious choice that had made her insist on Venice; it was her secret joke: she had married a conventional husband, and here they were in the conventional gondola. The conventional moon was the same red-gold as Aunt Simone's hair, as Iris's hair; she, Toni Rakonitz, Toni Goddard, completed the conventional picture by the conventionally romantic gesture: she held his hand.

And it wasn't so bad . . .

As for Giles, he held Toni's hand because he wanted to. His motives were always simple and unaffected; though, at times, startling to Toni, who pleased herself by arranging him always by the formula to which she had first fitted him. She did this in a high-handed sort of way, consistently following out her line of the wholly preposterous, because her love-affair of the Five Approaching Males towards Richard's duck-pond, had begun so preposterously; and she had no wish to alter the vein of comic exaggeration. So whenever Giles walked out of the rather narrow limits she had so imperiously set to his tastes and understanding, Toni either pretended not to notice, or else nimbly put him back again. Nevertheless, she had had one or two small shocks already. It was a joke, undoubtedly, that a Rakonitz should marry into a family composed entirely of strong men, of the English country-house and landed-gentry race; who looked their best in old tweeds and old prejudices; who talked about horses, and had been to public schools, and were as offhand about each other as was the North Pole, possibly, about the Equator. Therefore, she insisted that the joke should be kept up. As a joke, in fact, it excused her. It translated a marriage, to which he had consented for reasons that were plainly a betrayal of her spiritual fearlessness, into terms of buffoonery. Yet, after all the buffetings she had had, did she need excuse? So Toni petulantly argued with an adversary who was also Toni. There was surely a gallant swagger in the joke? If you did not expect romantic love any more, why, then you did not moan, but snapped your fingers at it; burlesqued it—with Venice, and two in a gondola, holding hands. You presented your Giles Maurice Goddard, aged twenty-eight, Charterhouse and Univ., with a very scrupulously bound Vellum Edition of Toni, trimming away such superfluities as an acute talent for business, and a keen sense of obligation to your kin —oh no! he certainly would not want that! nor a Family like the first eight chapters from Chronicles, who would expect to be asked to the wedding, and to the house-warming, and to the Baronitzutahs of many sons. So the family was carefully screened away behind Toni's casual: " I'd rather be married at a Registry Office, Giles. We don't want fuss and people, do we? "

And that other betrayal, of " Toni's "? the business which her driving energy, grimly and tirelessly, had pulled through crisis after crisis, as a child is pulled through its perilous infantile complaints, until at last, taut nerves might slacken, for at last a solvent " Toni's " was beginning to acquire personality in the dress world?—that, too, was recklessly tossed over her shoulder; slaughtered in some such phrase as: " Oh! yes, it was quite amusing, for a time, to run a shop; lots of girls do, you know; but we needn't be bothered with it any more. I've told them they can keep my name on, if

they like. . . ." Miss Thompson, the superlatively good
fitter, and Aimée Lequesne were running "Toni's" now,
though she remained a sleeping partner and Court of Final
Appeal ; arranging with the Bank for her signature to all the
big monthly cheques ; and reserving the right to look into the
books whenever she wanted to. It was she who had hastily
fixed Miss Thompson's present salary at £300 a year, and
Aimée Lequesne's at £200, though, by a system of payment
in closed envelopes, neither of them were to know what the
other was to receive ; Aimée would not have seen why . . . ?
Toni herself, who had drawn £500 a year out of the business
during the last two years, now fixed to draw only £200 a year ;
and this should go, every shilling of it, to her mother. Her
brother Gerald was beginning to earn quite adequately ;
between the two of them, Susie would be all right ; and Giles
need not know—here was the point !—that Toni had relations
who were dependent on her. It made such a dingy figure of
her girlhood, to have " dependent relations." Only—and in
this lay the ironic fun of the situation !—by placing herself in
such a pretty, amber limelight, softening all the angular
curves ; by wantonly remaining the charming, graceful,
demure girl in yellow, who had poured out the drinks one
afternoon, ten days ago, on Richard's lawn—Toni had left
herself entirely dependent on Giles. But how fantastic a
change, exulted Toni-of-all-people, to be actually a spoilt,
quiescent, soft, little plunderer of male pockets ; to watch
Giles pay the bills ; to yield her suitcase to Giles to carry,
because—with a little sigh : " It's so heavy—and, please, I
didn't mean to bring such a lot of luggage, Giles darling ;
but you *do* like me to look nice, and you know what shoes
are ! " . . . Val would have shaken her.

She was not staging herself as a fool ; that would have
involved too much conscious labour ; merely as a gay, irresponsible comrade in the frivolous good time they both meant
to have. Sternly, underneath the joke, Toni determined that
the future should solidify into fact, what she was shaping
herself, in play ; she purposed remaining this pirate to whom
gold was always accessible ; this slender, delicate, blossomy

creature, for whom burdens must be carried. Princess Parasite ?
But shameless Toni only shrugged her shoulders. . . . No
girl, she averred, can ever again shrug shoulders so lightly, who
has but once made the mistake of letting it be known that she
can carry burdens upon them. She had proved this. So let
Giles remain ignorant of her carrying powers.

As for love, you laughed at love, by taking your big, good-
looking, young husband to Venice, and lying with him in a
gondola under the moon, just to show that you were " Venice-
proof," and that they could not have you any more in the good
old way, with the good old stunts ! Coat of mail and cap of
darkness ! . . . but Toni had to admit that the overdone
" properties " which Venice shook out of her sleeve for lovers
on a honeymoon : lagoon and moon and gondola, were putting
up a pretty show, nevertheless.

Music, too. . . . " Oh, the darlings ! " exclaimed Toni, as
men's voices drifted faintly across to them, singing the melodies
which had dripped sentiment into the shimmering black and
silver water for the past fifty years, at least ; and—no, surely
this was too plausible to be true ?—

—" Good old Barcarolle," grunted Giles, heartily : and
their gondola glided easily to a place among the group of
gondolas that were floating round the stationary raft of the
singers. " Funny, though, isn't it ? the boats swing in time
to that music—hackneyed as the deuce, of course ! but it
just hits the gondola rhythm." Indeed, the monotonous
cadence seemed to appeal to the mating instinct in the proud,
dumb gondolas, as they rode, with high uplifted prows, on the
Lagoon ; to impel them, by mysterious force, nearer and nearer,
each stealthy two attentive to the spell ; so that you expected
that, in a final tempest of passion, the notched steel would
clash and clash together. But the flanks of the gondolas
touched silently like the rubbing of velvet upon velvet, and
glided apart again . . . till the melody drew them once more.

. . . Hussy of the Adriatic !—(" Bride," indeed !) . . . Yet
what more ridiculous than Toni's confidence that her lagoon
and moon, and her gondolas like giants' shoon, could no longer
work their rhyming, lapping magic ? " Hackneyed as the

deuce ! " Giles had said ; and Toni had chosen Venice because
there was not the faintest possible element of risk in being
taken in by it ! Gondolas ? Good Heavens ! Moonlight ?
Good God ! . . . But she felt a twinge of mistrust, inside
her enveloping coat-of-mail ; suppose it had broken slightly
apart at one of the seams, and suppose Venice were to
creep in ?

" Can you cope with any more of this syrup ? " she asked
her husband, uneasily. " Shall we go on to Rome ? " Or
couldn't she risk Rome, either ? Was there no place of enough
old-fashioned and conventional beauty to fit into the joke,
Toni's rollicking joke ? The places she had really ached to see,
the travelling she had longed for, now no less than always :
Vienna, Budapest, Constantinople—these she had not dared
visit, for fear of the tumult they might awake in her. And for
a deeper-lying fear . . . that the joke might not look so
funny, there. Besides, you did not go to Vienna, for the first
time, with the wrong man ; not if you were Toni Rakonitz.
You could go to Venice with the wrong man, of course, because
—oh ! well, Venice was an idiot !

" Let's stay here," replied a lazy and contented Giles,
answering her question. " Of course it's a dug-out—I said
so !—isn't that what you chose it for ? Isn't that in keeping
with the latest whim—fad—what d'you call it ?—to be
Victorian and put antimacassars on your jazz arm-chairs ? "
His eyes teased her ; Kitchener eyes, Toni had called them,
because they were set so deep under their gables ; but then
she had noticed how they lacked blue steel and keenness ; and :
" A loafer's eyes," she added, tempering her former description. And he had retorted, not inadequately, by describing
her as less a girl of flesh and substance, than an Immaculate
Silhouette of the Very Latest Fashion. . . . And there he was,
out of the formula again ! The Giles of her conception,
might, indeed, have realised, in a stumbling, infatuated sort
of way, that she always " looked all right, somehow. Her
clothes, I expect, or the way she puts 'em on or something——"
but without the power of being so articulate about it. Toni
was rapidly becoming impatient with these two truants from

her good management : this Venice of persistent enchantment ; and this Giles, who refused to talk in empty, well-bred tones about what was done and not done . . .

" It's the gondolas that get me," Giles went on. " What luck that the late Republic of Venice should have had that stingy fit, pandering to the Puritan Party !—when they gave orders that gondolas were not to be coloured any more, because the nobles were getting too damned extravagant all round. All this splendid, sombre black and gold is simply the making of Venice ; it must have looked pretty foul, before ! But that *is* Italy : they get most of their best effects by accident, I've noticed ; and usually when they're trying for the exact opposite ! "

Toni agreed that she would not have fancied a gondola in vieux-rose picked out with blue. And then, unnecessarily, she reverted to his question about her reasons for the choice of Venice, which still plagued her as might an unsuccessful burlesque that you afterwards try to justify by re-naming it a morality play :

" My great-grandfather married a Venetian woman ; so I was curious to come here. She was a Civrian ; there were five lovely sisters, and their father was a glass-blower, and they lived in an old palazzo up by the Rialto Bridge."

Giles did not look as disgusted at the mention of relations, as her hypersensitive feelings on the subject had led her to expect :

" How jolly ! then you've got it in the blood. But what a shame that you haven't tawny Venetian hair. I stood on the steps of the Rialto for about two hours yesterday, while you were in the shops, hoping to spot some of it ; but I believe it's extinct."

" My cousin, Iris, has got it." Now she had so fatally begun, Toni was curiously impelled to go on boasting about the family ; but she hoped Giles would stop her soon, by looking bored. " Iris isn't Venetian, and nor am I, and nor was Aunt Simone, though the colour of her hair was just that dark red-gold. My great-grandfather married twice ; Clementina Civrian was his second wife. I'm descended from the first, through Grandmère——" She stopped herself from further babblings.

" I haven't seen your granny yet, have I ? "

" You'd know it if you had," spoke a voice in Toni's soul ... but not aloud. If only Giles could be aware how far removed was the Matriarch, Anastasia Rakonitz, in all her rich and jubilant arrogance, from the pretty oleograph of silver curls, knitting, and a gentle voice, implied by the old-fashioned term " granny " !

The concert was over now, and the gondolas shot away, one by one, into the warm darkness. Presently, they were drifting back to their hotel; too soon for such a night; Giles rummaged among his forgotten tags of Latin, and produced some sort of order to the gondolier, that he was to take them a long way round by the little canals, dark crooked water-ways between high walls. Now and then he uttered a low, musical cry of warning : " Ohé ! " as they swung round a corner, or under the archway of a bridge where the water lay in a triangle of blacker velvet in the blackness.

" What are we going to do afterwards, Giles ? No, I don't mean Rome ; I mean after that, when we get back to the studio ? "

" Enjoy ourselves like Hell," said Giles. " You weren't expecting me to say that I must take up some form of regular work, were you ? I'll stop in Venice, if I've got to work, and become a dredger. Imagine the really exciting bodies I should have to haul out of the water on to the steps, while they dripped green slime down my trousers, and gondoliers wailed : ' Ohé ! '—which is awfully like ' Oh, I say ! ' when you come to think of it ! "

Toni shuddered. " I don't see myself as a dredger's wife, not even in Venice, with a shawl over my un-Venetian hair ! No, of course I don't want you to work. Why should I ? Though I suppose the right sort of wife would inspire you with lofty ambitions to Make Good."

" *Going* to make good," murmured Giles, prone on the cushions at Toni's feet. " Going to make good, having a good time. Had enough work. School and 'Varsity, and then

six years of war, two years more than nearly everybody else.
. . . I was some ass to get into the Occupying Army."

"What is your great secret ambition, Giles ? Surely every
decent fellow has a Great Ambition ? "

" Honest ? "

" Yes, honest." Now she could see if her formula were in
working order. What, according to type, should his great
ambition prove to be ? The lonely summit of Mount Everest ?
the North Pole by aeroplane ? making a century for England
against the Australians ? Toni ran them all over in her mind,
hearty, robust, manly ambitions, worthy of an Island Race ;
nothing morbid or exotic ! And he would be reticent, of course,
in revealing them ; shy, and rather awkward ; he would make
her promise not to rag him. . . .

But Giles's revelation of his most intimate feelings was
delivered without any preface or apology ; and with all the
suppleness at the joints of rhetoric, which one has learnt to
expect from one of Dostoievsky's Russians, meeting a stray
victim, dumb but not deaf, in a café in Moscow :

" I'd like to stand in front of a cheering, raving, hectically
applauding crowd, all because of me ; just for a moment,
focussing the sensation I'd won ; drinking it in. I don't quite
know what for, and it really wouldn't matter ; an opera-
singer at the end of his big act on a gala evening ; a dramatist,
taking his call on the first night ; or a soldier back from "—he
laughed—" a rather showy campaign ; or a K.C., who has
managed to get his murderer off against overwhelming odds ;
it would have to be a very public trial, of course, and millions
of people swarming round the Court-house. Or," added
Giles, with earnest and appealing directness, " a king ; not
that a king ever gets much of a show nowadays, unless one
had a revolution—oh, I wouldn't mind being guillotined, if
they'd stick it up in a really conspicuous place ! "

. . . " Ohé ! " cried the gondolier, as he delicately shaved
the corner of a bridge, and oared them for a moment into the
light of a rusty iron lantern out-thrust from the wall, as
though a rigid fist were holding it there. Toni was staring at
Giles in complete amazement : he could not really mean what

he was saying? but even as a form of chaff, it took an unexpected line; his Great Ambition was so acutely personal,
so ignoble and gaudy . . .

"You don't really mean all that, do you, Giles?"

"Why not?" replied a perfectly serene Giles, whose face
she could not see; they had passed, now, out of the light of
the lamp, into another canal that was a mere flowing strip
between the palace backs.

"Well," said Toni, sublimely unconscious how she, in her
turn, by a reversal of rôles, had adopted the public-school and
country-house outlook, which she had so confidently expected
from him: "it—it's not even adult! It's not the sort of
thing that you *ought* to want most of all, unless you're a child,
screaming for something glittering to hold."

"I didn't say it was what I *ought* to want most! I ought,
of course, to want to accomplish something by steady, patient
labour, that will benefit mankind, and nobody ever know that
I did it; like the cure for cancer, you know. But," he finished,
plaintively, "it's not my fault if I'm vulgar, is it?"

He could feel Toni's body shaking with laughter, close up
against his. She was laughing, as Providence had fortunately
enabled her to laugh, at her own discomfiture; for Giles's
ambition really had shocked her. And with the discovery,
that it was certainly hopeless to continue obstinate in her
belief that he was the kind of man, easy to deal with, whom
civilisation had known as long as it had been familiar with
maps, she began to wonder what their uncharted future
together would be like? It could not be left altogether without
plans, to haphazard, and to the doubtful good-nature of heaven.
One's grandparents—they had never discussed anything beforehand, and look what a mess . . .

"About children, Giles," said this 1921 Toni, "I'm not
keen on being a childless couple, are you? or even part of
one; but we do want, both of us, to let things rip, and
have a good time without any hindrances. . . ." She
hesitated.

"Kids needn't be hindrances, if you sling 'em over to a
decently expensive nurse," said this 1921 Giles. The scene

was Venice by moonlight, in a gondola, and they were on their honeymoon. . . .

"Of course we'd provide a decently expensive nurse. You don't think I mean to trail about in a nursery for the rest of my radiant youth, hanging wee under-garments over the fire-guard to dry? No, but the point is, shall we get it over, and have a child first, and a good time afterwards?"

"Why not the other way round?"

"That would limit the revelry, wouldn't it? I don't want to feel that in the middle of everything, one's Inner Policeman would bawl: 'Time's up! come along, now, and have a family!' A good time ought to go on and on and on, like a road over the hills."

Giles remarked, indolently controversial, according to masculine habit, over the symbol instead of its essence, that he would hate a road over the hills to go on and on and on, without any prospects of an end, and a halt, and a drink.

"But look here, Giles, I'm not going to dump a nursery on you if you'd feel it as any sort of check. . . . You know, when we got married, the notion was, that we weren't, either of us, to be stuck in a quaggy place, not able to get out without dragging on the other; we were each going to do as we liked."

"Of course," Giles agreed; "that was in the bond." He did not feel very strongly about it, because his manner of upbringing, mainly by his father, and a tutor, and then in institutes run by males, for males, with males, had always left him personally free, after he had done obeisance to an obvious mechanical routine. So that he took it for granted that marriage would impose no more "dragging" than the negligible amount within the scope of his imagination. He had wondered, idly, why Toni had been so insistent that he and she should continue morally, as free as gipsies? naturally, marriage did not prevent this! Toni, by getting hectic over their mutual freedom, was offering a gift of space and fresh air to one who had all his life dwelt solitary upon open moorland.

But when Giles had tentatively enquired whether Toni would, perhaps, as she seemed fearful of certain penalties and

bogeys in marriage, prefer something called a " free union,"
he liked to remember how her fastidiousness had curled back,
in disdain, from even the phrase ; which, from her point of
view, signified a muddle, pompously designated ; and only
chosen by marriage shirkers, who could not even properly
handle their so-called " freedom." Giles was heartily glad
she felt like that about it. But she was, surely, a bit morbid
on the notion of " dragging on one another," domestic
tyranny, and so forth ? . . . Toni a tyrant ? Ridiculous !
Then what was she afraid of ?

" Afraid of herself " . . . did not occur to him, as a solution ; nor that she was piling up barriers to thwart her own
matriarchy, should it ever become uncontrollable ; warning
Giles, warning her husband. . . . But he had decided that
Toni had heard of unfeeling husbands who forced motherhood
on their wives " because all women enjoy it " ! Well, she was
stupid for once. *His* was not an " all-women " type of reason-
ing. He set to work, reassuring her : " The main point is,
Toni, that if *you* don't want to have children, you needn't
think you have to, because of me, and because you're married.
However sensibly we behave afterwards, over nurses, and not
being sentimental, and all that, still, it *will* be your show and
not mine " . . . he stopped, suddenly, seeing a mental picture,
almost unbearably vivid, of the usual bedroom and furnishings,
during the time when a child was being born ; marionettes in
the costumes of doctor, nurse, anxious mother . . . tip-
toeing to the door—creak—creak—passing on the message :
" getting on as well as we can expect "—to the anxious husband,
who waited, racked with impatience, in the passage, on the
stairs, in and out of the dining-room. He had heard the whole
process recited a thousand times ; by married pals . . . and
in books. . . . It was all so familiar as to have contained no
meaning at all—until, as now, he visualised Toni in that room,
and himself outside it. Unbearable ? well—but how was he
going to bear it, then, when the time came ? Toni could face
it, nonchalantly, . . . for Toni had pluck. He wished those
beastly writers would not be quite so lush with their description of " a sound of low moaning," " a scream of agony which

wrung the man's heart "—not too late to prevent it happening, now, while he still had Toni safe in his arms, and she could
coolly discuss whether or not it would be convenient to have
a child. Anyway, he did not want Toni to have children,
just to please him. He felt absurdly unlike a father ; the word
still had dignified associations, or foolish and pompous associations, of grey beard and walrus moustache ; and of the
genial fellow represented in the advertisements, wearing a
bowler hat, and bringing home, while the Little Ones clustered
round him in the hall, special preparations of toffee, or oats,
or breakfast food : " *Father*, is it Dodson's ? If it's Dodson's,
it's RIGHT ! " . . . —Father ? . . . What did Toni want ?
talking about love and motherhood in that voice which always
seemed to him as light and as soft and as cool as falling snow-
flakes ? snowflakes that heaped up, and formed a hiding-place.
. . . Caves and hollows underneath the brittle snow. He had
learnt very little, as yet, of his carnival partner.

And Toni, who imagined that she had not married for love ;
who imagined that she wanted to have no more to do with
family or family obligations, who wanted her future to be
divinely carefree, without shackles upon her time or high
spirits, who had desired recklessly to spend money on enjoying
herself—Toni, not wholly a traitor, was quite determined
that one child, at least, they must have. One child ; and soon.
The racial instinct was still resilient in her ; so that she looked
upon the next generation as the generation that counted, and
the existing generation only important as parents. Her
individual life had fought to contradict all this. It was *she*
who wanted to laugh and dance and enjoy herself ; not her
sons and daughters, but she, Toni, now, most urgently ;
nevertheless—and here pride of matriarchy rolled up !—she
was the eldest of the eldest of the eldest of the eldest . . . it
must not be Toni Rakonitz who failed to carry on the Rakonitz
family. Her conscience refused that responsibility, worse
than any she had yet shouldered, of voluntarily being the one
to stop the progressive line. " Begat," that word echoing
through Old Testament Chronicles, was in the marrow of her
bones, commanding them. Toni denied that she was romantic ;

denied that she was religious; most vehemently would she deny that she was obedient. Yet she still found romance in the continuance of a great family; she was still obedient to what was demanded of her, in fulfilment of her share in it. But as for religion—oh, you called it a code, for present-day needs; or, with yet more wrappings of slang: " behaving decently! " . . . So she thought of having a child, not heroically, as of one dedicated to race, but as " a hell of a nuisance "—with the same impatience that she had felt, when she was a child, and received a circulating round-robin letter, during that trying fashion: you copied out a prayer, or a wish, or a page of poetry three times, and sent it on to three of your friends; and it all seemed quite purposeless, but it just had to go on, because it had started somewhere, and someone expected you to do it, and you dared not risk your luck—and not only your own, but, it might be, an accumulation of luck—by being the first one to say "stop!"

If you were a spinster, and could not help being a descendant but never an ancestor, that absolved you. But Toni recognised the decree, and yielded to it, which had kept the Israelites still a vitality to be reckoned with, through ages of persecution and exile. Only half an Israelite herself, and she had married a Christian; there would not be much of the Jew in Toni's child. Still . . . she shrugged her shoulders—you married and let yourself in for it; the world must go on!

" Postponing things is the devil," she remarked to Giles; " I hate going to a party, and being called away for an hour, just as I've really got going; and then coming back to it and having to get into my stride all over again. So let's have a child before we even begin to paint the town red. It needn't affect you, Giles, any old way."

" Lord, no! It needn't affect the Chinese Minister nor the policeman in Ludgate Circus, need it? Why do you suppose I married you, Toni? "

" Because I'm so attractive, darling! " She turned towards him, laughing, her eyes gaily crinkled, as they had been the opening moment he had seen her, in her yellow dress, with a thunder-sky behind her.

He knew, by now, that she was not really beautiful; that
had been his illusion of the first half-hour; but he knew, too,
that within her sedate and exquisitely dandified shell, she was
debonair, and nimble-witted; wild and tingling with life;
responsive to its limitless possibilities, as no other girl whom
he had met during his leaves, or since he had returned home
from Germany. Hundreds of girls there had been, who could
dance as well as Toni, and dress almost as well as Toni; who
had the same smooth, bobbed hair; and the same happy,
unscrupulous, piratical methods of gaining whatever they
wanted. But they did not want *enough* . . . they did not
know how much richness existed, that they ought to want and
to fight for. Toni did!—that was the difference. You sensed
that she was insatiable, but wisely, and not in tiresome ignorance. Leaven your greed with irony—Toni had learnt that
lesson, somehow. Pretty useful, the things Toni had learnt!
. . . Giles admired the consequences, without guessing what
rough experience had led to them. He was most of all relieved
that Toni did not take marriage seriously; he would have
been bored beyond telling, by a union of solemn ecstasies and
bated breath; too much trouble, after this long business of
war; too burdensome altogether, such a rarefied atmosphere:
" how different and how wonderful it's all going to be, my
darling! "—But Toni and he were good companions; they
did not believe that their life was going to be anything especially sanctified. Why should it be? Other people's weren't.
He loved Toni, but not—so he believed!—not uncomfortably
too much. As for Toni . . . had she any passionate feelings
for him at all? One old-fashioned love-scene, with "speeches"
in it, might have enlightened him; out-of-date! . . . You
must just puzzle along, then. . . . She was sweet to his silent
ardour, sweet and warm, as ripened raspberries flushed in the
sun, with that queer glamour in their flavour that is a surprise
every time you taste them afresh. That might be her acting,
of course. All the better—he could enjoy dealing with a
scoffing young rogue and hypocrite, if the rogue were Toni.
He was not very sure about any of Toni's qualities, good
or bad; though he had formed conclusions that she was

extravagant, lazy, and callous about home ties—— For just so
clever had his rogue and actress been, in the specially edited and
revised version of " Toni Rakonitz," which she had presented
to him; just so clever in omitting all mention of her fifteen
heart-rending, heart-hardening years of obstinate and dreary
service in hard work and payment of debt, for her family !

. . . Toni interrupted his reverie, by demanding that he should
share her pleasure in the sequence of superb poses, which their
gondolier perforce had to repeat over and over again in the
three movements of his oar. Giles cast an envious look over
his shoulder. A fellow who could wear a sash twisted round
his hips, and stand upright and remote with all the glory of
Venice for background, had obvious advantages over a recum-
bent Englishman without a sash !

" Would you love me better if I were a gondolier, Toni ? "

" No; I'm not romantic."

" You lie," said Giles.

" Not for gondoliers, anyway."

" Nor for me. I know that. But for somebody ? once ?
long ago ? some day ? . . .

" Well . . . but meanwhile—I'm here." She slipped down
the cushions, closer to his side. Toni was never niggardly.
Toni had merchant blood in her, and fair and honest merchant
blood at that; she had married Giles, if not so much for his
money, for ease and escape and change; yet she had nothing
but scorn for those tremulously sensitive martyrs who, when
they married for more or less the same reasons as herself, would
yet shrink away from their husbands, with ice-cold finger-
tips, and back pressed close to the wall, faintly murmuring :
" Please—oh, please "—in defence against his brutality.
" Damn it ! " argued Antoinette Rakonitz, whose name was
good enough, in business, for a business man to have advanced
her, two years ago, £1500 without guarantee, when she had
wanted to set up on her own, " Why, damn it ! it's indecent
not to carry out your share in a contract, squarely and whole-
heartedly, and even with something over the margin. And
what's wrong with letting the man you trade with think that
you're pleased with the deal ? "

And she remembered how Uncle Max had taken her, when she was about thirteen, to see Mr. and Mrs. Kendal in " The Iron-Master."   Maximilian Rakonitz could not have realised, before he was actually in the box, that this play was a translation of " Le Maître de Forges."   He had probably deemed the Kendals a solid and respectable education in themselves, for a young girl.   Toni, in frilly white, was very full, at that period, of chatter and pert opinions ; she had remarked, after the curtain had fallen on the famous bedroom scene :—" Here is your sleeping apartment, madam, and here is mine . . . ! " —that she thought it rather silly of Mrs. Kendal to have shrieked and shuddered and clenched with quite so much offended sensibility, when Mr. Kendal had approached her with kindly but amorous intentions.   Uncle Max's friend, Zillah Korishelski, who had been with them, and who was always on the look-out for an opportunity to snub either Val or Toni, had snapped : " Now you be quiet, Miss, and don't talk about what you don't understand " ; and then had added, in explanation : " it's a terrible thing, a terrible thing, for a woman to be touched by a man she doesn't love. You'll know, one day."   And here, right across time, and across Europe and the lapping waters of Venice, " one day " had come, and Toni knew. . . .

—And still thought that " Claire " had been kicking up rather an unnecessary fuss. After all, fair was fair ; and she had married the man !

She did not allow Giles, on his honeymoon, to be disappointed.

CHAPTER V

TONI and Giles were at breakfast in Val's studio. They had been occupying it for about four months. Giles was tensely engaged with his kidneys and bacon; Toni with her letters. A 'phone conversation had just ended, and probably they would be rung up again in a few moments; the telephone bell usually gave them very little rest, during fifteen hours out of the twenty-four. Ten minutes past ten; and they had ordered the car for eleven; but Toni was still wearing her dressing-gown, sprigged silk, coral-tinted roses set formally on an ivory stripe, quaintly out of place in the brilliant, rather jazzish scheme of decoration left behind by the artist who had owned the premises previous to Val. The Goddards had returned home very late, the night before: "About time I took a pull," reflected Toni; her child was expected in another five months. She did not, in doting fondness, think of the infant, already, as "my son," because, frankly, though she cared very little whether it should prove to be a son or a daughter, she had a slight bias towards a daughter; Toni's experience allowed less chance of a girl turning out to be flabby stuff, than a boy; most young mothers longed for a boy; prayed for a boy; spilt all their devotion in front of a boy . . . and then he became the usual man! If the very tolerable imitation of a fine young husband acquired by Toni were not sufficient to coax her from the immunity provided by a too early injection of scepticism, she was certainly not going to venture her emotions into the open again, exposing them to sure disappointment, for a son; she would admit no glamorous likelihood that her son would be nobler, kinder, more heroic, of greater moral sturdiness, than anybody else's son.

Well, one way or another, a son or a daughter . . . and no

55

more dashing round—after this week-end. Oh—and next week was packed with a specially cheery programme, not to be lightly sacrificed. But after that, quiet and rest.

And meanwhile, these bills ! . . .

Toni's eyes twinkled. Her elbows on the table, her chin cupped in her hands, she looked beseechingly at her young husband. . . . This promised to be quite a pretty scene, with the late head of " Toni's " playing chief part in it :

" Giles, darling . . . is your coffee all right ? "

Giles grinned back at her :

" I've had one or two bills, myself," he confessed. " It's damned expensive, keeping the Dook ; always lying helpless in the garage, under repairs. I wonder if I ought to have spent my gratuity on something more useful ?—ploughshares, for instance ? "

" We can't run about London on ploughshares," sighed Toni ; " and anyway, think what the Dook saves us——"

—" In 'bus and tube fares ? Yes, I know. That's the stock argument. I wonder if you've been more than about twice in your life in a 'bus, you wasteful hussy ? "

Toni's sentiments towards him were all of spontaneous admiration ; truly, it was marvellous that his usual intelligence —and she granted him that, now !—should so far have failed him as not to notice that her responsive sparkle for this good time they had been having, through the past autumn and winter, was largely due to its fling-back of contrast with her former poverty-stricken existence.

" These bills, Giles," she began again, with the air of one charmingly half-afraid, half-confident of being helped and comforted, even though she had been naughty. " They do seem to have mounted up a bit. I wonder whether it *is* extravagant to have one's shoes and hats especially moulded, to order."

" Not with your unique head and feet.—But don't you get trade discount ? "

" Only for my dresses from ' Toni's,' of course. And it's a fatal discount—it leads one on and on. I asked for my pass-book, when ' Féo's ' account came in last week, and that's

arrived too, this morning. And I suppose I *ought* to have paid
for my fur coat three months ago, when I said I did."

" Didn't you ? You are a scoundrel, Toni ! "

" And," finished Toni—" pass the marmalade, dear heart !
—and I seem to be overdrawn. What are we going to do
about it ? "

Giles began to look efficient : " What's the total ? "

And then the minx whom he had married discarded the
last remnants of her honesty, and simply wallowed in the
semblance of a weak but lovable woman : " I'm so bad at
figures, Giles," helplessly ; " and in a bit of a muddle over
the debit and credit sides of my pass-book. . . . What *is* this
sum that they've filled in with pencil ? ought I to subtract or
add it ? "

" My dear little girl," Giles's voice swelled and rounded, as
he deliberately burlesqued the pompous city husband ; for he
guessed that Toni wanted her bills paid ; and guessed that it
might be easier for her to ask this favour of him, as a figure of
exaggerated comedy, than if he remained Giles. As for her
behaviour in coming to stand behind his chair, and rubbing
an ingratiating cheek along his sleeve, he recognised, to the
extent of about a quarter of the truth, that she was bluffing
him into accepting this as the veritable Toni. " My dear
little girl, you'd better let your great big, strong, bull-and-bear
man know the worst ; he will then go into the city, and make
lots of money ; become a Director or a Preferential Dividend
Holder. . . . Sling your whole confounded post-bag *over*
here ! "

" Oh ! thank you, Giles. You *are* so good to me. I don't
know what I should do without you. Here are the minor bills,
and here is ' Féo's ' hat account, and these are shoes, and
here is the pass-book, and—wait a second !—I'll find the bill
for the fur coat, that came in for the fourth time, yesterday ;
and here's one summons that I quite forgot to mention
before."

Giles bent an absorbed head over the pile of letters she laid
before him ; then he jotted down some figures and added
them up. When he next spoke, his voice had considerably

less mock weight, and more real concern : " Great Scott, Toni ! you *have* been going it ! "

" The fur coat makes a difference. I shan't be wanting one every year, of course—— At least, I don't know, I might. . . ." Toni chuckled.

" This habit of squandering recklessly ought to have been checked in your youth, young woman."

" Ah . . . life has spoilt me, I fear," said Toni, pensively, her head a little on one side.

She was impenitent, and determined on one thing : never to worry any more over the sagging responsibilities of money, and expenditure, and debt. . . . Here was Giles—*he* could worry ; it was her time to grow young again ; Toni was looking after Toni.

They had managed their income, up till now, in a haphazard sort of fashion, always meaning to systematise it, and always being too full of engagements, or the after-effect of engagements. Jimmy Goddard's Bank had had orders to pay five hundred pounds a quarter into Giles' Bank ; and his idea and Toni's had been, as this came in, that he should pay half of it regularly into her bank ; and they would share expenses. But it seemed unlikely that they would ever do anything regularly. Most of the money was spent, or promised, or contracted for, before it had actually been paid in ; sometimes it was her doing, and sometimes his ; and they borrowed from each other, and gave each other I.O.U.'s, and lost them. Giles had already raised an overdraft on expectation of his next quarter's allowance, which would be paid in, in March ; this was what they had been throwing about for expenses that demanded payment in ready money. He handed Toni two or three pounds, or sometimes ten pounds, whenever she chanced to ask for it, or if her cheque-book were not handy ; and confidently hoped, that when her cheque-book *was* handy, and he was cleaned out, she would be able to stand treat to him out of the two hundred and fifty pounds which he had contrived to pay to her credit at the beginning of December. One look at her pass-book convinced him that he had trusted in vain : " Always a mistake to send for one's pass-book," he

murmured; " best to go on blundering in ignorance. As it is
—we're due at Teddy's by one o'clock; it's a two hours' run,
at least, and we haven't dressed, or packed our suitcases, yet."
He pushed back his chair, dug his hands deep in his pockets,
looked up at his wife, and said :

" Toni, I believe we are ruined."

" Yes ? " . . . But Toni had once played a conspicuous
part in a period of family ruin, and knew what the real thing
was like; she could not, therefore, be disturbed by its present
imitation in swansdown. " Well, we mustn't let Teddy down.
She's counting on us. It strikes me that those bills ought to
be settled, somehow, when we come back on Monday. Can we
plunder Jimmy any more, do you think ? " She had not seen
very much of her father-in-law as yet, because he had remained
most of the time down in Gloucestershire for the hunting;
but what she had seen of him, she liked.

" Oh ! I daresay.—Damn that 'phone ! If it's anyone
really chatty, say we're dead, Toni; we *must* get dressed now.
Yes, I'll tackle Jimmy. He's sure to be overdrawn, himself;
usually is; that's three overdrafts to one family ! " But this
was the year when overdrafts were rife in England. The
unwontedly hot summer may have sapped the nation's resistance to the notion of outpacing its income. Even the common
habit of reticence over personal money affairs had given way.
And : " What's your overdraft ? You should just see the size of
mine ! " was a phrase to be heard in almost any greeting between
friends. . . . " I think Jimmy ought to be able to manage on
over six thousand a year," continued Giles, sternly disapproving
of his father ; " even if he has to keep his profligate sons and
parasite daughters-in-law ! "

" It's not the 'phone," Toni remarked, without moving.
" It's the front door; callers, and not eleven yet; callers
before P.M. can't possibly want the whisky brought out, can
they ? And Murray finished all our champagne, last time he
came to breakfast. . . . The cellar's getting low, Giles. What
are we to do about it ? . . . I say, Giles, we're not really
going to be hard up, are we ? "

He heard the first break of genuine apprehension in her

voice; and remembering that, apart from his normal pleasure in cherishing Toni, there was now a special reason why she should be tranquillised, he thrust the crumple of papers, which he had been examining, into one of the baggy pockets of his tweed jacket, and said in a tone that carried conviction : " Don't get worked up, Toni. Leave it all to me. I'll see to this bunch. No, of course we aren't going to be really hard-up ; this is what's technically alluded to as a ' temporary embarrassment ' ; so ring up ' Féo's ' and ' Toni's ' and your Bond Street shoe-shop, and order another complete outfit, at once. That's not extravagance ; it's to restore your nerve, like riding, the moment after you've taken a toss ; very important thing, to restore your nerve. Who the Hell is this ? "

" This " was the visitor who had rung twice at the front-door bell, before Quimper, their cook's husband, who functioned as valet, butler and odd man, had quite finished polishing a set of wine-glasses to his liking ; polishing glass was his religion, and he allowed nothing to disturb it.

" Why, it's Miss Lequesne ! " . . . Toni was still dazed and stricken with awe at Giles's incredible performance of what she had hitherto deemed a remote legend : that a man should ever really speak those exquisitely melodious words to her : " Leave it all to me : I'll settle it ! " Her contrition was partly real, as she said :

" You're an angel to me, and I'm awfully sorry, no, not only about the bills—never mind what. . . ."

And Miss Aimée Lequesne, being just then admitted by Quimper into the studio, showed a vast amount of *savoir-faire* and aplomb—her own definition of a lady's most important assets in Society !—by quickly picking up the kitten. Burying her face in its fur, she exclaimed :

" Oh, you *darling* little whiskery thing ! Aren't you too *mignonne* for anything ! " which served the double purpose of revealing her presence to the others ; and of blurring her vision of the pretty, domestic tableau on which she had intruded : actually, Miss Rakonitz—no, Mrs. Goddard, she *should* say !—showering soft kisses up and down the nape of that good-looking Mr. Goddard's neck, while he—well, at any rate, he stopped when Aimée's tactful remarks to Shoe Lane, the cat told him that he and Toni were no longer alone. (" But just imagine it ! "—thus Aimée, afterwards, to Miss Thompson— " and she who was always so cold and keep-off-don't-touch-me while she was here.—His *neck !* my dear, I *was* surprised ! "

" I don't see why you should be," replied Millicent Thompson, in her nasty, bluff way : " People don't usually behave the same at their private breakfast-table as they do at business ; whose neck did you suppose she could kiss, here in Hanover Street ? "

" That's not a very pleasant thing to say, Miss Thompson," Aimée rebuked her. " I must say this about Miss Rakonitz, that she was always very particular to keep Hanover Street *nice*, and I'm doing my best to follow in her footsteps."

" See that you do, then," responded Miss Thompson. . . .)

—Toni straightened herself quickly. " Why, it's Miss Lequesne ! " . . . and Giles stood up, but not quickly, because, unlike Toni, he had no reputation for coldness to maintain in front of that suave and svelte young lady who was putting them both at their ease, from the door-way. Suave and svelte were the adjectives that at once occurred to him, in connection with Aimée Lequesne.

" You must forgive me, Miss Rakonitz—I *should* say, Mrs. Goddard. It's an unpardonable taime to come round, I know, but Miss Thompson seemed to think it might be best to consult you because of the responsibility, though I, personally, have very little doubt about what you'll say. You have to take risks sometimes, haven't you, Mr. Goddard ? " with a smile that brought him into the conversation, in case he should feel left out.

Never did Toni feel less inclined for a debate on any business subject. Her manner, when she invited Miss Lequesne to set forth the problem, wavered in an unsatisfactory no-man's-land, between Giles's pretty, petted, extravagant young wife, and the cool, competent head of " Toni's " whom Aimée had learnt to respect, and even, in emergencies, to fear.

" It's our account at Belworthy's," Miss Lequesne brought out, breathlessly.

Toni nodded. The name of Belworthy, combined with the girl's slight agitation, at once proved the difficulty to be of some magnitude. The mere fact that Miss Thompson had suggested coming to her, had already indicated as much ; this was the first time they had troubled her since her marriage ; and she and Giles had dwelt in such a hectic whirl, that she had not been able to get down to " Toni's " more than twice in five months ; she might have explained, in cab-parlance, that it was " outside the radiance." . . .

Belworthy's was a wholesale business whose stuff was well-known and most saleable ; and from whom, therefore, Toni—knowing him from previous experience with the Wolffs—had been buying very largely, during the two years of her own autocracy in Hanover Street. Mr. Edwin Belworthy, an astute gentleman, encouraged a large standing debt, of which a certain amount was paid off every month, and then, by further purchases, swelled again to its original size.

" How much is our account there, now, Miss Lequesne ? "

" *Voilà !* " Aimée's voice betrayed how gratified she was ; " I knew you would ask that very question ; I knew it, so I went to Miss Wildblood—Miss Wildblood is our good little book-keeper "—she threw in, aside, to Giles, again in the same kindly spirit—" and I asked her : ' Oh, Miss Wildblood, what is the exact amount of our account with Belworthy, now ? ' and she said : ' four hundred and seventy-two pounds, eight shillings, and ten pence, Miss Lequesne. How clever of you to think of getting it for Miss Rakonitz !—Mrs. Goddard, I *should* say.' . . . I should say : *she* should say. . . ." Aimée fumbled helplessly between herself and Miss Wildblood ; and then gave it up.

" Well, but isn't that rather a lot ? " asked Giles, getting interested.

" It is a lot, isn't it ? " Aimée agreed. " But, you know, we can always get rid of his stuff ; and it's usual, in our business, to have one or two permanent debts of that sort, as long as one goes on buying, of course ; convenient for them, and con-venient for us—but, of course, Mr. Goddard, I needn't explain business things to *you*; you are probably used to dealing in thousands, not hundreds."

"Millions," said Giles, briefly; "not thousands; millions. I say, Toni, we're going to be hellishly late for Teddy's, you know."

"Oh, I must apologise," began Toni's chief sales-woman. "It seems a shame to have come on a Saturday morning——"

"Oh, that's quite all right. But I was wondering whether you'd like to cut along, Toni, and get dressed, while Miss Lequesne and I confab together on this mighty matter of Belworthy's account."

Toni recognised the indulgent, semi-humorous note in his voice as being the other and less agreeable portion for her to swallow, of the same attitude, which had said, protectively: "Leave it all to me" over her bills, ten minutes ago. She had accepted the half; must she now accept the other half? Must the minx pay, so soon, for idleness, extravagance and self-indulgence? Standing, mentally, first on one leg and then on the other, in an indecisive fashion, she said: "I think, if you don't mind, Giles darling, I'd rather wait and hear, myself. Wouldn't you like to go and 'phone Teddy?" Anything to get rid of him!

"I promise not to take long, Miss Rakonitz—I *should* say, Mrs. Goddard! Please don't put off your friends; please, Mr. Goddard, don't trouble." And, now that she had reached an actual statement of the perplexing point, Miss Lequesne showed herself, after all, not such a fool as might be imagined from her social conversation:

"What Mr. Belworthy said, when he came round to see me on Wednesday, was just this——"

"*Wednesday?* To-day's Saturday!"

"Yes; you see, we've been discussing it ever since, Miss Thompson and I; between times; for we're very busy. My opinion was, that you meant us to be self-reliant and not always running round to you in every small difficulty, like schoolgirls. You that have your own life to live, now. But Miss Thompson was so worried—I'd rather not say obstinate——"

" What did Belworthy want ? "

" He said he was frightfully interested in our firm, and in how well we were doing, and what the trade was saying about us ; and that he thought that, having done as much as we had, we ought to be doing double the amount with him ; so he offered to let us have as much stuff as we like, and he will advertise us, into the bargain. Now doesn't that seem to you an offer to be accepted, Miss Rakonitz ? "

" Rather," answered Giles, heartily. " Congratulations ! "

Toni knitted her brows. Her one comment : " What's he after, I wonder ? " had not been meant for the others to hear.

Aimée Lequesne heard, though.—" Oh, surely, Miss Rakonitz, you can't suspect Mr. Belworthy ? I always thought he was a perfectly charming man ; so much aplomb. And no one could have been more fair and honest than he was, on Wednesday, with me and Miss Thompson."

" I'm shaw . . ." murmured Toni. " Did he say anything else ? "

" Well yes, he did. He was with us for nearly an hour ; just in the morning rush, too."

" I'm jolly glad to hear you've got a rush," Giles remarked ; and again, Aimée turned her attention to him :

" Oh, but this is our Spring season, you know. You ought to come down to ' Toni's ' sometimes, Mr. Goddard. Oh, you mustn't think me familiar to your wife, calling it that !— It's the name our establishment is known by, you see. Mr. Belworthy said that everybody was talking about ' Toni's.' He said that we ought to double the amount with him, that we are doing. He said that I had caught the note of *true* elegance, in the modes we are showing now ; daring without being *outré ;* and with such—*timbre !* That was the chief thing, he said, nowadays ; *timbre !* And then he said one or two quite nice little things to Miss Thompson, too, about her cut ; I was so glad he remembered to do that ! "

Toni controlled an inclination to settle Miss Lequesne's exuberance by one brief and business-like snub. " Did he say anything about our account with him ? "

" Yes, indeed, Miss Rakonitz. He said that, quite frankly,

though our account was large, it wasn't large enough to allow him to continue the arrangement you made with him when you first began."

Toni, anticipating that Miss Lequesne, in her infinite *savoir-faire*, would turn round and explain this arrangement to Giles, told him, herself, that she had arranged to buy from Belworthy's, on condition that he confined those especial goods to her, and did not sell them anywhere else.

"Hot stuff!" remarked Giles, approvingly. "I didn't know you had it in you, Toni."

She imagined that he sounded a trifle suspicious; and said, hastily: "Oh, I was helped a great deal; Mr. and Mrs. Wolff helped me; they were darlings; I could never have thought of all that, myself."

"Oh, but indeed, Mr. Goddard, Mrs. Goddard is much too modest; she's wonderful; all the trade say so; we're quite lost without her, indeed; she was so oh fay in every department of the firm!"

"I wonder why no one strangled you at birth," murmured Toni, only just inaudibly.

"Well, Miss Rakonitz, I'm keeping you; all we wanted to be sure, Miss Thompson and I, is whether we are to accept his offer, or not? If you say we are to, it's what I said all along, because it will pay us to be advertised by Belworthy's, and we have never yet failed to sell his stuff; and besides, if we did refuse, and he closed his account——" Toni's eyelids flickered, once, and then her gaze steadied again.—"It would be almost impossible to find such a large sum just now, in the tight season, with all the Paris stuff to pay for; they were showing such lovely things that I simply didn't stint, knowing we were likely to have a good season. . . ."

"Hi! wait a moment!" Giles leant on his folded arms, across the table towards Miss Lequesne, intent upon her disclosures: "Do you mean that this fellow Belworthy has said that unless you accept his offer and double your present orders with him, he'll close your account, and you'll have to pay up on the spot? Is that it?"

"How clear you are, Mr. Goddard! but I always say a

man's brain. . . . Yes, that's what Mr. Belworthy said, and one really can't blame him, because in a way, I suppose, our account up to now isn't large enough for him to get any benefit out of confining his stuff to us. And he knows we can't do without it."

(" *Thinks* we can't do without it," murmured Toni.)

" It would cramp your style terrifically, just now, to pay—what was it ? four hundred quid ? "

Miss Lequesne reeled off glibly : " Four hundred and seventy-two pounds, eight shillings and tenpence ; it would certainly cramp our style "—and her accents of pure refinement toyed daintily with the repetition of Giles's slang. " I saw that at once, and I told Mr. Belworthy that, if it depended on me——! but, of course, in a big matter like that, Miss Rakonitz—Mrs. Goddard, I *should* say—ought to be consulted ; and Miss Thompson was quaite brusque about it. One has to forgive her a lot, you see, she's such a marvellous cutter ; but at times her manner is—well—almost offensive ! Mr. Belworthy said I was a wonderful business woman."

" How long has he given you ? " asked Giles. Neither of them appeared to have noticed that Toni had dropped entirely out of the discussion. " I'm afraid he might think better of his offer, you see, and close right down."

" I promised, on Wednesday, to let him know this morning. He'll be at Hanover Street at eleven o'clock ; that's why I dashed round at this dreadful time, when I found Miss Thompson would *not* allow me to take a strong innishertive, as I was perfectly willing to do."

" How much is your turnover with him, per annum ? "

" Nearly two thousand pounds," said Aimée, after a minute's thought.

" Double your order, then, and double your turnover. It's a great idea ! don't hesitate a moment. It's an advantage to him, of course ; I'm not supposing he's a philanthropist ; but it's obviously a bigger advantage to you."

" Oh, I'm *so* glad we all agree about it." Aimée Lequesne sighed in deep relief.

. . . And Toni was just fifty seconds too late !

Directly Miss Lequesne had let out, in the midst of a jumble of minor facts, repetition of flatteries, and jealous little side-pats at Miss Thompson, that Belworthy was trying to force them to accept his offer by the threat of closing his account, Toni had grasped that, whatever happened, the offer must not be accepted. She had never entirely trusted Belworthy; he was clever enough, but not too straight. Possibly, knowing that Toni was only a figure-head, now, his simple, happy idea was to ruin the business by making them buy far more than they could afford, or easily dispose of; and so, finally, get it into his own hands. This much was instantly clear to her. What she was considering, while Miss Lequesne and Giles were settling up matters between them, and took her approval for granted, was how to circumvent Belworthy; and, at the same time, escape from instant payment of that four hundred and seventy odd pounds, which, as an alternative, would be almost equally ruinous. Then, the inspiration came.

. . . She saw it as a sculptor, in his mind's eye, sees before he begins work, the completed statue—glorious, simple, massively significant lines. She saw it . . . as, maybe, a hundred years ago . . . or, with another leap backwards, six hundred years ago . . . a merchant of the Rakonitz tribe had seen his adversary's game—and, with a more brilliant game, had triumphantly countered it.

"When you see Belworthy presently, fall in with his plan. But say that our account's a bit large : you would like to get it paid off gradually by bills, say a hundred pounds every three months—no, a hundred and twenty pounds—we could do that. Directly he agrees to take the bills, and the matter is settled, write to him, and close the account, and never buy another thing from him ! " . . .

—During the swift seconds that this was shaping itself in Toni's mind, and just before she could say it, her husband, with what Miss Lequesne had admiringly called a man's brain, and knowing nothing, absolutely nothing whatever, about the business, had reviewed the possibilities of the new plan, as they might appear on the surface to any normally intelligent layman, and delivered their joint verdict.

A wrong verdict.

Toni did not contradict it.

And now he was looking towards her, affectionately; pleasantly conscious of having, by his masculine, administrative qualities, saved her an enormous amount of bother and bewilderment: his darling little rogue, who couldn't understand figures, and got so tangled by the debit and credit sides of her Bank Book. . . . " So that's that, Toni! we shall be living on your firm, if it goes on booming in this way. Have a drink, Miss Lequesne? Whisky and soda? Champagne?— No, no, wait a bit—we're out of champagne; what about a cocktail? "

But tactfully, Aimée refused the cocktail; it was much too early in the morning—and anyway, Mr. and Mrs. Goddard were in a hurry. She was so thankful to have had this interview—and now she must rush off, not to be late for Mr. Belworthy. She stood up to go: " It's raining quite terribly hard," she remarked—and they all became aware of dull drumming on the skylight. " I do hope I shall find room in one of the 'buses. They're so crowded just at this time. . . ." She was not complaining; but setting forth as matters of commonplace but unalterable fact, that it *was* raining; and that the 'buses *would* be overcrowded. And so she ceased to be aggravating to Toni, now that her willowy elegance and refinement had dropped, like covers, leaving her natural, and rather pitifully apprehensive. Toni was reminded, and drew back from the memory with a pang of thankfulness, of past moments in her own life, when all buoyant expectancy of suddenly meeting glamour and grace and solace in life, suddenly shrank to a meek hope that there might be room inside a 'bus on a wet day. Lord! how *threadbare* you felt, as a business girl on your own! elbowing for a place—— She had almost forgotten, until now, the innumerable little things that first strained your nerves, and then tortured them, and did not stop, even then; did not stop for panic nor prayer . . . till at last you spoke as Aimée, just now, in a used-to-it could-not-be-otherwise voice. Almost forgotten—in the rush and dazzle of her overdue good time, with Giles to look after her. She was so incomparably stronger than she had been, and able to behave as though she were so much more delicate.

" Can't you run her up to Hanover Street, while I dress and pack our suit-cases, Giles ? You told them to bring the Dook round by eleven. And it's past eleven, now."

Giles nodded : " That's an idea. . . . Yes, the Dook *is* outside. Come on, Miss Lequesne ! . . . Darling, are you sure you don't mind just ramming my razor and pyjamas into the case ? No, look here ! leave it, anyway, and I'll do it when I come back. I don't want you to tire yourself."

" Oh ! " cried Aimée, " how lovely ! "

Toni was not sure whether she meant that it was lovely to be taken in the car, or lovely that Giles should not wish his wife to tire herself by putting a razor into a suit-case. But she smiled very charmingly upon Aimée, as she said good-bye to her. It was nice to think that for once Aimée need not cool her feet, waiting about at wet, blowy corners. For once . . . yes, occasionally the forlorn you of other days had been also in the way of a thrown-off splinter of luck ; one drive in a car with a man benevolently lent, to cherish you for ten minutes, by a girl who had somehow found her way into the zone of unearned increment : ten minutes' ease, *chucked* at you, from within the five-mile radiance. And Toni hoped, warmly, that Aimée, too, would marry quite soon, and also be kept-in-idleness for the rest of her life. . . . And then Giles kissed Toni, and went off with Miss Lequesne, Toni's bills bulging out his right-hand pocket.

. . . Toni reflected, not without humour, that they would all have liked each other a great deal less, and would not have parted in a spirit nearly as innocent and happy, if she had told Miss Lequesne exactly what ought to have been done in the matter of the Belworthy account.

Of course, it had been out of the question to make a fool of Giles, in front of Aimée Lequesne, by betraying his decision to be an ignorant blunder ; and correcting it by an inspiration that, both in contrast and on its own merits, proved her his superior in brain and judgment. She could not, nakedly, shame him like this, even to save " Toni's."

Especially as, ten minutes before——

——Oh Hell! those bills. . . .

Toni did not go and dress. She sank down on the same
divan, where she and Val had sat and destroyed the fetish of
sturdy self-reliance and the joy of earning a living. She sat
and, morally, kicked herself. Not Giles. Giles had inter-
fered in a matter which did not concern him—but his
interference had not been in the least unwarranted. To
him, the office of cherishing Toni had been carried out
equally by paying her bills, deciding about Belworthy's, and
refusing to let her pack his razors for him; saving her
trouble! . . . Toni's smile was tremulous! . . . " He *is*—
quite a darling!"

But he had made a mess of things, all the same. Or she had,
by controlling herself at the critical moment, and not giving
her orders to her sales-woman.

At the first instant of hearing Giles speak: " Double your
order and double your turnover . . ." all Toni's instincts had
leapt up, urging her at once, and at whatever cost, to put the
matter right again. She simply could not leave a wrong judgment to operate, when it was in her power to cancel it; when
she so surely knew that only her own solution had truth in it,
and the clear beauty of truth—no less beauty because it concerned itself with merchandise and not with art; she was a
god in her capacity to direct her spear straight to the vulnerable spot, neither to the right, nor to the left of it; she, Toni,
a girl of twenty-seven, could laugh at Belworthy and his plot.
The fun of being a trader!

. . . Those bills!

You cannot behave as two absolutely inconsistent beings:
one fundamentally and—using Aimée's phrase—technically
" oh fay "; the other, that helpless, charming little spend-
thrift whom she had wantonly pretended to be, before Aimée
had appeared. If it had been Nemesis who had sent Aimée
just then, Toni resented passionately such a punctual and well-
timed performance. She was ashamed of herself, self-tricked
into a position where she could not immediately and loyally
support " Toni's " in its crisis.

" I suppose it's not too late. I could 'phone Miss Thompson now . . ."

But it was a risk. She would be imperilling the miracle she had achieved, of Toni Rakonitz—Mrs. Goddard, I *should* say ! —presented to Giles as a creature tenderly to be considered, privileged, luxuriously kept ; a woman . . . and his inferior. Till now, she had not in the least minded being his inferior, on these terms. And she would not mind again, if this Belworthy business could be adjusted somehow.

—She rose, and took an indeterminate step towards the 'phone. Belworthy would be there by now. And Giles and Aimée also, probably. It was more than likely that Giles would accompany Aimée to the interview. If Miss Thompson answered the 'phone, and returned to the others with Toni's peremptory message—she might just as well not have been shifty and a coward, in the studio. The reprieve was useless, if Giles were to find out, after all, that she had been humbugging him. . . .

" Don't 'phone, then . . ."

" You ought to know, by now, that there's no compromise. You either pick up faggots, or you sit luxuriously by the fire for the rest of your life. . . ."

" I *won't* go back to picking up faggots. I've done too much of it, already."

. . . He had been so decent. Ungrateful and surly, if she had let him down, simply because her vanity could not suffer a bad deal to go through, in a business that hardly concerned her any longer, though it happened still to bear her name. So she had chosen, rather, to let " Toni's " go to ruin ; chivalrous Toni ! But she could not rest happily on that version, pleasing though it was, and soothing to the conscience. She could not altogether believe that chivalry alone had kept her dumb. Toni could be plausible and a sophist to everyone else in the world ; yet, somehow or other, could never be quite plausible enough, arguing with Toni !

The arguments for and against 'phoning Miss Thompson, reeled and jostled, in battle, over her mental area ; not two armies fighting ; but small, isolated squadrons, skirmishing ;

a victory here, and a loss over there, in another part of the field; so that the sum of victory remained always unresolved. Her strategy had been at fault in sending Giles along to Hanover Street, if she had meant to 'phone Miss Thompson directly she had rid herself of Aimée. But that had been genuine good-nature. It was raining. Nor would Giles's presence in the studio have simplified the task of 'phoning.

. . . Quite insane, when they were not really rich, and in debt, to throw away money by letting that mistake go through. Yet why was consideration for the material standpoint always the greater mistake? Perhaps, in her seeming foolishness, she was being saner than she had ever been in her life before; saner than almost anyone else had ever been, to sacrifice, at the imperious bidding of a vision, a problematic gain for " Toni's "? . . . " What shall it profit a woman——" And G les might have said, if then and there she had exposed herself, strong and clever and an autocrat . . . Giles might have said—Toni was nearly sobbing now, so painful was this to recall—" Oh ! you—*you Matriarch !* "

Another man had said it, and left her. Danny. " Not again. . . . I needn't do myself in *again*, need I ? You don't punish twice in the same place, or do you ? "

But it would not punish her with the same malignant brutality; for she did not love Giles. She knew he would let her down, some time or other . . . unless she were twice as clever as—merely displaying cleverness.

Vanity again took a share in the dispute. . . . Another part of the field—alarums and excursions—and enter the complacent ghost of Mr. Edwin Belworthy ! . . . " How can you bear to let Belworthy imagine that you don't see through him ? " Wouldn't it be fun to worst him ? show yourself the more merciless and cunning of the two ? For it really *was* an astute stroke. . . . Once he accepted those bills, he was helpless. Not likely that he would, for his part, insist on a more than verbal assent to his suggestion of doubling their order with him : he would rely on their pleasing incapacity to do without him. The proprietor of " Toni's " tingled with a nearly forgotten exhilaration, imagining his surprise when he

received no further orders from her firm, and his disgust at
having pledged himself, right across those bills, to receive
leisurely payment only, of the large amount owing to him.

Yet supposing Giles and Aimée were right; and they ought
to accept Belworthy's offer, and double their order to
him, and double their turnover? Toni's wisdom was not
omnipotent.

Or, even if Belworthy's intentions were what she suspected,
and he were scheming to land them into such a position of
difficulty and debt that he could eventually buy them in—
even then, it might not work out like that, by pure luck.
Luck, in business, ran in queer zig-zags.

But a ten-per-cent chance that, by pure luck, they might
succeed along the wrong course, did not in the very least
excuse Toni. She was gambling, and with no right to gamble.

What? not with her own property? "Toni's" was hers;
what if she lost it? nothing could be more dreadful than to
go back to being the old Toni, who looked after others, instead
of being looked after, herself.

" I'm going to have a child; I want to be cherished while
I am having a child." . . . All the Rakonitz women, down
the ages, all Israelite women, were cherished by their men,
while they were going to have a child.

. . . And just because this final skirmish seemed the con-
clusive one, and there were no more blows to be dealt for the
cause of ringing up Miss Thompson, Toni, very emphatically
and scornfully, walked across the studio, picked up the
receiver, and with over-elaborated clearness, gave the number
of " Toni's."

Perverse of her! but then Toni *was* perverse; and, having
stumbled through so many adequate reasons against her
present action, the last reason of all, that she wanted to be
cherished while she was having a child, appeared more than
adequate, more than plausible, more than wise and far-seeing;
it was, in fact, the true reason. Toni had a good look at it,
and said to herself, softly: "You coward!" . . .

For the sake of your share in holding the world's fortress
for those proud and lonely few who are clear-headed, coherent

and resourceful, you plainly could not, for any personal shirking, let stupidity go through, and range yourself on the wrong side, along with the fumblers; the clumsy, dense crowd who hold up action, while slowly, and with an immense and scrupulous sense of duty, they think out the wrong thing to do.

Therefore, Toni 'phoned Miss Thompson.

It could not be helped, now, if Giles and Aimée were already there; it could not be helped, now, what Giles thought of her; only—she just hoped, she still could not forbear from hoping, while trying her hardest to put things right, that some arbitrary happenings, beyond her control, might yet block her way, such as—such as . . .

. . . A loud, intermittent buzzing sounded in her ear:

"Sor-r-ry. Number-r-r-engaged; shall I r-r-ring you?"

"Yes, please," answered Toni, breathlessly; and replaced the receiver. But she did not go away. She stood leaning up against the door-way that led into the hall, where the telephone was, looking down at the instrument curiously, with a sort of humorous anger; and wondered who was the unknown stranger—a client, probably,—who, by ringing up "Toni's" at this exact moment, was prolonging the strain for her. She jumped, when the bell ripped the silence again, even though she was expecting it. "Oh, well, now for it! . . . Hello!"

Miss Wildblood would probably be at the other end.

"Is that the author of 'Uncle Tom's Cabin'?" minced a voice which certainly did not belong to Miss Wildblood.

For a dazed second, Toni tried to think it out. . . . Then she burst out laughing: "Colin, you idiot!"

"My dear, I simply *had* to ring you! Marvellous of you to be up already, and it isn't even lunch-time yet. I'm lunching at Rebecca's, of course, because of the sandwiches."

"Savages?"

"*Sandwiches!* You know she gave a party last night, so that we should have enough sandwiches for lunch and tea and dinner, the next day. It's really the only way to get sandwiches in any quantity. They were perfectly godlike: caviare, *pâté-de-fois-gras*, and those lovely ones, fresh walnut and celery with a dash of cream-cheese, which, thank goodness,

nobody likes except myself. She ordered thousands too many
of each kind ; I made her ; and I mounted guard at the buffet
so that they shouldn't be handed round twice. Darling, everybody went home so hungry—except myself, of course, and
Rebecca, and Michael, and Maurice, and Marion. We stopped
on, after the others. I don't know why anybody ever invites
any others, except to see them go home hungry ! Why weren't
you and Giles there, by the way ? I missed my Little Elegance,
and my Splendid Tweed-man ! "

" Oh, we were at Daly's : first night of ' The Lady of the
Rose,' and Gilbert made us go on with his party afterwards,
to Ciro's. But, look here, Colin, how did *you* manage to get
away ? Weren't you acting, last night ? "

" Leetle sprite, you couldn't have said anything more tactless and distressing ! And talking about first-nights too, to
me. . . . Didn't you know that my play, my ewe-lamb, my
ugly duckling, my first-born——

" Oh, Colin ! it *hasn't* come off, already ? "

" That ' already ' makes it worse and worse ! Yes, indeed,
dear, after a quite unique run of eleven nights and three
matinées, it came off on Wednesday. I don't think it can
have been a staggering success, do you ? Oh ! I *must* tell you
about last night ! my dear, I completely passed-out, last
night ! I was the Marquis of Pass-out ! ninth of the illus-
trious line !—but you'd better go and fetch a chair ; it's
going to be a long story, and if you were at Ciro's till late,
and haven't had your prairie oyster yet . . ."

" Go on, Colin ! I don't dabble in prairie oysters, as you
know ; not since the time when I bit the egg, instead of
swallowing it whole ! "

" My Wee, it must have been devastating for you ! I
know, myself, what it feels like to bite on a soft egg. It just
slips away from under you, doesn't it ? and leaves you with
one tooth positively grinding on the other !—Well, my dear,
the most glorious thing happened. We were all standing
round and ragging, and being frightfully well with each other.
Maurice had just sung : ' I-ain't-a-goin'-to-do-it,' standing
on his head, and I accompanied him on the piano, with my

well-known deft touch over the keys ; and Michael turned a
couple of debonair somersaults, forwards and back again, in
that killing style that's so irresistible to Duchesses—and can
you blame them ?—When quite suddenly, my dear, what *do*
you think ?—without any warning, a perfectly strange man
walked into the centre of the room, and began to recite. He
provided a most colossal sensation ; nearly put the party out !
You know that old-fashioned sort of recitation, with actions
that have nothing to do with the words. He pronounced the
title, first, in a slow, aggressive shout ; and the author's name
in full : ' Dollawrees '—by Algernon Charles Swinburne. . . .
Then he paused—and took one step forward . . . and we
could just hear Rebecca, in her clear, little, far-away voice of
agony, saying : ' Oh, my God ! '—plop into the silence !—
He recited it all through, word-perfect, without making a
single mistake from beginning to end. . . . ' Our Lidy of
Pine.' . . . And we were much too stricken to do anything
except just listen."

"Colin, it's too pathetic. He must have thought that he
and Maurice and Michael and you were helping to ' make the
party go.' "

"He almost did, my pretty ! . . . When he finished, nobody
said anything for a long, long while : then Rebecca remembered
that she was hostess, and squeaked in a flurried, absent-minded
sort of way : ' Oh, thank you so much . . . that was lovely ! '
. . . and he just disappeared, faded out again like a beautiful
dream. Nobody knows who he was, nor where he came from,
nor anything about him. We came to the conclusion that he
must do it as a profession ; he just wanders round the streets
till he finds a party—and then he goes in and recites all over
it ! Toni, aren't you thrilled ? "

"Not *quite* so thrilled as when I heard it all for the first
time, Colin darling, at 9.15 this morning. . . ." She paused,
for comment.

"That takes me *right* off," he remarked, pleasantly.
" Who 'phoned you ? Rebecca, I suppose ? '

Toni continued :—" But much *more* thrilled than when I
heard it all for the *second* time, at about 9.45. Because this

third time I was really anxious to discover whether your version tallied with Rebecca's or Marion's, which were entirely different. As it happens, your edition corroborates Rebecca's, so that must be the true one. It's nice to know. But I wonder why Marion went out of her way to tell me a lot of eye-wash about it ? "

" My sweet, this is interesting. What did she tell you ? "

" That the reciter was a Mr. Leslie Barlowe Curtis, whom Gwenda Lord brought along by special permission. And that he stayed on afterwards, later than anyone else, and told tiresome scandals about the Sargasso Sea. It's odd, because the true story is very much more interesting ! "

" I can't tell you how gratified I am ! " exclaimed Colin. " You must admit, Toni, that it was quite too marvellous of Rebecca and myself both to have made the same improvements on the original tale, spontaneously, to give you pleasure, without any agreement about it beforehand . . ."

" *Marion's* was the true version, then ? "

" Of course it was. It touches up the anecdote, though, and puts light and shade into it, to say that the reciter was a total stranger who had wandered in from the night outside. I had no idea that Rebecca and I were so exquisitely in harmony ! Perhaps I ought to marry her ! What do you think, Toni ? You who are so happily married, yourself ; can you and Giles tell the same lies, without agreeing on them beforehand ? It does seem to me the Supreme Test ! Are you going down to Teddy's over the week-end ? "

" Yes ; we ought to have started ages ago, and I'm not dressed yet. Will you be there ? "

" Yes, I might tootle down with Betty, this evening. Look out for me, mottled and bloated with too many sandwiches— particularly the walnut-celery kind ! Oh, by the way, Toni, before I ring off——"

—But Toni had already rung off. While Colin had been rippling on and on, she had forgotten everything, engrossed in the doings of this delectable, jubilant set to which she belonged. Constant succession of week-ends, and first nights, and dancing till kipper-time came round at the Night-Clubs

. . . what *fun* it was, to be rung up the next morning after a
party, and have time to gossip and laugh over the jokes which
had, and had not taken place, before dashing off, in your own
car or someone else's, to do some other imperative, amusing
thing! Colin's outlook was so infectious: he could make
trifles swell to such importance, that important things, beside
them, dwindled to mere trifles. . . .

So that, even remembering that she had to ring up Miss
Thompson about the Belworthy business, Toni did not pick
up her former ponderous and disturbed state of mind. It had
the aspect, now, of no more than a silly incident, and an
unwelcome clog on the day's swift progress! "Toni dear,
how *tiresome* of you to fuss!" would have been Colin's exasperated comment.

Still sparkling, flushed, and with that peculiarly witty feeling
which always remained behind after a talk with Colin, Toni
again approached the mouthpiece. She would speak to Miss
Thompson, now, and get it over. . . .

But, at the same moment, the key jarred in the front-door
lock, close by, and Giles came in:

"Ready? That girl *is* a priceless ass!" he began. . . .
Then: "You little rotter!—not dressed yet? What *have*
you been doing, all the time?"

"'Phoning Colin—or rather, he 'phoned me. I couldn't
help it. He only just this second rang off." . . . and Toni
replaced the receiver on its hook. "Give me ten—no, seven
minutes, Giles! I can be ready to start in seven minutes. . . ."

CHAPTER VI

THE very expensive nurse from St. Olaf's suggested that it might be better if she were to take baby down to her grandmother, Mrs. Bertrand Rakonitz, at Bedford Park, for the week-end, if Mr. and Mrs. Goddard were giving a party that night: "It isn't as though a studio were a house, is it, Madam? In fact, I'm not at all sure that studio life agrees with baby." The expensive nurse from St. Olaf's said this quite seriously; and Toni gathered that she was not referring so much to the possible influence on Babette's morals, of the continual dissipation which connects itself with studios, nowadays, rather than canvas and oils, as to the sinister influence of shape. And she admitted that there did exist a noticeable incongruity about a baby in a studio: even in a high-class studio such as theirs: the slant of the huge skylights, the too distant vistas from end to end of the vast room, patched with rich-coloured fabrics stiffly spread from column and balcony; the cubist angles which duplicated and broke and re-formed themselves, oddly doubled in trembling light and shadows, now that November had come, and big fires were roaring up the open brick chimney. All this indoor landscape might quite conceivably not " agree " with Babette, aged four months.

"And getting light from on top, Madam," Nurse went on, "instead of sideways; that's bound to make a difference to a child; and being all on the ground floor, too. It's not that I don't highly approve of new-fashioned upbringing when it's healthy—and, of course, in the old days, they did tumble downstairs a lot; but, even then——" She hesitated, doubtful of the point she was about to make—" a nursery at the top of the house——" She came to a halt, again; the point eluded her; she gave it up. . . .

But Toni remembered the nursery at the top of the house, natural region of banishment to herself and all her cousins, in the old days when each small family, within the great encompassing Rakonitz family, had had their own residence; their own dining-room, drawing-room, bedrooms; and then, up the third and steepest flight, that well-known room—most of their little friends had it, too!—before the clean, bright era of cork floors, and hygienic fireplaces, and animals stencilled in a frieze round distempered walls. That was the modern nursery; Babette should have one, perhaps, when their lease of Val's studio was up. But then, in the eighteen-nineties, it had been a Turkey carpet, too frayed and faded for the dining-room; wall-paper with a pattern on it—hers had been a looped bewilderment of tulips!—and a fire-guard, and a rocking-chair, and a small cosy fire that glowed between the three iron bars of the grate. In one corner stood the great mahogany toy-cupboard, nearly always with a door ajar, and a bulge of escaping toys; and the gas sang companionably inside its prison of pink, opaque glass; and Grandmère sent up cake from the drawing-room for the children's tea: Austrian Torte: luscious, flat slices of pastry with fruit spread on top; or that wonderful crumbling cake, smelling of hot spice and veined with cinnamon . . .

The old nursery days!—Toni looked at her small daughter with tender compunction; still, Babs was hardly old enough to recognise what she was missing.

And really, it was an anxiety to have a baby in a studio cottage, with revellers in and out at all times of the night; motor-horns blown frantically as the cars were backed down the lane into the street; the gramophone hardly ever at rest, from tea-time onwards; and no possibility of completely shutting off the bedrooms from the studio itself, which was dining-room, drawing-room, lounge, and smoking-room, all in one; and even spare-room, if you counted the musicians' gallery, with the divan in it, up the small twisting staircase; you could shut it off, if you wanted to, by tugging the thick cords which pulled heavy silk curtains, scrawled with green and gold and ginger and magenta, right across the studio, unequally

dividing it. It would have been huge fun, as a child, to have
played with those curtains ; to have drawn them aside, dashed
up the stairs into the gallery, made a speech over the rail to
the imaginary multitudes thronging the studio below ; fun
for one afternoon ; not for always ; you would get tired of it ;
you would want to go back to the nursery. . . . Toni roused
herself, with a start, to listen to what the nurse from St. Olaf's
was saying :

"Quimper seems to think, Madam—but I don't know if
it's right—that it's quite a quiet party you're giving, and in
the afternoon ; but that perhaps a few people may be expected
round in the evening, after he and Mrs. Quimper have left,
who couldn't get away from their work before. But I told
him that it was not quite what I expected, from hearing you
and Mr. Goddard talk."

"Yes," said Toni, hunted and guilty ; "I mean—no—the
fact is, Nurse, that we don't think that Quimper would enjoy
our evening party, so we haven't told him much about it.
Dancing, you know, and liveliness——"

"Quite so, Madam," the nurse agreed, sympathetically.
"The meringues *do* get about so !"

The obscure reference was to a fore-shortened vision, which
neither she nor her mistress had ever quite forgotten, of
Quimper's disgusted expression, as he staidly mounted a
borrowed step-ladder, to pick off a couple of limp meringues
that had somehow or other found their way on to the skylight
blind. This had occurred after their last dance, three or four
weeks before : dance that was an informal proclamation from
Toni, to all whom it might concern, that she was once more
ready to be included in "any rag that was going."

For Toni had by no means emerged from her phase of
glorious and irresponsible lunacy. Her bad, mad times, indeed,
did not occur along a level plateau, but pelted, spasmodically,
up and downhill, in imitation of the intoxicated sprawl of a
patient's progress in a fever-chart. Beginning with the day
of her violent reaction from work, when she had lain in the
sunshine by the duck-pond, and wished that the world would
fill itself with men and laughter, it had mounted quickly from

normal to, perhaps, a temperature of 101°; where it had remained until she had dutifully slackened pace, last March,
realising that she must give her baby a chance. From
March to July, then, a gradual descent towards normal again,
and July—darkness and the struggle . . . "a lovely little
daughter, Mrs. Goddard." . . . *That* was all right, anyhow!
she had preferred a daughter, and Babs really was lovely from
the very beginning. Another three months of exemplary
behaviour . . . and then the line began to waver up the chart
again—99°—100°—101°—until suddenly, it shot up an almost
precipitous incline, to the equivalent of 105°!—High fever!
—Call the doctor!—"Let things rip!"—Toni was done with
being good; Toni was tearing about again, spending money,
buying clothes; a fortnight in Paris with Giles; and dancing,
dancing, fox-trot and tango and waltz, waltz and Java and
Blues, till kipper-time came round at the Night Clubs. . . .

The very expensive nurse from St. Olaf's looked after Babs
so wonderfully, that really there was no need for Toni to take
charge; and Giles was impatient to have Toni beside him
again, wherever he went, and whatever he did, because she
was such a good companion; although, once the perilous time
had been well over, in July, he had not refused all invitations,
in order to hang about the studio, brooding tenderly upon the
spectacle of his wife with their child in her arms; as, inevitably, a Jewish husband and a Jewish father would have done.
Giles was remarkably popular; even more popular than Toni.
Women said it was because he was such a divine dancer. And
other men were not alienated from him by this, because his
dancing was of the kind that felt divine, and looked perfectly
ordinary, so that they never suffered from an uneasy sensation
that one of their number was performing, instead of merely
enjoying himself. Giles's dancing was the unexpected bonus
thrown in with Toni's already bursting sack of good fortune;
and as the Viennese side of her was most in evidence, this
year of her good time, so she was able to dance her fill at last.
They had danced for the first time together, she and Giles, in
Rome; among the pillars of Bragaglia's cellars; and they had
danced in Paris; and in London, they invariably danced six

nights out of the seven, and sometimes the seventh ; London was still in the grip of the dancing craze. Toni could nearly believe that she loved Giles, dancing with him. . . .

The studio had a good wooden dancing-floor, now, laid down at their expense. They had been quite incredulous when they had rolled aside the Persian rugs, and had perceived how rough and uneven the boards were, underneath. What could the succession of artists have been thinking of, who had inhabited the studio previous to themselves, not to have attended to this important matter?

They were giving a preliminary party, that same afternoon, for Quimper alone. He was liable to mope and to give notice, unless " company " were frequently invited. But it had to be " company " in his sense of the word, not theirs! He liked the kind of company that remarked afterwards : " How beautifully the silver shone, and how well everything was done! they must have a perfectly marvellous butler! I envy them their possession of same and aforesaid."

So that Toni and Giles were " At Home," on this occasion, to everyone they could collect who had either a portly presence, or a title. It was obviously Quimper's party, and they were merely in office to receive the guests and pay for the tea. And Quimper assured them afterwards, with much satisfaction, that he thought : " . . . It had all gone off very well indeed, and nobody went without!" Toni and Giles, now convinced that they would retain his services for the next few days, did not risk his golden opinion of them, by informing him that he had made a gross and unmannerly mistake by tip-toeing discreetly over to Toni, while she sat being charming to a knot of nonentities, and whispering in her ear : " There's a Person in the hall, Madam, who asked for you. I wasn't sure, so I left her outside." The " Person in the hall " had turned out to be Toni's most influential and dowdy client of other days, the Hon. Mrs. Wensley, of the type of county aristocracy before whom Quimper should have grovelled !

" Butlers don't get on to a breast-high scent, as they used to," remarked Giles, afterwards. " Never mind, I think Quimper enjoyed his party. Let's hope it'll help him to survive the wreckage that he'll find when he turns up to-morrow. That was a good wheeze of yours, Toni, to rope in all your old family silver, from Bedford Park. That man has a passion for silver that's hardly holy! I heard him singing: 'Pale spout I kissed . . .' to the teapot, in the pantry! How do you come to possess such a rich collection, with your grandmother still alive?"

Toni replied vaguely: "Oh, it just happened!" It was a matter of past routine, which she had kept from him, that she had always redeemed the family silver, and Maxine the family jewelry, whenever the Matriarch, in her bad times, had gaily pawned them, or given them away to chance acquaintances whom she had met and liked on her merry junketings. . . .

"I wonder why we take all this trouble to appease Quimper?" she speculated. "Mrs. Quimper's a great cook, of course. She calls him 'Quimper' when she speaks of him! I think I'll take to calling you 'Goddard!' She says: 'Quimper—he's funny about some things!' Have you noticed, Giles, that since the war, nearly all our friends have either acquired butlers, or else can't afford any servants at all?"

"I've noticed it, with a painful sense of loss. In my father's young days, he used to kiss the trim parlour-maid in the hall. I have exactly the same disposition and yearnings; but, wherever I go, I find the hall full of Quimpers, and they don't tempt me!"

Toni was lying outside her bed, resting after a bath; enjoying, idly, the slippery feeling of the loose, thin silk wrap against her bare flesh; and the pleasant hollow of warmth and comfort and luxury cast by the flames of the gas-fire, in the absence of all other light; a gleam twinkled here and there, in dragon-fly colours, from the outlying shadows of the room, where Toni had tossed down three or four evening-dresses, while choosing what she would wear that night. It was an iridescent season: dresses hung straight to the ankles; dresses that were just beads and beads and beads again; and women shot and shimmered across the ballroom, sheathed as in a fairy ballet. . . .

At the end of the bed, Giles squatted, and smoked his pipe. He wore a very stolid brown dressing-gown, because, as he explained when he bought it, he felt decadent enough, living in a studio, without extraneous help from the Burlington Arcade.

This was the lull between party A and party B. The Quimpers had gone home; and Nurse and Babs had left for Bedford Park; nobody arrived at a dance before ten o'clock, at the earliest.

"*Why* do you talk through your hat, Giles? You wouldn't really kiss parlour-maids, would you?"

"Good Lord, of course I would! Jimmy always did! Does!"

"That's no reason," replied Toni, primly. "How did your mother like it?"

"He didn't do it in front of her, of course; he used to confess like hell to her, later on, usually when she had a headache and couldn't be bothered to listen."

"Weren't you awfully fond of her?" said Toni, softly. This was practically the last time that she adapted her tones to the conventional response to be anticipated from a reserved young Englishman, who very rarely cared to speak of his mother. . . . It seemed inevitable that Giles would answer, briefly, and with a suggestion of huskiness: "Yes, she was everything to me"—and change the subject.

Giles answered, cheerfully: "No, not awfully. She died when I was about fourteen, but I can't remember missing her much. She was always rather scornful and detached. Quite decent to us kids, though, in lots of ways. I think Jimmy plagued her a lot, and so she didn't expect very much from us, being boys."

"How queer . . ." mused Toni. It *was* queer that this unknown Nancy Goddard should have felt as Toni herself felt, about boys and men. . . . And that Nancy Goddard's still more unknown parents were supplying the wealth which now enabled one Toni Rakonitz to lap cream!

"She was strikingly good-looking," Giles said. "*My* eyes," he went on, with pride; "My mouth, too," he added, as an after-thought. "And my profile," trying to help Toni form a conception of his mother's good looks.

But Nancy Goddard's daughter-in-law remained pre-occupied, puzzling out what might lie behind a former remark of his: "Jimmy plagued her a lot."

" About parlour-maids, Giles," she began again——

" *Trim* parlour-maids," he corrected, gravely. " One wouldn't want to kiss them, you know, if they weren't trim ! "

" Have you, since we were married. . . . I expected you would, you know, among—oh, our own friends. But parlour-maids——"

" Great Scott ! " exclaimed Giles, incensed. " You don't really imagine that I sneak about, kissing your pals in odd corners, do you ? Rebecca, or Betty, or Esmé, or any of the gang ? Except in front of you, of course ? There's a lot of indiscriminate hugging in our set. I don't approve, but I bow my head to it."

" I consider your outburst of virtue is suspicious," said Toni, accusingly ; " especially after yearning for trim parlourmaids."

" That's different. It isn't the kisses I'm virtuous about ; it's the people I put them on. That girl, for instance, from your business." . . .

" *Giles !* " Toni raised herself on one arm, in complete consternation and horror : " You didn't kiss Aimée Lequesne, that time you took her back to Hanover Street ? "

" What did you expect ? Over and over and *over* again ! I can never resist a sheer ass. You should have seen her being dignified, and saying, ' Oh ! Mr. Goddard ! . . .' " He chuckled reminiscently.

Toni subsided on to her pillows, with a groan : " This—*man* point of view is beyond me. Can't you see how you were letting me down ? "

Giles couldn't. " You're so naïve and wide-eyed, in some ways," he complained. " Aimée knew there'd be a spot of kissing, from the first second you suggested I should tootle her back in the Dook. She cried, ' Oh, how lovely ! ' don't you remember ? Aimée's used to it. *How* was I letting you down ? I didn't set her up in a flat. I kissed her, and told her she was pretty and a darling. It's all right, Toni ! "

" But it's so old-fashioned," Toni argued. " It's a relic of the period when girls' ankles were a treat to a man, and knees positively thrilled him ! Aimée belongs to those days ; so do you. Are you the same generation as Jimmy, after all ? "

He laughed: "Have you got a headache, Toni?"

"Oh, you weren't confessing, my husband. You were boasting."

"Boasting?" he repeated, wearily; "*boasting* of having kissed Aimée? My dear kid, it's you who are old-fashioned. In one moment, you'll be telling me I'm a sad dog with the ladies!"

Toni was becoming more and more interested. She felt as though she had inherited a trunk full of miscellaneous objects, and had not had time to rummage through them until now, to find out their contents. Had she been probing herself, instead of Giles, she might have been amazed to discover that she was not all calm curiosity, but, here and there, hotly angry. Parlour-maids! the Aimée type! (she ticked them off on her fingers)—but he wouldn't kiss my friends, except in front of me. . . .

"What about barmaids?" laconically.

"Oh, you don't kiss barmaids," Giles explained, meticulously exact in his definitions of male behaviour; "You go on in a way that makes them say: 'Now, saucy!' They don't say it as much as they used to; that tradition's dying out, too. You'd better talk to Jimmy about barmaids; his reminiscences are fruitier and more bloomy than mine! Hard luck you're not a man, Toni! It's a historical moment when you can draw a barmaid to say: 'Now, saucy, give over!' It'll be entirely lost to the next generation, I'm afraid. If Babs has any brothers . . ."

"Babs won't have!"

He raised his eyebrows, quizzing her certainty. Toni smiled serenely back at him . . . her closed mouth an uplifted crescent.

Abruptly he stood up, sauntered to the fireplace, and knocked out his pipe: "It's nearly nine o'clock, darling, and the snow lies heavy on the skylights. I doubt if any single person will come, this bleak November night, but you'd better dress. You can hate me just as well while you're dressing as while you're lying there, you know."

"Hate you? I don't hate you. I'm not a jealous wife of

the Edwardian era. I find an impersonal analysis most richly rewarding, that's all!"

"I'm shaw . . ." retorted Giles, using the favourite idiom of the moment. And he went whistling into the bathroom.

"Giles," she called, presently, through the open door; "can't you really see that you were letting me down, by kissing my sales-woman, who had been to see me on business?"

"Wait a moment, my heart; I couldn't hear you; I was splashing; now say it again."

Toni, with unnatural courtesy, repeated her question.

No, Giles didn't see that he had let her down.

"But you do consider," she persisted, "that you would be letting me down, if all this time you were flirting, with kissing accompaniment, say with Betty or Esmé?"

"Your friends? our friends? It's simply not done, Toni."

She had been eagerly expecting him to say: "It's simply not done, Toni"—for a year and two months. So that now it had actually been spoken at last, she could hardly believe that he meant it, and was not merely scoring a humorous point by playing up to her.

"I see. Thanks, that'll be all for the moment!"

Two minutes later, he called out: "How's the impersonal analysis getting on?"

"Nicely, thanks!"

"Unfolding like a flower?"

. . . No answer came from the bedroom. Giles had only just plunged into his bath, but he stepped out of it again, and dripped across the tiled floor towards the door that led into their adjoining bedroom. He stood on the threshold, and looked at Toni for a few seconds, before she knew that he was there. . . . She was sitting on a low, cushioned chair in front of the gas-fire, voluptuously drawing over her left leg a filmy stocking of pale oyster-coloured silk, with a faint sheen of rose on it where the curves took the firelight reflections. The silk wrap she had thrown over her while resting on the bed, had been abandoned, and lay in a tumble next to her chair. Her smooth, small head was bent low, as though absorbed in her task, so that he could not see her face. She had not begun to

dress yet, except for one highly decorative stocking on one
highly decorative leg. And now she stretched it out, straight
in front of her; most earnestly scrutinised it; knitted her
brows . . . then smiled, a provocative, secret smile, at the
exquisite ankle and instep.

. . . But Giles still watched what could be seen of her face.

—Toni suddenly looked up, and saw him standing there. It
would have been natural to speak; to carry on their bantering
quarrel; or to ask him if he had mislaid anything. But neither
Toni nor Giles said a word. He went back to his interrupted
bath. She pulled on her other stocking.

" I shan't need any rouge, after all ! " she murmured, in
front of the long mirror. Her heart was stuttering in movements wild and disturbed, as of a pigeon who has heard distant
gun-shot. Yet how radiantly well she looked ! And how she
was looking forward to the rest of the evening ! So much
more than ever in her life before. . . . This was going to be
the dance ! Yes, she was certain of it. . . .

It had chimed three times, for a quarter to twelve, from
the nearest church tower, when Toni said to her partner, who
was Giles, and had already been Giles over and over again :

" Colin and Betty ought to be arriving, about now; they're
not stopping to change after the show. Colin said he'd ask
permission for them to come straight on in their costumes."

Giles went to the studio door, and opened it wide. The
cold air shuddered in, and seemed to squeeze away warmth
into the far corners of the studio.

" Pitch black outside, and snowing; they won't get a car
up the lane; we ought to show them a light of some sort."

" Who? Colin and Betty ? "

" Are Colin and Betty coming? Good egg ! "

" Will they be wearing that ripping kit of the third act ?
Betty looks too gorgeous in it ! "

" Listen ! what's that ? it's a taxi, isn't it, stopping just
down the road ? "

" Here's a bundle of long, wax tapers," cried someone else.

They were snatched from his hand, quickly distributed, thrust into the fire, and then rushed towards the door. The men and girls in the rear of the crowd were pushing forward the others, willy-nilly over the threshold and into the lane.

The snow was falling very lightly now; soft flakes strayed vaguely in the air, before, at last, they fluttered to the ground. The out-thrust tapers were like slender twigs from a white tree, tipped with burning crocuses of flame.

Between the high blank walls, two fantastic figures moved slowly towards them, hand in hand, the clasp held high, as though in some formal dance. Colin and Betty. In the brilliantly lit studio, behind the crowd, the gramophone was still playing the last fox-trot:

" It's moonlight in Kalua. . . ."

Kalua. Sliding ripples of black and silver water on a warm night. Canoes slipping down the shallows. Black silhouettes in the canoes. Silvery light just struggling up through the black sinuous trees on the bank. . . . That was the music of " Kalua." . . .

And suddenly it seemed to Toni that at last, crystallised here, now, into this single moment, was her good time as she had always dreamt of it. No more than this had she dreamt; not magic nor fairy-tale, but just such a happy fusion of the whirling snow, the crowd of figures, half in the light, half out in the dark, brandishing their torches; Colin and Betty, beautiful and slightly grotesque, advancing towards them in full panoply: velvet skirts spread like a huge, inverted cup round Betty's feet, as she minced over the pure, sparkling strip of snow; the absurd dangle of plumes on Colin's helmet; pause in the dance, the melody still running on; everyone laughing; bare shoulders heedless of the snow; Giles pressing against her arm; and the universal shout of welcome:

" Come on, you two; we're nearly frozen ! "

It had been a diamonded evening, and this was climax. This, surely, was the quintessence of gaiety itself. It did exist ! it did ! and not, perhaps, to-morrow; or reminiscently, yesterday, and incomplete; but now; for one encircled moment lifted high. . . . " It's moonlight in Kalua." . . .

A quick wind whirled up the lane, and blew out most of the flames. Colin and Betty were dragged within, and the door slammed.

"You *are* sports, to come on a night like this!"

"I want *hot* punch, glowing hot," announced Colin, firmly giving trouble. "And Betty wants a posset of mulled claret with plenty of spice in it, don't you, Betty, my angel? None of your nasty, chilly champagne for us, Giles, so it's no good popping corks in that ostentatious way of yours! No, thank you, my pretty, *no* cider-cup! I *know* cider-cup, made with a sprig of borrage, according to Aunt Anne's recipe, or is it Aunt Sophia's?—'almost non-alcoholic, and *so* nice for the young people'! Toni, I've never seen you look so far from plain; come and dance with me! Sling on another record, somebody. Now, Betty, mind you change your goloshes!"

They were all dancing again. . . .

About an hour later, Toni, halting beside the gramophone to help Maurice find the Java record, noticed a girl capering past whose face she did not know; one of several who had been brought along by somebody else, who, in turn, might have been brought by an originally invited guest, in the ramshackle way that modern parties build themselves up. "I could swear that I've never seen her before," mused Toni; "and yet—*have* I?" . . . But then the thought was cut off sharply by the freakish rhythm of "Java":

"Can you do it?"

"No, I haven't got the hang of it."

"Watch Toni; Toni and Giles do it beautifully."

"They oughtn't to be encouraged to show off, ought they, in their own studio?"

"It's not really *in* yet, is it? at least, it hasn't come to stay?"

"No, I don't think so."

"Colin, can't *you* Java?"

"If I could find a partner worthy of me," said Colin; "my shoes are a little pre-Java, but still! . . . Betty?"

Betty shook her head. With her voluminous olive-green skirts ballooning stiffly around her on the divan, she bent her tiny, sharply-carved black head over a bowl of mulled claret ; and pronounced the spicing to be amateur but nutritious. Colin swung round with arms appealingly outstretched for a partner. The strange girl, whom Toni had recently noticed, leapt into them. Two couples moved up and down the studio floor, elated at the space that their solitary proficiency had procured for them. Two couples, Giles and Toni, Colin and the girl whose mouth, closed but smiling, was curved like an uptilted crescent ; dodging, zig-zagging, while the rest of the party languidly criticised or generously applauded, according to their natures. The strange girl called over one shoulder, to Toni, as they brushed very close :

"We're relations, you know ! " . . . just before Colin swept her on again.

"How funny ! " laughed Toni, next time they passed close enough ; "How do we manage it ? "

"Oh, some great-uncle or other ! "

And that was all, just then.

But when Toni was a child, and before life became a breath-less and unmannerly scamper, Rakonitz met Rakonitz in a very different way :

First, rumours of arrival ; then a deprecating letter, in pointed handwriting, addressed to the Matriarch, as head of the tribe, announcing definitely that the relatives settled—perhaps —in Vienna or in Budapest, intended sending their loved son or their loved daughter on a visit to London, or for a long stay; so would the dear Anastasia be a little bit kind, yes ? . . . The letter was passed round ; read to Aunt Elsa and Aunt Henrietta and all the other aunts ; read to the Uncles ; all the history of that particular branch of the family was dis-cussed ; all the anecdotes that richly encrusted their past, were taken as circumstantial evidence of what might be ex-pected from this unknown : "He must have a little attention paid to him, isn't it ? coming over for the first time ! " And the "little attention" would swell and materialise into an overwhelming pageant of hospitality ; starting by a big dinner-party, the first of many, given by Anastasia ; to which the principal and most important Rakonitz members would be invited. The abundant and indigestible dishes that were cooked! The ceremonious compliments that were exchanged! and the messages that were delivered, from Vienna or Budapest! One foreign embassy despatched to another would hardly have evoked such scrupulous assemblage to do honour to the arrival of a stranger who was yet a unit of the family. A vast amount of bustle, a vast amount of graciousness and warmth; and a great deal of dignity too, were qualities that the family paraded, in quite unconscious obedience to the laws of their tribe and history, on these occasions. And Anastasia could be relied upon to say to the new-comer, in her genial, domineering tones: "You must tell me just exactly what business you wish to do, over here, and if you are looking forward to meet some nice young girl"—or "a nice young gentleman!"—"And I will see to it all! Ach! I remember your grandfather well. It was he who was always so careful about his cravats, and *would* go about Paris buying antiques, and order them all to be sent home to him—but dreadful shams, some of them! but his valet, who knew his ways, saw to it that they were all taken back to the shops the next day; and your grandfather was so absent-minded and such a dear fellow, that he never noticed, and sometimes even bought them twice or three times over! But as he never had to pay, and they always went back, it did not matter. A charming man, your grandfather!" . . .

When Rakonitz formerly met Rakonitz, in the old spectacular days . . .

But now:

"We're relations, you know!"

"How funny! how do we manage it?"

"Oh, some great-uncle or other!"

. . . The party went on. Toni did not think she could ever feel sleepy again. Once or twice, she remembered that moment when they had all crowded with torches into the doorway, lighting Colin and Betty up the lane powdered with snow . . .

PART II

THE YOUNG MATRIARCH

CHAPTER I

LORAINE was the great-granddaughter of Andreas Rakonitz, who was the fourth son of Simon and Babette. Therefore she was of the same generation as Toni Goddard and Maxine Silver, Val Power and Helen Czelovar and Richard Marcus.

In about the year 1840, Andreas and Eugène left Vienna; and travelled, the one, West, to Spain; the other, East, to Constantinople. Of all the long line of brothers and sisters that began with Sigismund and ended with Rachel, they were the two who vanished most completely. Their mother, Babette, never ceased hoping for their eventual return. For the benefit of her grandchildren, and most of all for the edification of little Anastasia, who used to squat at her feet beside the great china stove, holding her ball of knitting, Babette's comfortable, maternal arrogance built up a purely fictitious legend of the strength and the beauty and the admirable gifts of these two dashing young sons. No more was heard of Eugène, until, in about the year 1904, his widow, a dark dingy little Greek woman, had suddenly appeared in London, destitute, with four children, all more or less idiots. Eugène had assured her that his family would look after her; and the family had forthwith met in tribal council, and had abused Eugène, and squabbled exceedingly over bye-issues . . . and had vied with each other in bursting and abundant generosity; until Uncle Maximilian, in his testy, high-handed fashion, had commanded that no more should be said about this tiresome Greek woman and her children; which had merely meant—as the rest of

94

the family well knew—that he would supply funds for her whole support, and his elder sister Anastasia would administer them.

Andreas, in some mysterious fashion, had managed, by his marriage with Manuela Panja, to link himself with the family of a Spanish travelling showman. . . . And three generations later, out of obscurity, Loraine appeared, to dance the Java with Colin, at Toni's studio party. At once she had looked at Toni with those portentous, light eyes of hers, one so much smaller than the other, as though she and Toni shared a secret, but Toni might trust her not to betray it. . . . This was a trick of Loraine's. Later on, she would invent a secret about you, that you did not even know yourself; and make you believe in it; and then tell you how she had leapt to it from her very first encounter with you.

She was not at all beautiful; her lids slouched heavily over her eyes, in a raffish fashion; her small face was quite colourless; and her hair was colourless, too, and fell in flat angles, like painted wood, across her brow, and over her cheeks and ears. Only her mouth was beautiful; it was the Rakonitz mouth in shape, but the curves had a deeper sweetness and subtlety than any of theirs; it was a child's mouth still; but the rest of her face was old, too old; older than Loraine herself, and she was not very young any more. She hoped that she was ageless, like Cleopatra . . . people who came under her spell, told her so. Loraine's Spell was a very important part of her equipment; it would have been easier to cope with, had it been entirely her illusion; but it worked, sometimes; often enough to encourage her; and when it worked, it was a forceful spell. It worked most frequently on children, and animals, and servants, and old people; and moony girls were easily enough entangled in it. And every time that Loraine came into conflict with a human being who was spell-proof, she was first incredulous, and then uneasy, and then dangerous; and finally, ill and broken by the horror of her failure.

She was in conflict with her cousin Toni, now.

Loraine saw a lot of Toni, following their meeting at the dance.

The fiercest love of which she was capable, strangely enough, was for her unknown family. And it was a genuine obsession. She had caused her entrance into the family to be deliberately sensational. For some weeks before her advent, she had been hanging about on the outskirts, waiting for her chance; until at last it came, through a girl whom she knew, who knew a man who knew Giles! All through the evening, until she chose to declare herself, she was exulting in the knowledge that Toni Rakonitz was as yet unconscious of the very existence of Loraine Rakonitz; but that Loraine Rakonitz had the power to enrich the family gravy, by the additional substance and flavouring of herself, at any moment that she wanted to. Loraine had planned, moreover, that a sudden warm love would spring up at once, between herself and Toni. She was not sure that she wanted Toni actually under her Spell—not too easily enmeshed, at any rate; she despised people who were caught too easily. Eventually, of course—but, meanwhile, a sort of passionate cousinhood. She would hear all about Toni's life. They would sit, for hours and hours, talking. And she would contribute, diffidently, a few of her own nomad experiences . . . nomad and eerie, because she subconsciously placed herself as a spiritual offspring of Lavengro and La Belle Dame Sans Merci. And most of all she wanted to hear all there was to hear about the rest of the family; and to meet every one of them, often, and touch them, and be near them, and grow familiar with their oddities and characteristics, until she fulfilled at last her furious longing to be identified with Rakonitz and Czelovar and Bettelheim; absorbed in their most minute interests; knit closely into the fabric where she belonged.

But she had arrived among them so very much too late; and the fabric was torn and threadbare.

"Toni wasn't having any," was an out-of-date idiom in 1922, but it exactly expressed what Toni felt about this unexpected bombardment from Loraine. The family, to Toni, during her present phase, was not any more a fascinating and succulent chronicle, as it appeared to Loraine, who had only seen it from a distance. Toni had lived all her life in the very dust and heat of it; and only recently had managed to get away; she was not at all ready yet to go back to it, even in endless narrative. The family was tiresome . . . and she was enjoying herself with her rabble of happy-go-lucky contemporaries. A long time ago, she, too, had been capable of romantic excitement about the Rakonitz legend. . . .

And now Loraine, insistently pelting her with questions, saw it still as the child Toni had seen it: " Well, but surely-to-God I can visit my Aunt Anastasia? sit with her, even if she *is* ill? But why not, if I want to pay tribute to the old warrior? . . . She'd enjoy hearing about my grandfather's story of his father's escapade that night of the feast of Saint Ignatius Loyola. And where's my Aunt Elsa? Staying with Val in Italy? And Franz Rakonitz was killed during the war, you say? Ah, but I'd have adored my cousin Franz! Don't the San Remo lot ever come over, any more? Do you know Aunt Berthe, in Paris? And the two old dames who are both over a hundred years old. . . . Dead? dead? Ah, but the bad luck I've had. . . . So many of them dead. And the Uncles . . .? It's not so very long ago, is it, that Uncle Louis died? Where's Richard? Richard Marcus? Why won't you give me his address? Toni, darling Toni, let's have a party and invite them all; all who are left. Aunt Truda's a sweet darling woman, that she is, and I love your mother and Iris and your Babs. . . . But—where be all these dear dead women——? Where's Raoul Czelovar and Aunt Henrietta Solomonson and my cousins Neil and Sylvia and Helen? I want to see them all at once, in their glory, sitting at a long table, and eating Apfelstrudel! "

. . . Loraine was a fanatic, and—here was the worst of it! —a parody of Toni's former self. Toni, rather cool, rather bored, very full of engagements; Toni Goddard, wife of Giles Goddard, could not forbear from wishing, at first courteously, and later wearily, that Loraine would go back to Spain or to Ireland or to Lower Beckenham—wherever it was that she really came from!—and stay there. Her sentiments towards Loraine, were those of all mortals, except the very noblest, towards their parodies.

Where *did* Loraine come from? and what was her past?

Toni never quite found out. The background that she created was a kaleidoscope, perpetually shaken and jogged into fresh patterns. Apparently Loraine saw no reason why anything within reach of her imagination should not be looted for inclusion into her own personal history. The time and space and probability of these varying tales perpetually contradicted one another; but Loraine quite simply denied yesterday's pattern for the sake of to-day's re-arrangement. Her travels made geography into sheer bewilderment; her ancestors were of every known European nation, with a wayward dash in the direction of the South Seas. She had apparently been married, and not been married; she had had three adoring husbands; and she was a lonely, frightened elf of the woods and streams, who had never been loved by anyone. Gipsies and convents and circuses, and other picturesque flora and fauna, suddenly dotted the landscape of her childhood, and then as suddenly disappeared again, or were planted down in another place. She was an international vamp, and the Portuguese police would like to trace her whereabouts. . . . But sometimes, never a stain appeared on the white escutcheon of her virginity. She had, apparently, a glorious gift for singing, and the greatest singer of the world had once said to her . . . But then she had lost her voice, rescuing a Hapsburg drowning in the mouth of the Humber. . . . She had the finest seat to hounds of any woman in County Wicklow; and the Duc de Richespan, after she had lived with him in the old Château de Richespan for eleven years—for there had never been another man in her life! how could there be, after that fine and witty gentleman?—had once said to her: "Ma belle et fatale Loraine, avec toi, plus on trouve, plus on perd . . . mais ça vale bien les deux sous . . . !" . . . She had embroidered for him a set of tapestries depicting the obscurer portion of the Leda legend, which, with a wicked chuckle, he had been compelled to hang in the private closet that led from his dressing-room—for discretion's sake! And there wasn't a cabin nor hovel on the west coast of Ireland, nor an arena in the length and breadth of Andalusia, that did not know her and love her . . .

" My father took me wherever he went, good luck to him, until he died last year, preventing injustice to a Basque smuggler," said Loraine. " I was with him then, too. . . . We were used to the rough of it and the smooth of it, together. He always said to his friends that his scapegrace of a daughter had a palate for Madeira and port that, by God ! he'd never met the like of it ! "

Now this tale, although it was only a trifle, scratched at the portals of Toni's wrath. A connoisseur's palate for wine happened to be one of her own reasons for pride ; it was un- usual, in a woman. The fact that Loraine, with her Basque smugglers and her stage Irish, had followed her down into the very cellar, at once made this talent appear over-stressed and rather ridiculous. Anyway, Loraine was probably lying. . . . Toni took a cigarette, leant back in the arm-chair, and said, nonchalantly :

" Have you ever tasted a '74 Château Margaux ? Uncle Maximilian always called it *my* wine. . . . I was rather a pet of his, you know. I remember the first time he and I had a bottle together——" She was bragging, royally ; but Loraine had an evil effect upon her, and she did not care. If her cousin Loraine could be flamboyant, why, so could she, and not less effectively. " *Really* brilliant people never boast. . . . Do *I* boast ? "—It had been forgotten which Rakonitz had originally made this remark, but it expressed the immortal Rakonitz spirit, in a phrase.

. . . Those two small heads bent close together over the fire, gossiping like old friends, seemingly like good friends, bore a freakish likeness, one to the other. So did the oval faces, and that haunting lift at the corners of each mouth. Only the eyes were different ; Toni had the advantage there. Toni was by far the prettier of the two, and the younger by about eleven years ; and Toni could select and wear her clothes fastidiously, with just an allure of impudence, never a shade too much. But the two silhouettes were the same, and the type. Here was Rakonitz, expressed in terms of the twentieth century. The breed conformed to the modern cut of youth ; soft, short hair ; small bones ; boyish hips. And yet Rakonitz

women used to be large, and bountifully built; their superb
limbs disguised by bustle or crinoline, shawls, swelling leg-of-
mutton sleeves; their quantities of long hair plaited and rolled
and piled high, to hide the shape of their heads. These women
of former generations used to grow, and leave their maiden
hood behind; they became definitely adult, matronly, middle-
aged, elderly, old; at any rate, in appearance. This process
of development was now, in the physical sense, a lost secret;
thin girls might be seen flitting, unencumbered, through the
years; and, in time, they would wither a little, but they would
never grow, and grow old, with the massive dignity that their
ancestors had achieved. Maxine, perhaps, who was big and
dark, might do so; and Val, who was big and fair; but never
Toni and Loraine.

Toni and Loraine strove to out-boast each other, now, in
the same irritated, swaggering spirit with which those two old
women, Aunt Anastasia and Aunt Elsa, might have competed,
when they were fine young matrons in their thirties.

"I was rather a favourite of Uncle Max," repeated Toni,
musing. Then she laughed a little: "He called me an impudent chit, but I think he liked it when I cheeked him! The
other children were all afraid of him!"

Loraine laughed: "Afraid of Uncle Maximilian? And what
would they be afraid of him for? Of all the darlings——!"

Toni raised her eyebrows, astonished: "But you never
knew him, surely?"

Loraine smiled mysteriously: "I'll tell you, later. What
was the story about you and the wine, first? Ah! do pour
it all out, Toni! If you only knew how I ache to hear the
little things about the Uncles, and their rubies, and their
dressing-gowns, and their valets, and the houses they lived in,
before the whole grand structure crashed down. It was my
bad luck to have been out of it, until now! Uncle Maximilian
once said something about taking me home to live with him
and to run his house for him. . . . He said I'd amuse his
friends when I didn't shock them—and when I did, ah, sure,
it would do them good! and he said I could be trusted to order
the perfect dinner for twenty guests or more, and he would

never insult me by looking at the menu beforehand, even if the
King of England were invoited ! I always cooked the dinner
myself, when Uncle Maximilian sent one of his telegrams, across
half Europe, to say he was coming. And then I'd slip on the
dress he said suited me so well—that funny, old fashioned
brocade, striped plum-colour and smoke-blue with the little
posies of myrtle worked on it—I must show it to you, Toni ;
remind me ! . . . Uncle Maximilian found it himself, in a
fusty old shop in Barcelona, and he bought it for me, because
he said I had quite a rare sense of period and would wear it
with the right air. I loved hearing him say : ' Ecco ! here
comes our little Gräfin' ! ' That means Countess."

"Thanks," said Toni, drily. " I'm partly Viennese, too, as
it happens, and I've picked up a few words of the language."

She simply could not understand why Uncle Maximilian,
her late idol, should, apparently, have been so intimate with
Loraine's branch of the family, as to have sent them telegrams
across half Europe, to announce his advent ; to have refused
food, except when cooked by Loraine's own hands ; and to
have insisted on her wearing that dress which he had bought
for her in Barcelona. Not to mention the unspeakable idea
that Loraine should ever have been installed as his favourite
niece, and head of his household ; a beloved and trusted little
housekeeper to amuse and shock his friends. . . . Toni had a
distasteful vision of Loraine being lifted by Uncle Max on to
the table, to dance for them ; and all the dudes and dandies
leaning back in their chairs, glasses of Château Margaux up-
raised—Toni's '74 Château Margaux !—applauding and crying :
" Brava ! Brava ! the little Gräfin ! " . . . Had Uncle Max
not realised how his proposal was letting Toni down ?

" It's most peculiar," drawled Toni, in an endeavour to
restrain Loraine's officious thrust for a place in the very heart
and sanctuary of the family, " that Uncle Max should never
have mentioned you."

Loraine winced. Glanced at Toni, and quickly glanced
away again. Fidgeted with the bellows. Then, lifting her head
proudly but sadly, she said : " You see, there was a reason.
. . . However much he adored me, and made a favourite of

me, he wouldn't be likely to bring me where I could be with the rest of you."

" And why the Hell not ? " growled Toni.

" Because," Loraine replied, with haughty distinctness, " at that time there happened to be a prejudice, still, in your safely curtained drawing-rooms, against being connected with a bastard ! "

. . . It was about a year later that Toni discovered, and completely proved, that Loraine had never known Uncle Maximilian, except by recent hearsay : a photograph seen at Aunt Truda's, and one or two words the latter dropped in explanation : " Uncle Max—the Grand Seigneur, we used to call him. . . ." He, for his part, had been as completely unaware of the existence of any of Andreas' descendants, as were the rest of the family ; and, finally, Loraine's mother and father had been, from the first, most impeccably married by both Church and State.

An hour or two after Loraine had hugged her impulsively, and gone away, it occurred to Toni that in spite of all attempts, she had been baulked of telling that picturesque incident about a pretty, wilful child called Toni, who had always insisted, whenever she dined or lunched alone with her favourite Uncle, that a bottle of '74 Château Margaux should be brought up for her special benefit ! and the cork given to her for a relic, and a sign of initiation ; in the same sporting tradition as a child of a hunting family would be given the brush. But the Rakonitz family of cosmopolitan epicures would only think of " blooding " their young in rare wines. " Darling Uncle Max ! —I suppose it amused him to indulge me," Toni had meant to remark, in an off-hand sort of way. " How I loved to think myself sophisticated, then ! "

And her anecdote happened to be true ; but what was the good of truth against Loraine ?

Loraine, the scornful little Gräfin, a love-child and a wanderer, had decidedly scored in narrative ; Loraine, con-spirator in the dark but glowing life led by the Grand Seigneur outside the pale, when he escaped from family respectability !

Toni was cross ; she *had* been Uncle Max's pet niece !

CHAPTER II

. . . " I AM *very* glad to hear it," said Toni's grandmother, emphatically. "This time, it will be a boy. Boys are better." And this she said, tended lovingly in the house of her daughter; supported by her two granddaughters. She said it in the utmost good faith.

Toni herself was rather less glad. She had made up her mind to have one child, so she had behaved nicely over the advent of Babette. And Babs had proved adorable. Perhaps, in a great many years, she might possibly choose to have another. . . . But just now, to have to retire from the very rush and torrent of her amusements, was an interruption and a bore; worse than that, even; it was what Colin would have called bad stage-management. Toni, understudying Destiny with some efficiency (as she thought) for the entire pleasure and benefit of Toni, was very perturbed indeed at the prospect of this second child. Toni, in May, stared at the end of December, and gave it what almost amounted to a dead cut! She would continue enjoying herself, anyhow, up to the last possible moment; and begin again at the first possible moment.

"Well, good-bye, Grandmère darling, I must fly home and dress, now; we're all going to 'Lilac-Time' to-night. It's laid in Vienna, you know: 'Drei Mädchen-Haus'—Schubert's music, and the story of his love-affair with——"

"You will *not* go to the theatre to-night," said the Matriarch, positively. "After what you have told me? No, you will lie down!" She indicated a doubtful space beside her, on the canopied bed. . . . It was littered with a miscellany of interesting objects, necessary to the invalid's immediate comfort and happiness: two old but excellent boned corsets, black satin brocaded with red flowers, and purple satin brocaded with black flowers. A collection of open tins, containing sardines and other *hors-d'œuvres*, in a fair state of repair. And,

principally, a "set" for the writing-desk: six different "parts,"
in gilt squirligigs and marble-like crystallised raspberry ice;
blotter, ink-tray with duplicate inkpots, and four accessories,
use unknown. It had been the Matriarch's wedding-present
from her cousin Josef, and she had commanded it to be unpacked this very morning—one of Truda's busiest mornings—
because she said she could not make her Will without it. "Her
umpteenth Will . . ." grumbled Derek, despatched to the
attic where the trunks were kept.

"You will lie down, Toni. Now and here. If I do not run
behind things myself, nothing ever gets itself done."

"Grandmère darling, I can't lie down for seven months.
Going to the theatre to-night won't hurt me."

"Me, you can teach nothing!" cried Anastasia, beginning
to get shrill and excited. "I have had five splendid children:
Bertrand and Truda; my two beautiful boys, Ludovic and
Blaise——" Five . . . but she had forgotten who was the
fifth; Sophie had never been of any importance. "And I
lay down for all of them," finished the Matriarch, resigning
poor Sophie to limbo.

Toni, to quieten her, promised that she would go home and
rest. Grandmère must not be over-excited; there was always
a fear that another stroke might prove fatal.

"And tell that husband of yours that he is to give you
plenty of *bouillon; bouillon* as the French make it. Do you
understand? Tell him I say so, and that he is to have it prepared with a raw egg in it, and give it to you himself—— It
will not hurt him, though he *is* a Goy, for I have seen an
advertisement on all the walls of a young husband giving soup
to his wife who has had a baby in naval uniform, and your
Giles is not even in the army any more, so you see? And also
this, that if our Empress Elizabeth had not been so colossal
fond of England and the chase . . . The English soup is hot
water, and so we had all that Meyerling tragedy! And her
lovely hair too. . . . But you *would* have it bobbet, as they
call it, and now look at you! A young married woman like
you should be both virtuous and *séduisante*. So, she will have
many children. Strong French *bouillon*——"

" I'll tell Giles," Toni promised obediently.

" You still have our Maria in the kitchen, isn't it? That is right!"—But Maria had been dead, now, for over fifty years. "And come to see me more often, yes? No one comes to see me now except that silly girl whom I do not at all like, and her dress falling off her shoulders because she has no figure to hang it up. But Truda lets her in, and so she is always here, calling me Grandmère. . . . I am *not* her Grandmère!" Anastasia sat up in bed, and began to show signs, once more, of a turbulent spirit. Toni, being human, could not help being glad that she was still the Matriarch's favourite, and had not been replaced by Loraine. So she kissed the old woman even more tenderly than usual; and scolded herself, as she drove the Dook rapidly back from Ealing to Kensington, for so seldom going to see her. But there was too much going on; too much to do and see; too many companions clamouring for her; most of them originally introduced by Colin, who had been in hospital with Giles in 1917; they had become close friends, then; and when Toni brought in, as her share towards the nucleus of a set, two or three of Val's late intimates, they had enough and more than enough to start on; all the others followed, inevitably. The constant demand for Toni's presence by every fresh group thrown in her way by the last group, in an endless chain, gave her a giddy, elated feeling of being indispensable. Surely it could not all go on, after she had once dropped out? Surely, she was both the egg and the egg-whisk? . . .

In London, if you are young, gay, if you love dancing; if you have the trick of throwing money about without looking in which direction it goes; and if, moreover, you are not tiresomely conscientious on any particular point of religion, duty, or reform; if, finally, you have personal magnetism, a knack of putting on the right clothes at the right moment in the right way, and if your existence in the past had been a drab thunder-grey, so that its present golden-yellow shines in brilliant contrast against it; then there is only one asset still required for your complete enjoyment, and that is robust health.

Toni would never be robust ; but she lived on her nervous vitality.

And so the good time went on. . . .

As for Giles, she did not see as much of him as formerly ; very often, now, they agreed to revel apart, instead of together. They had been married for nearly two years. . . . On the whole, she knew rather less of Giles than when she had first confidently enclosed his entire individuality into the space of the conventional nutshell. His capacity for rushing round with a laughing, drinking, dancing throng, equalled, if it did not outdistance, hers ; but it remained an astonishing faculty, in an Englishman, to continue to want, vigorously, no more than evanescent gaiety, that never resolved itself into a solid chunk of gain, some purpose fulfilled, some win in a game, some trophy of sport.

Toni would have hailed it as natural in, say, her Viennese cousin who was killed in the war : Franz Rakonitz, that nonchalant and well-dressed cynic, who had composed songs ; and played on the pianos of every cabaret in and off the Kärntner-Ring. . . . She could remember now, how he had sat down in Aunt Elsa's drawing-room, on a visit, and accompanied his own singing of that serious and enchanting lyric : " Wass macht ein Kuh am Stefansplatz ? "—roughly translated to : " How the deuce *can* a cow occupy herself in Regent Street ? " . . .

What, ultimately, did Giles want out of it all ? His drinking was only a cheery accompaniment to an evening's amusement ; he did not gamble ; nor, as far as she could see, did he make love more promiscuously than the fashion of the day demanded. Yet what did she expect from him ? A wheel could leap nowhere, except, at a break-neck pace, back to its own beginnings ; and, outstripping these, round and round again. . . .

How old was Giles ? Twenty-nine ? Thirty ? yes, but in his enjoyment of a good time, as in Toni's, was a feverish element ; six years of the war, matched to her twelve years of monotonous work ; they had both been robbed ; they were both refusing to submit to such robbery. His nominal " job " was selling motor-cars ; the job of nearly every post-war young officer who was not crippled in nerve or body, and who could afford to ignore the serious question of earning a living. In partnership with another ex-officer who played tennis all day long, covered courts in the winter, Giles was agent for Rolls-Royce, Vauxhall, Bentley and Morris automobiles. Toni found infinite amusement in contemplation of the way these two men grimly fought their way to the top, inch by inch, in a business career. . . . Most of the time they forgot about it altogether !

May, June, July. . . . " I'll break off in November," said Toni. At the end of November, unwillingly, she began to shut out the crowd, and the lights and the music. It all died down. This time Giles remained on the thronged and noisy side of the curtain. He stayed on with the swing-boats and the merry-go-round : " All the Fun of the Fair ! " . . . A good time, during the post-war years, naturally expressed itself in Revue titles : " Dover Street to Dixie," " London Calling," " Yes," " Mayfair and Montmartre," " Snap," " Brighter London," " Carte Blanche," " Rats," and " The Little Revue Starts at Nine." . . . Here was the summary of Giles' career, in the hurried jargon of Giles' generation.

Paul was born on New Year's Day. The Matriarch had asked that the boy should be called after her long-dead husband ; and Toni had humoured her ; it was such an easy little thing to do. Paul would probably develop into the usual selfish, charming, unreliable Rakonitz man, one day to make glad the heart of woman—some woman or other !—so he might as well have one of their names from the beginning ; it would remind his mother, at all events, not to expect much from him. Better to start with fixed disillusion, than have to grope for it, later on, through bewilderment and agony : " We happen to know where we are with each other, Paul Goddard, don't we ? " she said, half laughing, to the baby in her arms. Paul Goddard gazed up at her, with as much adoration as though she had said : " Goo-goo-goo, was it my own pet lovums ? " . . . Perhaps Toni's voice had been warmer, kindlier, than her intention. He was plain, but already very dear.

She did not find it possible to pick up the good time again.

It was not as it had been before the break ; you could see the rivets. To the modern crowd, five minutes before to-day was already the past ; the jargon had altered ; the steps of the fox-trot were not, in March, what they had been in November ; November was alluded to as " ages ago ! " Different plays were on ; different stunts were the rage. Toni could adjust herself, within an hour or two, to whatever change had been in clothes. Once, and once only, she went out with an apache scarf knotted round her throat in the style which had been absolutely " it " when she had retired from sociability and the world, before Christmas ; she found that all apache scarves had been in the meantime swept mysteriously from the universe, and that she was looked at askance, as though she were a leper ; an unaccustomed experience for the head of fashionable " Toni's " ! She went home and presented her entire stock of apache scarves, numbering about eighteen, to Mrs. Quimper. Ever since the Belworthy incident, as reported by Aimée at the studio, she had stopped going to " Toni's " for her clothes, even though the discount profited her so enormously. But . . . " Toni's " ?—what was going on in Hanover Street? She did not want to know. She was uneasy, afraid to know. Probably everything was swinging along famously. As long as she kept away, she could corroborate none of her fears, and they might therefore be impatiently dismissed. But if she were always running in and out of the show-room, trifles might indicate, to an eye as experienced as hers . . . Oh— rubbish ! What trifles ? But she signed her monthly cheques with, metaphorically, her head turned away and her eyes screwed up. And she bought her clothes deliberately else- where, choosing the very smartest West End firms, of course. " Toni is looking too marvellous again," her friends said.

But to catch up, in dancing, was more difficult ; her graceful proficiency in the blues won her very little applause, now that the latest mania was to keep rigid knees in the fox-trot : " *No*, Toni, you mustn't hold yourself like that. . . . It's all wrong, I tell you ! quite straight the whole way down ; move as though you were made in one solid piece. Look ! watch Betty ! " . . . Toni did not want to watch Betty, when Giles told her to. It

was all Giles' fault that she *had* to watch Betty, in order to
acquire the correct poise for the fox-trot as it was now being
danced. . . .

And another small incident occurred to upset her :

The last time her mother had brought Babs to the studio,
Toni had commented on the child's curious aloofness :

" She seems to hate being kissed, even by me."

Susie looked worried : " If I were you, Toni——" she began,
briskly ; then swerved, and started again on another tack :
" What are you going to do, young lady, about taking a house
large enough for you to have all your children and belongings
in, now that there's Paul too ? "

" Oh, we've got the studio for nearly another year. You can
manage Babs and Nurse till next autumn, can't you, Mummy ?
They seem so happy. If not, of course, we must charge round
and find a house ; but they are difficult to get, and foully
expensive."

Susie did not seem comforted : " Well, but how are you
going to arrange things ? Are you going to have a second nurse
from St. Olaf's, for Paul, here in the studio, when the Monthly
leaves ? "

Toni laughed. " Do you know, it sounds incredible, but I
honestly hadn't thought about that. No, we couldn't afford
two nurses ; so I suppose we shall have to unload Paul on to
you, too ! What a mercy you've got room enough ! I shall be
down there staying with you more than half the time, of course,
so it's very much the same thing as having the children at home
with me. I mean, I shall see just as much of them."

" Just as little of them," contradicted Susie.

" Mummy darling, aren't you being a bit cantankerous ? "

" You were complaining just now that you didn't find Babs
affectionate. She's affectionate enough with Loraine. . . .
That girl is always rushing down to Bedford Park, morning,
noon, and night. She's a warm-hearted little scrap—I'll say
that for her ; and very nice to me, always ; gets me talking for
hours, sometimes, so that I forget all about getting supper.
But it's mostly Babs she comes to see ; she's crazy on the child,
and the child's all over her ; eyes for nobody else when

Loraine's about; and when she isn't, for ever looking out of the window to see when she's coming."

"Oh?" said Toni, laconically. "Funny girl, Loraine! How's Gerald getting on, Mummy? Has he had his rise yet?"

. . . And that was all, for the moment. But a fortnight later, Toni astonished her husband by informing him that she had all but taken a house in a "pretty useful" neighbourhood —Regent's Park; and if Giles had time that afternoon, perhaps he'd bring round the Dook; and she'd take him to see it; "I might as well have your approval before I finally settle on it," she said, cheekily.

"I appreciate your old-world courtesy and consideration," laughed Giles. "Seriously, Toni, what on earth do you want to take a house for, when we've got this studio for another year?"

"We can sub-let," said Toni, dodging the question of why she wanted a house. Their landlord was now, not Val, but the owner of the studio from whom they had directly taken over the remainder of Val's lease; so there could not be any question of being let off their contract.

"I suppose we can?" doubtfully.

"My dear old boy, people are simply waiting in queues for studios; artists, especially; they can't get them, since the dancing craze began."

They proved too late for the house in Regent's Park; somebody else had slipped in a claim first. So they took a furnished flat near Knightsbridge, instead. It was a nice flat, and Toni was wildly enthusiastic about it; but after they had signed on for a two years' tenancy, they heard from the agents who had the Regent's Park house in hand, that the contract with the other tenants had fallen through at the eleventh hour; and would Mrs. Goddard like it, after all?

"We must have it, Giles; it's a gem of a house and a chance in a million; so wonderfully furnished; almost nothing in it, and yet everything that one could possibly want; hot and cold water in every bedroom makes such a difference to my soul's well-being. We can sub-let the Knightsbridge flat quite easily."

" That's two," remarked Giles. " Let's take on some more ! "

He had never really known Toni's Grandmère, beyond a few perfunctory visits to her bedside. He had never seen Anastasia at the jovial zenith of what had been called, by her grandchildren, a " bad time " ; or a certain uncanny resemblance might have struck him . . .

The Matriarch had taken houses, too, and flats—thousands of them ! Toni and Maxine had had to see to all that ; clear up the mess when the bad time had toppled again.

The Goddards were luckily able to arrange to sub-let, profitably, both the Kensington studio and the Knightsbridge flat.

" You see ! " said a triumphant Toni ; and they marched into their Regent's Park house in May. The Quimpers came with them. Babs and the nurse from St. Olaf's joined them at once. Even Shoe Lane, the studio cat, expressed herself satisfied with her new quarters.

And now Toni knew definitely that she was going to have another child the following January—exactly a year after Paul's birth.

This time, strangely, she did not feel the same resentment about it ; she said that it was the atmosphere of a house that made all the difference ; a thoroughly up-to-date and well-arranged house was, after all, very much more luxurious than a studio, even Val's studio. Her mood was lazier and more oriental than it had yet been, since her marriage ; she did not want to be bothered with anything ; nor to strain to keep up with the latest capers and fantasies of Colin and his gang. There were plenty of people to wait on her, to attend on her caprices. As the autumn drew on, the little Sybarite, who had once been noted for her driving energy and her power of ascetic endurance, lay back in deep arm-chairs ; ate pleasant fruits ; read the sort of books that recalled, once more, that mellow and yet tingling feeling of being a grape of Sauternes, bursting with over-ripe sweetness in the sunshine. It was nice, thought Toni, cosily, returning home in the Dook after exercise dutifully taken in Richmond Park, nice to have nothing to do, and no worries. " Toni's " never badgered her for advice in the business nowadays, except nominally, to sign the usual out-going cheques. Miss Thompson and Aimée Lequesne had obviously learnt to be self-reliant, as she had intended they should. Giles, in consequence of her beautiful management over the Belworthy affair, still took responsibilities—there were few enough!—upon his own shoulders, thinking Toni unfit to cope with them. How wise of her to have married Giles! How cleverly she had found this house, and sub-let the flat and studio! How good to feel that two children were playing in the nursery upstairs! . . . And she was conscious of a mysterious sense of rightness, too, in reminding herself that a third was on the way; and for that reason, and no other, she was privileged to be quiescent, dreamy, full of whims; securely lodged in a dwelling with many comfortable rooms. . . . It happened to resemble the state of marriage as it used to be, for women of Israel. And Toni settled her small slim body, boyish still in outline, deep into the arm-chair, and laid her shingled head back among the soft silk cushions, and told herself, without any hint of irony, that this was as it should be! . . .

"But I ought to go and see what's happening at Hanover Street!" This was the only jagged, strident thought that interrupted her pearly content. She could not help remembering "Toni's," over and over again, now that she was no longer restlessly on the move, all day and most of the night. And every time she remembered it, the more nervously her mental gesture of recoil pushed away from it. If she once gave in—oh, responsibility again! And she had had too much responsibility, while she was too young. Business dreariness. . . . And supposing a long sequence of mistakes had accumulated from the initial mistake of accepting Belworthy's proposal? No—well—that was altogether unlikely . . . but *supposing?* Then it would be her job, all over again, to re-organise and re-systematise and put the trouble right. . . . Why *should* she? This was surely better, to be flexible and acquiescent and womanly, to lie among cushions, to exact petting, to let things tire her easily . . . little Toni! Little slim scrap of a child—doesn't she deserve her rest after her hard time ?—well then, why forfeit it ? Shut up, Toni, and drink the beaten-up egg and port that Quimper has just brought you. As long as you never let yourself be driven by a fool conscience back to Hanover Street, you're all right. So shut up ! . . . lie still and lie soft, and croon lullabies to your conscience. For those who lie still, they lie soft, among plump cushions, blue and purple, that have the shape and the bloom and the hues of giant grapes. . . . What cushions did you have, Toni, when you pushed forward, too soon and too often, and said : " *I* can do it—leave it to me ! "? . . . It all came afterwards, didn't it ? with the unearned increment, with the pampering fur coats, and the dancing, and the mellow wine, and the fine handsome young husband who will not let you tire yourself. So don't be a fool, little Toni . . . leave Hanover Street and the business alone. They're all right. Haven't you learnt yet that it's not by doing things well, but by letting others do them, that you are suffered to lie still and lie soft ? Stir, and the spell is broken. . . . So :

" Loraine, darling," voluptuously, " *would* you mind closing that door ? There's a draught."

For Loraine still came rather often ; and Babs could not be weaned from her fidelity. That had been another stroke of fortune gone awry ; but here Toni trusted to time ; presently, when things began to matter again, when she recovered her energy, she could so easily deal with her small daughter's ridiculous obsession ; so easily win Babs' affection for herself. But meanwhile, she could not altogether bar Loraine, warmly confident of her welcome ; she was, after all, Toni's own flesh and blood. During this period of fecundity and languorous content, the antagonism between the two cousins drowsed : Loraine was a witty and amusing companion with whom to fill in the tea-to-dinner hours of early Autumn, chatting in front of the fire ; while Giles, who had recently " chucked " his car agency, spent a month down in Gloucestershire, hunting with the Berkeley. She was no fool, either ; you came across deep wells of knowledge where you least expected them ; and—still more astonishing—deep wells of commonsense. That moment, for instance, when Babs had swallowed a fish-bone, at lunch,

and had begun to choke!—but Loraine had had her off the
chair and out on to the balcony, where she had deftly removed
the bone and soothed Babs' terrified crying, before Toni had
even time to be agitated, or herself to help in the matter.
The way Loraine had done it all, had reminded Toni of someone else's quick, cool methods in an emergency ; she could not
think whose ? . . . As a matter of fact, they were her own.

"And she has managed to fit Quimper with one of her
made-to-any-measure Spells, which is odd," Toni remarked to
Helen Czelovar, another and very much younger cousin, who
had strolled in, one afternoon. "You saw Quimper in the hall
just now, Helen ; wouldn't you say, after one look at him,
that he'd be the type who would shudder at the sight of
Loraine wearing a jade-green velvet evening dress, arriving here for lunch, with Giles's ex-Colonel, and Aunt
Constance ? "

"But actually Mother liked her, too," said Helen ; "and
Mother liked Quimper ; we know Quimper liked Loraine ; the
only thing we're doubtful about is whether Quimper liked
Mother ; will you ring, Toni, and ask about it ? Tell him
she's a Dean's daughter ! But, do you know, I sympathise
with Loraine over jade-green velvet ; it's what *I* really ache
to wear, deep down in the bottom of my soul ; rose-red velvet,
too, and lots of bright-coloured beads and ear-rings and orange
silk shawls ! However, as I was born the most blatant type of
Whitechapel Yidd, I have to confine myself mostly to sober
blacks and whites. Hard luck, isn't it ? "

Toni looked at her, and smiled . . . appreciating Helen's
courage in the face of great odds ; for, indeed, this youngest
child of Raoul Czelovar and Constance, the Dean's daughter,
was an outrage on her parents' austere mansion in Chester
Square, so acutely did her characteristic hooked nose, her small
beady eyes, her fuzz of black hair, and white, bold flash of
teeth, remind the beholder of faces usually to be encountered
only in alien roads, east of London : dark, ghetto faces ; over-
mobile, too expressive. Helen, as a child, had been the family
joke ; she had seemed such a just retribution, appearing, as
she did, after the cool, English good looks of her elder brother

and sister, Neil and Sylvia. But Helen had brains, too, and a whimsical and exact knowledge of her own exterior; and now, at the age of twenty-two, she provoked the exclamation: "how smart!" instead of "how hideous!" when she was first introduced to a stranger. Like Toni, she selected and wore her clothes with that touch of individual genius that declared them her own, and impossibly anyone else's. She had a supple, lightly-balanced figure; she discarded all colours and trimmings; her hair, shingled, and brushed hard and straight back from her forehead, anticipated the Eton crop.

"No, I wouldn't give way to red velveteen," said Toni, with an approving nod for Helen's three-piece suit: "That's a good cut. You can beat Sylvia hollow along your own line, you know, Helen. What a pity I didn't have you at 'Toni's'!"

A still brighter gleam showed in Helen's eyes: "Oh, I wish you had! I want to do something; going to, in fact. Not music, nor any of the graceful arts; they bore me. Business. Business must be topping!"

"Glorious!" said Toni, briefly.

Helen missed the sardonic inflexion. "I suppose you won't be going back to it?" she asked; "I'd rather be in with you than anyone. You know your job, you see."

"No, I'm not going back." This was spoken positively. She had a sudden freakish impulse to tell Helen about the queer, considered choice she had been called upon to make, at the moment of the Belworthy incident. Then she decided not to; Helen might think her a fool; Helen knew a few things by intuition; but she had not been battered by years of poverty and anxiety into the ultimate wisdom of knowing when she was well off, as Toni had been. For the Raoul Czelovars were tolerably wealthy; and the correct Raoul adored his ugly little Yiddisher girl. "I *must* go round to Hanover Street to-morrow or the day after, without fail," Toni decided. Then suggested aloud: "Why don't you get your father to start you off in something, on your own. He'd let you have a thousand or two of capital, like a shot, wouldn't he?"

"Not exactly like a shot! He'd let me have it to buy a

ruby tiara! . . . It hasn't struck him yet, that jewelry doesn't suit my quiet, fair beauty! But he's still rather horrified at the idea of a sordid commercial career for me. I began on him wrong, you see: I let out, one night, mostly to annoy Sylvia, who was dining with us and being objectionable, that I intended to be the first lady pork-butcher, and already had the premises for my shop, in the Euston Road. It *would* be rather fun, Toni! Think of the trotters!"

"I refuse to think of trotters in my present state of health. I'm not surprised Uncle Raoul jibbed!"

"Well, then I went on quite mildly to ask him if I could go in with Eileen Moss; this was a year ago, before Eileen had made her great success."

"*How* casual we've become about each other, in the family. I didn't even know Eileen had made a success of anything at all. She's inclined to be intense, isn't she? I haven't seen her for about fourteen years. . . . What's the joke, Helen?"

"She started an atelier," said Helen, darkly twinkling. "An Atelier for Portrait Studies; not common photographs, but Portrait Studies; rather impressionistic! She started off on Basil Courtland—you know, little Benny Kohlbach that was, before the war! and by a sort of happy accident, she got him looming out of a fog, looking like a Christian! She was bothered about it, at first; but Benny was simply delighted; sent all his friends there. Now Eileen's made a big thing out of subduing—subjewing her clients! a sort of trick-work with high lights; frightfully profitable. She's never dared to try on me, though; I suppose she's afraid I might be her first failure."

Toni leant forward, deeply interested: "And can she reverse the process? Can she photograph Goys, I mean, and make them look like the best Israelites? I'm sure Giles would love to loom out of a mist with a Hebrew nose!"

"What does Giles *do*, all day long?" Helen asked.

A curious little smile was Toni's only answer, piquing Helen's curiosity.

"What *does* he do, Toni? What do . . . they all do? Those with any money of their own?"

" My husband is a man of business," Toni explained, respectfully ; " or rather, he was. I think he gave it a pretty useful whack, and then chucked it ; bit of a wash-out, d'you see ? " —Helen laughed outright at the burlesque of Giles' manner of speech.—" He and his pal, Captain Murray, very energetically didn't sell cars, every day !—unless they were doing something else,—from eleven thirty-five in the morning until about quarter to six in the evening. They didn't sell Vauxhalls, Rolls-Royces, Morris cars and—I've forgotten the other that they were agents for ?—oh yes, Bentley's ! I watched their method with humility and awe. It consisted mostly of casually barging into places of entertainment and refreshment, in the West End, where they might be likely to meet some fellow or other who knocked about with some other fellow who had a perfectly decent 'bus already, but might be thinking of getting a better one. Having spotted this would-be purchaser, in itself a subtle and difficult process, they stood him drinks. Then he stood them drinks. Then they stood him a meal. Finally, they offered him a trial run in whichever make of car he had no active objections to. Giles usually drove on these spins because Murray couldn't miss tennis on any account. Except during the football season, when it clashed with a match that Giles had to play in. Then Murray drove. After that, the client was stood more drinks. And then he didn't buy the car. If he had, Giles and Murray would have split the firm's commission. . . . Follow ? I can't tell you any more, because of course I don't understand business. . . ."

" Scoffing young blackguard ! " said Helen. " Is this the way you talked to your husband when he came home, tired and dispirited, from a long day's toil ? "

" They had a dear little office and stamped note-paper," continued Toni, being thoroughly naughty. " Oh, and the tweetest files and racks. . . . I *did* so want to be allowed to hang up a few pretty pictures, there, and choose some cretonne curtains for them. But they fwowned at me, and made me feel I could play no part in men's daily stwuggle for a bare living. Oh, Helen, I *do* think it must be dweadful to be a man, don't you ? Business is so difficult, so mysterious . . ."

Her cousin agreed that a woman was only a nuisance when she tried to participate in the dark and smoky ritual of earning money; and that her rightful sphere was the home and the nursery: "So stop being an ass, and let me see your offspring. I can't remember that I ever have, yet. What are they like? Do they revert to type, at all?"

Toni rang the bell.—"Oh, Quimper, ask Nurse to bring the children. No, I don't think they revert to type, much, if you mean the Rakonitz type. They are three-quarters Goy, after all. Babs is staggeringly lovely—this isn't a mother's partiality; you'll see. Paul's plain enough, but quite inconspicuous, and very nice indeed. They are on the stairs. Thank goodness, Nurse doesn't 'dress' them for visitors! Do you remember how we were scrubbed, Helen, when the Uncles turned up?"

Babs ran into the room——

"My hat, *isn't* she what you said!" exclaimed Helen, appraisingly. But she did not gush over Babs; nor try to lift her on her lap; nor say: "Do you temember *this* Auntie, darling?" nor even ask for one of her pretty curls; because such feelers were bad form, nowadays, between Drawing-room and Nursery. An exaggerated off-handedness was judged *de rigueur*. So strong was reaction, in Toni's and Helen's generation, from what they had once suffered at the lips of enthusiastic amateurs in child-worship, that Helen just gave Babs a comradely nod, and said: "You'd hate to be kissed, wouldn't you, Babs? So would I hate being kissed back again. So we'll call it quits!"

But when Toni's daughter had fully taken in the dire fact that in the arm-chair, talking to her mother, was not her beloved Loraine, but a stranger, she burst into desolate weeping; and nothing could make her stop, nor make her tell what had so disappointed her.

CHAPTER III

O N the same day that Antony Goddard was born, his great-grandmother died.

So they did not tell Toni; not yet.

Anastasia Rakonitz had been at her merriest, all day, and had given a great deal of trouble : " She wears me out when she's like this," Truda had complained to Maxine; " always insisting on rich things out of tins, and I'm sure she ought not to have Gänse-Leber-Pastete, but it seems to do her more harm saying no, than giving it to her; you know what Mama is like, when she wants something and can't get it ! "

Towards evening, the Matriarch, abandoning the question of cold goose-liver-sausage, began to agitate for a certain tortoiseshell comb; a richly carved ornamental comb, which she had been wont to wear high in her black hair, among the curls and rolls and plaits, in the days when the Uncles had entertained, and she had acted as gracious hostess. She declared that she must have the comb at once; you never knew when unexpected callers might arrive, and find her without it; she had seen it only last week in the drawer of her Second Empire bureau, with the Venetian lace; someone had stolen it without asking her; Iris, perhaps, or Aunt Gustava, who had visi ed her last Thursday; or the gifted little Belgian pedicurist whom she insisted on interviewing professionally, once a fortnight : " No, stay a minute, I remember now; Susie always admired that comb; so then it was Susie's mother who took it—Mrs. Lake, always a woman not to be borne; she was afraid I might leave it to you, Truda, in my will, instead of to Susie—not that I mean to, for you have been so disagreeable all day !—but Mrs. Lake could not know that, isn't it ? I remember very well, but very well indeed, now, that I had it with me last time I went to Bedford Park, showing that one ought never to leave one's bedroom, but especially not when staying with your son's wife and her mother who owed me a grudge. And now, how am I to get back the comb in time, to-night? Iris must go at once to fetch it for me. Tell her she is to take a taxi all the way; I pay for it," continued the Matriarch, grandly. "Me, I grudge nothing."

Wedged firmly in her brain was the delusion that to wear the comb at some obscure but splendid social entertainment, non-existent, at which she was to preside as in the old days, it must be in her possession by 7 p.m. Truda and Maxine and Iris found it impossible to calm her. When seven o'clock came round, and the phantom tortoiseshell comb still did not, could not, materialise, the Ma riarch scolded, clamoured, and threw herself about on the bed, still littered with sardine-tins and old satin corsets, and the pink marble and gilt writing-set; she issued a hectic confusion of orders in all directions; she cursed Susie's mother richly and profusely in every language that poor Mrs. Lake—dead now for some years—could not have understood; she sent a peremptory message to the Head of the Ealing police; and, finally, choking out something inarticulate about a Chinese cloisonné vase which poor Louis had never liked, and a bad deal in Nong-Khan sapphires —she burst a small blood-vessel in her head, and lay quiet at last. . . .

Three hours later, when the Doctor had been sent for, and had declared there was no more to be done, she suddenly uttered, with piercing sweetness, the words: "*Sponge* over it!"—and on that apology, died.

CHAPTER IV

"' *SPONGE* over it?'" Giles repeated, in a mystified way. "What could she have meant?"

Iris explained: "There's a Viennese slang expression: Schwammdrüber. I couldn't make out first what she meant, and then mother remembered. 'Sponge over it,' is the literal translation."

But their Christian cousin-by-marriage was still fogged: "Sponge over it?"

"'Wash it out,' we'd say," Maxine informed him, laconically. She had not shown much surface emotion over what had happened; but somehow she was not inclined to discuss the Matriarch's last words with Giles, who was not a Rakonitz. Perhaps it had been accidental that this magnificently troublesome Grandmère of theirs had died with what sounded like a plea for pardon on her lips. Such turmoil! such splendour! such ruthless tyranny! the thousands she had spent! the marriages she had forbidden, and the marriages she had arranged! the quarrels she had initiated! Her sublime lack of consideration! Eighty-nine years of gay and irrepressible junketings, crossed but not cancelled by much wailing and sorrow: four children dead out of five; or it may have been three dead and one lost—if Ludovic were, after all, still alive; three beloved brothers dead: Felix, and, worst of all, Maximilian, and Louis, the youngest; and Paul, her devoted husband, dead. The power broken, and the glory departed. And then the younger generation in revolt; and the younger generation victorious; and the younger generation kind and indulgent and tolerant. A restless, crowded life with a great deal of superfluous furniture in it; a life that had held much talk and much movement, and very little thought. Grandmère's good times and—Grandmère's bad times. . . . Enter-

taining on a grand scale, for the Uncles : " Anastasia Rakonitz
is a marvellous hostess ! " A career that was like the uprushing
curve of a rainbow—one end rising from the old house on the
banks of the Danube in Vienna, the other end dipping into the
angry confusion of her bed in the little room in Ealing. . . .
Ah, well, " Sponge over it ! " . . . nothing left but a few bits
of brocade and feathers and lace ; a few trinkets hoarded in
empty sardine-boxes . . . and over this, she had been troublesome, too : " You will clean out these boxes—yes, Iris, you,
who have nothing to do all day in the holidays except work
for your degree and that will soon be over and no sense in it
when it is. But these little tins are just what I want ; they
are useful ; I lose things on the bed when you all come and
sit on it. It is not for my sake ; it is for you children I must
keep the things ; you will wear them, one day, and be glad ;
at balls where you meet young men, it will make a difference.
. . . You see, I think of you all the time ; clean me out these
boxes, now ! " . . .

" I won't go through her things till next month," Maxine
told Giles. " I'll wait for Toni ; there's a terrific accumulation—mostly rubbish, I should think. You haven't told Toni
anything, yet ? " For this was the day after the funeral. A
very quiet funeral. According to Jewish custom, only men
could follow the coffin ; the women stayed at home and wailed.
And not many men were left ; Anastasia's grandsons, Gerald
and Derek ; her nephew, Raoul Czelovar ; Raoul's son, Neil.
And Deb Marcus's husband, Samson Phillips, had punc-
tiliously turned up ; but Richard Marcus had not been able
to leave his farm in Gloucestershire—perhaps he had not tried
very hard ; Francis Power, Val's father, was laid up with a
bad attack of influenza. So that Giles was the only alien of
the tribe, who was present. He looked strangely incongruous
and detached from them all, listening attentively while the
young Rabbi, who had not known the Matriarch, spoke a few
words commending the good qualities—which she had never
owned—befitting an Israelite wife and mother ; for indeed,
her virtues were too lively and erratic, too wholly genial, to
form an appropriate graveside oration.

—" It'll do if I tell Toni in about a week, I should think. I don't want to upset her; she's getting on so well; and she seems so much more content with this new little beggar than she was, last time, with Paul; content to lie still, and not get back to things. She was frightfully restless over Paul."

Maxine nodded: "Yes, I know. Mother thinks she——" then she stopped. Truda's grieved discourses on the sin of leaving a baby to be bottle-fed, so that one could get quickly back to one's dancing and pleasures, had impressed her with the feeling that this time Truda was right, and that Toni had behaved, indeed, badly over Paul, both before and after his birth. But she was no mischief-maker, so she did not say any of this to Toni's husband.

"You're calling him Antony?" asked Iris, eagerly.

"Yes; nearest thing to Antoinette; Toni chose it. She seems to want them to have family names."

Maxine raised whimsical eyebrows; "*Her* family names— Babette, Paul, Antony! I don't seem to notice any of yours, Giles; wouldn't your father like——?"

"No, Jimmy doesn't mind. Why should he? Nor do I. And, by the way," Giles looked suddenly very young and chubby and serious, "oughtn't Jimmy to have written to somebody—you or your mother, or Toni's mother? He's thoughtless, is Jimmy, but I don't want you to think we're barbarians."

Maxine concealed a desire to giggle. The death of the Matriarch, in her house, and the subsequent scenes with the worn-out Truda, and all the fuss and bother and emotion of the funeral—though only a bloodless and attenuated version of what it would have been in other days, had, nevertheless, left her feeling somewhat hysterical.

"Oh, it's all right, Giles. Don't bother, old thing. I'll let your father off; I'm sure he'd have written if he had thought of it."

Giles looked relieved: "You people think such an awful lot of funerals and ceremonies; and writing letters to each other. We don't, you know. I forgot Toni's birthday, last time; she didn't remind me, but her mother let it out! Toni pretended she didn't care a broken boot-lace, and then, ten days after, I found her in a hell of a stew about it ; I suppose the stew had been going on all the time ! "

Truda went into mourning for her mother. Aunt Henrietta wore black for a period ; so did Aunt Elsa, weeping tempestuously, out in Italy, with Val to comfort her. None of Anastasia's grandchildren wore mourning ; it was an incongruous custom, somehow, in these days, when time scampered on so quickly, and when even death was spoken of in a casual sort of way. Bereavement had ceased to be practised as an art, needing time and technique, and a special costume ; nowadays, you were not bereaved ; if you lost someone you loved, you were lonely, perhaps, and unhappy ; but you were not bereaved. Bereavement wears a decorous black ; loneliness puts on its brightest colours and hurls itself into the noisiest thoroughfare of pleasure.

A month later, nearly five weeks after her third child was born, Toni was able to spend an afternoon down at Ealing, with Maxine and Iris, Helen and Loraine, looking through the Matriarch's things, and deciding what should be given to whom ; what should be sold ; what kept, and what thrown away. It had not seemed necessary that the boys—as Gerald and Derek were sometimes still called, to their great disgust—should be present ; and Maxine had sent her mother away to the seaside for a week, to grow strong again, with every extravagance that filial affection could suggest, and Rakonitz extravagance provide. Truda was naturally inclined to be a sentimentalist over the past, and her daughters thought it better for her that she should be out of the way, while they rummaged in the lumberroom and on the scrap-heap of ninety years.

Neither Maxine nor Toni had any notion why Loraine should be included in such an intimate job as this promised to be ; but somehow or other, she was there ; and so, to balance her presence, they sent for Helen, too. Helen's relationship to the Matriarch was about the same as Loraine's ; Loraine could not, therefore, imagine herself included on equal terms with the grandchildren. Toni and Maxine and Iris were the grandchildren ; Loraine and Helen were there to help them look through the things and dispose of them. . . . And that was that !

Toni and Maxine were, in manner, almost too business-like to be quite normal. Toni, in particular, was determined that her very real grief for the loss of Grandmère, should not be suffered to spill itself in a sickly, silly way, over Grandmère's material possessions. But, gradually, as the numerous packages and boxes and trunks, which Derek had previously hauled down from the attic, and which they pulled out from under the Matriarch's bed, and down from the top of the huge cupboard, were unpacked, and their contents were piled on to the purple satin eiderdown, and overflowed from the drawers and bureaux on to the chairs and on to the floor ... gradually a dim, musty richness of old Rakonitz began to engulf them, and to sap their defences.

And then they found the Matriarch's last wills and testaments.

They found them in old blotters and jewel-cases, and in the pockets of dresses, and under piles of clothing, and among the gloves and handkerchiefs in quilted sachets. And one was sewn up carefully in a silk lamp-shade, but the silk frayed and split as they lifted it. There was one will in the key-basket, one in the Sèvres coffee-pot, and three between the album leaves of smudged and faded photographs. Altogether, they unearthed twenty-two ! But more may have been too carefully hidden for discovery. It was obvious that the Matriarch had taken impulsive though hardly cunning precautions to ensure that whichever of her relations was temporarily deposed from favouritism and inheritance, during the period of her wrath, should not have the chance of finding and destroying the document that enriched the succeeding favourite ! Only seven of these wills were dated, and none of them were drawn up legally, nor properly stamped and witnessed ; Anastasia had mistrusted the cold formalities of lawyers : " Me, you can teach nothing ! " She had been too fond of sprawling over the limits of their precision ; while the law tried to jostle Anastasia into a corner, she would escape by the window, and re-enter, radiant and plausible, by the door. So that her wills were personal letters, addressed to collective humanity; and achieving, in the Matriarch's own sublime fashion, a wonderful gossiping intimacy with collective humanity. Whenever Truda had upset her, or Toni had made her angry, or Maxine had been ungrateful, the Matriarch's voluble sense of injury bubbled up in the will of the moment; snatches of inner Rakonitz history were thus fully reported for the first time.

It was practically impossible for Toni and Maxine to get any system of disposal into the stuff which was collecting around them, or any fairness into the allotment, while these virile, autocratic epistles in the Matriarch's pointed handwriting, kept on turning up, and cancelling each other, and lop-siding every arrangement; impossible, if now Truda were to have the Dresden figures on the mantelpiece, and now she were to have nothing at all, but *nothing*—with furious emphasis !—and now again she were to have all the sables and all the beautiful Bohemian linen—what was left of it. Two minutes after they had imagined they were satisfactorily through with their troublesome job, they found a will with quite a recent date upon it, absolutely cutting off Iris from any participation whatever in the Rakonitz treasures :

" That mu t have been made on the day when I threw away those jars of sprats that she was trying to pickle according to some old Viennese recipe," Iris enlightened them. " I had to ; they were stinking the room out ! She raged for hours, and I remember that she ordered her writing things to be brought in, after that ! "

" Look here," said Toni at last, amused but despairing, " it's no good. We can't pay any attention to these. I don't believe Grandmère would have wanted us to, really, in her nicest moments. Disinheriting us each in turn, was like a form of drink ; she indulged herself sometimes, because she thought it did her good ; we needn't take any notice of it."

Maxine said : " You mean, scrap the lot ? "

And Toni nodded.

Loraine, who had been reverently fingering a really lovely old brocade frock of the 'sixties, looked up from where she knelt on the floor, and said huskily : " We can't do that."

" Why not ? "

" We *can*, of course ; I didn't mean we couldn't ; but we oughtn't to. It's a shame. Mourning and so on—well, she would have liked us to wear it, but that's just a wholesale fashion going out ; I can understand how it is we're not wearing mourning "—her " we " identified herself entirely with Anastasia's grandchildren—" but to ignore things written down, and that she wants done after she's dead, God rest her soul, that's different ; it's not decent ; it's crude, and failing in respect."

Toni and Maxine silently looked at each other, as they had done several times since the beginning of the long February afternoon in the gas-lit room. . . . They did not wonder, aloud, whether Loraine would have talked with quite such a flourish of respect for the late head of the family, if she had gone through with the Matriarch all that their mothers, the mothers they had loved, had gone through. Loraine, indeed, had been irritating in other ways besides an attitude of subtle reproach at their continued callousness, their harsh modernity. She was far more at home in the past, than they ; both romantically and technically ; her admiration of certain bronzes and china, of the craftsmanship in the setting of gems, was sophisticated ; she had picked up, in some way or other, an enormous medley of " period " knowledge. She brooded in a dream of delight, that was not affectation, over the last Bokhara rug which lay on the floor beside the double bed ; over the bed itself, with its carved rosewood pillars supporting the canopy ; over one of Uncle Felix's snuff-boxes, solitary relic of a collection once famous, but long since dispersed. Chinese cloisonné ; Venetian crystal candelabra ; a crumpled umber silk sun-blind, probably also from Venice ; two old Chelsea wineglasses with twisted stems, left from the original dozen which Toni remembered to have seen in use when she was a child, at Anastasia's glittering dinner-parties ; a Salviati glass dragon, gold-powdered, that had once lifted a fruit-dish high above the great mahogany dinner-table in the house in Holland Park. . . . All of these, Loraine was able to sort out from the stacks of lumber and valueless imitations—cheap, gaudy stuff, bought later by the

Matriarch herself, when her judgment had failed, and the rich Uncles were dead.

—" *This* is wonderful! No, no, Toni, you mustn't throw that away . . . Can't you see that it's a lovely specimen? That's no good! That's awful! . . . how can you admire it, Iris? But those buckles are genuine French paste, Louis XV; you'll see how they'll come up when they're cleaned. Wait a minute, and I'll tell you what that dress is made of?—bombazine?—*No*, my dear, never in this loife! *Bengaline*, that's it! Bengaline silk; it was very fashionable in the 'seventies . . . it actually does stand by itself, look! And she wore it with a small round hat, perched high, and tilted at *this* slant, with quantities of feathers on it. . . . We ought to be coming across some ostrich feathers, soon. No old lady ever threw them away. Do hand over those panels, Maxine. Look out! You're trampling on them. They must have been torn out of their frames, and they look to me like Vernet Martins. If they are, they're priceless. . . ."

Toni and Maxine were beginning to get a little tired of it all The ostrich feathers, when they did turn up, very much out of curl, filled a whole trunk; and another large box contained nothing but limp bunches of artificial Parma-violets. Loraine exulted joyously over the quaint fashions recalled by these findings; and called the others ungrateful, utilitarian and—worse still—unimaginative, for seeing no more in ostrich feathers and violets than their cubic dimensions. . . . " All the time : ' yes, but what are we to *do* with them? ' or ' where are we to find room for them? '—Glory be! these are not souvenirs of Brighton or Dieppe! They belonged to the *family*. . . . You'll be saying next that you think of throwin' away these darling Silhouettes! "

" I do," said Toni, briefly. But she put the Silhouettes aside, all the same. . . . Her own father, Aunt Truda, Uncle Ludovic, Uncle Blaise, and Aunt Sophie whom she had never known, each profile done in sooty black with a sort of gold shadowing to indicate the waves of hair; each portrait in its oval gilt frame. She had, indeed, meant to be tender to the Silhouettes from the first moment of unpacking them; but

she was averse from displaying, in front of Loraine, any secret
kindness to the Rakonitz legend. Resentment of the biter
when bit. Fifteen years ago, and she was herself playing
Loraine's part, passionately striving to stimulate her own
romantic enthusiasm among her more indifferent cousins. But
Loraine, as usual, was overdoing it—overdoing what Toni
might have done, and making a burlesque of it. . . .

A loud squeal from Helen drew their attention : " What is
it ? What have you found ? "

" About four dozen tortoiseshell combs, in a portmanteau,"
said Helen, displaying them. " And every one of them broken."

Toni and Maxine and Iris gazed almost in awe at the combs.
The sudden presence among them of four dozen tortoiseshell
combs in a portmanteau, every one of them broken, made it so
impossible to believe that Grandmère was dead. . . . This was
such a vivid manifestation of her personality. " I remember,
now," Maxine said at last, in a hushed voice. " She bought
lots of them from some bogus South American firm that
advertised a great bargain, cheap. They broke very easily."

" They can be boiled down," Toni declared, quickly resuming
her utilitarian disguise ; " sold and boiled down. No use keeping them in this state." She looked defiantly at Loraine.
Loraine said nothing about the combs ; merely twitched her
brows in impatient scorn. But she waxed clamorous again,
when, as a climax to their weariness, the lace appeared. Not
beautiful lace, like Anastasia's Chantilly fan ; but stacks, un-
ending stacks, of that expensive ugliness in machine-made silk ;
brittle now from long disuse and burial ; most of it still folded
over and over on to blue cardboard blocks ; lace which ladies
had once looped and flounced into petticoats to wear under
the voluminous skirts of their ball-dresses.

—" ' Blonde ' was the name of it," announced Loraine.
" You'll find it over and over again in the fashion-books of the
'seventies and the 'eighties . . ."

More and more blonde was fished up. And yet more. The
legatees were all worn out, by now, and anxious to get home !
The room was too full, and the air smelt of naphthaline and
camphor, and everybody's head ached . . . and still they went

on unpacking blonde . . . and still they went on unpacking blonde . . .

And Loraine insisted that it must all be kept : it would be a—a sacrilege, not to ! She accompanied the unwinding of blonde by a series of quaint, irresistible word-vignettes about the sort of people who had worn it ; deliciously funny anecdotes of their dining-rooms, and their ball-room suitors. . . . " *What* a memory you've got ! " said Helen, not in admiration.

—But when the bewitched flow of blonde terminated abruptly in a very short sealskin jacket, with very large sleeves, the fur eaten away in patches by an energetic picnic of moths, even Loraine dropped into silence ; gazed at it, without once proposing that it should be kept. . . .

Anastasia's most valuable and obvious treasures—the silver and the china, the cameos and the jewelry, brooches and bracelets crusted with rubies which the Uncles had given her at the height of their prosperity—had either been sold, during the course of years ; or many times pawned, and redeemed by Toni and Maxine ; and were already in their possession. It would have been more restful to have assumed that the remaining lumber was no more than lumber, and need not be kept. Had Loraine not been present to identify the various " good " bits and pieces, and to be officious about them, they need not have had all this bother. Now, without further discussion, they began to divide up the relics. Toni looked queerly, now and then, at Loraine ; Maxine took no notice of her at all. Slowly, order began to shape itself out of the bulging confusion. Iris, of course, was to have the portrait of Aunt Simone, painted by a famous Hungarian artist of that time ; it had always been promised to her, in virtue of being the only one in the family to have carried on the red-gold hair. Truda and Susie inherited most of the household treasures. Derek and Gerald were to share whatever could be of male use. They gave Helen the Vernet Martin panels ; and they offered Loraine the Chantilly lace fan, and the Louis-Quinze buckles, which she said were of such beautiful paste. Loraine smiled, and shook her head :

" No, thanks. I won't have anything. At least, I won't have anything valuable."

This was a nuisance. It gathered her in more effectively, instead of, as they had hoped, disposing of her claims.

" What do you want ? " said Toni, coldly.

Loraine flashed an angry glance at her : " Is that what you say to the beggar at the back door ? "

" Oh, don't be melodramatic ! You said there was something you would rather have, instead of what we offered you ; and I asked you what ? That's all ! "

" These, then," answered Loraine, and she pointed to two oil paintings, large, dim and undistinguished, in ornate frames, which hung opposite the bed in which the Matriarch had died. They were the paintings of Simon Rakonitz and his wife Babette, Anastasia's grandparents.

" Those ! . . . What on earth do you want those for ? "

Loraine took no notice of Maxine's question. Her eyes were fixed on Toni, who said slowly :

" I'm sorry, Loraine. It's out of the question."

" You mean, you're going to have them for yourself ? "

Toni ignored the interruption. " The frames are hideous, and the paintings fairly awful. They're clumsy, bulky things, too."

" I wasn't considering them as objects of art, you see." And then she repeated her question : " You mean, you're going to keep them for yourself ? "

" Do you mind, Maxine ? " said Toni, elaborately polite.

" You're welcome, old thing. I've lived with them too long ; they're no pleasure to me."

" And yet," persisted Loraine, " you hadn't even noticed them, until I put out *my* hand. That's queer, isn't it ? One would have thought, if they were so precious, that you would have mentioned them hours ago. We've been shut up here the whole afternoon, now."

" I'm afraid," said Toni, in a voice so maddeningly charming and well-bred that it would have brought a dormouse raging out of its winter-quarters, " that I took it for granted about the old family portraits. I'd no idea that they would appeal to you."

" And why shouldn't they ? Aren't they my family as well

as yours? Our great-grandfathers were both sons of those two up there in their gilt frames. Isn't that true? Why do you try to push me out?"

"Nobody's trying to push you out; and do remember, Loraine, that we're not keen on grand scenes and quarrels and feuds nowadays, especially over property. You can have my whole share of the collection if you like, except those portraits."
—But Toni was as exasperated as Loraine, although she suppressed it under an exterior with a cool and most effective glaze upon it. Loraine must be taught to understand, once and for all, that she was an interloper, and that Toni was now head of the family—yes, Toni, who for years had been trying to forget that such claims and offices existed. . . .

"I've told you that I'll accept nothing of value, haven't I? You're slow in understanding me! I'd like the portraits of the founders of our dynasty, ugly and cumbersome as they are; just for sentiment's sake."

"I suppose you think *we* have no sentiment?"

Loraine shrugged her shoulders: "I think that *I*, personally, would have respected my grandmother's will. . . ."

"Your grandmother's twenty-two wills?"

Silence. And the strain in the room tightened!

"You've been trying to shoulder me out ever since I came," Loraine blazed. "I don't know what you're jealous of. That's what it all is—jealousy. I don't belong here, and I don't belong there; this and that isn't my business; and I'd better not go and see my own relations in case I'm in the way; and I'm a nuisance asking about them. . . . That and all that! And you who marry a Christian, and don't ask the family to the wedding, and don't even tell the old woman who loves you best, and tear up her last wishes—*you* are the cousin who is to count, I suppose? *You* take the throne! *You* couldn't sleep in your bed to-night if the old portraits weren't hanging on the wall opposite you!—It's just to anger me you want them. You'll put them away in the garret with their faces to the wall, and the dust gathering on the backs of them. I don't want anything from any of you except a little bit of warmth and friendliness—but you hang back, grudging me that—and after

I had longed, these lonely years, to be counted in ; longed for you to see that I love the family, too, and its history and people. . . . Aren't we all one flesh and blood? First you insult me by telling me it's gain I'm after ; offering me something that I can sell for a nice round sum——" She paused, as though hauling up all her strength for some grand rhetorical climax that would crush Toni utterly. . . . "And anyway, if you're so keen on the family, if you're so damned keen on them, if it's you that's now head of the family entoirely, then it was a pity, wasn't it, to have let poor old Aunt Eugène die of neglect and starvation ! "

CHAPTER V

"READY to come home, Toni? " called out Giles. He was already in the room; they had not heard the bell downstairs, nor his approaching step. Loraine turned away from the others, and began to extricate a bunch of monster keys from a tangle of jet ornaments, which had all been flung down together on the bureau. Her fingers trembled.

"Aunt Eugène?" Iris repeated, in tones of wonder; "Why, she. . . ." A look from Maxine stopped her. Maxine knew that Toni would not want any family revelations, especially if they were painful, bursting out in front of her husband.

"Lord, what a mess!" exclaimed Giles, who seemed to be in boisterous spirits. He caught up a heavy, black velvet, beaded cloak, slung it from one shoulder, and waving ostrich plumes from his head and hands, strutted through the usual fool attitudes that associate themselves with dressing-up—till, quite suddenly, it occurred to him that ragging was out of place in Anastasia's clothes, in front of Anastasia's grandchildren, in the room where Anastasia had recently died; and very uncomfortably, he dropped the ostrich feathers, and said quietly to Toni : " You look all in, Toni. Can't the rest of this, wait? You've been at it the whole afternoon." And then, even more disconsolately, he remembered that he still had three feathers waving waggishly from his head, stuck through a sort of tiara of paste brilliants! So he removed them, hoping fervently that Toni had been too preoccupied to notice, or to think him a b aying ass. She did seem preoccupied, but she roused herself, now, with a sigh :

"Yes, I'm coming home at once. We've done more than—than it looks as though we'd done," she finished, limply, as though even to find ordinary words to express herself, were, for the moment, too onerous a task. "Loraine's coming back with us to dinner."

Loraine started. "I wasn't," she cried out, panic-stricken; "I mean, I'd like to, but I can't! I—I don't think I can."

And Maxine, with a desire to protect Toni from a scene alone with Loraine, said swiftly: "You see, I've already asked Loraine to dine with us."

"You won't mind giving her up to me?" Toni answered, steadily persistent.

Giles laughed: "My word, you *are* popular to-night, Loraine! The whole gang fighting for your company!"

And it really looked as though they were; and as though none of them could bear not to be with Loraine, that evening. For Helen, guessing what was passing in Maxine's mind, pleaded with Toni, in whimpering imitation of a child: "Oh, please, mayn't *I* dine with you as well as Loraine, please? You *said* I was to invite myself whenever I wanted to."

"Hello!" thought Giles, with an inward whistle of amusement, "so young Helen's got a rave on Loraine, has she? Toni doesn't seem too keen about it." For Toni was very gently and plausibly explaining to Helen that, of course, she *loved* Helen to come whenever she wanted to, but just to-night, after all this unpacking, she was terribly fagged, and wanted only one of her cousins with her, to have dinner in her room, and put her to bed, and make a fuss of her; for men weren't very much good at that sort of thing; and Giles, anyway, was probably going out dancing: "You said something about the New Quadrant, to-night, didn't you, Giles?" Toni was determined to hear what Loraine had meant by her sinister hint regarding Aunt Eugène; and the others recognised that there was nothing more to be done but to stand back and let her cope with the situation as she willed. Loraine, now that she was no longer at the tip of rage, would remember, surely, that Antony had been born barely five weeks ago.

An hour later, and the two cousins were alone together, seated in front of the fire in Toni's pretty, luxurious bedroom, the dinner-tray on the table between them; but neither were in a mood to eat.

"Now then . . ." Toni led off. But Loraine saw that, for all her bluff, she was frightened.

She felt, herself, partly exultant at having driven this gay, careless, spoilt Toni to the point of fear, and partly apprehensive—wishing she had controlled her temper. She sprang out an impulsive : " Look here, Toni darling, don't bother any more about it. If it weren't done with, and past our helping —but it is, you see, so why look backwards ? "

" Please, Loraine, I'd rather not be shielded. What's the good of throwing open a door and window, and then telling me, tenderly, not to sit in a draught ? "

" And supposing I had made it all up ? " said Loraine, with a queer elvish look from under the slouch of her lids.

And this was the most decent thing that Loraine had ever yet done : where she really had a tale to tell, and a true one ; where she really had arrogant Toni at her mercy ; this attempt to use her undeniable reputation as a flamboyant liar, in order to save Toni from bitter self-reproach, was very nearly heroism.

Toni was only too ready to grasp at such relief ; and to be rid of that sick, icy panic which had squirmed and plunged like an octopus in the pit of her stomach, ever since Loraine's : " Aunt Eugène died of neglect and starvation."—But of course Loraine had made it all up ! of course she had ! . . . and how like Loraine ! That was why she had been so reluctant to go home with Toni to Regent's Park. " —Why did you let Aunt Eugène die ? "—Just a meaningless reproach she had picked up, a strand of the blowing winds, because she had been in such a blind fury. For an instant of counter-fury, Toni could have stamped on the other's face, for causing her such agony. . . . Then she smiled lazily, and poured herself out a glass of claret.

" I ought to have known. But why not choose something you can substantiate, my dear, when you're really wanting to do me in ? You must have guessed that you'd be found out," Toni went on, fatally, fatally, dancing on Loraine's vanity, " just talking empty rot about Aunt Eugène. It wasn't even amusing, which you usually are when you let your imagination rip ! "

" And when is it that I've been amusing in that way ? "

asked Loraine, watching her good intentions begin to scatter and to fly, like bits of waste paper before a breeze. But Toni was too thankful at her release, too light-headed, to notice the ominous mutter in Loraine's voice. She did not see why Loraine should not be teased, punished even, for her flaming bad temper, for her idiocy, and her habit of making wildly untrue statements that upset everybody and did no good to anybody ; so she sipped her wine, and murmured, appreciatively :

" Mouton Rothschild . . . it *is* quite true that a second growth of a good year, in a claret, very often beats an inferior Château Lafite or Latour. . . . Well," aloud, " what about Uncle Maximilian ? Are you *quite* sure that you were such a favourite of his ? Are you *quite* sure, for instance, that he used to send you telegrams, ' across half Europe,' and come and stay with you, and buy you old-world dresses with full skirts, and praise your cooking, and call you ' the little Gräfin ' ? " For it had been easy to prove from a dozen different sources that Uncle Maximilian had, indeed, never known of the existence of this Spanish branch of the family ; and that Loraine's account of him failed and crumbled under steady questioning. Toni laughed at the other's discomfited face : " Good Lord ! don't be such a little goose ! What does it all matter ? He *was* a darling. . . . You would have adored him if you'd known him ; and it's quite possible that he might have called you ' the little Gräfin ' ! Let's drink to his health ! It was he who first taught me to know one wine from another—did I tell you ? "

" So you think I can never ' substantiate,' as you call it ? " Loraine half whispered. Her temper was in that white phosphorescent blaze which illuminates an habitual liar whose solitary effort at truth has met with nothing but mockery and disbelief. Very precisely, and planting her facts in front of Toni with the delicate precision of a cat placing its velvet paws, she related how, in October, 1923, soon after she had first come to London, she had gone to stay with another girl, down on her luck and in need of Loraine's nursing, in a little knot of slums at the back of Kilburn ; and how she had heard, casually, from the landlady, and from the girl herself, about a death which had occurred several months before in the top

rooms of the house. This lodger who had died was an old
woman, over eighty, and foreign, they said; not a German,
because they had got in a Swiss waiter who was a friend of the
landlady, to talk to her in German, just to find out, but she
had not understood that language; she could speak English,
but not well; she did not speak very much at all; and she did
not go about shedding beauty and charity from her mere
presence, as garret lodgers of fiction are so often reputed to
do; in fact, in a negative sort of way, and from all accounts,
she was an unlovable crone. She owed the landlady two and
a half months' rent of the rooms; she said she had rich relations, but, somehow, they did not come to see her, and she had
lost their addresses: "They have all moved away from where
they were before," she kept on saying, which the landlady had
not thought a very likely story; and she had a son who came
to her sometimes, but he was very nearly imbecile, though he
was earning a little money in some shady sort of job that didn't
need any brains, but the landlady couldn't say what it was.
She only knew he brought a few shillings, and then disappeared
for weeks together. The old woman was under-nourished, and
she caught a cold, and lay up there shivering and shivering . . .
and presently she died: pneumonia and lack of strengthening
food; she was very old and wizened. What the landlady
wanted to know, now that she was underground—for the
Doctor had given a certificate, all right—was this: would she
be justified, did Loraine's friend and Loraine herself think
she'd be doing any harm, in keeping the few things that the
poor old soul had left behind, as against the two and a half
months' rent, and the cost of the Doctor and burial? "Well,
but you *have* kept them, haven't you?" Loraine pointed out,
cheerfully. But the point was, apparently, that the landlady
was asking for approbation, now, not because she wanted to
keep the things, but because she wanted to sell them; in fact,
sell them to Loraine, who, to her mind, looked better off than
the majority of her tenants' visitors. She had brought the
"things" in, for Loraine to see. The foreign old woman had
had, apparently, a taste for false jewelry. Perhaps, once, and
long ago, she might have been accustomed to wearing real gems,

and later on consoled herself with buying sham stuff when she ought to have been spending the money on food and wine. 'Oh! but she drank wine whenever she could," put in the landlady; " awful, cheap, sweet stuff, and she walked for miles to get it, to a part of London I don't know. But are none of these real?"—She was terribly disappointed when Loraine shook her head over all the gaudy trinkets except one large brooch: bars of coarse silver filigree work, crossing in a round silver setting, with a small garnet set at each intersecting point.

" This is all right; I'll buy this; it's Turkish work, I should think, from this hole left in the filigree for the material of your dress to be pulled through and pinned; that's the way they always do it. Your old lady may easily have been a Turk."—At which the landlady cried out in holy horror, not fancying the idea of having had anyone in her house connected with " them nasty harems, which I didn't even like in skirts, Miss, and very glad to see them go out, what with my daughter Mabel not even able to step on a 'bus without spraining her ankle. She called herself Mrs. Raikes, not that I thought that was her name, ever, but it didn't bother me, the war being over; but they rummaged for the usual papers and I don't know what, when she died, the way they always do; and it turned out to be a name that sounded as though it might have been a heathen Turk; and there was a book too, which I'll show you, that she read sometimes, but it wasn't by any means the Bible!" She produced the book. It was a novel of the kind that a Parisian would describe as : " un peu risqué, tu sais, mais rien d'épouvantable"; and the language was modern Greek, or rather, Greek that had been modern some seventy years ago, which was the date on the frontispiece.

The owner's name, written in faded brown ink, was Chryse Stefanopoulos; and underneath it, in ink almost as faded, and in the same handwriting: Chryse Rakonitz. 1861.

. . . " That's all," said Loraine, staring into the fire. " I've got the book, and the brooch; and I can, if you like, introduce you to my friend, and to the landlady in Kilburn who will introduce you to the Doctor who tended Aunt Eugène in her last illness—as you seem to think I can't *substantiate* my stories."

Suddenly she looked at Toni—and was shocked out of her dogged mood of vengeance. " Toni *darling*. . . . Toni, you mustn't !—It wasn't your fault. Nobody could help it ; it was just accident ; I happened to stumble across it. . . . There was nothing more to be done. I wouldn't have told you. . . . I didn't tell you, then, did I ?—although I managed to trace you, and all the rest of the family, soon after that ? but what was the good ? I wouldn't have told you now, if you hadn't jeered at me over Uncle Max."

But Toni, who very rarely cried, was crying now. For years, no one had seen her give in. . . . And even through her piteous collapse, she did wish that it need not have been Loraine !

But Loraine had dreamt of just such a moment of intimacy ; of Toni clinging to her ; of hers being the arms to tighten round Toni. It had come true, at last. Humbly enough, she hoped that as she had been granted this privilege, she would find words that were comfortable for Toni to hear. Loraine had already forgotten that it was she who had wantonly created the sorrow she was now trying to heal.

But Toni's self-reproach was like a hard and bitter lump in her heart, that could not quickly be yielded up nor soothed. For this which had happened was shame on the whole family ; and most of all was it shame on her, who had flitted away to her good time ; talked airily of not being " bothered " any more ; of having had enough ; of chucking the family. All the younger generation had jabbered about escape, freedom from tyranny ; they could see no good in the old ways, the interference, the tribal councils ; the over-vehement curiosity shown by the Aunts over everyone's affairs. . . . But was there no good in the old ways, after all ? Tightly as the net had been drawn, restricting their liberty, yet because the mesh had been close, no one was allowed to slip through. Could this have happened in the old days of Anastasia's rule ?—when at the least hint of trouble in the family, Aunt Elsa put on her best toque a little bit awry, and hurried round to headquarters ; when Aunt Henrietta and Aunt Gustava were on the spot almost without summoning ; and when Anastasia imperiously used to send for the Uncles. . . . Could it have happened,

then, with all that unfailing bustle and solicitude and abundant
benevolence, that poor Eugène's widow, as they had always
called her, would have been left just to slither down and be
forgotten? to die of cold and starvation? . . . Toni shuddered.
In 1923, Loraine had said; and how she had enjoyed herself
in 1923! Thrown money about, danced, drunk wine!

. . . But *how* could it have happened? she moaned; how
could it have happened? Someone, surely, had been looking
after Aunt Eugène, paying for her, responsible for her? Some
Rakonitz, besides Toni? Toni could not remember even
having seen the old lady, and had but rarely heard her name.
She plunged about, desperately searching out a loop-hole for
guilt to wriggle through. Loraine was as anxious, now, to fix
the blame elsewhere, as Toni herself; she listened to Toni's
bewildered recollections of the family's huge organisation
fallen into confusion, ready with a quick: " There, you see, *he*
ought to have seen to it! " or " *She* ought to have seen to it,"
if opportunity should offer.

" You see, Loraine, one never met her personally; otherwise, of course, she couldn't have been forgotten like that. But
from the very first, it wasn't as though she actually were our
own flesh and blood; she was just a queer little Greek woman,
not very nice, I don't think, from what I heard Grandmère and
Aunt Truda say; they none of them liked her much—I mean,
she was never asked to dinner as though she were a real Aunt,
nor for birthdays; she didn't fit in. But she was poor Eugène's
widow, so, of course, she had to be provided for. And there
were four idiot children, I know; you talked about one son;
I wonder what can have happened to the others? I do remember the fuss when she first appeared, because she went to Aunt
Constance by mistake; Aunt Berthe, from Paris, had sent her
there, and Aunt Constance was afraid the Dean would see
her! " . . Toni began to laugh uncontrollably. " And then
Grandmère and all of them threw open their doors—is that
melodramatic?—but they always did, you know; they were
darlings, in that way. . . . Oh! what would Grandmère
have said if she'd known? "

" Wait a moment. . . . Who *did* provide for her? "

"It was Uncle Max, originally, I know, because Mummy told me about the high-handed way he lost his temper with all of them, and told them not to talk so much! which just meant he paid for everything and wanted to get out of being thanked. And then came the crash—that was about fifteen years ago now, when Uncle Max "—Toni stopped . . . and then scampered on hurriedly, as someone who skips two or three pages of a book, and does not bother if an irrelevant join betrays the act. She could not bear, even now, to let her memory linger on that ghastly time when her father and Uncle Max and Uncle Albrecht, and the family grandeur, were all swept away together. . . .

"So Uncle Louis took over, then. Well—I suppose he took over Aunt Eugène, too, along with the other responsibilities. I haven't the faintest idea where she lived, or how. I imagine he sent her weekly or monthly payments. I don't know. And then Uncle Louis died. . . ." Toni groped for some logical sequence of Aunt Eugène's fortunes. "Is that where I ought to have—yes, I suppose so—I don't know. I did see to a lot of things, but I was just beginning 'Toni's,' then." And suddenly Toni knew, quite certainly she knew, that she had failed "Toni's" as she had failed the family; and that all her apprehensions were bound to be justified, sooner or later, by a summons from Hanover Street; she might, indeed, continue to combat feebly, ineffectively, the necessity to take up in person this responsibility again; she might continue to pretend to believe that things were all right, there, but——

"What is it? Oh, Toni, *don't* look so tragic! What is it? Go on telling me!"

"I've shelved my job," whispered Toni. Then, with a sigh, dismissed the intruding worry; pulled herself back again to the subject of Aunt Eugène: "I hadn't actually been given control of the money, even after Uncle Louis died. That was the trouble."

"Who had?" asked Loraine, intensely absorbed in these items of Rakonitz history.

"Grandmère. The Uncles worshipped Grandmère. She was much older than they. She had always been more like a

mother to them, than an elder sister; especially to Uncle
Louis. However mad she got, he always remembered her and
talked of her as she had been when she knew such a lot about
precious stones, and the ruby trade was booming, and she had
acted hostess for all of them. So in his will he said that his
sister Anastasia must administer everything until she died.
There were several people to be provided for,—oddments of
family, and widows. . . . After Grandmère should die, he left
it to me to carry on, not Aunt Truda; I think Aunt Truda
was a wee bit hurt over that; but he counted Grandmère first,
and the younger generation next; and Aunt Truda was neither
one nor the other. Anyhow, Maxine was rather glad that her
mother wasn't to be bothered. Uncle Louis must have made
that will, of course, long before Grandmère had had her first
stroke. He died four months after she had it. I daresay he
would have altered it, after all, if he hadn't died."

"It was Uncle Louis' fault, then?" cried Loraine, joyfully.
"It wasn't yours; not a shred of it."

"Well—he knew Grandmère had her bad times; but he
couldn't know that she was going to get a stroke, or that he'd
die so soon afterwards. You can't tell, with heart failure.
None of the family were at their old addresses, if Aunt Eugène
had tried to find any of them. And Grandmère forgot lots of
things. Loraine, *do* you think I'm like Grandmère, at all?"

"Not in the least," Loraine lied, heartily. She could not
bear to see Toni afraid. . . . "Of course, in an old family, and
where there's been a lot of intermarrying, certain characteristics——"

"What nonsense!" very quickly and petulantly did Toni
dispose of that. "Why should they? I loved Grandmère,
but I hated her characteristics. And everybody knows that
you don't inherit things, from your grandmother, like over-
excitement and rushing to extremes. Especially if you're
quite different yourself. When Maxine and I took over the
sort of general trustee-ship from Grandmère, she may have
reminded me about Aunt Eugène; I don't know; she talked
such a lot, and so many names tumbled in and out."

Loraine did not say that Grandmère was to blame. Somehow, no Rakonitz ever did; and she made a point of sharing in every family fetish that her uncannily quick instincts could divine. But she suggested Maxine as at least co-partner in Toni's responsibility.

Toni merely snapped and glowered at this. Maxine, she said, had performed her share, and more than her share, always. Why, she had actually and for years lived in the same house with the Matriarch. "More than I did; lately, anyhow!" But then, that unmerited punishment had been Toni's during all her childhood, till she was fifteen. No wonder that she responded with such savage denials to self-accusation and proof that she could be as forgetful, as capricious, as blatantly and overwhelmingly inconsiderate, as the old woman whose tyranny she had been forced to watch, at close quarters, manufacturing hell upon hell for pretty Susie Lake, Toni's mother. . . .

And then, suddenly: "Aunt Elsa!" suggested Loraine, triumphantly. "What about Aunt Elsa? According to you, she was in at the very beginning, when Aunt Eugène first arrived from Constantinople. How did she come to forget?"

But Toni was being searchingly honest with herself, now; and she would not lapse on to a whining, too-easy accusation of Aunt Elsa : "She *did* come to me at once, I remember now. It was during my busy time at 'Toni's'; the first real rush of clients. I was frenziedly over-worked, and frenziedly keen to give them my best and create a splendid first impression!"— Oh, *damn* "Toni's"! why did it always keep on cropping up, to-night?—"And just then, Aunt Elsa marched into the show-room, looking determined and auntish in her silk mantle trimmed with jet—spouting a whole lot of talk about 'poor Anastasia!'—and was this being done? and was that being done? and had I remembered to see to this and that important thing? And where was Louis' will? and I was only a child still, and could not be trusted. . . . Oh! you know Aunt Elsa —no, you don't, I forgot! She was just in one of her most trying moods—buzzing round with questions, and insinuating that Maxine and I were just out of the nursery, and couldn't be expected to deal with family affairs without help—Good Lord ! after all the rampages we'd both been through with Grandmère, clearing up her affairs time after time. . . . Never mind all that now ! And Aunt Elsa's the kindest old dear in the world, but she just got my goat on that occasion, and I let fly at her —not too visibly, of course ; the place was full. I just whipped out that I had all the arrangements in hand, and that I was quite competent to see to them, and that she needn't be in the least afraid that Grandmère's affairs were being neglected. And then she went off in a huff, saying : ' I ask nossing any more, but *nossing*, ever, you see ? ' And anyway she's out in Italy with Val, every winter since 1922. No, it's no good, Loraine," Toni cried, miserably tossing away every arduously collected fragment of consolation ; " everybody thought that someone else was seeing to things ; it was just a muddle, holes in the knitting, but it's too damnably easy to say : ' Accident— no one to blame ! ' . . . The fact remains that Aunt Eugène died—that way ; and that I oughtn't to have allowed it. It doesn't make any difference if you know your relations, or not ; birthday parties—silver weddings—presents—just the froth on top. But the family all stuck together, once, and that was what counted. I've been a sleek, selfish, complacent swine, and you can't excuse me, though it's generous of you to try."

And it never occurred to either of them, not to Toni, nor to Loraine, that the late Eugène Rakonitz had had several brothers and sisters ; and one of them was Sigismund, who was Toni's great-grandfather ; and one of them was Andreas, who was Loraine's great-grandfather. So that Toni's responsibility was Loraine's too, and in the same measure. . . . But it did not occur to either of them.

And now Toni's conscience gave her no rest. The final swing had been given to the pendulum of her moods ; and reacting violently from her good time, from careless friendships and heedless spending, she began laboriously to tell her tale of the family, as a shepherd tells his tale of sheep ; counting them over and over in her mind, fearful lest another might have dropped down among the dead men, and might somewhere be starving and cold. She had just accounted for all her relations safely, in safe houses, within her reach and aid, if necessary : she was just about to make that final jerk at her reluctant will, which would bring her attention round to " Toni's " and Hanover Street,—when Little Klaus could not be found.

Had he been forgotten, like Aunt Eugène ? just like Aunt Eugène ? Was it two, three months ? a year ?—since he had last been heard of ? Followed a hectic scrabble of days when Toni pelted all her other cousins for news of this lost unit of the family, till they cursed the very day of his birth. She was in a panic lest he should slip away entirely, as, some twenty years ago, her Uncle Ludovic had slipped away—Anastasia's darling son, who had gone to Nicaragua, and presently had forgotten to write, and forgotten to send his address. Twenty years ago. . . . But where, now, was Little Klaus ? He had not any very near relations to bother about him, as he was the only son of Klaus and Babette Sellabach, of the Viennese branch, who had both died when he was quite a little boy. So, obviously, the care of him had devolved upon Toni ; and she could not even remember very clearly what he had been doing since the war ? He had distinguished himself in the war, and won decorations, to the astonishment of all of them. But since then——? . . . So, with all her reawakened energy, and using every clue that presented itself, she pursued little Klaus from one address to another. . . . Thereby causing that young man, and the lady under—as the phrase goes—his protection, a great deal of inconvenience and tribulation. He had been at some pains to hide his temporary misalliance from the family ; and hitherto they had not bothered him.

Thus, Toni's frenzy ended in a most uncomfortable tea-party, and Little Klaus begging her, in his shy, stammering way, as he accompanied her to the front-door, to " please not b-b-bother about me, Toni dear. It's most awfully kind of you, and we've loved s-s-seeing you ; but, you see, as things are . . . and I'm not making enough to marry yet. . . ."

CHAPTER VI

"MY dear Mrs. Goddard,

Having just finished my holiday which I badly needed, and went down to Torquay, though it's not always as fine there as one might expect from the word Riviera, I certainly think I ought not to start on my new engagement, without letting you know that I have left Hanover Street, and how sorry I am. I assure you, Mrs. Goddard, that I stayed on as long as I could, though it was never the same from the moment you left, and never could be. The truth is Miss Lequesne and I don't hit it off. First it was one thing, and then it was another, and I'm sure, though it's not for me to say, that you would have agreed with me over that matter of the Agnès model and Lady Penstead; but what really brought things to a head, as I might say, was that Miss Lequesne was vexed when she found out at the end of December, that I was getting more than she was, and I expect it *is* difficult to understand the high wages that a first-class fitter can always command. But we never hit it off, and Melville's have been trying to get me, with tempting offers, as you know, even before you left, and much more after. So, when we finally didn't quite hit it off, I said: 'Very well—next season I go to Melville's!' Of course, I ought to have come to you straight away when I decided this, but thought it better not, hearing you were just going to have and now have a dear little boy, and oughtn't to be worried with extras. Please let me offer you congratulations, and I hope you will let me come to see you, as though this hadn't happened.

With best wishes,

Yours sincerely,

MILLICENT THOMPSON.

P.S.—It sounds mean to say this, Mrs. Goddard, but I must tell you that I could have done better last season, if I'd had

more Paris models and at the usual time, instead of being
loaded up with all that Belworthy stuff our clients are getting
so sick of."

—" And here it is," said Toni, recognising, almost with a
deferential salute, the materialisation of a nightmare.

" Toni's " ! her business, which she had shaped from the
very beginning ! She had been proud of " Toni's " . . . until
she forgot it ! What had they been doing with it, these two
women ? Mauling the edges of her clean-cut method, pulling
it this way and that, messing about. . . . *What* had they done
with " Toni's " ? She telephoned an imperious message to
Hanover Street, saying that Miss Lequesne was to come round
at once ; Mrs. Goddard wished to speak to her.

. . . " She's in a funk," thought Toni, the second she confronted Aimée Lequesne. Toni's eyes were keen and very blue ;
her voice was like a stretch of taut silk. Giles, had he been
there, would hardly have recognised the Toni he only knew as
a personality gay with pretty, coaxing, feminine caprices ; this
was not the dancing Toni any more. But Giles, this time, was
not present at the interview.

" I've heard this morning from Miss Thompson. She tells
me she has left the firm. That's bad news. Couldn't you
have managed to cope with it, when you saw it coming ? "

Aimée burst into a flood of excuses. She was full of indignation, and very near tears—and, as Toni had opined, badly
frightened : " It was really no good, Miss Rakonitz. I was as
tactful as I could be ; any of the girls will tell you that. Gwendoline Moore said to me over and over again : ' Well, really,
Miss Lequesne, I wonder you put up with it ! ' or sometimes to
one of the others : ' Really, I wonder Miss Lequesne puts up
with it ! ' But I knew that you valued Miss Thompson's
services. . . . And, of course, it was quite right, feeling like
that about her," Aimée went on, her breath getting short, and
the tip of her nose, pink, " that she should have been receiving
a hundred pounds a year more than me, though I must say,
Miss Rakonitz—Mrs. Goddard, I *should* say—that you would
have found me perfectly agreeable about it, knowing what

fitters are, if you'd consulted me at the time when you made the arrangement; I'd have said, quite agreeably and reasonably: ' Certainly, Miss Rakonitz '—you *were* Miss Rakonitz then, you see!—' I know that fitters get very high wages, especially when they are as good as Miss Thompson. So even though it's a joint managership——' for that's what you called it, Miss Rakonitz—' you won't find me unreasonable.' Yes, that's exactly what I would have said, if you had consulted me then."

Toni's brows drew down into a straight line: " I don't consult; I decide," she said, in that cold, intimidating, Napoleon-of-the-costume-trade manner, that Miss Lequesne had been so relieved *not* to meet, on the last occasion that she had been in her employer's house.

Toni did not waste time in discovering how Aimée had found out the difference of salary; that did not matter. She struck out for information on essentials: " What sort of Autumn season did you have ? "

" You paid out the big monthly cheques, and the cheque for petty cash as usual, Mrs. Goddard," Aimée replied, getting flustered, as she felt the probe nearing all her sore and unprotected places.

" Yes, I signed the cheques; they were about as big as usual—bigger, once or twice. I didn't look into them; and obviously I could have had no idea of what we were doing, unless I had seen the corresponding cheques that had been paid in."

" That's not *my* fault you hadn't, is it, Miss Rakonitz ? " There was bound to be a point of the interview at which Aimée's dignity, her fear and agitation, should degenerate into veiled pertness. " It was your arrangement that Miss Wildblood should have the power to endorse those. And really, it isn't as if you'd been near us for months, not even for your clothes, as you used to."

Toni passed over the latter portion of this speech. " Yes, I'll send for Miss Wildblood, presently, and ask her to bring down the books, and the firm's pass-books. Only, quite naturally, I come to you first, to hear what orders we have had ; and how last season's Paris stuff has done, and if the clients were generally satisfied. When did you get the models over here? By the middle of September?"

Aimée became very haughty: "Indeed, Mrs. Goddard, it's certainly not for *me* to tell tales whatever anyone else may have been doing; but if it was not quite such a good season as usual, it's quite as much due to Miss Thompson's extravagant whims, as to my sister's wedding having been put off, which really only made a week's difference in my getting over to Paris."

"Ah!" . . . Toni's experienced mind, hitching on to this disclosure, raced swiftly alongside the hundred-and-one troubles which would have followed on such a beginning: The postponement of the journey to Paris, if only for a week, meant that Aimée had arrived there when everybody was too busy to attend to her, so that she would not have been likely to get her models over until the first week of October. This delay would have put Miss Thompson all wrong. Customers would have been in already, ordering dresses for the Autumn. Miss Thompson would have had to start cutting out without the new models. No wonder Aimée's slackness had infuriated her.

But before Toni could express any of this, Aimée had gone on to say: "And anyway, it wasn't very much good; I mean, it wouldn't have made much difference if I hadn't gone at all, as I could afford to buy so very little. We were simply overstocked with Belworthy's stuff . . ."

—This time, Toni did not say: ah! Here was what she had all these months been dreading and warding off—here it was in actuality. She acquiesced almost with relief to this establishment of her instinct that the Belworthy incident would lead "Toni's" delicately, from season to season, into the very pit of ruin.

Aimée did not like the silence; she deemed it especially threatening to her, and would have preferred what she called "a good rowing." With truly prodigious dignity, she proceeded to deliver rope for her own hanging: "Of course, Miss Rakonitz, it's quite natural that the firm should get into debt, when Miss Thompson insists on having an expensive dress made twice over; the first one scrapped—and, as you know, we have to pay ready cash for Rodier cloth—simply because a client fancied a dress she saw afterwards more than the one she'd already ordered. I'm not a snob, myself, and titles make no difference to *me*; but it's very different with Miss Thompson. That's the worst of women in business, I always do say !— though naturally I don't mean you, Mrs. Goddard—but then you weren't there; and I don't let myself be annoyed by little feminine reasons like that; it's not my policy. It's Miss Thompson's one idea to satisfy Lady Penstead just because she *is* Lady Penstead; and directly Lady Penstead saw that model from Agnès, while she was being fitted—the cloth already cut —she said if she'd seen it beforehand . . . well, that's all very well, Miss Rakonitz, but she'd already ordered a copy of a Belworthy model, and naturally we put those forward, having so many of them, and now she was not satisfied with it; and, if you please, Miss Thompson insisted that we should take her order all over again."

"Quite," said Toni, being human, and "taking it out" of Amy Lecky, to stifle, for a few moments longer, her contempt for her own past insanity; "Miss Thompson was perfectly right. The model from Agnès and every other model, whether few or many, should have been there already, when Lady Penstead first came in with her order. You could hardly expect her to understand how that little matter of your sister's wedding postponed your journey to Paris. Our clients are not expected to, you know. The idea is to satisfy them at all costs, not to reveal the domestic predicaments of our staff."

. . . Aimée began to cry. She could not bear sarcasm. She hated it when Miss Rakonitz became sarcastic. Toni gathered, from the few hysterical sentences which gurgled and oozed through the tears, that poor Aimée, in accepting the sole management of the show-room, and buying side of "Toni's," without any authority behind her, had bitten off decidedly more than she could chew; and that things were in a pretty ghastly muddle—far worse than could be revealed by this sole anecdote of Lady Penstead and the model from Agnès.

"I'd better go down and see for myself"—Toni had just

reached the door, when a torrential Loraine, in high spirits, hurled herself into her arms :

" Darling—and aren't you glad to see me, and this is just what comes of telling me that I'm welcome here at any day or hour of the day, for sure, it's not yet ten o'clock, but it's a horrible bleak morning and something was after bidding me come and cosset you and make chocolate fudge for all the babies the way only I can make it in all this world, and so back you go in the arm-chair and be a baby yourself, because I've come for the day and you can't get out of it ! But kiss me first, Toni, my dear, dear little piece of elegance, because I love you better even than I love Babs and that's saying a lot, I may tell you . . . and here's your visitor wondering if I'm mad entirely, so tell her I'm your long-lost cousin, Toni, which is nothing but the truth, and that you hated me hard for over two years and so you did, but that we've tenderly made it up over our last big quarrel, and we ain't a-going to fight no more, no more. . . ."

Loraine was, indeed, going straight on from the place where she had last left off, with Toni ; confident, because once a disconsolate little cousin had given way and cried in her arms, clung to her, accepted her heartening consolations, that the same little cousin would continue loving her, and never be irritated by her again. She was so buoyantly sure of her welcome, that Toni might not have disillusioned her, however differently she were feeling on a sane Friday morning from her shocked and desperate mood of the Sunday evening before,— had not other events suddenly been hurled into the gap of time. She could not stop, now, for Loraine nor Loraine's endearments ; nor to betray affectionate need of Loraine. She wanted to get down to Hanover Street, to " stop the rot," there ; get government into her capable hands once more. Her mind was full of Aimée's exposures . . . " Toni's " was what counted ; " Toni's " was in danger. So she merely put Loraine aside—she could not remember afterwards by what words she had checked all that exuberance, nor whether, indeed, she had been beastly and snubbing, or simply somewhere else already and not any more in the room with superfluous Loraine and weeping Aimée—" Tell them to bring round the car *at once*

Quimper ! " . . . A hat pulled on, up in her room, and leather-lined coat—" Not now, Babs, I haven't a moment . . . but Loraine's here ! "—and a squeal of joy from her small daughter, following her own light run downstairs, front-door slammed—ah ! and here was the Dook—good ! Toni was impelled by a fierce compelling energy that was a queer delight in itself, after these years of mental inertia, even though disaster had brought it about.

Miss Wildblood proved quiet and helpful, with a hint of reproach in her mild eyes behind her owlish spectacles. Half an hour's consultation with her, and a quick preliminary scrutiny of the books, revealed to Toni the unpleasant certainty that they owed Belworthy thirteen hundred pounds ; and that he had already been hinting pretty strongly, among his business cronies, that in another six months, a ruined " Toni's " would fall helplessly into the snug hollow of his hands. The happy arrangement made by Giles and Aimée to double their order with him, had landed them with far more stuff than they could dispose of, and very little variety, because they could not afford to buy much from other firms, as well as such an unprecedented quantity from his. This, combined with the incidental matter of delay in getting in such Paris models of the Autumn season as they could still afford, had lost them a considerable number of influential clients. The rack was full of small unpaid bills for silk, for cloth and trimmings, down to the very bill for milk for the workroom teas, all of which should have been settled out of the petty cash fund for which Toni had signed an inclusive cheque, every month ; but Aimée, demoralised by the state of things, had also believed that slackness did not matter, as very soon the firm would come under Belworthy's sway, and *he* could put all that mess right, if he liked ! She had been too frightened to tell Toni, too frightened to do anything except talk charmingly to the very few clients who were still coming in to give their orders—" a mangy lot ! " Gwenny Moore called them ; " suburbs, mostly ! " Since Miss Thompson left, a month ago, they had been working with a totally incompetent fitter ; Aimée warded off enquiries for the sort of Spring models that she had not yet bought, knowing, helplessly, that there was no ready money to go to Paris during the first week of March, which was the latest date to which she should have postponed this important bi-annual journey.

Toni, metaphorically, dug her hands into her pockets, and took a good hard look at the few fragments and splinters of the prestige she had so enthusiastically built up. . . . Then she laughed! Let Belworthy have "Toni's"? not she! The Dook was waiting for her outside. She dashed round to the Czelovars in Chester Square. She could do nothing without capital; and had not Helen most providentially asked, last November, was it?—if she were *never* going back into the business again? Helen would do; she had brains and excellent taste and a level judgment; her father had plenty of money. Toni laughed again, as she started the car. Miss Wildblood and two of the girls stood staring after her, amazed at such levity.

She found Helen at home. Ten minutes' explanation with her, was enough. What a relief to be dealing with Helen's quickness, after Aimée Lequesne's muzzy and self-important explanations, with the emphasis all in the wrong places; though Toni still contended that Aimée in the showroom was all right, and just what was needed; probably she need not be sacked. Still, all that could wait. She and her cousin went off to Gray's Inn to interview Raoul Czelovar.

. . . "This," said Raoul, "is a thing that must be considered slowly, Toni, my dear; not decided all at once."

And Toni answered: "I quite agree with you, Uncle Raoul; but I must leave for Paris to-day week at the latest; earlier, if possible. By that time, Helen must be installed and in authority at Hanover Street, if we are to pull off this season at all; and I intend that we shall."

Raoul hated being rushed like this; but he adored Helen; and Helen and Toni together were too much for him. Besides, he was impressed by the way this ultra-modern young woman was able to answer every question relating to the past and present of the firm, on the financial side. She did not attempt to hide the trouble they were in, but she made him realise that two thousand pounds immediate capital from him, in purchase of a partnership for Helen, would pay off Belworthy ; and buy some attractive fresh stock ; and after that, all which was required to lift it back into the profitable concern it had previously been, was Toni's personal and whole-time supervision brought back into it.

" You needn't be afraid about that," Toni promised. " I've done with being a figurehead. It's Hanover Street for me from nine until seven every day, now ; more, if necessary. I'm ever so much stronger than I used to be."

Raoul asked : " What will your husband say to that ? "

Toni had not once thought of Giles the whole day, except to damn him heartily over his share in the Belworthy business ; and even then, she had damned her own share in that incident still more heartily. . . .

" Giles won't mind," she said. " We're each free to do as we like with our lives. That was part of the contract."

Raoul was just about to utter a few sound views on modern marriages, when headed off by his disrespectful daughter, who saw, with Toni, that there was not a moment to be wasted.

" I should just like you to tell me this, before I lightheartedly put every penny I possess into a ramshackle business with a hole in it," said Raoul . . . and Toni winced. " Why are you suddenly so anxious for Helen to come into it ? "

Toni replied : " Apart from the fact that she's keen, and that I'd like to work with her, and that she has a distinct *flair* for clothes, I need your money. That's obvious, isn't it ? "

" Why not your husband's money ? or the money of your husband's family ? "

" Because," replied Toni, in the manner of the old-fashioned French exercise-book, " the Bank overdraft of my husband is very big, and the Bank overdraft of my husband's family— which is mainly his father—is bigger still ! "

" In other words, you've been spending too much, young lady ! "

" A damn sight too much," said Toni.

" With three children ; and knowing that your name on a business makes you responsible for its debts ? "

" Yes, Uncle Raoul."

" You're quite as bad as your grandmother, poor soul ! "
But he had never approved of Anastasia ; " you're as bad as
your grandmother, and your father, and your Uncle Max.
This is poor Max all over again, this business ! "

" Yes," Toni repeated, meekly taking her scolding. That
was the worst of going to the family ; they usually ended with
some loyal rescue work ; but you always had to bear, first, with
reminders that you were like the very worst manifestation of
somebody else in the family. And especially she resented with
all her strength, any allusion to the undoubted likeness that
existed between her own curious phases, and her grandmother's ;
both of them reacting from strong clear sanity to a sort of gay
madness, and then back again. . . . Had she hated the sight of
the Matriarch in her " bad times," because of all the misery her
unbalanced extravagance had brought on the family ? On
herself, and her mother, and all of them ? . . . Or most of all
because she felt, deep down within her own nature, a potential
longing to behave just like that, with the same pendulum
rhythm ? and was never sure how far she would be able to
control the oscillation, or its fantastic consequences ? She
minded far less being told that she resembled Uncle Maximilian,
even though he had brought their family prosperity crashing
down over the Nong-Khan sapphire mine. As for Uncle Raoul
. . . she weighed in her mind all that she had ever heard about
his temperament, and all that her own intuition told her now.
And it amounted to a conviction that he was one of those
people, far commoner than those of the opposite type, who can
be driven and not led. So she resolved to risk the whole issue
of her appeal to him, on one bold stroke of sheer inexcusable
bullying :

" Look here, Uncle Raoul—it was you who mentioned Uncle
Max, not I. . . . You didn't help him when he was up against
it, I know. I've heard the family say so, and that you easily
might have ! "—Raoul Czelovar made an inarticulate sound.—
" Well . . . won't you help *me* now, instead ? Sentiment
apart, it will make you feel more comfortable about it all. And
you'll get it back, this time, with interest. You know perfectly
well that I *am* reliable, in business, when it comes down to

brass-tacks. It's simply bluster to pretend that I'm entirely Grandmère."

. . . And the next thing to do, directly she knew that Helen's partnership and Raoul Czelovar's two thousand pounds were —with due precautions—safely hers for the business, and that Czelovar was giving another lawyer instructions at once for a proper contract to be drawn up—the next thing to do, was to see how far Miss Thompson could be managed. Miss Thompson must be won back for " Toni's," at all costs. There was nothing harder, in that trade, than to find a fitter who was a genius in her line. But Toni now had that full-tided feeling that nothing could stop her ; that she could dash down all difficulties in her way, as easily as an oncoming wave disposes of frail sand-castles. Melville's, the firm to whom Miss Thompson had recently promised her services, was the sand-castle in this instance ; and Melville's claims went down before her irresistible onslaught. Miss Thompson had always liked Toni, and had always got on well with her. Reassured, now, that the old régime had come back, and that sufficient money was promised to deal with the Belworthy menace, she faltered, hesitated, and gave in.

" You know, Miss Rakonitz, I never really would have left if you'd been there ; I wouldn't have dreamt of it." She was sporting enough not to say anything more about Aimée's rule and the devastation it had caused ; in fact, she agreed with Toni that Miss Lequesne showed off the goods well, and had a manner which made her a favourite with clients, so that it would be quite a good thing to retain her.

" She hadn't much head for business," said Miss Thompson, " and nor had I, you see ; and there we were ; and I thought I might as well clear out and find myself a place before Mr. Belworthy took over ' Toni's,' lock, stock and barrel—for that's what it looked like."

" Mr. Belworthy is not going to have lock, stock *or* barrel," Toni prophesied, happily. And went home, her small head arrogantly tilted, her eyes blue and unsmiling. . . .

To-morrow, she would get her brother Gerald to go through the books with her and Miss Wildblood, more carefully than to-day's rush had allowed. To-morrow, also, she must certainly try and see Mr. Caley, who had originally financed ' Toni's,' and ask his sanction to the new arrangements ; and ask his permission, too, to continue on a basis of two-and-a-half-per-cent interest, for another year or two beyond the agreed limit of time, instead of beginning to return him his capital by instalments. Then there was that question of taking on the downstairs premises, as well as the two rooms they now rented on the first floor. Helen seemed keen. And a sudden launching-out, a bold and expensive-looking " splash " just at this crisis of " Toni's," might work out as a prudent business investment, for it would soothe and impress the clients who had been dropping away, just when it was most urgently needed. The new premises would have to be investigated at once, because some other, and not too desirable tenant was already bidding for them. And Helen would have to be initiated, as quickly and yet as thoroughly as possible. And, most important of all, Paris !

—" I hope to God, I shan't be too late for Paris," thought Toni, aloud, at her belated dinner.

And Giles, who had already reached the dessert stage, said curiously : " What's this about Paris ? Anything wrong with one of your relations there ? " For during the past ten days, he could not help being aware of Toni's anxious pre-occupation over her family, in single units, and as a whole ; and he was growing used to the fact that everything she said or did, seemed to hark back to Rakonitz. Truth to tell, he was a little bored by Rakonitz. For the first three years of their married life, Toni's attitude towards her relations had been the famous one of the legendary Queen of Spain towards her legs . . . they simply did not exist. But the death of the Matriarch, and, topping that, some jumble that Loraine had told her about the dead wife of a still deader great-uncle—Giles had never quite got the rights of it !—had appeared to upset Toni, and to encumber her mind out of all proportion. So that he was rather glad when she answered :

" No, not family. Business. I'm going to take on ' Toni's ' again, Giles."

" That's rather sudden, isn't it ? "

Toni hoped he was not going to be importunate about the claims of home, husband and children. He had better hear the worst at once, so that he should realise that naked necessity, and not whim, had prompted her decision.

" Aimée Lequesne has muddled things hopelessly ; and the firm is in debt to the tune of about thirteen hundred pounds ; and as it's still run in my name——"

" My dear kid ! " at once Giles' protection sprang up all round Toni like a ring of pikemen, steel turned outwards : " Why on earth couldn't you let me know ? I'd have seen to it all. You must have had the very deuce of a day—simply puts the lid on it, with all the other rotten luck you've had lately. But why tire yourself by rushing over to Paris, alone ? It's absurd, of course. Look here, you sit tight, and let me take it on for you."

" Good God, *no !* " cried Toni, before she could help herself.

The symbolical pikes were slowly lowered . . . and **Giles** said, in quite a different tone :

" You'll have to explain that, Toni."

The time was past for Toni to manœuvre a scramble back to the ranks of the petted feminine. She spoke with as much forbearance as she could muster ; and for very weariness, her voice was gentle :

" You see, old boy, you don't know the technicalities. I was in it for twelve years."

" Isn't it just a matter of common-sense ? " he asked, knitting his brows. " Over that Belworthy business, for instance——? "

" Quite," said Toni. " Over that Belworthy business."

Immediately, Giles' solicitude and innate kindness sprang once more into evidence : " Did we go wrong there ? Is *that* to do with the present smash ? I say, Toni, how absolutely foul ! I'm damned sorry ! *Is* it that ? "

" Mostly. It originally led up from there, I think ; and, of course, Aimée is God's own mutt ! But I think I may be able to swing it all round again, Giles, if you'll just allow me time and space. I hate neglecting the infants, but just for a couple of years, Mummy and Nurse can carry on with them. I left them alone, for nothing but to have my good time ; so I might as well leave them alone a bit longer, for a rather better reason."

" Well," said Giles, cheerfully, " no more giddy cocktails and what-not for me either, then. I must barge round and get work again, of some kind, if you work."

Toni had envisioned her husband just dancing on. . . . His matter-of-course announcement was, therefore, a surprise, and not altogether a pleasant one. Part of her change of attitude towards taking up a business career again, the relish, the curious jollity, the buoyant sense of power with which she viewed the prospect, contrasted with her girlhood's tired distaste, arose from the wordless but blessed security of a background ; of Giles being there, emphatically there—a warm, robust, definite Giles to start from and go back to, with ' Toni's ' between. She belonged at home, with Giles ; but she went forth to " Toni's." . . . She had the responsibility of " Toni's," but her husband had the responsibility of her. All this, so much more satisfactory than in the old days, before her marriage, when her shoulders were spared no burden, and she was solitary and not strong, fighting against odds all the time. But : " I must barge round——" She felt dimly that an entirely new set of psychological bothers, exactions, changes of household habits and general upheaval, might be involved by Giles discontinuing his present happy-go-lucky existence, and bargeing round in search of employment, more definite than his late agency for motor-cars ; employment which might even lead to his leaving England—("Orange-farms in South Africa——!" flashed through her mind)—just at the precise time when she most desired from him a corporeal presence, combined with a negative temperament.

" Why should you, Giles ? "

He produced one of his totally unexpected formulas : " A man can't let his wife work, if he doesn't."

" But a man needn't work, as long as his wife doesn't ? Is that it ? "

" My dear kid, can't you see the distinction ? Good Lord ! "

" I'll try, presently, working it out with pencil and paper," said Toni. " I'm hungry now. . . . What are you thinking of ? " she asked, two minutes later ; for his gaze at her, over the wild-duck and orange salad, was unseeing and fixed.

Giles reverted, most inconveniently, to the subject of devoting his energies to the firm in Hanover Street. " Your business interests me, you know ; what I've seen of it. You'd better take me in as a partner, Toni."

" Got any money to put in ? "

" You grasping little devil ! I've got my overdraft ! Every penny of it my own ! "

" Well, has your father got any money ? "

" He's got *his* overdraft," said Giles : " about four times as big as mine ! Jimmy was always a swanker ! "

Toni laughed : " Don't accuse me of swanking, but I've got an overdraft, too. Three overdrafts won't make a summer for Hanover Street. As a matter of fact, I'm taking in Helen Czelovar as partner ; she's got brains and ' timbre,' as Aimée would say ; and Uncle Raoul is going to plank down two thousand pounds. That ought to save us ! Thirteen hundred of it goes to Belworthy, worse luck ; but I must get rid of our debt to him."

" What *was* Belworthy's little game, two years ago ? Where did we make our mistake ? "

" His game was to force us to double our order with him, by his threat of closing down our account. He knew it would have been terribly inconvenient for us to find such a large sum of money just then. He knew, too, that the firm couldn't carry so much of one man's stuff ; and wouldn't be able to afford to buy elsewhere ; so we'd get a name for having no variety, and a lot of his stock would remain on hand, and——"

" Yes, but look here," interrupted Giles, " what's the good of that to him ? It would simply mean a growing debt, and he would have no hope of getting paid."

" Yes, that's right. Belworthy was looking forward to buying in ' Toni's,' cheap, when we were in such difficulties that it would practically have to flop into his hands. He was just within a month or two of realising his ambition, too, if I hadn't got wind of it all."

" Didn't that mean that he had us in a cleft stick from the very beginning ? If we couldn't pay then . . ."

" There was one thing we *could* have done," said Toni, who had forgotten that Giles was her husband ; forgotten all the subtleties involved, and was talking to him as two business men talk across a table. " And it would have been considered perfectly honest, too, in the trade. We ought to have told Aimée and Miss Thompson that they were to have an interview with Belworthy, and fall in with his plan, but to say that the money owing was a bit more than we liked, and that we preferred to get it paid off, gradually, by bills. You see, Giles, a business man would have been glad to take bills accepted by a firm of good repute ; and he'd be sure of his money."

Giles frowned : " Go slow, Toni ; as you say, there are technicalities. What exactly do you mean by bills ? "

" Well, supposing Miss Thompson, speaking for me, said : ' Will you take my bills ? ' He would probably answer : ' For how long ? ' And then she'd say, perhaps : ' nine months.' And then I imagine Belworthy would answer : ' Very well ; I'll send you the bills for acceptance.' Accepting is done by writing one's name across the bills, agreeing to the terms. He couldn't claim a penny until the bills became due in nine months' time. Do you get that ? "

He nodded.

" Well, that's where we'd have scored, you see. Directly the matter was settled, and he had agreed to take the bills, we'd have closed our account, and never bought another thing from him."

Giles gave a long, low whistle. Then admiration gave way to contrition : " I'm damned sorry, Toni. That was an unholy blunder for us to have made—not to see what he was after. Entirely my fault, too. That's one thing : you needn't blame yourself for a second. It was I who made the mistake, not you. I'm an interfering ass, and I don't quite know what to do about it."

Toni cried impulsively, seeing that he was in genuine distress : " No, it wasn't your fault as much as that, Giles. If anyone stands in the dock, I do. How could you be expected to understand what you were doing? But I 'got' both Belworthy's scheme, and my own counter-scheme, from the very first, while you and Aimée—— And I shut up about it, and let the mistake go through. So you see, you needn't have a burdened conscience at all. All the guilt is on mine."

. . . She had been so anxious to relieve him, that she had miscalculated the effects of her confession.

Giles said : " Are you—mad, Toni? Do you mean that this brilliant stroke of business that you were just telling me about —first getting him to accept the bills, and then never ordering any more stuff from him—do you actually mean to say that you were inspired by all that, when Aimée first—while she and I . . . You mean, I suppose, that you thought of it when it was too late? after they'd already seen Belworthy? "

" No," Toni said, slowly and honestly ; " before it was too late."

" In the studio? While Aimée and I——? "

" Yes."

" Then why the Hell didn't you come out with it? "

" How could I? You had already given your advice. More than your advice—orders ; you had told Aimée what was to be done. You were my husband ; a man. How could I make a fool of you by contradicting you, then, in front of her? "

" Thanks for your chivalry," said Giles. . . . They had been married four years, but Toni had never seen him angry until now—ordinary, swearing anger. " I didn't know anyone could be such a bloody fool! " he shouted.

" If you remember," Toni retaliated, at once mutinous and disdainful, as she always was at such moments ; and in her coldest, most concise tones : " If you remember, just before Aimée came in, I'd been coaxing you into paying my personal bills for me—shoes and hats and fur coats—that sort of thing. It would have been ungracious, wouldn't it, on top of that, if I'd come slashing in with orders that exactly cancelled yours, in front of my saleswoman? "

" Your saleswoman! Hell! I can't see what she's got to do with it, and I can't see what your shoes and hats and vanity-bags have got to do with it. You're apparently an exceptionally competent business woman——" He stopped dead . . . and though, when he went on again, his voice and manner had calmed down, Toni felt that he was, if anything, angrier than before. " Oh ? . . . yes, I'm beginning to see. I remember, now. You were spoofing me. . . . Just a pretty, gay, little thing, with no head for business ! No head for business—— Good God ! And the quickness with which you must have jumped to what Belworthy was up to, and to that way of getting on top of him. . . ." He brooded on the matter for a few moments. . . . Toni watched him prowling about among the ruins of her helplessness and frailty. She had seen a great many things crumble and fall in, during the last few weeks, and was too intent on holding up the pillars of " Toni's," to be resourceful in any other direction. Her thoughts wandered in the direction of shaded colours; was it really going to be the season's fashionable material ? And if so . . .

" You were incredibly dense, Toni," Giles interrupted her queerly impersonal musings. " Didn't it really occur to you what a perishing fool you were making of me, by letting this mistake go on ? go on, and lead to worse ? this mistake that I'd made, and that you could have put right at once ? It's—it's almost unbearable." He was still bewildered, beyond adequate expression of his smart, under the indignity which Toni had laid on him. Giles was not a stupid man ; and once he was on the right trail, his understanding went forward at a terrific pace. He winced before this picture of himself as an innocent, well-meaning, officious boy, shoving forward the wrong ideas when they were neither wanted nor asked for. He hated Toni's humiliating forbearance : " You weren't to blame, darling ! " . . . Not to blame, because *she* had known all the time exactly what had to be done—this brilliant, clear-minded, efficient Toni. But because Giles had been clumsily nice to her, because he had played the little man, and had put her bills into his pocket, and slapped it, and said : " Righto ! I'll pay 'em ! "— or words to that effect—because of that, Toni, male of the twain, thought it up to her to smile and be indulgent. . . .

Abruptly, Giles got up from where he was sitting, and walked over to the window. He simply couldn't face Toni.

That was what she had done to him . . . this was what women did to men, in the new way of things. " You've got me all wrong," he exclaimed, exasperated. "I apologise for swearing at you ; but it was blasted *silliness* to think that I'd have minded your knowing better than I, over this one thing, over this Belworthy business. Silliness, to have imagined that I'd mind just because it *was* business, and I was a man and you were a woman, and men are supposed to know better in business."

" Most men would have minded, because of that," from Toni, still at the dinner-table. She was meticulously peeling an apple, so that the peel should curl round into one long unbroken initial. . . .

" Convention. I don't believe it ! Anyway, I'm not such a vain ass ! I'd have been proud of you. . . . Don't smile in that way—I tell you I *would !* If you'd treated the situation— it hardly was a situation—straightforwardly, as men would have done ; instead of tying it round into psychological knots ! Talk about equality !—who can possibly object to equality ? But it's having to say thank you for your damnable *tolerance* . . ."

" Giles, I——"

But he had lashed himself into a state beyond listening ; words were banging about in his head, and though they did not always fit his anger, he used them, to relieve himself.

" Tolerance ! . . . Completely wise to us, you think, and putting up with our charming futility, because we're decorative, and indispensable to dance with. . . . ' Ladies—the Gentle- men ! '—and then you sit down to the serious concerns of life, but mentioning it that he was *rather* sweet, wasn't he ?—It was perfectly adorable, the pretty way he gave his orders over business that he knew absolutely nothing about ! . . ."

" I didn't say all that ! " Toni protested, furiously ; and she tore the strip of apple-peel into little bits.

" Something like that, anyway. Well, I'm overwhelmingly grateful to you, Toni, for having spared me ; for having kept me from knowledge of my inferiority, and not made a fool of me in front of your saleswoman. I'm not sorry your infernal business has gone smash, because I imagine you'll so enjoy your glorious competence in putting it right again. Let me know if you want my help, won't you ? and be sure to keep it from me how absolutely fatuous it is !—The dear little chap would *love* to think he was helping ! " . . .

Toni was left alone. Her husband had crashed out of the room ; she heard his steps trampling up the stairs ; she heard the door of his dressing-room bang. She was glad that he had lost control of his temper. It would have been awful if, at that moment, he had been able to close the door in a spirit of softly mocking irony.

. . . " Friday, to-day," she murmured ; " Saturday, Sunday, Monday—I ought to leave by Wednesday morning, at the latest." . . .

.   .   .   .

On Tuesday afternoon, while Toni was superintending a re-arrangement of the showroom, and at the same time instructing Helen in a hundred different professional secrets, and scattering a few last directions to cover her next week's absence, and trying to decide which of the girls she would take with her to Paris as her aide-de-camp, an express letter was brought to her. It was quite a short letter ; she glanced at the handwriting : it was from Giles. Then : " One moment, Miss Wildblood," she said, apologetically ; for the book-keeper was standing at her elbow, with fountain-pen and blotting paper, and some urgent letters to sign.

This was the letter :

" I'm leaving England now, with Loraine. She's in a dreadful mess, and only I can help her out. I'm not certain when I'll return ; but I'll write when we've got some fixed address. You always said we were both free to do as we liked. Nothing is going to stop us. And you won't miss me. I've written to Jimmy that he's to pay three-quarters of our income into your Bank instead of mine. Good luck with the business.—GILES."

Toni read this through. Then she signed the letters that Miss Wildblood was holding for her, first reading these through, too—seven of them, relating to fairly complicated dealings.

One did not please her, and she made several corrections, and told Miss Wildblood that it had better be done again.

. . . Giles. . . . Giles . . . !

Feeling rather dazed as to her next immediate action, her eyes wandered round the showroom; then she nodded to Gwendoline Moore, selecting her for the Paris expedition: " You, Miss Moore, I think, as you've been to Paris before. Can you be ready early enough to-morrow? Miss Wildblood will tell you the exact times and arrangements."

. . . She had been right all along, of course : men were no good; men failed you, whenever you most wanted them. Only, this time, it did not matter, it did not hurt, because she had known that men were no good. It did not matter. . . .

—She noticed Aimée Lequesne standing by a glass show-case, looking very tall and willowy, in black marocain silk. And Toni's mind twisted back to an old bewilderment : How could he have kissed Aimée that time? or rather, *why* had he kissed her that time? Why? . . . She had never quite understood.

PART III

THE WAR OF THE CHINESE COAT

CHAPTER I

AT the foot of the mule-track, where the carriage stopped, one lighted window showed in the villa.

"We get out here," said Val to Richard Marcus, who had just arrived in San Goffredo. "It's the only way up to my cottage. They'll carry your luggage up from the station presently." She gave some directions to the coachman, in Italian. Just as they were starting up the track, the window with the light behind it opened, and a slim figure stepped from the room on to the balcony, and called out a gay greeting to Val; spreading her arms along the balcony rail, she leant over still further:

"Is that my cousin Richard? Welcome to Italy, Cousin Richard!" And then, laughing away her own affectation, she added spontaneously: "We've all been longing for you to come."

"See you later on, to-night," Val cried, over her shoulder, and began to trudge upwards under the bending olive trees.

"Some time to-night," was flung back by that low, joyous voice in the dark.

"Good heavens! Who was that?" asked Richard; and Val replied in slightly mocking tones:

"That, dear Richard, was your Cousin Loraine. You haven't seen her yet, have you?"

"Loraine? Do you mean that little tick who did a bunk with Goddard? Do you mean that they are *here*?" His inflexion was like a wedge of stolid British horror; if there was one thing more than another that Richard disliked, it was a

168

situation—an irregular situation. " Does Toni know they are here ? Why doesn't she do something about it ? "

All Toni's relations had been asking this.

" Toni knows. I sent her a telegram, of course, as soon as the happy pair turned up, about six weeks ago ; the middle of September."

" And Toni answered that you were to pack him straight back to her, I suppose ? "

" She did not, Richard. And it would have been a difficult thing to do, anyway. Toni, being a spirited young woman, sent back a telegram which amounted to a shrug, a laugh, and her blessing ! "

" I still don't see why you kept them here," Richard went on, irritably. " Why, good Lord, they first met on my lawn, he and Toni."

" That," Val answered respectfully, " would naturally bring you in as a main factor in the present deplorable disintegration of the marriage."

" Don't be a triple ass, Val. I meant—he seemed to me all right ; sound, you know. County family. I don't like his brothers much ; one of them's a waster, but quite an ordinary waster. And I often see his father, Jimmy Goddard. He's in the same hunt as Molly."

" That's making it worse and worse ! "

" I like you, Val," said Richard, laughing, " but I growl when I'm ragged ; I'm that sort of dog. And as for your Loraine——"

He had taken a violent dislike to Loraine—partly for Toni's sake, of course ; and partly because of the little incident when she had come out on to the balcony and welcomed him warmly to a strange country. He felt, without being able to express it, that she had arranged this fleeting moment of drama in the dark, anticipating that he might treasure it for ever in his heart, as a sudden oasis in the wilderness. " And I still don't see why she was longing for me to come."

" You'll adore her. Everybody adores Loraine ! "

" I hate people everyone adores. What do *you* think of Goddard ? "

. . . Val did not answer for a few moments, as the path

slanted up at a sharper angle, and the stones were slippery from recent rain. Then she said slowly: " I don't think Giles is at all well."

That, in fact, had been her real reason for encouraging them to remain where, for Toni's sake, she could keep an eye on him.

They had reached the top of the path, now, and there was a wan stream of light from the cottage which stood on the crest of the low hill. Richard was able to see Val's face. He said affectionately:

" You don't seem over fit, yourself, Val. There's a sort of— of pucker in your tranquillity." He was, indeed, very fond of Val Power ; she had helped him out of what had promised to be the worst scrape of his life, a few years ago ; and he had talked to her, then, with all his reserves broken down. . . . That awful business when the family had tried to marry him off to Jeanne-Marie ! . . . And thinking of the family, reminded him that a once formidable member of it, was said to be staying with Val at San Goffredo ; and that he would presently meet his Aunt Elsa.

" Look here, I say, Val—this business of Goddard and Loraine. What does Aunt Elsa say about it all ? Surely, *she* doesn't put up with it ? She's with you, isn't she ? "

" Rather ! She's with me," Val chuckled. " I foresee," she said, " that I shall have the delight of watching you and Aunt Elsa at last in alliance—spiritually in alliance ; but all the same, she's struggling on the edge of being fond of Loraine."

" You never allow her up at your house, I suppose ? I can't see Aunt Elsa putting up with that."

" Of course she puts up with it. We've coaxed her into being quite genial."

" Then she's no right to be genial," grunted Richard, feeling that a bit of the ancient auntly severity was badly wanted in this home, where Val encouraged runaway cousins, and runaway husbands of cousins, who had run away together. . . .

Val said: " You can write to *The Times* about it, and sign yourself ' Father of Two,' or ' Shocked Paterfamilias,' or ' A Clod of Gloucestershire Soil,' whichever most appeals to you ! But don't unsettle Aunt Elsa's mind, there a dear. She doesn't quite know where she is, any way : what with liking Loraine, and loyalty to Toni, and family tradition, and my arguments, and Giles looking thin. . . . You know what Aunt Elsa was, when anyone looked thin ! And now suppose we stop lingering in the damp garden, and go in where it's warm, and have some food." She whistled, and a small West Highland terrier, a scuttling patch of shaggy white, dashed down the path towards them, and began leaping all over Val, with sharp joyous barks.

" Down, Mac ! Down, old boy ! Make friends with the new gent ! Where's Terry ? Oi ! Mac, where's Terry ? "

And a voice from the front door, a deferential, girlish voice, belonging to a figure in pale pink, said :

" I'm afraid Terry's down with Loraine again, Miss Power. I hope you don't mind. We tried to shut him up, but Marietta opened the door for something, and he dashed out. You know how Terry adores Loraine ! "

" Who's Terry ? " asked Richard in an undertone. " And who's that girl ? "

" My other dog—a Kerry blue ; and that's Queenie, who runs the house for me while I paint."—But then all undertones were drowned in a voluble burst of welcome in a foreign accent, from the hall behind Queenie :

" My dear, dear boy, but this *is* a pleasure ! No, come—I *must* have a kiss ! But you are looking splendid, I will say ! And grown ! And how I vish you could have brought those *good* little boys with you. I always say to Val, one can never have enough in ze house, especially children ! You nottee, what are you doing, too, coming so far and not bringing your vife ? But come in now ! You are wet and frozen and you must have your dinner ; you will not be sorry now—no ? yes ?—to try your old Aunt Elsa's cooking again, isn't it ? "

Richard infinitely preferred Aunt Elsa's welcome, to Loraine's. He felt, too, that it was a good thing for Val, dwelling erratically in a foreign country, that she should have Aunt Elsa saying vehemently : " No ! " and " I forbid ! " and " It isn't right ! " and " Never, never ! " at frequent intervals, even if Val took no notice of such adjurations. There was something eternally warm, eternally jocund and coquettish, in the personality of Aunt Elsa. She and Richard were ancient enemies ; and she had been chief among those who had accused him and trapped him, thwarting all sullen attempts at escape, in the Jeanne-Marie episode. But " Wash it out ! " thought Richard, unaware that he was repeating the Matriarch's dying words.—" Wash it all out ! " . . . Here they were together in Italy—he and Val and Aunt Elsa, heartily pleased to be under the same roof. He gave the pretty, dimpling old lady a hug that was far too robust for her strength, and told her that he was ready to eat largely of anything she had cooked ; but—a whiff from the kitchen helping him !—he would most of all prefer those ripping things like dumplings only in a sort of rich gravy and stuffed with eggs. . . . " Or was it plums ? " a little vaguely. For he and Molly and his sons ate proper food, joints and roly-poly pudding and the like, so that he had almost forgotten what might be the ingredients of a Rakonitz dish, spicy and mysterious.

It was difficult to be articulate in the chattering, noisy welcome that seemed to have unloosed itself from every corner and archway of the vaulted room. . . . Kindly flames leaping from the logs of olive-wood ; Aunt Elsa, wildly excited, explaining that it *was* " Eier-nöckeln," but how could Richard have guessed—but no, how *could* he have guessed ? The dog Mac still hurling himself from one to the other of them ; Val hurriedly interviewing a sort of Italian infant school, that had poured in from the kitchen—Marietta and Stefania and Lola. . . . " How do you do ? " said Richard, awkwardly, to these, responding to Val's matter-of-course introduction, and to their shyly outstretched hands and bright beaming faces. Queenie was saying in discreet, rapid undertones to Val :

" Did you see Loraine, coming up here, Miss Power ? Did she seem all right ? She seemed a little depressed when she went, after tea. I wonder if you'd mind if I took down my hot-water bottle, in case she doesn't sleep again, and needs it ? Or did you say she was coming up to-night ? She wasn't sure if you wanted her, though I told her of *course* we did ! "

—Richard looked questioningly at his Aunt Elsa, who fluttered, twinkled, shrugged her shoulders, spread her hands, nodded and sighed ; trying to convey, by these conflicting

signs, her utter perturbation of spirit over the monstrous
advent, at San Goffredo, of Toni's husband; her bewilderment at Val's acceptance of such a situation—(but a disgrace!)
—her reluctant beginnings, nevertheless, of motherly affection
for Loraine; her secret understanding of Richard's point of
view, promising him a long confidential talk later on; her
amusement at Queenie's very obvious rave on Loraine; and,
finally: "But come, we must be a little modern, isn't it?
After all, zat poor Loraine is not quite English! . . ."

Stefania put in a question as to whether the Signorina
Loraine was coming up to dinner that night? Her mobile
little mouth drooped in disappointment, when Val said: "No,
after dinner."

"Stefania adores Loraine," said Queenie, and Richard
muttered: "Oh, God!" Queenie, not noticing, went on
with enthusiasm, reciting her saga into space, telling her
rhapsody to the reeling constellations: "All the little Italian
peasant kiddies adore Loraine. She is wonderful with children.
Stefania and Lola forget to be servants when they're playing
with Loraine. She races up and down the hills with them, and
climbs trees. Luigi, the son of the man at the wine-shop, is
simply crazy over her, though he's only sixteen; and she tries
to laugh it out of him. He brings her a bottle of his father's
sweetest Moscata wine every day; he steals it for her, because
she once said she liked it. Old Pulcini will be furious if he ever
finds out; Luigi always says such a romantic thing whenever
he gives it to her: 'This is for the Signorina; it is a beautiful
wine, because *she* is so beautiful!' Loraine's own cook,
Manuela, adores her, too. Manuela is half Spanish; she says
she will knife anyone who hurts her little Señorita. Loraine——"

Very firmly, Richard requested to be shown up to his room.
You could not too virulently dislike Queenie, so pretty and
breathless, with a faint flush on her blossomy skin, and a look of
sudden timidity as she realised, perhaps, that she had been
talking too much, in front of a strange man. But he had had
enough of hearing about Loraine worship, for the moment:
Terry, the Kerry Blue; Queenie; Stefania; Manuelo;
numberless Italian children; and Luigi, aged sixteen, son of a

local vintner—all, so said the legend and the disciple, were centred in this adoration; and, it was to be supposed, Giles Goddard, Toni's husband; and, imminently, Aunt Elsa, who, according to Val, was struggling on the edge. Apparently, only Val had succeeded in remaining immune; and of Val's feelings he could never be quite sure. He would have to see her with Loraine before he was satisfied. She was not as serene as usual: there were signs of disturbance in her indolent voice; in a mournful, tired way, her eyes seemed at times to contract, until the pupils were merely black specks. Val had an attractive trick of suddenly closing her eyes, and then quickly opening them again, just before she laughed; as though, before laughter could have its way with her, she must first, for a fleeting instant, shut out sight of the visible world. . . . Richard imagined that, without being a victim to the spell that Loraine seemed to scatter around, Val was yet too acutely aware of her cousin's force for destroying peace. Then was it upsetting her work? Val had made her name on a certain concentration of savage irony that burst its way through the paint in whatever she did; a curious tendency, considering how lazy good-nature to those around her, was her main characteristic. Did Loraine like Val? . . . "As though it mattered!" remarked Richard, to the empty room about him; and he banged his hair-brushes down on to the table with quite unnecessary vehemence. *Did* Loraine like Val? Richard was not impressionable. His was a nature that, as a rule, instead of responding sensitively to vibrations and harmonies and subtle signs of conflict in the atmosphere about him, solidly resisted them, remained impregnable, hewing out his own slow, sure way towards the mental destination on which he was originally intent. That was why he was the more disgusted that he should now find himself in a strange house, in a strange country, speculating about a strange woman, and her strange effect upon those around him. This was the sort of damn-fool mood that artists had, and sometimes foreigners; or, perhaps, invalids; not sensible English farmers! As though good old Val could not be trusted to keep in place a gaudy creature who would presently appear to vamp him with a red camellia in her mouth! Richard clumped down to his

dinner. . . . Thinking of Loraine and her artificiality, he
found perverse pleasure in accentuating his own farm-labourer
characteristics, easily enough shed as a rule, directly he was on
holiday, and out of the fields.

But when, a couple of hours later, Loraine materialised, with
Giles by her side, and Terry squirming along behind, ostenta-
tiously and willingly her slave, she did nothing so obvious as to
chew a red camellia, or attempt to vamp her hitherto unknown
cousin Richard. She was, indeed, frankly and exuberantly glad
to see him ; but her second welcome, in its essence, had the
same note in it as Aunt Elsa's : claiming kin with him, stressing
the warm fact that they were, though distantly, blood relations.

She wore, not the jade-green velvet that ought to have
shocked Quimper, and did not, but a sedate nut-brown frock,
cut in the way that her fingers shaped all her frocks : long,
pointed bodice and wide skirt down to her ankles. It was
subtle of Loraine, with the feet of a goddess, not to yield to
the cheap temptation of wearing short skirts. And she came
running in, calling :

" Ah now, where's my Aunt Elsa, the only friend I have in
this house ? "

" Oh, Loraine ! . . ." gasped Queenie, protesting. But
Loraine swept aside Queenie's very existence ; Queenie had
been too easy a conquest.

" You *are* my friend when I'm not there, aren't you, darling,
wicked Aunt Elsa ? Tell me truly, Cousin Richard, hasn't she
told you nothing but noice things about me ? She scolds us to
our faces, but sticks up for us behind our backs ; and don't I
know it ! "

Aunt Elsa tried very hard to frown her disapproval ; but an
irrepressible dimple, which sixty years ago had been one of the
toasts of Vienna's young officers and " gigerls," showed suddenly in her left cheek, just under the eye. " I do scold you,
yes, when you wear that thin dress and no cloak after all I have
told you," she cried ; and succumbed to Loraine's flattery, to
Loraine's embrace. Then, remembering that Richard was
there, and that she and Richard were allies in the cause of
respectability, tried to pull herself together again—too late—

and added pettishly : " But do not, I beg you, sit about all over me like this ! You are one of those who never finds themselves a chair, no ! "

But, meanwhile, Richard and Giles had met. The last time had been nearly a year ago : November, in Gloucestershire, when Giles had gone down to his father for some hunting with the Berkeley ; that had been just before Antony was born. Richard expected a measure of embarrassment from Goddard, which would at least equal, if not double, his own. But Giles was not embarrassed ; he was not even self-conscious nor defiant, as far as Richard could see. At the first second of encounter, Richard had thought Val was talking rot when she had remarked that Giles was not well. . . . Why, he had never seen the man look quite so alive, nor so full of vitality. But straight on top of that, followed the contradiction ; and he understood, with a resentful shock, both the reason for Val's comment, and the reason for her slackness in censure. There was surely something not quite natural about a fellow who was not a bad fellow, and yet could leave his wife, and, a few months later, appear among his wife's relations with that air of sunny exuberance—well, not sunny, exactly—starry was more the word : Giles seemed to be kicking his heels among the stars ; he was not on firm ground any more, and he had forgotten that other people could still keep to firm ground and firm conventions. This pair—Giles and Loraine—damn it all ! They were assuming themselves the centre and nucleus of a happy family party : " Here we all are ! Isn't it amusing ? " Their entrance had been—well, Mercury and Psyche . . . demi-gods, half-mortals. . . . No, Mercury was a whole god, wasn't he ? But here, in Giles, was mortal faculty to be happy, with a god's severance from the consequences. In *Giles*—public school, young English army man ; father in Gloucestershire now ; type that hated all forms of freak conduct, freak clothes. . . . His evening-dress, his manners, his close-cut hair and short clipped moustache . . . all in order. . . . You couldn't *place* it, that effect he brought in with him, of sparkle and irresponsibility. He was not acting, but this entrance—it was surely part of a show ? It would have been glib and insolent, had it been meant insolently. But it was not even that, Richard could see. They were expecting no reproaches; they were just happy and full of charm.

Val, watching the encounter with concealed anxiety, observed with relief that the hackles on Richard's neck had ceased bristling, the bulk of his opposition had subsided. . . . And, in the way of Aunt Elsa, he slowly succumbed—but to Giles, not to Loraine.

Loraine was comfortably settled on the floor, now, her brown skirts billowing round her, her head against Aunt Elsa's knee; Terry lay in her lap, blinking up at her through such a thick mat of untidy fringe, that it was hard to believe that he could see anything at all! "Terry ni houlihan" . . . or words to that effect! . . . she murmured affectionately.

"She talks to him in Pidgin Erse," Val mocked; "and to Mac, in a sort of bastard Gaelic. I don't know what language she'd achieve if we kept a Pomeranian!"

Did Val like Loraine? Richard was still not sure. No doubt but that, out of the whole crowd assembled, Val's approbation was the only one that Loraine really cared about, or sought to win. He could not accuse her of showing off; she was quaint and old-fashioned that evening—a little princess of the rigid Spanish Court, very courteous to Richard, quietly affectionate with Aunt Elsa; she checked Queenie's exuberant services; and, in her low, husky voice, made them all laugh with a really funny account of how Queenie had despairingly brought her the household books to check, that very afternoon; and after Queenie herself, and Aunt Elsa, and apparently Marietta, had already been tampering with them, with the best will in the world and in three languages, striving to get them right . . .

"What I always say is, everyssing or nossing," cried Aunt Elsa. "It is true that Val has her work and does not want to lead the house, therefore; but if it were all left to me who was taught to be domestisch and practisch in the kitchen when I was yet an age when girls now sit in school and learn nossing . . ." And she nodded vigorously at Queenie, whom she detested. "But how can I make economies and prevent ruin, yes, for that will be the end of it, when that one there calls herself the house-keeper and interrupts her coquettings with the cobbler and carpenter and all the other Italians whom she thinks barons and counts because she knows nossing of the world and has read a lot of quatsch ! Yes, calls herself the housekeeper here, and gives a lot of silly orders and adds up the figures all wrong ! "

Queenie protested with tears in her eyes, for she was not used to Rakonitz frankness and open hostilities : " Oh, but really, Mrs. Rakonitz, you mustn't, please. I did my best, but I am with Miss Power to housekeep for her, you know, and how can I get the accounts right when you make Marietta bring them to you first, and turn all the ' ones ' into foreign ' sevens,' so that I can't read them any more ? "

Aunt Elsa was heard to observe in a perfectly clear aside to Richard ; " It would go that child nossing on, if she *could* read them ! No head, I tell you, Richard, no head at all ; and what Val wants with her—one of my reasons for stopping, is naturally to save my niece the expense and worry——" Not for the first time was Aunt Elsa hinting that Queenie should be sent about her business, leaving her in entire lordship of Val's domestic arrangements. But Val preferred remaining Aunt Elsa's hostess, to allowing her full powers of ministration. It was comfortable and entertaining to have this really delightful specimen of the best and most highly-flavoured Viennese aunt, *being* an aunt from room to room, and as good as a fire in them. But Val knew that an Aunt Elsa on whom you were dependent, would speedily become an Aunt Elsa of whom to be afraid ; not merely lovable, as now. So she retained Queenie, nominally as a housekeeper ; actually, as a safeguard from old autocracies. Aunt Elsa's persecution of " that-one-there " was unflagging, and a real pleasure to behold, for those who had gauged the thickness of Queenie's pale skin. " And you don't know what a mouth she has for eating," she still confided in Richard, but fortunately during Queenie's absence in quest of drinks. " You think it pretty now, yes, but wait until you see it full ! Ach ! I have no patience ! And zen she runs about with a vase full of blooms and moch *too* full of water, and puts it in ze middle of the table, spilling a big pool for me to put my needlework in, later on, and vonders if everyone, yes, everyone is wondering how Val could ever ever manage to get on without the help of that *sweet* young girl who arranges blooms from the garden so nicely? . . . Nöebig ! "

But Queenie was quite determined that nothing on earth, except sheer booting, would make her quit Val's establishment while Loraine was at San Goffredo and at the foot of the hill. Loraine could compensate her for everything. Queenie Bell, brought up entirely between Potley Green High School and Potley Green Tennis Club, had never met anything so dazzling, so unique, as Loraine. She could not understand how anyone could look at Val Power, although she painted very good pictures in their way, when such a thrilling Loraine was about ! So she swallowed as much as she could of her resentment at that terrible old woman's persecution, and said, smoothly—hearing Aunt Elsa's final denunciation, and having been taught to be polite to the aged, insane, and decrepit : " Mother always told me it was an inspiration to artists to have flowers about the house. And I do my best to save expense, Mrs. Rakonitz, indeed I do. It's not easy in Italian, and I'm nothing like as good as Loraine at figures. Loraine——" muzzily, into space, once again, " Loraine is a marvel at figures."

Richard was surprised to hear it ! It was easy to believe that pretty pink-and-white Queenie, her sleek fair hair and demure eyelids, and that self-conscious wiggle of the hips, almost imperceptible, reproving the non-existent but always possible license of men, had been that type of school-girl who had sat with her friends as near the back of the class-room as she could get, and far away from either the sporting or the intellectual group ; paying no attention whatever to the lessons, except as a form of oft-repeated joke ; and giggling violently, especially in the mathematics class, at an earnest mistress's efforts to instruct her. But Loraine?—Richard looked enquiringly at her : her eyes were shadowed to an expression of soft and serious supplication, as though she were saying : " Please don't hate me—I can't help being unattractive, can I ? " He was to learn, later on, several of her other characteristics which would strike him as equally incongruous with the sturdy aptitude for figures. She was not to be got by heart, all in a flash. Not only was she, as Queenie had said, an expert accountant—neat and accurate—which was absurd, when you looked at her !— But she also gloried in hard and incontestable substances : coarse food, for instance : large quantities of coarse food, like macaroni and pungent onions and rough bread ; she enjoyed digging in the garden ; and it seemed to give her the same odd comfort to plan systematic and daily performances of such un- adorned hard work as this, as to balance dreary and complicated sums in arithmetic : " I'm coming up here, every single morn- ing early, at seven-thirty, without fail, Val knows, don't you, Val ? to dig over this large bed for potatoes. Who says I won't ? But I'm going to, and it'll be splendid for me, and that it will, indeed ! " . . . And no amount of subsequent lapses from such a time-table, would kill her illusion of her own fixity of purpose, next time she made such a resolution. " If you do things regularly, like that, sticking to it, you can't die ! " she had cried out, once, passionately. And a truth lay like a small patch on the spectacular streamer of rubbish. She had any amount of quick, practical knowledge of what should be done in ill- nesses ; how to cook vegetables ; how to take a stain out of silk ; she knew about laundry, and useful carpentering odd- ments. It seemed as though, with these qualities and prefer- ences, all of them genuine, she were holding her sides with ribald laughter at those people who would inevitably expect her to be richly-coloured, dreamy, full of wild romances and other-world longings. Val had asked her what it was that gave her such a vehement satisfaction in the smell of strong soap, for instance ; or in the sight of a column of double-entry ; and she had answered, abruptly : " It's because they keep one to earth —things like that. And I want to be kept to earth."

" Afraid of dying young ? " Val quizzed her. She always pricked Loraine's heroics whenever she could ; and Loraine had replied, angrily :

" Afraid, yes. . . . But not of dying ! And you're unfair to me, Val, as Toni was. . . . You'll always, always, always try to show me up at being theatrical, even when, like now, it's I and no one else who have shown you how to get the red-and-white tiles of your verandah floor properly polished, and you using water on them! You clever people, who push away exciting things for fear they're not real, you'll end by never settling near anything real at all!"

But Richard, too, who had visualised her along purely decorative and fantastic lines : useless, bewildering, ensnaring, found, bewildered and uneasy, that she did not try to ensnare him ; not, at all events, with any of the usual flutter of sex ; though she had a way of perpetual, silent appeal that he would back her up and be on her side ; even when no one was attacking her. And every now and then : " Yes, I know your secret. . . . I knew it at once! But don't be afraid ; it's quite safe with me!"—thus her soft and inscrutable rain-coloured eyes both warned and reassured him. " Damn it!" thought Richard, " I haven't *got* a secret!" . . . This girl was going to be a nuisance. Why did she so fatally force upon them all the conviction that they were taking sides, or that there were any sides to take? Why did she make loyalty and enmity, their liking or dislike of her, so much more significant than it really was? Richard thrust down a schoolboy desire to growl : " Yah—no one's even thinking of you!"—and see how she met *that*. And yet, as she gathered up Queenie-worship and Terry-worship ; and bits from Aunt Elsa, and fragments from Stefania, flitting in and out to draw curtains and fill the log-basket ; as she casually mentioned Luigi and his votive bottles of Moscata, and repeated the incredible compliments of an old gentleman with whom she had accidentally scraped acquaintance on the hills, that day ; and read them a paragraph of a letter from somebody-or-other's governess, wanting to leave her present employment for the sake of being with Loraine for no salary at all—yet it still struck Richard that childishly she was heaping up all these rags and tags and treasures, only to build an impressive pile to be laid at Val's feet ; in some cases, she was actually working to draw away from Val, what Val already had, in order, generously, to be able to offer it up again as a personal tribute from herself.

. . . Giles was teasing her, now, by enumerating a list of her odd preferences : " Roots of garlic, Kerry Blues—she doesn't like you, Mac, does she, my white angel? "—(" No," growled the West Highland; "and 'cos why? 'Cos I don't like *her!* Quod erat demonstrandum! ")—" Black bread; washing up dishes, preferably greasy ones, from a dinner-party of twenty-four! Smuggling on the coast of Dalmatia—which I don't believe in, not for a moment . . . but it makes a good tale! Trigonometry; hard mattresses; and relations! Have I got the list right, Loraine? "

Loraine answered, serenely, for she seemed less aware of Giles than of any other person in the room: " More or less right; but you might add that you were asleep during the smuggling—fast asleep, at the bottom of the boat, with the net thrown over you. And I like bathing healthy babies, with round, strong limbs that kick the breath out of me. *You* have two little boys of your own, haven't you, Cousin Richard?— the darlings! "

" Are you going to call him Cousin Richard, all the time? " asked Val. " It reminds me of an old-fashioned children's book —the Sir and Madam kind—when the young were too respectful to accost their elders without a prefix."

" Maybe that's how I feel about Cousin Richard," laughed Loraine; and Aunt Elsa interrupted:

" Vot nonsense! Richard is younger than you, yes, a good deal! Richard is—let me once see—twenty-three? twenty-four?——"

" Give us a chance! " said Richard. " Twenty-six. Jimmy's two, now. *My* Jimmy, I mean, Goddard; not your governor! "

" And such a love! " cried Aunt Elsa, leaving it vague as to whether she meant Jimmy Goddard or Jimmy Marcus!—But anyhow, she had never seen either! " Such fat little legs! "

" Ah! But you should see Babs! " said Loraine. . . .

A shocked Aunt Elsa cried: " You dear God! "

. . . They were all, except Giles, appalled at Loraine's calm mention of Toni's daughter.

In the after stillness, you could almost hear the apparatus of Queenie's modesty sending its message to her eyelids, so that those blue wells of innocence that were her eyes might remain veiled. " Lower them! Quick! Danger! " . . . Loraine

could do no wrong, that was understood ; and as for Giles :
" —It's a sin, yes, I know, but how can he help it—for *her* ? "
But in this rather dreadful house of Miss Power's, people
actually *talked* about sin . . . which was worse . . . And
Miss Power never stopped them. Never even tried. " I
expect she herself . . ." thought Queenie, vaguely.

Val, with her habit of indolence, always with the hope that
if she did nothing whatever about a difficulty, sometime somebody else would conveniently do it first, Val, indeed, was just
waiting ! She noticed, however, that Giles was abnormally
unembarrassed ; and that it was, in fact, merely a graceful
deference towards possible inhibitions of Aunt Elsa or Richard
Marcus that restrained him from agreeing quite simply and
heartily with Loraine, that his little daughter Babs was, indeed,
extraordinarily fascinating and attractive. Giles had not been
gripped by a set of new and lawless notions ; he just appeared
to have been cut loose from any moral centre of gravity, and
to be floating in a serene haze, midway between cool earth and
dark heaven. . . . But Richard, whose feet, in heavy boots,
were well and firmly planted, thought that everybody about
him, not alone himself, was in a state of hot anguish. Generously, for the first time in his life, he made one stupendous and
pugilistic effort to be tactful ; when an uncomfortable remark
had been made, a man well versed in the art of graceful
diplomacy, at once and with a deft wit, changed the subject,
and turned the conversation. So :

—" By the way," said Richard, laboriously building his
bridge, " talking of your people, Val, I've brought out a present
for you : from a chap I don't know ; but he said Aunt Haidée
had told him I was going out to visit you ; . . . he just caught
me at Victoria, and whanged a great lumpy parcel into my
arms. He said his name was Greenways, and that he'd been
staying out here . . ."

CHAPTER II

BUT if the calm had been pricked before, now it was ripped across, beyond all repairing. Stephen Greenways? . . . Richard paused, not understanding why his sudden effort at tact seemed to have been lifted off its hinges . . . swung in mid-air . . . and then gently lowered and replaced again. . . .

"Yes," said Val. "He's a pal of mine. But he's always trotting off to China and places like that—inconvenient, if you want him in a hurry. He stayed out here about two months ago, was it, Loraine?"

"Less than that; six weeks ago. Giles and I found him here when we came. Ah, now, do fetch down the present, Cousin Richard, and let's see if it's worth having."

"What is it?" Queenie asked inquisitively.

"I don't know," said Richard. "D'you think I opened it?" And he went upstairs; while Val, Loraine, and Aunt Elsa exchanged glances of amusement over this characteristic male, who could bring a present the whole way from London to San Goffredo, without even prodding it to find out the contents, or tearing away a little corner of the paper!

"Let's guess what it is," said Queenie, who was youthfully thrilled by presents, even when they were not for her.

Giles said promptly : "Mocassins. Travellers from foreign lands always bring home mocassins and yashmaks."

"I want a necklace of shark's teeth, more than anything else in the world," cried Queenie. And gazed limpidly at Giles, who answered, "Your personality doesn't suggest shark's teeth, Queenie. D'you know what *I'd* bring you?"

Queenie immediately began to flirt; which meant, in her case, that she assumed a creamy demureness, as though her girlhood were a pearl in a locked white velvet casket, and she had recently lost the key.

" *What* would you bring me, Giles ? "

Aunt Elsa interrupted, vindictively determined that Queenie, if she could help it, should never hear what Giles would bring her. . . . She condemned Giles for running away from Toni, with Lorraine ; but, once with Lorraine, at least, thought Aunt Elsa, he might as well stop where he was, and not add to the complacencies of the Belle of Potley Green, who called him " Giles," so cheeky !

" But zat is *not* true, Giles, vot you say before. Often have I been abroad ; I have told you, have I not, that I vas not born in England ?—but never have I brought home to my girls anything so sillee as yashmaks."

She thought they were a form of waterproof coat.

. . . Richard returned ; and they all clustered round Val while she opened the parcel, which was elaborately swathed in several layers of thick brown paper, and then in coloured tissue paper. Marietta and Stefania stole in from the kitchen, with that sense of happening which always beckoned them forward at the right moment.

Finally, Val removed the last crinkled black wrappings. . . .

For the first moment they were all startled by the flare and whirl of colour which beat out on their eyes. The jade and blue and anemone pink were like three distinct shocks ; then Loraine, with a cry of joy, plunged her hands into the brocade and embroidery, and shook it out before all of them, so that they could see that it was a Chinese coat—even before they heard the clank of the little gold Mandarin buttons, three at the throat and three at the hem.

Gazing at it, you might think that you had never seen embroidery before, for it was the very climax of all that was brilliant and exotic. The flower-petals were worked in a flaming pattern round the broad bands of kingfisher blue embroidery ; and again round each oval plaque that was woven of a silvery heron with a long green beak, and behind his outstretched wings a rainbow. All among the silken arabesques, butterflies were delicately poised, golden butterflies and black butterflies, and butterflies that were gold and black. The closer you looked, the more there was to see ; intricate markings

on the butterfly wings, purple and grass-green and apricot;
tiny stamens springing from every flower; circles that wisely
ringed the eye of each separate stork. Not one stork was like
another, and not one butterfly; nor was it incredibly foolish
that this discovery should make you happy. And when you
had looked closely, you looked again, from a distance, to exult
in the perfection of the whole coat, stiff and gleaming folds of
anemone pink, lining that was a flash of green lightning, bands
of a blue so intense that for very depth of colour it appeared to
stir and shift and shudder, as the depths of the sea will stir
while you look down into it.

—"By Jove!" muttered Giles. "Finest specimen I've
ever seen!"

"But it is colos*sal!* It is wunderbar!" simultaneously
from Aunt Elsa.

And Queenie cried out: "Oh, Loraine, how perfectly
gorgeous you'd look in it!" Furthermore, she told the constellations: "Loraine looks gorgeous in things that most
people can't wear without looking queer and funny!"

Loraine said, in a voice that sounded harshly, as though two
metals had been struck together: "Put it on, Val. Queenie's
quite right, you'll look gorgeous in it."

Giles, struck by the twist she had given Queenie's burst of
enthusiasm, glanced swiftly, apprehensively, at her. . . . She
was not happy and restful any more, and her hands trembled
with impatience as she helped Val on with the coat. Val was a
superb woman with nothing frail nor exotic in her appearance.
Health was clear in her brown skin; in the curves of her mouth,
firm and yet indolent; in the burnish on her ash-gold shingled
hair. The Chinese coat hung upon her impersonally as though
on alien shoulders. The Italian children burst into enthusiastic
admiration at seeing their mistress so radiantly apparelled.
She pivoted slowly, displaying herself, spreading her arms to
show the wide square of her sleeves.

And Loraine turned to Richard, and said confidentially,
as though she could not withhold her admiration any longer:
"Wouldn't Val look magnificent in riding kit?"

"COUSIN RICHARD'S going to take me home to-night," announced Loraine, at the end of a boisterous evening—boisterous as far as she was concerned. She had changed quite suddenly from the little-Spanish-princess mood, quaint and old-fashioned, to a fury of restlessness, attracting attention in every hectic way she could. She had given negro imitations; she had flung her arms about Aunt Elsa's neck, tom-boy fashion, and swung her off her feet, at the same time pacifying her with soft, Irish endearments; she had made Terry dance with her: " Oi! First unique performance of our special Kerry Blues . . . dedicated to the plural of his race! . . . An' was this the way of it, me sweet heart of a dog?" And she had shown off Queenie's thraldom by first snubbing the girl brutally, and then restoring her to favour. None of this exhibition was meant, individually, for Richard or even for Giles; it was all hurled at Val :—" *You* have the coat! But these gifts, and these, and these, are mine . . ." Thus Giles, who, after eight months, was learning to know his Loraine, interpreted her defiant looks at Val; her stolen, longing looks at the treasure which Stephen Greenways had sent out to Val.

And then Loraine had told her maddest stories, in which brigands, smugglers, elephant-trainers, and any handy form of potentate, flung their admiration round her like a dark cloak with a rich lining. She whirled her hearers along by the roads and seas which Giles and she had travelled, since last February : down the Adriatic coast on the Dalmatian side, into the Grecian Archipelago ; up through Roumania ; up the Danube ; and to Vienna in September, after their long solitudes in wild places : " And it was like a breath of home again, to me, though mind you, I'd never been there in my life before. But the trail of my own family was in every street I saw, and on every tongue I heard speaking. . . . And I said to Giles : ' I've got to follow it up. Now I know what it is that I've been lone and hungering for, these months. For I must be with my own flesh and blood again, or die. And if none of them are left in Vienna, then, du lieber Gott ! what's to prevent us going South to Italy, where my cousin Val is, and my Aunt Elsa, and settling down near them for a while ? ' "

" What indeed ? " murmured Val. . . .

Giles did not contradict any of Loraine's tales and rhapsodies. Now and then, under his clipped moustache, his mouth twitched humorously ; but his eyes remained angry, deep-set under his brows ; that fixed spark of anger which last February and a scene with Toni, had brought along.

Loraine had them all with her in Vienna now, and Aunt Elsa was getting excited. . . . What a noise the two of them made, like a crowd—a chattering, sparkling crowd, in a café. Val, too, lay back in her arm-chair, and, like Giles, was content to watch them, half-abstractedly. . . . Now and then her eyes strayed towards the coat where it lay spread upon the divan. She was happy that evening.

And Richard thought : " Foreigners ! "

And Queenie, from another angle, thought : " Foreigners ! "

. . . While Loraine and Aunt Elsa danced their eager, hilarious memories :

" Those sandwich at Demmel's—you went in there ? The Hof-Konditorei ? Ach, delicious ! And especially the Lachs— the smoked salmon ! " " Aunt Elsa, one morning we took a droschke and drove up to the Kobenzl, and had our coffee and rolls there—high up, oh *high* on the terrace, with all Vienna below us. The sun smiting the tall, tall Stephanskirche, and the dome of the Karlskirche, and—oh, do you remember what a sunset was like, downy raspberries solemnly crushed between the two spires of the Votif, when I went in for Chorale every evening . . . And one morning I passed, and the Tailors of Vienna were inside, consecrating their heraldic device. . . . They came out in mediæval costume, and rode on horseback with banners, and all the crowd cheered. . . . It was so like

Vienna, to take their tailors so seriously, and almost nothing else ! "

Aunt Elsa metaphorically ducked her head and rushed in under Loraine's whirlwind of enthusiasm : " Ze Prater-Allée. . . . Straight straight down many miles between the green trees. And there the officers rode, so fesch ! And the Royal family—ach, die arme Elisabet !—Tell me, then, Loraine, did you enter the Spanische Reitschule ? Did you see the vonderful horses from Arabia that no one else but royalty must ride, effer ? "

" And the blue trout, at Schöner's, in the Siebensternengasse —swimming in their tanks ! And the cool restaurant down in the vaults of the Rathauskeller——"

" Schöner's ?—but did you not go to Sacher's ? All the finest people went bummelling to Sacher's—— It was gay in Vienna, in those days when I was a girl—ach, yes ! And we bought plums cheap, you would wonder yourself, in the old Hoher Markt ! "

" . . . Drank heurigen Wein at the Rockenbauer—and the students sang : ' Mädel, ruck ruck ruck—— ' "

" —An meiner grünen Sei-ei-te ! " chimed in Aunt Elsa. And they finished the chorus together.

" You went to the Opera——"

" Rosenkavalier ! Oh, Aunt Elsa——"

" New music, that. Good, yes ! but I vos taken to Zauber-flöte ven a young girl. Mozart ! Himmlisch ! If I had not married so young, I meant to sing, myself, at the Opernhaus in Wien, one day.—Fancy this, Loraine, it vill make you laugh : at my Aunt Laura's wedding I was a little bridesmaid in white tulle mit silver dots and a wreath of coral on my curly hair ! Goldig ! Your Uncle Leon—or was it Karl ?—or was it not your uncle ?—but still, he put me on ze table, and ' Hoch ! ' they all cried, and at once I sit myself into the middle of the big Chocoladen-Torte . . . Quatsch ! "

—Giles was getting restless. He broke in, two or three times, in attempts to interrupt them ; persistently trying to fix attention on a certain Viennese musical-comedy—the very latest, which they had heard and liked : " It hasn't come to

England yet; it won't get there until next year, of course.
They start from Vienna, and only come to England later.
' Grafin Maritza.'—You look out for it, Marcus; it's jolly
good! But it won't be over until next year. There's a
wonderful fox-trot in it. Do you remember, Loraine—
' Varasdin '? All London will be humming it, next season. . . .
But it won't be new to us. We'll have heard it already in
Vienna . . . ' Varasdin ' . . . this is how it goes . . . gorgeous
rhythm. . . .

Tempo di Fox Trot.

> " Komm mit nach Varasdin,
>   So lange noch die Rosen blühn;
>   Dort wollen wir glucklich sein—"

. . . Impetuously, he pulled Queenie to her feet, and fox-
trotted with her, still trolling the jovial chorus. . . . If Queenie
had only known it, he was not dancing with hin er a room in
Italy. . . . He was once more back in the studio with Toni—
having a good time—popular—the best dancer. . . . He had
not dropped out yet! Why, this melody, this tune of the
season—he was ahead of them all . . . he had heard it in
Vienna! Didn't that prove——?—He was sick of it before
Colin and Toni and all their gang had even heard of
it. . . .

" Hel-*lo!* " thought Richard; " he's home-sick! " . . .
Home-sickness was a thing Richard could understand and compassionate, when it was for England; he could perceive home-
sickness sensitively, before anyone else; and perceivlng it
hidden behind this pitiful outburst, actuating every jerky
irrelevant boast in it, he felt the friendlier towards Giles
Goddard. Everything here was so beastly exotic: Italian
servants; Chinese coat; Aunt Elsa and Loraine with their
Vienna and Vienna. . . . " Poor devil! He's home-sick! "

—And Giles danced with flattered Queenie, out into the
hall, and out through the open door.

" Not raining any more, and it's moonlight," he called back
to the others. ". . . It's Moonlight in Kalua." . . . And
then they heard Queenie's :

" Oh, do let's go up among the olives for a few moments.
It's so lovely there, with the moon ! "

> ". . . Denn meine Leidenschaft
> Brennt heisser wie der Goulasch-Saft ! "

which means that my passion for you, Queenie, is hotter than
gravy with red pepper in it."

" Oh, Giles, you *mustn't* . . ." Queenie giggled.

Their voices died away.

Richard supposed that there would be an immediate outbreak of tigress-woman from Loraine, at seeing her mate thus
snatched away from her ; tempestuous scenes and dagger
threats ! But Loraine, on the contrary, appeared peculiarly
satisfied by the departure of Giles with Queenie, as though it
coincided with a plan of her own, as yet unrevealed. She
gave a low chuckle, echoed by Val.

" At it again," said the latter, softly. " Happy Queenie ! "

Aunt Elsa rose to her feet in some excitement : " It is not
right, after ten o'clock, and she a young girl, up there is ze
olives where no one is. Loraine, you should call him back.
Val, you should call her back. She is in your charge out here,
isn't it ? How does it look to those who see zem ? "

" Darling Aunt Elsa," Val pacified her, " Queenie's flirtations
wouldn't hurt a fly ! At heart, she's just a little prude. I've
heard her put a man through his paces so often. So has Loraine."

" Yes, this is how it goes," said Loraine ; " we were listening
once, after Queenie had got off with that Taylor man, at Santa
Nucia. She was standing at the window, flicking the blind-
cord about, her back to the room . . ." Quite remarkably,
Loraine became Queenie : it was a complete transforma-
tion ; her movements were Queenie's, and the way she held
her head.

. . . " And he came up behind her : ' Why are you so cross
with me to-night ? '

" ' Oh, I'm *not* cross with you.'

" ' Oh yes, you are.'

" ' If you think so, I suppose I am. I didn't know I was.'

" ' What have I done ? '

" ' Nothing.'

" ' Perhaps I should have done *something*, then ? '

" ' You must do as you like, of course.'

" ' No, I want to do as *you* like.'

" ' It doesn't make any difference to me.'

" ' Sure ? '

" ' Oh, I'm never sure about anything.'

" ' Some people are quite sure about one thing.'

" ' Some people isn't everybody, are they ? '

" ' No, but they wish they were.'

" ' Do they ? '

" ' You know I do. . . . Are you ever going to forgive me, Queenie ? '

" ' It can't make any difference to you.'

" ' Can't it ? '

" ' Can it ? '

" ' That's for you to say.'

" ' Of course I forgive you, silly boy.'

" ' Then you aren't angry with me any more ? '

" ' I never was. I said so.'

" ' You didn't ! You said—oh well, never mind. What are you going to give me to prove you forgive me ? '

" ' I can't give you anything that you want, can I ? '

" ' *Can't* you ? ' "—Young Taylor, as assumed by Loraine, was growing deeper and more intense with every dive below the surface of his emotions ; and still Queenie—Loraine flicked her personality with marvellous ease from one to the other—stood by the window, her head turned towards him over her shoulder, her fingers airily flicking the blind-cord :

—" ' Perhaps I don't mean what you mean.'

" ' I can only mean one thing.'

" ' Is it what you were saying so seriously to Miss Carlisle, last night out on the terrace ? '

" ' What did I say to Miss Carlisle ? '

" ' How should *I* know ? . . . She's very pretty.'

" ' Oh, yes, she's pretty. She dances prettily. But what comes next ? '

" ' I don't know,' " said Queenie—Loraine, archly provocative.

" ' There's nothing in her.'

" ' Ah ! there spoke the embittered man of the world.'

" ' Are you never serious ? '

" ' It's nice to be serious sometimes,' " wistfully. " ' Only one's afraid, isn't one, to let oneself go ? '

" ' Is one ? "

" ' Well, isn't one ? '

" ' Do you mean what I mean ? '

" ' I don't know what you mean.'

" ' Don't you ? Well, do I ? '

" ' You ought to know ! ' "—

—" Oh, shut up ! " cried Val. She and Richard were helpless with laughter. " She's never as bad as that ! "

" I sink it is dreadful, dreadful," said Aunt Elsa. " I do not know vot they were talking about all the time ! "

" No," shrugged Loraine, " nor did I ; nor did they. I believe there was some question of a kiss playing hide-and seek under it all ! But I can't be sure, even now ! "

" But do you mean to tell me," protested Richard, " that Goddard plays up to that sort of footling game ? That that's what they're doing now ? "

" Not quite, no. Giles confides in her ; confides in her more than in any of us. We try to rag him out of it. But he says he can't help it ; it's a fatal fascination ; his one unconquerable vice. He makes most lurid revelations to Queenie, some of them almost true, just to hear the damn-fool things she'll say, and watch her eyelids flutter, and hear her trying to make him a better man ! There's something prettily religious about our Queenie, in addition to all our other troubles with her. She's rather ' Mercy among the heathens,' in this house— ' Sign of the Cross,' you know, especially church-time on Sunday morning. What Giles won't see is that it's very trying for us, when he singles out Queenie to hear the story of his life. She's simply thick with sweet importance for hours afterwards ! "

Loraine put in: "Like a white blanc-mange that's had a cherry stuck in it!"

"Thought you were keen on her," growled Richard.

"Not at all, Cousin Richard. She's keen on me. Such a difference! She calls me 'Loveliest,' when really moved. And anyway," Loraine added, shaking back her head, "I'm not going to wait about for them, while Giles throbs his soul inside-out, up yonder in them oonlight. I'm for home. Cousin Richard will see me down the mule track."

"Now zat I *vill* not have!" Aunt Elsa rose to a crescendo again. "Richard is tired. He's had his long journey, isn't it, and must go to bed? And you, Loraine, vill vait here quietly with me, while Val sends one of the little servants to fetch down the ozzer two, and you and Giles can go home. So, nobody will be disturbed or put out of their way. That poor, poor boy can hardly keep his eyes open," glancing at Richard, who grinned, and asked Aunt Elsa if she thought sitting in a train all day, and walking once up the mule-track and once down again, was equal to a day's stiff ploughing, single-handed, after frost!

"Of zat, I don't know. I may be nossing but a syphon in zis house; but in zis, I *vill* be obeyed!"

But Loraine hugged her, and laughed, and cried out: "Come on, then, Cousin Richard!" And Val laughed, too, and murmured sleepily:

"I don't think I can send Stefania after the truants, Aunt Elsa. They're all right, really. I expect Queenie will be along home, presently."

Richard and Loraine were already gone.

"I'd rather be vamped by Loraine than by Queenie, on the whole," Val was beginning, carelessly—— And then she saw that Aunt Elsa was crying, her eyes screwed up into a dolorous grimace, and the little tears chasing swiftly over her wrinkled crab-apple cheeks. . . .

"Aunt Elsa, *darling*, what is it? Have we been rude? Have you hurt yourself?" But she could not think of anything that had transpired during the last few hours, and certainly not during the last few minutes, that could have had the effect of making Aunt Elsa cry. Surely they had all been petting her ; making rather a fuss of her ; waiting courteously, even with deference, to hear what she had to say on any subject, before in actual fact, they took no notice of it ?

And Aunt Elsa, for her part, could not explain to Val that she was weeping because no one was afraid of her any more, and she had suddenly realised it. . . .

It was true, then, that they were old and done-for, the aunts ; their force broken for good. What Aunt Elsa had enjoyed in former days had been, not so much tyrannising over the weak, ordering them hither and thither, and striking panic into them by her scoldings ; but doing battle with those younger ones who presently grew strong enough to rebel against her. Those were, indeed, fine times, when they disobeyed her ; defied her ; told her what they thought of her and she had screamed back ! Now, instead, they were all kind ; so kind ! She could not rule them any more ; the mysterious power had left her ; she had forgotten the trick of it. Now, when she uprose wrathfully, and said : " I forbid it ! You shall not go up in the olives ! " and " You must not go down the hill ! "— they, instead of subsiding, terrified, as Truda's generation had done—Truda and Wanda and her own Freda ; or else shouting back : " I'll do as I like, I tell you. I won't be told what to do. It's my life, isn't it, not yours ? " as Val, Richard, Maxine, Toni had dared to do, while they were still in their teens— now, they smiled, and took such constant care not to hurt her feelings : " *Darling* Aunt Elsa ! " Their manners to her were charming, now ; they could even afford, occasionally, when not too inconvenient, to give in to her ; to make a show of obedience . . . The aunts were growing old. . . .

Aunt Elsa wept ; it was humiliating, and not nearly so much fun as when they had been afraid !

.   .   .   .

Down on the mule-track, under the colourless shimmer of the olives, Loraine was saying impulsively :

" Look here, Cousin Richard, I wish you'd tell me—I've been so anxious to know that it's all right—about Val and

Stephen Greenways? . . . Did he send her any sort of message, when he gave you that coat for her? Did he say nothing, nothing at all to show that he knew, already, that our Val was different from all the rest of the world? Ah, now, did he?"

Richard remained stolid. "He'd hardly be likely to, while running beside a moving train, would he?"

"You know very well what I mean," impatiently. "Why do you pretend you are dull or slow-witted? Two or three words would be enough to show. What exactly did he say, then, when he gave you the parcel? Had he spoken about it before?"

"I'd never met him before. He knows Val's people, doesn't he? It was they who told him I was coming out here. I like the look of him. He seemed a capital fellow."

"One of the best!"—Loraine mocked the hearty tones of one man when he speaks of another.—"A capital fellow!" And then she persisted: "What *were* his exact words when he handed you the parcel through the window of the train?"

"He said, more or less: 'Had an awful job to catch you; thought the train went at eleven instead of ten-thirty. Look here, I want you to take this out to San Goffredo for me. Will you?'"

"Is that absolutely all?"

"Absolutely all. Why?"

Loraine, who had been skimming to and fro between the trunks of the trees, stood still in the middle of the path: "I want you to take this out to San Goffredo for me."—She was not irritable nor truculent, any more. Indeed, she was looking rather as Val had looked, an hour ago—dreamy, with lips now wayward, now tender; the corners of her eyes tilted with laughing surprise, as though someone had given her a present....

"I'm used to this way down," she said at last, abstractedly. "Go back now, Cousin Richard; Aunt Elsa was cross that I took you away, the dear woman! It was just the company I wanted, for a part of the way. Good night! good night!"

"I'm coming as far as your door," Richard persisted. "It's lonely here, and—you can't tell, I suppose. . . . Quite likely there are dagoes about?"

"Quite likely, in Dago-land!" echoed Loraine, but not

unkindly. " Listen, though ! Aren't they after calling you, from up there ? Good night ! " She ran so quickly ahead of him, down the uneven, stony track, that he did not vainly try to overtake her, not knowing his way ; and with a shrug of the shoulders for her caprices, turned to climb back. He had thought she was only pretending to be rid of him, when she said that they were calling him from the top. Presently, however, as he drew nearer, his ears—not as fine as hers— caught Val's : " Richard, Richard, do make haste ! "

. . . " Giles has sprained his ankle, or done something to it," she assured him, hurriedly, when he reached the top, where she stood waiting. "—Fox-trotting about on the terraces, the idiots ! Can you help us bring him in ? The stones in those loose walls often give way, if you're not looking out. He's going to sleep in our sun-room, to-night. And probably for the next three weeks. Aunt Elsa said : ' Vat did I tell you, isn't it ? ' at least seventeen times, bless her."—All this, breathlessly, while Richard strode beside her, up the garden, past the house, and over the terraces to where a grove of olives grew thickly on the lower slopes of the hills behind. Richard, who had the shoulders and muscles of a young bull, was, as Giles thankfully declared, the man out of all others he would have chosen—the very pick of English heroes, in fact !—to carry him the two hundred yards or so from the scene of his accident, to the divan in what Val called the sun-room.

. . . " If you don't mind, Miss Power," Queenie broke in, rather pale and agitated, " hadn't I better run down and sleep with Loveliest, to-night ? She'll be alone, you see ; and she won't know what's happened. We can't leave her alone, can we ? If I go down, I can look after her."

" I suppose you'd better," Val conceded, for the moment more preoccupied with Giles' foot, which, indeed, had received a pretty serious wrench, than with the vital question of who was to look after Loraine. " Richard, see Queenie down to Loraine's, will you ? It's just at the bottom of the mule-track, you know."

" That poor boy ! " wailed Aunt Elsa. " He must be, quite surely, dead with sleep from all he has to do to-night ! "

Queenie hesitated : " I shall be all right, alone," she began. Richard grinned. " I think that poor boy can just manage to stagger a few paces further. I shan't have to carry you, at any rate, shall I, Miss Bell ? " And they heard a sweet girlish voice imploring him to call her " Queenie," as the front door banged behind them.

" She's a priceless ass ! " murmured Giles ; as, years ago, he had said of Aimée Lequesne. Queenie a little resembled Aimée, though she was younger, prettier, less elegant, more pink-rose and dew-drop. The type held a perverse fascination for Giles. He could not prevent himself from leading them on to display their full pricelessness ! Besides—as he explained to Val—by confiding in them, you had all the pleasure of getting it off your chest, without any of the after-sorrow of knowing that you had parted from your secrets, because they never even began to understand what you were driving at !

. . . All this, while she was bathing his foot, under Aunt Elsa's directions. Aunt Elsa thought him mad, and told him so :

" When I vas a young girl, the young gentlemen admired me, or zey did not. If zey admired me, zey took me for a walk, or a drive in the Prater, and there was a little—a very little, coquetting and compliments ; but zey *meant* ze compliments ; and sometimes zey were—oh, but in despair ! " Aunt Elsa went on, dimpling at the recollection. " But if zey did not admire me ; if, for instance, zey preferred girls who were tall, with a fine figure, blonde and serious ; zen zey did not take *me* for walks ; zey took another, and I was not offended ! Why should I be ? There were always plenty ! Plenty ! "

—" Oi ! " Giles cried out, in pain ; " that's hot ! You hell-cat, take it off ! " but Val serenely went on bathing his ankle.

" But," finished Aunt Elsa, " as for this modern silliness : ' I take her out and flatter her because she is an ass ; and not because I admire her von little bit '—of zat, there vas nossing ; and very glad I am to live then, and not now, when one never knows, and young men use ugly words like ' hell-cat ' when a clever girl does her best for them."

" —I apologise, Val," said Giles.

" I accept your apology, Giles," said Val.

"Put the gramophone where I can turn it on, before you go to bed."

"In ze *night?*" shrilled Aunt Elsa. "I beg of you, Val, you vill do no such thing that he asks! He can have a nice book and one aspirin."

Giles looked shocked. "Dope? Aspirin? Ought I, really? Wouldn't the gramophone be more wholesome?". . . And Aunt Elsa twinkled appreciation at him. She loved being teased by a good-looking man:

"You nottee boy!" and then followed a slap.

They made him comfortable, without the gramophone within reach, and went up to their beds.

"Tell Richard to lock up when he comes in, will you, Giles?"

"And you two boys are not to talk through half the night," was Aunt Elsa's parting adjuration. Her tears had eased her; and while she had one of her rampageous children—as they seemed to her—ill under her roof, or even under Val's roof, she would be entirely happy.

Presently Richard came in.

"You don't seem worn out, yet," Giles remarked. "Sit down and have a pipe before you turn in, won't you?"

Richard nodded. "How's the foot?" as he sank down at the end of the divan.

"Throbbing like hell! It would be better if you got off it, you know!"

Richard got off it. "Sorry!"

"Don't mention it! It was the other one!"

There was a long silence.

"Started hunting before you left, I suppose?"

"Barely. Foot-and-mouth broke out, down there; it didn't come near my farm, luckily; but it'll do in some of the hunting."

"You haven't seen much of my guv'nor, then?"

"No; he's been in town a lot, this autumn."

"Old scoundrel!" affectionately, from Giles.

A long silence again.

"Don't you ever get bored, down there? You never go up to London, yourself?" asked Giles.

"Bored? Good Lord! With two-hundred-and-seventy

acres to attend to? Not to mention a wife and a couple of sons! But I should think you get bored out here, doing nothing, don't you?"

The talk was nearing a perilous subject. . . .

"Doing nothing?" Giles repeated, with sudden bitterness. "Why, what have I ever done, since the War? If you are a born loafer, you don't notice it when you're doing nothing."

Richard began, awkwardly: "You had four years of fighting, and two out in Mespot afterwards . . ."

"Cologne, the last year," Giles corrected him. "But in an odd sort of way, you know, Marcus—I don't know if it has ever struck you?—the War has done us in. We'll never do anything else. I don't mean fellows who've got to tear round and find something, or they'd starve; they may end in pulling off a career; but when we needn't, like myself, we can always say: 'Oh, well, I fought in the War!'—and there it stands; an excuse, if you like; but a definite achievement—something done—we *have* fought in the War. Now in the days before there was a war, a man couldn't just slop about and dance and loaf and damn-all else, for the very shame of it; for the shame of having nothing whatever to put to his credit. Well—here I am, a useless waster; but the landscape isn't quite blank. My war service, such as it is, sticks up out of the flat, like—like the monument to the Dover Patrol on the cliffs at St. Margaret's."

Richard thought his companion was a trifle feverish; but there was sense in what he said, too. "Well, and here *I* am," he countered. "And I didn't fight in the War. Wish to God I had!"

"Too young, weren't you?" But Giles knew Richard's story. He had heard it first from Toni, and then from Val.

"Too young until 1917, and then I was interned. I'd been born in Germany, you see."

"Hard luck!"

"Yes," Richard assented. . . . He knocked out his pipe and got up. "We shall have Aunt Elsa down on us if we talk any longer." He was definitely liking Giles more and more; less for what had been said, than for a strange sympathy between them regarding the much, as yet, left unsaid. "Do you want anything before I leave you? How's the foot, now?"

"Still hurting like hell, thanks! No, I don't want anything. Good night."

"Good night."

He caught a flash of the other man's smile, just as he turned to leave the room . . . Giles had realised the sudden melting of Richard's prejudice, and had silently acknowledged it. They parted that night without a single mention of Loraine, or of running away . . . or of Toni.

CHAPTER IV

LORAINE began to make trouble.

From the moment she was inspired with the notion that the coat might have been meant for her, she did actually succeed in believing it. There had been just one angry hour when Val had worn it, and Val had owned it, and had dared to look happy about it . . . Loraine coveted that coat as never before in her life had she coveted a gift. It meant so infinitely much more to her than it could ever mean to Val, who preferred truth stripped of the hangings of romance, and bare lines that never pranced into arabesques. But Loraine was infatuated; she felt that if she could live with this coat, and touch its richness whenever she was appalled by day after day's dull and tepid routine; if she could learn, and learn by heart, the gracious poise of every butterfly on the deep-sounding blue of its background, she could be entirely content. She had been given beautiful things before now, but never yet such decorative perfection as these folds of brocade, stiffly encrusted and weighted down with their embroidered fantasies.

. . . Stephen Greenways, of course, had meant the coat for her, and not for Val. She had not been sure whether her legendary spell had fallen upon Stephen and entranced him, while he had been staying up at Val's cottage. He had teased her and argued with her, and he had looked at her very often, and they had gone fish-spearing on the Mediterranean, and he had talked about travel, a matter-of-fact Othello; and about drugs with perilous uses. "I'm utterly a nomad at heart!" Loraine had said. . . .

During one of the hours they had been together, he had kissed her, choosing for his sudden subjection an odd, a grotesque moment, when she had not been expecting it, out of all the

hours when she had felt herself fascinating and inscrutable. . . .
What had possessed the man, at sight of her light-hearted
clowning? It was at twilight on a muddy evening, when they
had gone to dig up plants for Val's garden, from around a
deserted house in the hills. One of the dogs had fallen into a
sunken tank, nearly hidden by a tangle of laurels and fig trees
and wild myrtle, and had been unable to haul himself out.
Loraine, always ahead of the rest of the party, had forthwith
plunged in and handed him up, dripping, to the others on the
bank. It was a wet, but not in the least a dangerous rescue,
and she did not try to make heroic capital out of it. She
simply took off her soaked woolly skirt and jumper; and
accepted any stray clothing that Queenie, Stephen, and Giles
could contribute. The result might have been a spirited
painting by Caldecott, or any other nursery artist who rendered
his pirates more highly-coloured than fearsome : bright blue
knickers and gum-boots—those were her own. Then a copper-
orange jersey and a shaggy lemon-yellow scarf, gaily clashing,
and both hugely too large for her slimness ; and Giles' old
green broad-brimmed hat-of-all-shapes, which she clapped
rakishly on her head to cover one eye ; and went capering and
dancing down the track, glorying in the shouts of robust laughter that must greet her comic appearance. Loraine never
minded making a fool of herself. Giles and Queenie had gone
on ahead ; and only Stephen was waiting. . . . And that was
when he had so surprisingly kissed her. " You *did* look such a
jolly kid ! " was his sole remark, afterwards.

But now, triumphantly, she knew that he had sent her the
coat as a proof of the affinity between them, of the silken thread
stretched tight between soul and soul. He would know that
she would look strange and marvellous in that strange coat.
Stitch by stitch, her mind worked a complex pattern of his
actions ; every sentence he had spoken, she cunningly altered
to express what his silence had never yet expressed. Loraine
had not cared over-much about him—then ; but she cared now
about the man whose intuitions had prompted him to such a
dramatic acknowledgment of her spell, as deliberately to wait
till just so long afterwards, and then, without any accompanying

babble, to choose such rich mysterious vehicle to express him —or to express her as she had appeared to him.

And now a foolish, an idiotic mistake had resulted in the coat going to Val, and not to her. Richard Marcus, Cousin Richard—he was a born blunderer! Loraine had seen that from the first. And his blunder had worked itself out antagonistically to her, influenced by his subterranean dislike.

" What am I going to do ? " Loraine wondered. Straightforwardly, she could have gone to Val and said : " Stephen Greenways meant the coat for me ; give it up ! " Or she could have written to Stephen : " The Chinese coat which you meant for me, has gone to Val. Please tell her at once that I am to have it." But these were not Loraine's ways of accomplishment ; she saw plot after plot unfolding, flower-like in front of her ; and her spirit trembled and thrilled and was exultant at the prospect of so many exquisite, minute devices. She had set up Val on an eminence to be worshipped—head of her family ; she, a little tribal outsider, for ever wandering about, seeking a pretext for submission to her tribal instincts ; she was ready to be extravagantly generous, in spirit and in service, both to Toni, and, after Toni had rejected her, to Val. But Val would have nothing so theatrical as worship or prostration ; nor even a specially encircled, specially consecrated duo of kinship,— Loraine and Val against the world, as Loraine would so gladly have made it. Very well then, since Val would not be her goddess, Loraine, bored with conditions of level tranquillity, was glad now to be able to invest her with a part of at least some significance, and one with the possibility of sensational development in it. The fact that Val, unconscious of what was being woven around her, would have hated such a part, amused Loraine all the more ! She cared, temporarily, not a whit for Val's natural reactions. Val had the coat ; so Val was a creature to be destroyed. Afterwards, when she had stripped her, Loraine would love her, and be sorry, and make a coat for her out of caresses ; and Val would be beholden to her for this. They were all arrogant, these—royal Rakonitz women. They all thought they could go their way, unchallenged, doing as they liked : rejecting love ; choosing it ; mocking at it . . . Val had advised Loraine, once, to leave amateur theatricals at the bottom of the hill, when she came up ! Right ! she should have theatricals forced upon her, and not so amateur at that ! . . . Loraine went up the hill.

But she was not going to ask to have her coat back ; nothing so crude ! It was enough for her to know, from a distance, that it *was* her coat ; enough, that Stephen should have meant it for her. Naturally, she was not going to take it away from Val, nor even let Val know that she had this power to claim it. Val must be protected ; allowed her coat, but by Loraine's sanction only, and by Loraine's sacrifice. . . . And Val need not know this, either. It was enough, again, that Loraine should know. "Praise unto Loraine, the Magnificent ! " . . . And, feeling exactly like that, she swung herself into the sun-room through one of its wide, open windows, on the morning following Giles' accident.

Queenie had already left Villa Bel Respiro, where Loraine lived, and gone up to her housekeeping duties, a couple of hours earlier. Loraine found her, now, looking fresh and sweet in pale pink, ministering to Giles' foot ; the very sight of her a refreshment—so Loraine was sure Queenie was sure !—to his hot, feverish eyes ; as her fair head, unconscious of self, bent pityingly over the injured ankle ; and her deft, cool little fingers massaged it the wrong way. . . .

" Oi ! " cried Loraine. " What the hell do you think you're doing, Queenie ? "

" It's got to be rubbed the way the blood flows," said Queenie, positive but vague ; and Giles' eyes threw a silent, anguished appeal for help, at the new-comer.

" And which way *does* the blood flow ? " enquired Loraine, with deep interest.

Queenie began : " I'm sure I heard the Doctor say when Norman, my brother, sprained the muscles of his calf——"

" All right," said Loraine, brutally. . . . She deemed it a fitting lesson for Giles that, fox-trotting with Queenie by moonlight, he should later have to submit to Queenie's un-technical nursing. " Go on ! I'll watch." But she could not watch for long ; the punishment to herself was too great, as it

always is to those who are aware of how a job ought to be done.
" Ah now, be gone and see about the laundry, Queenie, do !
Are you having the Doctor for this foot ? You'd better send
for him. It's badly swollen. Wait a minute while I see if
there are bones broken. No—no, I think not. But there
might be a tendon snapped, or more than one."

" You do everything like a professional, Loraine ; and a good
'un at that," said Giles, with a sigh of relief, as Loraine took
over entire control of the fomenting, massaging, and bandaging
departments ; and Queenie, a little hurt and offended, with-
drew. " Queenie's idea of nursing a fellow is to offer to read
to him. She seemed to think I couldn't read for myself, as
I've hurt my foot ! "

" What were you just telling her, last night, when the gods
tripped you up ? " Loraine enquired, severely ; and Giles
warded her off with an evasive :

" Oh, we were talking about Colin's play. First night
yesterday, you know."

" Do you wish you had been there ? "

He did not answer. Presently, with seeming irrelevance, he
said : " Queenie told me that every man had it in him to do
something, if only he tried."

" I'm shaw ! "

Giles made a quick, restless movement under her hands.
. . . Don't use that phrase. It's—silly."

" And why not ? All the gang were using it, two years ago.
A bit out-of-date, perhaps, but Colin's play will be pumping
some new slang into the waiting world, I've no doubt. Though
it'll be stale again, by the time it drifts out here."

Again, Giles did not reply. He was humming a tune—
" Varasdin " . . . " Queenie said," he began once more, " that
a man ought to do manly work. She didn't quite think that
acting and writing plays and dancing—and all that sort of
thing—*was* manly. I asked her if she meant the sort of work
that should be done in a sun-helmet ? She said : ' Yes, something like that.' And she was quite sure that I had something
in me which would make me a good leader of men. I told her
that I felt a most dreadful blighter, loafing about and doing

nothing; and she said that if I really loved you as you ought to be loved, being so wonderful, I'd feel I had to be doing something—something rather grand and big, so that you shouldn't despise me; and that even if I failed, that failure is sometimes better than success, and very often brought out the best in a man. . . . It was all very beautiful, Loraine ! And I meant to hew down a whole forest of trees, for your sake, with an axe, and wearing a sun-helmet and brawny muscles. . . . But then part of the wall slid and toppled, and me with it; and I shan't be able to get down the mule-track for a week at least, I should say. How will you manage without me ? "

" I don't know which of all that monologue I'll be answering first. It's full of good points, that it is. And of course if you like to get yourself laid up here among all my enemies, and no road where a carriage can drive up or down to fetch you away——"

" What enemies ? "

" Cousin Richard, to begin with. He hates me ! "

" My dear old kid——"

" He hates me," repeated Loraine, making entirely expert and practical movements with her hands, and wildly false and fantastic gestures with her temperament. " He'd do me harm if he could. He'll turn everyone against me. He'll make them disbelieve every single word I say. He'll make me feel I'm not welcome, like a blow in the face, every time I enter this door."

" You never do," Giles interrupted, good-humouredly. " You always leap in by the window, even when the door's nearer ! " He tried to beguile her from rhetoric, by teasing her over trivial matters. " It's one of your theatrical tricks, as Val calls them."

" Ah . . . yes, does she ? " . . . Loraine brooded a moment on this. " Where is Val ? "

" At the end of the garden, in the studio, working like a maniac to finish off something on hand now, because she's got a new idea she wants to carry out quickly. Something to do with painting that coat of hers, I think."

" Coat of hers," repeated Loraine, enigmatically. ". . . You're not to be telling anyone what I'm going to be telling you, Giles?"

" You're pulling that bandage infernally tight ! " said Giles.
" All right, go on ! I won't tell."

" It's got to be tight. That coat of hers—that coat of
hers——"

" Well ? " impatiently. " Gorgeous thing, isn't it ? I
thought at the time, when we turned up here and found
Greenways, that he was keen on her."

" And he might have been, if we hadn't turned up here.
Ah, it's my old curse, Giles——" Her eyes grew large and
haunted. . . . " It's my curse and my destiny, and I can't help
it, and I hate myself ; I long for peace, but there's trouble
wherever I go, following me ; where there was quiet before,
comes catastrophe. . . . It's my curse and my destiny and my
fate, and I wish it were different ! Oh, how I wish it were
different ! I'm not articulate, like all you clever people—I
can't express my meaning. . . . It's dreadful when your tongue
is tied on a short string. . . . And now here's sorrow again ! "

Giles kept to himself his slightly sardonic rendering of all
this : that Loraine did indeed create trouble ; but not in the
mysterious, foredoomed style of Deirdre of the Sorrows, and
Helen of Troy : " Where'er I come, I bring calamity." . . .
Not as she preferred to picture it—herself a victim, helpless in
the meshes cast by her own inevitable and unwilling bewitch-
ments. . . . No, there was trouble wherever Loraine came,
simply because Loraine brought trouble, Loraine made trouble,
Loraine *liked* trouble. It was eight months, now, since Giles
had run away with her. For eight months he and she had been
constantly together. You cannot be the fool of an illusion for
an indefinite period. Besides, Loraine permitted her fools to
break away quite easily, and without effort to keep them, when
illusion was over. She did not mind. Not in that way was she
tiresome. All her energies were bent on attracting, by enchant-
ments crude or subtle, those who might be reluctantly drawn
towards her ; and she wasted none on those who had already
walked beside her in the flowering meads . . . " Belle Dame
Sans Merci " . . . and were rubbing dazed eyes, not quite
awake, upon the cold hill-side.

She and Giles had almost, but only quite lately, reached the stage of being frank with each other. At any moment, so Giles felt, so Loraine felt, one or the other of them might break down the last filmy pretext—he of being infatuated, and she of needing his infatuation. But he did not want to encourage Loraine, just now, by plainly calling her a mischief-monger— no more and no less. For he could see that she was on the threshold of one of her bad times. He knew the swift course of them. He had known last night, when Val had tried on the coat, by something Loraine had said, then, and by her voice in saying it. This morning she was even more excited. Secrets were in the air : " Richard hates me ! " . . . " You're not to tell anyone ! " . . . " That coat of hers ! " . . . Loraine would allow no state of indifference in any group about her : friends, enemies, plotters, haters, lovers, victims—they would all be allotted their parts to play, and their sides to take, by Loraine, during the next days, hypnotised by her will ; all except Giles. Giles had been through it, and for him it was nearly over. He had a dwelling-place now, in his own private inferno ; and nobody was taken to view it except, sometimes, and most perversely, Queenie, who said of it, with earnest, girlish encouragement : " Oh, but I'm sure you can make this house look quite nice if only you put a few fresh flowers on the table, and dusted the corners ! " . . . and went away again without having seen it. His dwelling-place in Hell ! Giles grinned . . .

" Well—and what about Val's coat ? " he asked.

" Just that it isn't Val's coat ! It isn't ! Just that Stephen Greenways sent it out to me, and that clod Richard made a mistake, thinking, perhaps, in his comely Gloucestershire way, that I being with you, no other man would be sending me a present at all, nor thinking of it." And she told Giles what she had gathered from Richard, the night before—how Stephen had only said : " I want you to take this out to San Goffredo for me."

Giles looked disturbed. " It might equally be for you *or* for Val."

" It might be," Loraine retorted, " except that if one of us knows for certain—if one of us had had a hint, before he went away, of such a gift coming from him——"

"Did he give *you* any hint of that sort?"

"'I'll be sending you a message painted in silk,'" Loraine quoted dreamily.

. . . Memory or inspiration? She hardly knew herself. He must have said it, surely. So very much the perfect thing to say—with a secret intention behind it, proven now, of sending her the coat . . . "a message painted in silk."

"That does look as though he meant it for you," Giles admitted. "But why couldn't the silly ass say so?"

She shook back her hair, triumphantly. "He thought there would be no question. Of course he thought that. When a man is in a state of folly, does it ever occur to him that anybody in the whole world can think he's meaning any other woman? Besides, the train was moving already. Richard said so."

"It will be a blow for Val."

She blazed round at him, indignantly: "And what for in the wide heavens are you thinking that I'll tell her?"

"You'll not tell her?"

"No," sternly.

"You'll let her keep the coat?"

"Yes."

Giles concealed his astonishment. "It's rather—decent of you, Loraine."

"Why," Loraine said, softly—and truly, "I love Val beyond a thousand coats. But I suppose she'd call this one of my 'theatrical tricks.' Mind, Giles, you've promised not to tell anyone. Not Queenie. Curb your inconvenient vice, if you can, this time, for unburdening to Queenie of all the world. She's not safe."

Giles acquiesced, but absently. He was trying to work out what Greenways would do on receiving Val's letter of thanks. Greenways, too, would be rendered fairly helpless by his messenger's mistake. Unless he were a cad—and he was not a cad—he could not but imitate Loraine's *beau geste*. Nor could he even present Loraine with another coat from Pekin, always supposing that another so superb could be ransacked from the bales that unloaded their Chinese treasures down at the docks. Two girls going about wearing Chinese coats?—

one of them beloved, and the other not?—ridiculous, surely!
No, Val alone would have to possess the coat, and the rest of
them would be pledged to assist Loraine in protecting Val from
truth, and from a wound and an after-scar deep beyond their
knowing.

—"Damn!" muttered Giles. "I shall be deadly uncomfortable, now, every time Val snubs Loraine or makes fun of
her. Wish I weren't stuck up here!" But there was no road
down; only the steep mule-track; and no legitimate excuse
for him to raise a fuss and insist on being carried back to the
Villa Bel Respiro, when he was so comfortable and well looked
after in Val's house.

Meanwhile, Loraine had gone off in search of Aunt Elsa.
"Where's my Aunt Elsa?" she was heard calling, on the
stairs. "Where's my best friend in this house?"

Her voice was buoyant, relishing life. She was glad, tremulously glad and thankful, that she was going to let Val keep the
coat; that thus she had decided, for herself. Coming up the
hill, she had not been quite sure, you see—not quite sure what
she was going to do when she reached the top! It would so
depend on whom she first met; on how they spoke to her; on
the quickly altering flux of mood and event. . . . She had been
a little afraid that she might be led to behave badly over this—
or not as well as Val would have behaved, had their positions
been reversed. Then she had told Giles proudly, impulsively,
how of course she meant to say nothing; of course Val must
continue to own the coat, confident that it belonged to her.
And having once announced the sacrifice, Loraine knew herself
pledged to follow it by deed. So that was all right! Good
Loraine! Splendid solitary little heroine! . . . And there
would be any amount of fun to be had round the outskirts of
sacrifice! As long as life was not dull; as long as the hourly
wheel was spinning at perilous speed, not crunching, creaking,
monotonously around and around; as long as Loraine was at
the centre of the spin, she would not ask for more. And still
that glorious coat remained, indestructibly in being, where
she could sometimes see it, and secretly know it hers; and no
one else, no one else at all would know. . . . Yes, of course,

Giles, because she had told him ; but only Giles. So she ran, singing, into Aunt Elsa's bedroom. What she saw there, pleased her again : Aunt Elsa, wearing huge horn-rimmed spectacles, in a big arm-chair, a gigantic and overflowing work-basket beside her, was taking the trimming off one antiquated evening dress, with the obvious intention of sewing it in quite a different pattern on another. It was a cosy spectacle ; the trimming was not exactly sequins, and not wholly chenille, and not entirely beads : the three warred for place on the strips of lace sewn firmly on to stiff satin. You did not see trimming like that, nowadays ! And there were sheets round Aunt Elsa's feet, too, like waves of the sea, billowing, subsiding into hollows —Val's sheets, badly in need of mending. And, not content with evening-dresses and the sheets, Aunt Elsa had already been in Richard's room, and found all the socks he had brought with him, and triumphantly carried them away with her, to go over Molly's darns all over again—because she was quite sure that Richard's young English wife could have no idea how to darn a sock : " She who is out hunting ze foxes all ze year ! " . . .

" You darling ! " cried Loraine, gathering Aunt Elsa and spectacles and sheets and trimming and socks and the work-basket into a generous embrace ! She darted about the room, exclaiming, touching, taking up photographs of Melanie, Freda, Gisela, and Pearl—Aunt Elsa's four girls ; here they were separately, and in a docile group ; and here an extra one of Pearl, to show that she was the youngest and the favourite : " Hadn't she got lovely fat legs as a baby ? " cried Loraine. . . . But, truth to tell, pretty Pearl had them still, though she was now a B.Sc. And here was Anastasia—poor Aunt Anastasia, who had died the previous January . . . Aunt Elsa wept a little : she and 'Stasia had been such friends when they were girls together in Vienna ! And she recounted a few of the tricks they had played on their brothers, and on their dashing admirers. It seemed to Loraine that this laughing, mischievous generation had " played tricks " with terrific gusto ; she would have liked to have been born among them, and played tricks, too. And here was a dingy oil-painting of

Uncle Albrecht, Aunt Elsa's husband, and yet Aunt Anastasia's uncle, which was a funny mix-up, when you came to think of it! What a kind, mild face he had! He had died when the Nong-Khan crash occurred . . .

"His heart was broken," sobbed Aunt Elsa, luxuriously. "And also, he was eighty-eight—old enough to have been my fazer; but they all said it was good I should marry a man so much older; it would sober me a little."

"And of course it hasn't!" laughed Loraine. "You're just an incurable ruffian, Aunt Elsa! I knew it, the very moment I first saw you. You'd play tricks now, if you had the chance. I believe you *do!*"

—And Aunt Elsa's shoulders shook a little, and her dimple came and went, as she remembered how, only yesterday, she had played a fine game over the contents of the linen-chest, to upset that imbecile Queenie. . . . "Na, na!"—She prodded Loraine in the ribs, and Loraine prodded her back, as though they were of one age. . . . And then Aunt Elsa pulled her down, and whispered some spirited recital in which the phrases "lavender-bags" and "pepper" and "You dear God, how she sneezed, that stupid one!" recurred hilariously! . . . They chuckled together, and Loraine said:

"Poor Queenie! It'll do her good!"

And Aunt Elsa bade her bring out a large box of *marrons-glacés*, which she kept concealed in the cupboard, and they had a private munch together, and planned yet another trick for the bewilderment of the pink-and-white girl: "I vish I knew why Val keeps her!"

"Val keeps her, honey, because she's afraid of being left to *your* tender mercies," said Loraine, realising that you can always tell the truth if you do it directly enough, and with such scandalous boldness as not to be believed.

"Ach! Val knows I would break the last bone in my body for her! She is a dear girl—not as dear as my own girls," added Aunt Elsa, quickly; "and I hope soon she is going to be happy. . . . Yes? You think so too? That coat? It must mean somssing, you think?"

. . . Loraine knelt on the floor, among the sheets, her hands clasped, her arms on Aunt Elsa's lap. She felt very snugly in the heart and bosom of the Rakonitz family, up here in Aunt Elsa's bedroom, talking secrets. How sweet the old ones were, compared with the younger ones who did not like her: Toni, Maxine, Richard, Val—did Val like her? She was never sure. She cared most of all, lately, for Val's affection. And she felt, a little wistfully, that it was lonely making sacrifices that nobody praised you for; and that it would be nice if just Aunt Elsa knew—no one else *could* know what she was giving up for the sake of Val's happiness!—and perhaps praised her a little, and called her a " dear girl," in the same warm tones that she had just used for Val. There could be no harm, surely, in telling Aunt Elsa, in squeezing a little closer to this darling, middle-of-the-family, old great-aunt?

In the meanwhile, Aunt Elsa was going on: " I am so glad, too, zat it should have been Richard to bring it, and to see Richard here, and all of them so friendly. He and Val used to quarrel—oh, but terribly! He was always a little too serious, that boy—and zen during the War—but now he is very, very happy too. He has a sweet little wife—I have never seen her! —English, and zey hunt together, and she helps him with the farm. But it pleases me to see him out here and to see all you young ones together——" Aunt Elsa had forgotten, for the moment, exactly what it was that had brought Loraine together with the rest, out here in San Goffredo!—" Because we all used to be such friends in our family; always in each other's houses —I and 'Stasia and Henrietta and ze Uncles, as the children always called Felix and Max and Louis; always such jokes; and all of them so generous. You would have wondered yourself! But then after that—it used to make me sad, I tell you, when we gave up our houses and zere were no gemüthliche Sunday afternoons all together—scart and solo-whist ... till it vos bridge!—Ze pantomime at Christmas, and your Uncle Max had a box at the Opera; you remember? But I forget, you were not there; it was a pity. Where were you all ze years, Loraine? Ach! And Anastasia's sons: poor Bertrand! . . . And Mrs. Ischl never forgot to bring chrysanthemums on a birthday—never, never; and Zillah, who sang Schumann's

Lieder so beautifully, but one never sees her now; and Louis never liked her like the rest; but anyhow, she could only have married one of them. But often I used to say to that dear Anastasia: ' But what a shame the young ones do not keep together as we used to. They miss so much! I sink some of zem hardly know when the others' children are born! '—which would not have been possible, no, in the old days; and the wedding-presents not what they used to be when one of you married, and I always gave ze dinner-service and Truda ze fish-knives, and you shall get the same from me, Loraine, when you marry. And so," finished Aunt Elsa, beginning to sew again with renewed vigour, " it pleases me very much, it makes me feel warm and young again, to see you all together here such friends, and Richard coming all ze way, leaving his farm, to visit Val, and Giles with his bad ankle "—this, too, was apparently included in the list of blessings—" and only zat stupid girl who doesn't belong, to spoil it all."

And still it seemed to Loraine, luxuriating in the opulent sentimentality of this jumble from Aunt Elsa, that she herself was not quite placed where she wanted to be, with all the lime-lights beating on her at once; standing where all the rays crossed; the centre and the focus. . . .

" Aunt Elsa, I don't know what to do. . . . Darling, do advise me; there's only you—and I'm so worried; it would be so awful for her if she found out. But if we both work to keep it from her—Richard had no *right* to make a terrible mistake like this. You'll hate me for it, but it isn't my fault; it isn't! It's Richard's."

" But vot is it? " cried Aunt Elsa.

" That coat. The Chinese coat that Stephen Greenways asked Richard to bring out to San Goffredo. What *am* I to do, Aunt Elsa? Oh, do guess. Don't make me say it! His actual words to Richard were: ' I want you to take this out to San Goffredo.' If only he'd said ' to Val,' but he didn't, he didn't! Aunt Elsa, can't you guess? *I* was out here, too, when Stephen Greenways was staying with Val. I—I saw quite a lot of him——"

" Um Gotteswillen! " Aunt Elsa slowly realised what

Loraine was trying to tell her. " You mean—that beautiful coat——? "

" Yes. He sent it out to me, not to Val. I suppose he took it for granted that it would reach me ; that no one could possibly imagine—— Oh, I don't mind about the coat ! Let it go hang ! It's Val's happiness I mind. She mustn't find out, she mustn't ! Help me to keep it from her, won't you, Aunt Elsa ? Oh, perhaps I shouldn't have told you, but you won't tell anyone else, will you ? Promise ? "

Aunt Elsa, very upset, promised. And she praised Loraine with great emphasis for her generous behaviour in not laying claim to her property. Until, suddenly, her approbation clouded over, and her bright eyes beamed suspiciously from under the rim of her pushed-up spectacles. " But you must have encouraged him, that he should send you a present like zis, which I am sure must have cost much money ; whether he can afford it or not, I cannot tell ; yet however that is, you should not have coquetted with him, Loraine. It is very wrong. Yes, I am angry : one must be faithful, isn't it ? " . . . But then Aunt Elsa, too, tripped up over her sententious fault-finding, and came to a dead stop, faced with the moral situation of which the ethics were bewildering : one must, indeed, be faithful ; but in this case, to whom did she exhort faithfulness ? To Loraine ? in connection with Giles, who was Toni's husband ? Should Loraine be faithful to Giles who was being faithless to Toni ? And if she should, or if she should not, Aunt Elsa surely must not primly preach a wife's duties to her who was no wife ? For the hundredth time, the perplexed old lady asked herself how she could ever have been coaxed into this unrespectable attitude of pretending to sanction what was so shocking ? Supposing, for instance, any of the older members of the family—that dear Amélie, who lived so close, at San Remo, not much more than three hours away—supposing that they should ever find her out ? Find her sitting, as she was now, with her plump hand on Loraine's head, having secrets with Loraine ; the two of them so intimate that she had not even taken her front hair out of its little tight, steel curlers ? " But Val assured me zere was nossing . . ." murmured Aunt

Elsa, piteously seeking to put a wash of rose-colour over lurid scarlet, to cover it up. " But if there is nossing why are they togezzer, she and Giles ? " For, to her mind, being togezzer was everything, not nossing. And now all this further complication about the coat which that nice man, Stephen Greenways, had sent to Val ; and it was all so appropriate and as it should be ; and her own most fortunate presence in the house during his courtship—there must have been previous courtship, for him to have dared send such an expensive and such a significant gift—had added the last pleasant aura of convention around the whole satisfactory affair. Val had had her chaperon, and no one could possibly say a word ; yes, for even though she was in her thirty-fifth year, it would not have been right for her to have had a young man—an " admirer " was Aunt Elsa's favourite word for those who came a-wooing—if she had been living here alone, or with only that stupid girl. She did so want so see Val happy and with babies, and she did love a wedding—yes, even though it meant giving a dinner-service. But now—Loraine and not Val ? They had all been so peaceful, before Loraine came ; in a way, it was a pity. . . . And yet Aunt Elsa could not wish her away, with her affection, her spontaneous flatteries, the sound of her loud singing up the hill, the wind and the glow of life that she brought in with her whenever she appeared. No one else was such a real companion to Aunt Elsa, as Loraine. The others were all great dears to her, but Loraine was her contemporary !

It was, indeed, Loraine's especial talent and reward, to have been able to make her feel like this.

Even if Stephen Greenways cared for Loraine, and not for Val, and Loraine were to leave Giles who would go back to Toni—Aunt Elsa would have to produce her dinner-service, after all, this time for Loraine and Stephen ; because, to her, an affair must end inevitably in marriage or in broken hearts. Yes, but all that could not settle Val ; the poor one, her heart would be broken. It was time, too, that Val should have married—thirty-five, you dear Heavens ! and still a maiden !— (Aunt Elsa was taking a lot for granted.) Aunt Elsa herself would have looked on such an age as hopeless ; and, certainly she had hailed Stephen Greenways as Val's last chance. Yet Loraine was more than thirty-five, and also deserved a chance. But she had Giles. Yes, but she should not have had Giles !

. . . Ach ! it was all too dreadful and too puzzling ! And anyhow, Loraine had said Val was not to be told; that they two were to keep the secret, and shield Val. She was a good, kind, sweet child, although naughty, sometimes—but very naughty, this Loraine ! Aunt Elsa took the small oval face raised beseechingly towards her, firmly between her two hands, and gave her a smacking kiss. . . .

A light step outside, a knock on the door : " Please, I don't want to disturb you," said Queenie, resentfully ; " but Giles told me—is Loveliest here ? Yes, she is." Queenie's jealous eyes took in the attitude of the conspirators. " Loraine, are you stopping to lunch ? Because Stefania wants to dash down and get some of your favourite mascalponi ; and Luigi's here with an enormous bunch of yellow chrysanthemums that he said were for you because they are like the sun, and so are you ; only Stefania won't let him give them to you because she says they are cemetery flowers—you know how superstitious Italians are !—and Luigi says not when they are yellow ; only I really believe it's because she's jealous : they both adore you so, Loveliest ; they are fighting now, down in the kitchen."

—Terry rushed clumsily past Queenie, and rolled over on his back beside Loraine, barking delightedly at having found her.

.　　.　　.　　.　　.　　.　　.

. . . Why, they all loved her ! How could she have tormented herself with the thought that she was isolated, left out in the cold ? That she had enemies in this house—this dear, dear house on top of the hill ? They all loved her. . . . Loraine went down to lunch in the sweetest, gentlest mood, her heart like melting strawberry ice-cream, her tongue like velvet pansy petals ; putting forth life like the green plush shoots from the hedges on the first soft day of spring ; rippling with eagerness for a chance to be kind to somebody who felt pathetic and needed her kindness; to polish away sharp corners; to create laughter.

And this was Loraine, self-forgetful : for, once she was there where she craved to be, popular, sunning herself, Loraine did not bother about Loraine, any more; she could, indeed, achieve then a certain tender dignity that sprang from grace within; she could give, then, without taking; her ego entirely subdued, she would fling herself with all her soul and curiosity and warm interest, into the lives of others around her. It was only when the rays were withdrawn; when they lit on another head than hers; when she was neglected, left to the shadows, that Loraine began instinctively to fight for notice, as the normal creature fights for air. It was then that she bragged desperately, flamboyantly, waving her rags and tags of past conquests, past compliments; retailing them; reading aloud fragments from her hoarded letters, as though they were the tattered banners of old victories that could still make her glorious. And if all this boasting and clamour still failed to attract the notice she must have . . . watch Loraine growing hoarser, paler ! Watch her slowing down, dying. . . . That was what it amounted to : a gradual death-in-life, from lack of air . . .

Until, from the ashes, from the grey ashes whereof the licking, greedy flames had taken their toll, a phœnix Loraine would rise again . . . sweet, tender, humble, so that all those around her would marvel at themselves for not having loved her enough before !

But for the moment, all was well. The party gathered round the lunch-table were in excellent spirits.

" Here comes Cousin Richard," laughed Loraine, " wonderfully true to type, and just about to say : ' I can't eat your foreign kickshaws, Val ! Have you got a round of cold beef in the house ? ' "

" Oh, I can eat 'em all right," Richard said, very seriously; " I can *eat* 'em ! I don't say I like them, of course—— What are you all laughing at ? "

Giles, in an arm-chair, with his foot up on another chair, remarked : " You know, Richard, your eventual punishment for all this Anglomania will be that your sons will turn out rabid Internationalists, Pacifists and Esperantists, who will refuse to live anywhere except abroad ! "

Richard looked startled at the notion. " Good God " he muttered. . . . Then shook it off, as a nightmare that could never possibly be fulfilled. Yet it flitted across Loraine's mind that this would be a sort of tipsy tragedy that might well happen to Richard : his sons' complete reaction from his own fanatical love for England. Her apprehension of such a stroke of skilful irony from the high gods, amounted, for a few seconds, almost to prophecy. . . . Her eyes met Richard's. Could he have guessed what she was thinking ? . . . He thrust his hand down into his pocket, as though he had there a talisman against any such evils to come. "Had a letter from Jim, this morning," he announced ; and produced it for Aunt Elsa's reading. Part of it was printed in huge red chalk capitals ; the other part of it evidently dictated to Molly : " Darling Dad, I have been bluddid again "—This was Jim's only unaided effort. The hand of Mollie did the rest, and then added a foot-note : " Young Jim's got the very devil in him, lately. I heard Tommy howling the house down, so I ran upstairs and found that Jim had bitten him. Jim was tightly curled up in the blankets on the bed, trying to make me think he wasn't there ! He was pulled out with a very red face, and explained that he'd *got* to bite Tom, because, though he bore him no personal ill-feeling, he was a tiger, and a conscientious tiger couldn't do otherwise than bite ! So I used my worst and most preachy mother-voice, and said : ' But darling, even tigers don't bite their little brothers, you know.' But Jim got the better of me, even then. He said that he *had* no little brothers—— He was a *lonely* tiger, without relations ! I can't do much with him while you're away, Richard. And for other reasons, too, I like it better when you're here ; so don't stay too long in Italy, will you ? ' " . . . Molly was not coherent in conveying her feelings, but it was at least plain that she and Richard were delightfully far from being an unhappy couple.

Aunt Elsa scattered into ecstasies over " zat Bubele's letter." But she was shocked about " bluddid " ! She did think that

Molly really should not allow the children to use such dreadful, dreadful expressions !

" ' A lonely tiger, without relations . . .' " mused Loraine. " Ah, well, I don't suppose he *meant* it as a reflection on the Rakonitz family ! And haven't you often wished, Cousin Richard, that you were that lonely tiger ? "

" Oh, my relations don't bother me much, down on the farm."

Loraine sang, teasingly :

> " How're you going to keep him
> Down on the farm,
> After he's seen Paree ? "

" Beastly town, Paris ! " growled Richard. " Stopped a night there, coming through. Beastly guide chaps tried to take me round their beastly shows . . ."

" I do wonder you ever braced yourself at all to come out here, to the beastly continent ! "

" Oh, I'd do worse than that for Val.—Not much worse, though," he added, a slow gleam of humour in his deep-set eyes.

Val roused herself from abstraction. " Who'd do what for Val ? " She had not heard a single word of what had passed at the lunch-table. Val the hostess was temporarily submerged in Val the artist. The arrival of the coat yesterday, had materialised all her brilliant dreams ; not only one, but all, and in all directions : not only the coat itself, not only Stephen, but a new picture. . . . She was intensely alive, now, after a long and rather somnolent and non-creative period. The gift from Stephen had been as a single trumpet-call, before the full orchestra crashed into sound and movement. . . .

" You're looking quite dreadfully inspired, Val," Giles ragged her. " Come out of it, and tell us all about it ! I didn't know artists ever really looked like that. I thought it was a legend."

" Tell us, Val," pleaded Loraine, suddenly catching, from her affinity to Val, that quality of quivering excitement. And she was glad, now, again, that she had done or said nothing that might have destroyed it.

Val pushed back her plate, and smiled lazily round at the ring of faces turned towards her. " Oh, I don't mind telling you. Just an idea, and I want to begin to make sketches for it this afternoon. That was why I was finishing off that old stuff in a hurry. It's the Chinese coat, of course, that started me; I was crazy to paint it from the first moment I saw it."

Loraine's eyes flashed a message, first at Giles, then at Aunt Elsa: " You see ! And don't you dare to tell her ! " was the message. But they had not meant to tell Val, either of them.

" I've been up in your room, Queenie. I hope you don't mind, but I knew you had just the thing I wanted—that sort of kimono dressing-jacket affair, that you wear sometimes after you've washed your hair."

" It was a present from Aunt Irène," Queenie interrupted in rather an offended tone, pronouncing the name in the French fashion. " She said it was quite a good one, really. Not so lovely as yours, of course. But she bought it in Regent Street."

" My dear, I'm sure she did. It's a lovely dressing-jacket. I'm not running it down. Only—well . . ." Val was a little puzzled as to how she could proceed ; but artists must be ruthless, and she could not spare Queenie's feelings over that pseudo-oriental rag in cotton *crêpe*, with its bit of imitation embroidery round the edge ! And so she went on : " I want to paint you wearing it, Queenie. You do look so nice in it. I want you to look as though you knew you looked nice in it while you are wearing it. Do you see what I mean ? "

. . . Loraine was leaning across the table, her lips a little parted, her eyes sparkling with wicked joy. She knew well enough what Val meant !

" And I'm going to have the Chinese coat—mine—flung empty across a chair in the background," Val went on.

After a long silence, Queenie said : " I expect it will be a very nice picture, Miss Power, and of course I don't mind lending you my Chinese coat, and sitting for you. But I don't see much sense in it all. Do you, Loveliest ? "

" Yes . . ." said Loraine, breathlessly. And then she burst out with : " Val, you're a genius and a devil, and I adore you ! "

Giles, over in his arm-chair, chuckled, and said nothing. And Richard lumbered up in Queenie's support, saying : " If Val wants to paint that Mandarin's coat I brought out, why doesn't she do it ? But I must say, I don't quite see the sense of dragging in the other one."

Giles chuckled again.

Aunt Elsa, never long to be left out of a discussion, and quite unable to fathom why her clever niece should want to paint that stupid girl, cried shrilly, in terror lest Queenie should be too flattered by the selection of herself for the model : " Vy do you start calling it a Chinese coat, Queenie, now, all of a sudden so grand, when always it was a dressing-jacket before ? I cannot understand these silly affectations, no ! "

. . . Loraine's brain was light and flashing with an idea ; but she waited until she could get hold of Val alone, after lunch, and then rushed up to the studio in her wake. " Oi ! Val ! Wait for me ! "

" I thought you'd be coming," said Val, pleasantly. ". . . Well, what do you think of it ? "

" You know what I think of it ! . . ." Her tone was enough.

" Thanks. And what's Queenie thinking of it ? "

" As though Queenie mattered ! What's the good of pretending you aren't a brutal savage, Val, where your work's concerned. But now . . . look here—this is what I was after asking you "—for the moment she faltered, felt actually shy. Val, in her workshop, was rather a supreme being. " I want to be in the picture," said Loraine, with an effort of courage. " I want to wear the real coat. It'll be better than having it thrown empty across the chair . . . won't it ? "

But Val did not even reflect on the possibility. At once and decisively, she shook her head. " No, old thing. Sorry. Spoils my conception. Cuts right across it."

" Ah, but it doesn't ! Don't treat me as though I didn't understand, Val, what you're aiming at. I do, I do. It's the Modern Girl . . . trumpery ; sham little Queenie in her sham oriental jacket. And then, showing it up—ah, it isn't a picture at all !—It's a slice of cruelty. It's one of your mocking epigrams. You're too clever to live, Val, I always said it, and too articulate : showing it up, the real thing ; a real thing from the old world ; the work of a hundred eyes and a hundred hearts in it ; mayhap, a hundred years. They run them up by machinery now ; it's just as good, they think. But your picture—that will shout the difference. Ah, but Val, *I* am real ? You don't deny my reality, do you ? *I'm* not one of your Queenies ? Ah, see now, haven't I got your whole meaning plain ? Do you have to explain things to me ? Then what's wrong with my wearing the coat ? I know it's an honour to be painted by you. I want that honour. Say yes, Val. Say you will." For it had seemed to her, when Val had proposed the picture, at lunch, that here was the divine solution of the problem of ownership, and the quick, full answer to the sacrifice she had made ; far, far rather than possessing the coat, did she want to be painted by Val, wearing it. The substance was only the shadow, here. For Loraine was an artist too, at heart, though without a creative outlet. Her worship of beauty was sincere ; long after she was dead, she felt, instinctively, that her portrait would live, stiffly robed in the magnificent coat that Stephen had sent her, and immortalised by Val, who was one of the family and whom she loved. Thus would be quieted Loraine's consuming desire to be identified with the family. Not, of necessity, noisily, and for some shining gain ; flamboyantly self-assertive in all else, where honour to a Rakonitz was concerned, it was good enough, to Loraine, that Val should be the flame, if she might but feed it ; Val's fame, if to Loraine might be allowed the privilege of silent content, knowing she had done all she could in helpfulness. She was proud of Val. Proud of Toni, too. . . . (" *But I won't be left out !* ") She reflected, too, on contributory pleasures that would be involved, by sitting for Val in this picture : she would have, here, an excuse to wear the coat ; to be wearing it for long, silent, happy hours shut away in the studio, while the picture gradually grew and took shape—she sharing in it, understanding every subtle inflexion of the brush ; delicious hours, alone with Val—for Queenie hardly counted ; Queenie was the foil, in this case, to the close-woven unity between the cousins. Of course, she need never say, now, that the coat was really hers. What did that matter? She was not going to have said so, in any case. . . . But ah, how happy she was now, only needing Val's " yes."

But Val would not say " yes."

" Don't you see, Loraine—— No, it's no good interrupting, saying that you see everything. You see part of it. But I meant, among other things, that nobody was quite good enough to wear that coat—the real one. It can stand by itself—a sort of impersonal miracle. I know it's only stuff and embroidery, but it actually has achieved, along those lines, perfection. It has the indifference of perfection. It's not—a pragmatic proposition. It doesn't need human wearing. It's just solitary . . . a comment, a caustic comment, if you like, on shams and imitations.—Oh, I know I'm talking like a prig and a pedant, but there you are, Loraine!—You asked me. You must realise that you and the coat together would be too much of a good thing—a sort of vulgar over-emphasis."

" I don't know why you should call me vulgar," said Loraine, sullenly and deliberately blunting her receptiveness to Val's ideas.

" I'm not calling you anything," Val retorted, exasperated by the other's persistence, and badly wanting to get to work while the light lasted. " I'm not calling you anything. When the sun shines on the fire, it neutralises it, doesn't it? Makes the flame seem shabby and ineffective? Well, that's what I'm going to paint in this picture of mine. But I don't want *two* suns. Of course I'd like to paint you. I'll do you, one day, by yourself. Naked, probably; I like your straight, thin back— the back of a native African child. You can stand alone, too, you know, without a Mandarin coat to back you up."

" Thanks," retorted Loraine. " But I happen to want to wear the coat, and I don't see why I shouldn't ! " . . . She was struggling to fight down the impulse to cry aloud, passionately, that it was *her* coat, and that she could wear *her* coat whenever she pleased ! And that if she allowed Val to paint her coat, it was she who would be doing the artist a favour. She just succeeded in vanquishing this impulse ; but she glowered like a baffled, angry goblin, at this insolent and unconscious—

robber, so calmly rummaging among tubes and palettes and canvases.

Val smiled suddenly over her shoulder at Loraine : " Don't plague me, there's a good kid ; not just now. It's really quite out of the question, what you're asking me. I simply couldn't do it, and that's that ! Now, be a pal and clear off ! Tell Queenie I want her, plus Aunt Irène's dressing-jacket from Regent Street. And do take Richard for a walk, or do something to amuse him. It's stopped raining. What a nuisance, Giles being laid up ! He and Richard could have ' tramped ' together, lovely long-day tramps. . . . I detest tramping ! "

CHAPTER V

. . . SO Loraine walked slowly down the garden again.
She might as well take Richard for a tramp as do
anything else. A roystering wind from the sea
was hustling all the grey clouds over the mountains ; shoulder-
ing them apart to show, underneath, strips and patches of vivid
blue, the colour of a Renaissance Madonna's cloak. Presently
all the clouds would be gone, and the whole sky would be just
that deeply-dreaming blue. And if Val had only yielded her
what she wanted, Loraine would have been really happy.
Almost enough colour, even for her, collected into her small
space in the universe, counting the coat, and that blue sky
after rain. She called to Richard, and to Terry and Mac,
without bothering to re-enter the house.

" What's up ? " said Richard, strolling to the open door.

" Coming for a walk ? "

" I don't mind—I mean, thanks awfully."

" Well, come on, then ! " Loraine cried, impatiently,
standing three terraces above him.

" Oh, haven't you got to go home first, and put on——? "

" Put on *what* ? "

" I don't know," said Richard. " I imagined women always
put on something for walks ! " Even Molly, who was hardy
enough in all weathers, would change into stout brogues, and
put on a sports coat or a short suède jacket—he liked her in
that !—and jam a felt hat down over her curly, brown hair.
Loraine was wearing her favourite shape of dress: long, pointed,
tight-fitting bodice, and full skirt that flowed down almost to
her ankles. She dressed like this for day or evening alike. It
was rather a jolly dress, Richard thought, in its own way and
for its own purpose—a sort of rough, *crêpe* silk, patterned red
and blue. And she wore scarlet sandal-arrangements, in plaited

straw. . . . " What for would I be changing ? " said Loraine, simply.

" Aren't you cold ? "

" I'm never cold and I'm never hot ! Glory and gracious, Cousin Richard !—one would think you were a lounge lizard, yourself, instead of a farmer ! "

" *I'm* all right," said Richard. " I was being considerate." He joined her at once, and they swung along one of the paths that led up through the olives into the hills.

Loraine very soon left the worn track, to beat out a path of her own : down, for a while, into the valley, and then climbing again. She dropped from terrace to terrace, ignoring the roughly-hewn steps that were sometimes to be found ; as though steps were nothing to her, or as little as heat and cold. Richard was amazed at her suppleness. Although ready enough, usually, to believe that Loraine was showing off, he could not believe it now, on this walk. It was just natural for her to run and climb and leap ; she had been given the freedom of earth and air.

The olive trunks were bright black velvet stripes in the mist of silver foliage. " They always go black like that after rain," Loraine explained carelessly.

Out in the open, they could hear the wind ; and presently it banged and buffeted their faces, as, rounding a corner of the terrace, they found themselves on a small exposed plateau of grass and broom and wild thyme ; the valley was below them, first a wavy shimmer of yellow and purple and coppery-red, where the late leaves still clung on in the vineyards ; then a shimmer of silvery-blue, where the artichokes were planted, flat field after field. In front of them, across another dip and on a higher level than their eyes, was a small village, crested by three admonitory cypresses, pointing upwards in front of the church ; and a bell in the tower, clanging a wild, golden chime, as though that too were swung by the wind and not by human will. On a further slope, San Goffredo di Monte, a tiny forti- fied city, swarmed in a huddle of pink and white and lemon- coloured houses, behind prim battlements that were like a picture in a child's book of enchantment. Between the niches, you could just catch a glimpse of little magical orange trees, shining golden specks in their glossy foliage. And behind the walls again were the further mountains, lifting tier upon tier, purple and indigo in the shadows ; their eternal olives spotted by occasional crimson of the wild cherry in its November hues, drawing to a pause wherever was carved the single, sombre holiness of cypress. Whichever way they looked, Richard and Loraine, the whole landscape seemed to be tossed and insurgent, shaken in the jovial swirls of the wind ; plunged hot into the gold swim of the sun. For everywhere was gold, and everywhere was movement : the golden bell ; the rumpled glitter of the olives ; a telegraph wire, that looped the abyss from one village to another, gleamed, where the rays caught it, a quivering bridge of pure gold. A flight of small, dark-gold birds through the dusk into the sun . . . into the shadow again . . . back in the sun ; the flame of the red wild-cherry ; the flame of the spread vineyards. A wet, swaggering, turbulent scene. . . .

Loraine flung herself prone on to the ground ; the dogs rolled gleefully over and over beside her.

" What's the bell for ? " asked Richard, who had always heard that Italy was a highly-coloured country, and was now compelled to believe it. " No cattle anywhere ; they're all stall-fed, hereabouts. I was talking to a fellow in the train, about their chief produce ; he spoke a bit of English. They get frosts down on the level, sometimes, but practically never higher up. In a good year, he says, he can get as much as ten lire a dozen for the early artichokes. Sounds quite profitable. What *is* the bell for ? It isn't Sunday."

" Oh, a *festa* or something. You can always rake up a saint, here, if you feel like a holiday. How do you like it, Cousin Richard ? " Her cheek pillowed on her arm, she watched him under her nonchalant, unequal eyelids, ready to mock should he stick to his habit of British unenthusiasm ; though she would hate, too, any lyrical outburst in celebration of the landscape. She didn't quite know what she wanted. Anything would do to mock at ! Val had been horrid, and the devils were loose. . . . " Apart from the soil and the produce and the profits, how do you like it ? "

Richard said, after a pause : " Sharply cut everything is, except just the olives, and they're a sort of hazy background to the sharpness. In England you mostly get the farms and the fields and the hedges and trees, even the sky and the clouds, running into one another—blurred. But here—that village is such a brilliant white, and you can easily run your fingers along the edges of it—d'you know what I mean ? And the shape of the cypresses, and the clean round oranges, and the hills cut out with a knife along that awfully hard blue sky ; it's as though somebody were trying to make up for the olives ! "

Loraine said, in answer : " Oh. . . . Why do you hate me so, Richard ? " And this was not total irrelevance. She had been startled at his noticing such an essential quality of Italy, which had not yet presented itself even to her, with all her quick sense and appreciation of beauty ; nor even to Val, the artist ; Val had never pointed out what Richard, in his slow matter-of-fact tones, had seen in the shock of his very first encounter with all this brave riot of sun and wind, gold and blue and purple. So that Loraine, suddenly brought to knowledge that a Richard existed who was, after all, capable of response and utterance, a Richard whose friendliness would be worth while, and whose antagonism was a matter of fastidiousness, not, as she had scornfully deemed it, mere British stolidity, Loraine cried straight from her heart : " Why do you hate me so ? "

But Richard disliked being forced into personal arguments ; he thought Loraine was simply being tiresome, and incapable of seeing, in cypress or vine or mountain, aught but a background for Loraine. So at once he turned gruff, and said shortly : " I don't hate you ! Why should I ? " He might have added : " I'm just indifferent to you," which would have been, to Loraine, the most deadly insult. But he checked this, telling himself with his habitual honesty that, anyhow, it would not have been quite true : he was not wholly indifferent to Loraine ; most of the time she irritated him intensely, but : " I like her in spots," added Richard, not aloud !

Loraine said no more ; her chin cupped in her hands, she continued to gaze at him steadily. The bell from the church tower across the valley and above them, was silent now. Richard threw a stone for Terry, who, however, wagged his tail and did not move from his post at his idol's side. Mac was careering away somewhere, out of sight; but now and then you saw the bushes move, and heard a short squeal of delight, announcing some precious find.

" If you want to know," Richard went on—for he preferred silences that were of his own making, and became uncomfortable when they were, so to speak, the property of someone else —" If you want to know, you seem to me——"

" Yes. Go on ! "

" —Dangerous."

Loraine smiled, her mouth like a crescent moon, the corners tilted upwards. Dangerous ! This was the old story : Babs, Queenie, Luigi, Giles, Terry the dog, Manuela—how many more ?—" Dangerous to whom ? "

" To Val ! " he blurted out.

Loraine stopped smiling. " To Val ? Why—I'd do anything for Val. Why . . . I love her."

Richard stirred uncomfortably : you never used the word " love," especially in the open air and in daylight, and speaking of another woman—and of your cousin, good God !

" Perhaps," doubtfully. " But she's not as serene as she used to be ; and her house isn't happy. Because we're all bothering about you, all the time, one way and another." He felt himself helplessly committed, now, to being rude ; and though regretting it, thrust on his accusation : " You're a kind of obsession in the house." And when Richard did find words, they were apt to be extraordinarily on the spot. " It's unrestful, and it isn't good for Val, nor for her work."

Loraine sighed . . . closed her eyes, like a child snuggling down into sleep. He did not notice the furious clenching of her fists. " Not good for Val," she murmured. " Fancy that ! Not good for Val ! "

Richard began : " Sorry if I've put my hoof in it——" but Loraine's sing-song crooned across his apologies, oblivious of them—" And he brings out a Chinese coat, and gives it to the wrong woman, as a fool might do—as a fool might do . . . but I'm not good for Val."

"What the hell do you mean ? The wrong woman ? "

Loraine opened her eyes, sunnily : " You see, Cousin Richard, the Chinese coat was a present for me ; a present from Stephen Greenways. Who told you to give it to Val ? Did he ? "

—The man paused in the act of pressing down the tobacco into hisepipe, and stared at her in consternation, " Lord ! " he exclaimd, ruefully. " But why the deuce didn't you——? "

" Yes ? Didn't I what ? Should I be after saying : ' Hands off ! That's mine ! '—when you bring out a parcel, and tell Val—Val that I'm bad for !—that it was a present for her ? . . . And she trying it on, so pleased. . . . And all of them there : Queenie, Aunt Elsa, and Giles, and the servants ? Should I be shaming her ? Leaning forward, and snatching it off her very back, and putting it on my own, saying : ' It's a mistake—the messenger's a fool—it's a mistake—it's mine and mine and mine ? ' No. She's got to have it now. She's got to keep it, and never be told. *I'll* not be hurting Val. Don't you know yet, Cousin Richard, that it's people who are stupid do all the hurt ? not who are dangerous ! "

" Are you sure—that Greenways meant it for you ? " But Richard had not much hope, really, that she was lying to him. True conviction had sounded in her voice.

Loraine said, simply : " He told me, before ever he left, that he would send me ' a message painted in silk.' Mind, Richard, you have to keep this a secret. You've not got to tell anyone. And especially not Queenie, who's a babbler. It mustn't get round to Val."

Richard assented. But he was still troubled. " Well, but won't Greenways write or come out himself, eventually ? Something of that sort ? "

" And if I choose to let him drift ? " Loraine argued, mournfully. " He'll follow the coat. Don't I know men ? Why, there's hardly a man knows the difference between one woman and another. I'm not vain. It just happened to be me. It might have been Val. It shall be Val." She sprang up restlessly, and in a few seconds he had lost sight of her. She had darted round the walled corner of the terrace, and so was hidden to view. When Richard found her again, some ten minutes later, brought to the spot by Terry's frantic barks, she had found a new pastime, and had apparently forgotten all the world besides. A lissom olive sapling was growing from its parent trunk. Loraine had discovered that from half-way up the old olive, she could fling herself on to the crest of the other young one, embracing it, and her weight would be just enough to carry it in a wide, outward curve, almost down to the grass. Directly she leapt away, loosening her hold, the sapling sprang elastically upright again; and once more Loraine, scuttling like a wild-cat up the old tree trunk, could enjoy the glorious flying sensation of her sweep and dive to the ground. She did not know that Richard was there. He stood for a few moments, smoking, and watching her, and he could not help admitting the unconscious loveliness of her performance. The quaint, unsuitable dress she wore: wide-skirted, vivid blue and red, gave the beauty of her flying act its touch of humour, and humour always enhances beauty where it does not kill it. Grey-green and silver for background, and Loraine rushing past it like a jewel, like a bird. . . . Presently, in flight, she caught sight of Richard, and cried out:

"It's glorious! Come and do it! No, you're too heavy; you'd break the branch!"

Richard laughed. "Eleven stone ten! No, I won't risk it! Good sport, though! You look as though you hadn't any weight at all!"

. . . A temporary lull had occurred in their antagonism. They went home good friends. Richard thought it jolly decent of her to have shut up about the coat.

CHAPTER VI

—BUT, back at the house, it was hard to forget that Val was all the while painting her picture of Queenie and the Regent Street dressing-jacket and the Chinese coat. Val was absorbed in her painting. Loraine found this nearly unbearable. Even Queenie, so she imagined, was putting on slightly superior airs. Queenie, after all, was a participant, selected by Val to sit for her. It occurred to Loraine, maddened by this pantomime of preening and strutting, that she had only to inform Queenie, in words of one syllable, *why*, precisely, Val had chosen her, what was the subtle meaning of her inclusion in the picture, to put an end to all this ; but it would have put an end to the picture, too ; Queenie would hardly be likely to lend herself as model to Val, once she had fully grasped the symbolism which hitherto had only been clear to Loraine, and, in a lesser degree, to Giles, not counting the artist herself. Loraine would not consent to such a betrayal : a part of her nature was too big to be packed away into any enclosure of spite or petty jealousy : she reverenced beauty and the brilliant soft meanings hidden away in beauty ; and she worshipped the romance of the Rakonitz family, and all that went to build it up. Because she guessed already that the picture had in it the element of a masterpiece ; because it struck a blow for beauty against shams ; because it was Val painting it, and Val was the granddaughter of Simone Rakonitz—tall Simone with the red-gold hair that flowed down to her ankles when she stood ; because of all these things, Loraine would not wilfully deprive the picture of its chances of fulfilment. So she thought, at first, that she would behave with wonderful dignity and forbearance, and stay away from Val's cottage altogether. This would remove her from temptation—" And, thank God, I can always be happy by

234

myself ! " reflected Loraine . . . but with inward misgivings. The kind of people she most admired were those who could be happy by themselves : nomads, explorers, anchorites—that gallant, lonely, laughing race that never settled anywhere ; that depended neither on land, house, kin, nor friends. Loraine deemed these folk the salt of the earth : " I'm a nomad," she cried, when she most passionately desired to settle down and never move on again ! " And I'm happiest alone ! "—which was even more of an illusion ; for whether in love or in war, the fundamental Loraine was entirely gregarious ; so that her three days of haughty and solitary withdrawal to the foot of the hill, away from all the pleasant possibilities of warm, human strife on top of it, were, from her point of view, not a success.

The first half-hour was splendid : Loraine was convinced that she was doing the right thing, and that they must be sitting up there, respecting her for it ; respecting her hard and ceaselessly. She sang, because she was so happy by herself, and danced into the kitchen to chatter with Manuela . . . and was annoyed when she found her out. Before the day was over, she hardly knew what to do with herself, so tormented was she by the desire to run up the hill and see whether they were still noticing that she was keeping away. . . . It was all right, as long as they were noticing it. As for Giles, he was a traitor. What business had he to be up there in the thick of it, among her enemies? Up there, where Val owned the coat, and Queenie sat for the picture, the while Loraine, to whom belonged the coat, and who could have destroyed the picture, sat forlorn and outcast ? " I'm not going where I'm not wanted," half sobbed Loraine, that evening, when, looking up from her balcony, she saw the lights turned on in the sun-room, and imagined the sociable after-supper hum and busy-ness : Richard with his pipe ; Aunt Elsa with her mending ; Giles on the divan, confiding in demure Queenie, or pleading for the gramophone—old fox-trots and new : his favourite " Kalua " of 1922 ; " Varasdin," which he had recently heard in Vienna ; and that latest London success, " I'm a little bit fonder of you " ; Val, dreamy, tired out, her big limbs inert in an arm-

chair, absorbed in thoughts of her work, thoughts of Stephen
. . . Marietta and Stefania running in and out ; Loraine
envisioned them all, even the dogs, Mac and Terry—yes, ungrateful Terry would have forgotten her ! If Terry were but
half a faithful dog he would be down the hill by now, and lying
patiently on the steps in front of the closed door. " Ah well,
I'm biding my time," said Loraine, trying, against odds, to
work up melodrama. But it fell rather flat. *Was* she biding
her time, indeed ? Whom was she threatening ? And anyhow,—the same trouble again !—were they aware that she was
biding ? If not, then biding could bring no satisfaction. . . .

She wandered into the kitchen, and this time found Manuela,
and began to talk, and felt better, becoming more and more
voluble under the lubrication of Manuela's flatteries—sincere,
but artful in their placing ! She told Manuela the whole story
of the Chinese coat, and what a marvel it was, and how the
tall, handsome Englishman had sent it to her ; but the other
Englishman—not tall and with broad shoulders—yes, her
cousin, the one up at the cottage now—had given it to the
Signorina Val, by mistake ; but, of course, the Signorina Val
must never know : " because you see, Manuela, though one
can accept kindness from those one loves, it is very hard to
accept it from an enemy, and still find pleasure in it. And, I
don't know why, but they all hate me up there, and it would
spoil her pleasure—do you see what I mean, Manuela ?—it
would spoil her pleasure in that marvel of a coat if the Signorina
Val knew that she had to take it from me instead of from the
English Signore. So I don't tell her, I don't tell anyone but
you, Manuela ; and I keep away. I am happier alone."

" You are a princess," cried Manuela. " Yes, indeed, a little
princess, and they are all pigs ! The Signorina Val, moreover,
will look like a *carabiniére* and an elephant, when she wears a
coat such as you describe to me. That is a comfort, at least."

" Hush, Manuela. I cannot permit it, that you speak so of
my cousin."

" Like a whole brigade of cavalry, I say," repeated the
obdurate servant. " For there is no doubt that the gift is
appropriate to my beautiful queenly little Signorina, and meant

for her. When a man thinks hotly of a woman, day and night, then he knows by the movements of his heart what to buy for her, what to send her, what will express his passion. That garment, as you describe it to me, could have been meant for no other than *my* Signorina. Certainly not for that big slow Englishwoman. Ho, ho! I laugh at the idea. . . . *He* would laugh too ! "

Manuela held her sides, and rocked in mirth. She had said some shrewd things, and a whole heap of foolish ones. A benefactress of lovers was Manuela, hot and strong. Because she was too plain and angular ever to hope for one of her own, she relished love by proxy, and Loraine's conquests were meat to her. She yearned, now, to see her mistress arrayed in the embroidered splendour that must have cost the ardent Englishman so many *soldi*. But the situation created by the other Englishman's blunder did not displease her, either, for she gloried in intrigue and confidences. . . . In the days of Philip of Spain, you might have seen the prototypes of Loraine and Manuela, mistress and maid, court lady and faithful tire-woman, whispering behind fans, plotting while the lady's hair was being dressed and her face painted for the King's ball that night. . . . Masks, and grated windows, snatches of a gallant ditty sung outside. . . . Manuela's figure, close-wrapped, flitting on her mysterious bawdy errand down a dark street, the houses on either side as tall as towers. . . . And in consequence, later on, flowing blood that soon stiffened into a dull brown pattern. And then a new lover. That would have suited Manuela. She was puzzled when Loraine had ceased to be interested by Giles, who was so tall, with such a thin, handsome, distinguished face. . . . But now Manuela understood. Another cavalier. Life was so simple, after all. Two cavaliers suited her better than one ; they clinked coins in her palm, in rivalry, and she could play off one against the other. And two still fell far short of the numbers due to her mistress, her graceful, high-bred, imperious, fascinating little Signorina Loraine !

She hated Val, and commented freely, now, and scornfully, on Val's figure, which she deemed useful only for breeding

purposes—" And for that she does not use it, because she is
not one, she, to attract the men ! "—Val's clothes, her rough
tweed skirts and woollen sports coats, were too expensive and
well-cut for Manuela to recognise their origin, but sagged and
pulled out of drawing by bad and incurable tricks of digging
her hands into her pockets, and lounging. . . . And these
mannish habits, too, Manuela censured freely. She was blazingly
jealous of Val, and of Val's influence over Loraine.

. . . Loraine was aware that she ought not to encourage
Manuela's intimacy. But she was impressionable to atmosphere. . . . Loraine swayed and tumbled, half-hypnotised, into
her suggested rôle of the capricious little Spanish princess,
adored by her servitor, cruel to her at one moment, haughty
and snubbing. . . . And the next moment, a warm-hearted
child again, embracing her, pouring out penitence for that hot-
tempered box-on-the-ears . . .

And was the scene not richer, more interesting, played thus,
than in a style which dingy people called " natural "—" Mary,
you can go now. I don't wish to hear any complaints about
the fishmonger's boy. It isn't your place . . ."—Natural !
But now and here, Loraine, defying their criticism, talked with
Manuela, her servant. The talk rippled on and on . . .
Loraine went to bed, feeling much better.

The whole of the next day she spent up in the hills, picnic-
king with Luigi and with Luigi's little brothers and sisters.
This was not such a bad day. She could whole-heartedly play
games with Italian peasant children, and enjoy it as much as
they. And when she came home, she found that Queenie had
been down the hill three times in vain search of Loveliest. As
long as anxiety about her was active and not stagnant, she
could bear her self-imposed isolation. She wondered, in quite
a rosy humour, what Val was thinking about it ?

As a matter of sober fact, Val had not noticed. Val had
been in the studio all the morning. A rather petulant Queenie
had apparently been allowed a half-hour's rest—that was the
occasion of the first rush down the hill and back again—but no
more than that ; her services were relentlessly commandeered
again. At lunch-time, there was no sign of either of them.

Stefania, when questioned whether she had called the Signorina Val, said, in her pretty, distinct voice, that she had indeed been three times to the studio door, and at last had entered ; but that the Signorina Val was " molto occupata," painting : " She is painting the beautiful new jacket that the Signore brought from England," said Stefania ; " and she will not stop. I have never yet seen her *così*. Perhaps it is because——" —a rush of shyness overcame her.

" Vell, and go on ! " cried Aunt Elsa, more accustomed than the others to the foreign type of servant, who is at once so much more, and so much less, familiar with her employers than the English kind ; more intimately concerned with their welfare, and yet more feudally acquiescent to the differences between slave and master ; so : " Go on ! " Aunt Elsa bade her, inquisitively. Thus had she gossiped with that good Rosalia in her mother's kitchen in Vienna, when she was a girl ; Rosalia, who made such a speciality of Nusstorte and Zimmt-kuchen.

" Perhaps," Stefania obediently went on, and a hard note sounded in the usual pretty softness of her voice, " the Signorina Val is working so hard, painting the beautiful jacket, because she does not know how long she may keep it. . . ." And she put down a flask of wine on the table, raised her eyelids for one quick, inscrutable look towards the assembled Signori, and returned to the kitchen, where her little stolid Egyptian face broke into flashing mischief, as she recounted to Marietta what she had dared to say, and how it had been received ; and then dodged Marietta's elder-sisterly lecture !

Meanwhile, Richard, Giles, and Aunt Elsa, looked at each other uneasily . . .

" She knows something," said Richard. " How the devil did that come out, I wonder ? "

" She must have seen Manuela this morning," from Giles.

Aunt Elsa contributed : " But Manuela would not know, isn't it ? "

And then all three realised, one by one—Giles first—that neither of the others were in the last puzzled or surprised ; in fact, that they were talking quite naturally about a secret that

Loraine had divulged only to Giles, only to Aunt Elsa, only to Richard. . . . Giles laughed ; and Richard, making a laborious and belated attempt to cover up what had already been fully uncovered, said :

" Who *is* Manuela ? And what have she and this kid been talking about ? I can't make out what you're driving at, either of you."

" No good ! " Giles replied curtly. " You can safely open up, Richard. Finesse isn't your line. And anyhow, at this rate the whole of San Goffredo will know by to-morrow morning that you handed out Greenways' coat to the wrong woman."

.   .   .   .

Loraine's endurance gave out on the following afternoon. She provided herself, as excuse for going up the hill again, with a flask of rather special Orvieto wine, which the infatuated Luigi had stolen from his father ; and comforting herself with the reflection that whatever else awaited her at Val's cottage, there would be, at least, a grand scene of some sort, she started forth. Hardly was she a quarter of the way up the mule-track, however, when she met Queenie coming down.

—" Loveliest," said Queenie, after several hugs and where-were-you-yesterdays, " I've been sent to ask you if you would be too awfully sweet and come up to massage Giles' foot ? No one else has the knack of it like you have. The Doctor said it had to be done a certain way, you know—the way the blood rolls—and he doesn't seem to like it when it's me or Aunt Elsa or Richard. I don't mind a bit, of course, and I don't think Richard minds much either ; but Aunt Elsa gets in a terrible state—she's such an old fuss-box ! "

Loraine, ever an opportunist, considered the proposition in relation to her pride. " I *was* going up into the hills by myself all day long, with a bottle of wine and some cigarettes ; it would have been glorious, right, right away from everybody ; but still, if Giles' foot "—she paused, still indecisive——

" Loveliest," Queenie coaxed her, " it's so dull up at the cottage without you."

" It's not *that* would be bringing me back," said Loraine.

" No, no, of course not. I know it wouldn't. But I really
do think," Queenie went on, seriously, " that Giles' foot ought
to be properly massaged : it would be rather an awful thing
if he got lame for life—people do, sometimes—just through
wrong treatment, or through no treatment at all."

" You're a helpless lot ! " laughed Loraine, giving in with
good grace. " Ah well, I suppose I'd better be coming along
with you."

" You could go on for your day in the hills, afterwards,'
Queenie suggested.

" Don't you see I can't do that, when once I've . . . broken
through ? "

" What is it, Loveliest ? I don't quite understand. Broken
through what ? Has there been a row ? You and Val—is it
anything to do with the picture she's painting of me ? I
shouldn't mind a bit giving up my place in it to you ; you know
that, don't you, Loveliest ? But she's already begun, and you
know what Val is, in one of these moods." Queenie jauntily
called her " Val," away from her actual presence.

" It's nothing, nothing whatever to do with the picture ;
and I hate sitting still, anyhow. I can't sit still for more than
a minute or two. It's no good at all I'd be as a model, that I
wouldn't. It's nothing you would understand has kept me
away, Queenie, so you'd far better not be prying nor asking
questions. And look here, if I do go back with you to the
cottage now, to massage Giles' foot, you're not to say one word
about my having meant to go away from them all for the day.
It might make them uncomfortable ; it might make them feel
that I was doing them a favour by giving it up ; and I don't
want that. I hate these rows and scenes and intrigues. Peace
is what I want—peace, and a lot of it ; and lying about in the
sun. So mind that, Queenie ! and let's race along now ; and
look here, we'll pretend this bottle of wine was going to be a
present for Val ; I can't be bothering to take it back home
now. Luigi gave it to me for myself ; it's a very special Orvieto
—oh, I forgot, you don't know about wines. . . . Ah, never
mind, Luigi wouldn't be grumbling if I told him I wanted to
be sharing it with a friend or two."

" It's wonderful of you, Loveliest, taking it like that,"
Queenie sighed, admiringly. She did indeed feel that Loraine
had a way of adding colour to the smallest and pettiest affairs
of everyday, which merely ordinary people transacted with far
less generosity of spirit.

Val accepted Loraine's presence as though there had never
been an absence. Val was working furiously. Occasionally she
emerged from the mists and was lazily good-humoured all
round—she wasn't the snappy type of artist—and then disappeared again. Her blurred sense of observation was quite
incapable of making clear little mental foot-notes such as :
" Loraine's here "; " Loraine wasn't here yesterday ";
" Loraine is displeased "; " Aunt Elsa is fussed." She took
all this come-and-go for granted. She was neglecting her
household, in addition to neglecting Loraine's temperamental
displays—and not to mention the invalid's sprained foot :
Queenie was terribly shocked that Val omitted to say, at every
first daily encounter : " Good morning, Giles. Is your foot
better ? I do hope it is. Did you sleep well, or was it paining
you ? "—enquiries which punctilious Queenie never failed to
make herself. Moreover, Val also disgracefully neglected her
guest, Richard, considering that he had made a very special
effort of will and of convenience to leave his farm and leave
England and come out to Italy to see her. She had not any
formal ideas about entertaining, but took things haphazardly
and just as they rolled in from the future to the present; though
it did strike her, in proposing that Richard should take the first
available chance of leaving the farm to the superintendence of
his head man, and pay her a visit, that he might prove, in Giles'
case, a quite excellent antidote to Loraine ; and that the two
men could together fill their days by those useless and athletic
performances which the vigorous male adopts as a matter of
course. Then, too, Val had been going through a slack period as
far as her work was concerned, and had imagined she would have
plenty of time to devote to her cousin from Gloucestershire.
But with Richard had arrived, unexpected, the Chinese coat
from Stephen; and with the Chinese coat from Stephen had been
stimulated a mood of long-awaited inspiration. And now Giles

had twisted his ankle; and Val was shut up in the studio all day; and Richard was having, as he expressed it, rather a dud time. He took it philosophically, however, until the reappearance of Loraine in their midst; when he groaned in spirit, anticipating further pageantries and demonstrations of the kind his soul abhorred.

. . . But Loraine was behaving like an angel, and it was certainly not due to her that even Val, preoccupied as she was, gradually became aware of a curious discomfort in her home and in herself; yes, queerly enough, in her own body. It was certainly not Loraine who told Val that she was large and hulking; and yet, somehow, the words seemed to have been insinuated into the atmosphere, and Val began to behave as though she were both these things; as though she were blowsy, milkmaidish. . . . Yet it was not Loraine who was responsible for the idea. Loraine, indeed, was always defending her against any such absurd notion. Even when there was no one against whom she could prove the contrary, Loraine seemed to be proving it. Her loyalty went so far as to call Val's attention, over and over again, to the advantages of not being slim and supple and formed like a boy—" as I am, for instance," said Loraine. Also she helped Val by advising her over the choice of clothes, the sort of lines that would tend to make her appearance more slender, tone down the generous sweep of her bosom and hips. Loraine knew exactly what Val ought to wear; what she ought emphatically not to eat; and was quick and stern to check her disobedience to these rules; and so generously eager to point out to everybody—Aunt Elsa and Richard and everybody—the times when Val's figure was really not looking too unattractive at all, that, somehow, Val found it difficult to be unconscious for any length of time of the limbs that had hitherto carried her carelessly forward, not unlike the Winged Victory rushing down the steps in the Louvre Gallery.

Val had reasons, just now, for being peculiarly sensitive about her appearance. She responded to suggestion. . . . Gradually she avoided sight of herself in the mirror; gradually she avoided sight of Loraine running, Loraine climbing like a cat, Loraine slippery and boneless, leaping down from walls with hardly a jar in her contact with the ground, or slinking from bough to bough in the tree-tops. Val wondered if Stephen Greenways had ever looked from Loraine to her, and used the word—no, she could not use it herself, thinking of Stephen ; it was such an uncomfortable little monosyllable, like a germ in the air. She did not know how the obsession had glided in. Even the Winged Victory might not have carried herself so superbly if a tourist had once murmured in her hearing : " Fat " . . . and passed on.

And then, too, Val felt diffident and uneasy, now, whenever she wore Stephen's gift. At first she had often slipped it on, from an artist's delight in it, and her woman's profounder delight to appear, even in the man's absence, as he must have envisioned her when buying the coat. But Richard and Aunt Elsa looked at her so queerly whenever she wore it, so anxiously, as though they feared some unhappiness in store for her, and would have warded it off if they could. And Stefania, instead of murmuring with an appreciative gleam in her huge brown eyes, " Ma, chè bella, Signorina ! " whenever she saw Val in the stiff, glowing sheath of cyclamen and blue and emerald, would walk past with her small head held high and turned away, and afterwards they could all hear Marietta rowing her in the kitchen. Mysterious quarrels in the kitchen were frequent now, and they bothered Val, who was fond of the " infant school," as she called her diminutive staff. Now and then, too, she interrupted conversations between Giles and Aunt Elsa and Richard and Loraine—for Loraine was always up at the cottage lately—and she knew she was interrupting them, not from anything she overheard, but because whenever she came in, an entirely fresh subject was at once introduced, usually by the resourceful Loraine. . . . It was odd that at her entrance they had always just finished one particular subject of conversation, and were starting another.

Loraine, however, was the only one who did not suddenly lapse into a stricken and self-conscious condition whenever the coat was mentioned. Loraine knew a lot about Chinese art and old Oriental customs :

—" There you are, Val ! " Triumphantly she pounced on Val's rather silly mistake about hereditary Mandarins. Loraine was abnormally well acquainted with details about the difficult examinations that had to be passed before any Chinaman could become a Mandarin. " *There* you are, Val ! That proves you're absolutely Western at heart, or you'd have known that. You think of the East in terms of cheap bazaar. You're only interested in your own limited outlook ; your whole philosophy is Occidental ; any man who had travelled would laugh his throat dry if you should be after saying anything like that to him ! "

Queenie said : " What a wonderful chum you'd be, Loveliest, to a great man who travelled. Do you know——" to the patient others—" Loraine can toss down fiery *rum* without drawing breath, even, and not feel it ; like a man. And I simply don't know how you can remember things, like all you told us about the Pekin stitch, was it ? And all the poor little Chinese embroiderers who went blind doing it, so that it was stopped by law."

" Is it in my coat anywhere, that special Pekin stitch ? " Val asked, her interest aroused.

" Do you actually mean you can't find it yourself ? "

" If I could, I shouldn't ask you, Loraine."

After a pause, Loraine said, " Yes. It's in the coat. I noticed it at once. That's how I knew it must be genuinely old, because the Pekin stitch doesn't exist in the modern Chinese stuff."

" I should think not, if it cost the worker his sight. No stitch would be worth that."

" It might be—to the artist ! " Loraine blazed out, truculently bent on forcing Val into displays of ignorance and stolid mediocrity. " But I suppose you proud painters don't grant the title of artist to the poor souls who only know how to use a needle with a thin silk thread at the end of it."

The proud painter in question merely replied that she would rather argue with a hurricane than with Loraine. . . .

" The patient men and women who called into creation those storks and dragons and flowers and butterflies and rainbows on your coat, who never allowed their eyes time to rest on real blossoms and birds flying—don't you think they disdained the shoddy Western folk : little grey beings who performed dingy hasty work under a dingy sky ? don't you think they disdained their meagre sacrifices, and their hurried scramble to get things *done* so as to see the results quickly . . . These workers, who thought a lifetime and their eyesight too little to squander for decorating a square half-yard of silk—perfectly ! "

" I'd give up the coat, gladly, to leave them their sight."

" And that point of view they'd despise too ! To them it was just worth while, to achieve these controlled and minute arabesques, for me, lover of beauty, to appreciate two hundred years later . . ."

" Never did I let Melanie and Freda work too long wiz the bad gaslight on a sideboard-cover wiz crochet lace even though I knew I must not be seeing because those dear girls meant it as such a nice surprise for my birthday ; but, I said, eyes come first and surprises second, isn't it ? " Such was Aunt Elsa's warmly personal contribution to the discussion on Oriental aspects of philosophy.

" I once knew a girl," Loraine darted off at a fantastic tangent, " who bit her nails, but otherwise she was glorious as a lyric by Shelley. And there was a man who would have loved her, but for the blemish of her finger-tips. He was an artist as the Chinese understand it, you see, Val, and could only be satisfied by perfection——"

" Is this going to be a story specially invented to bully me ? " Val asked, a trifle apprehensively.

" Or is it all about something that happened to you, Loraine ? Oh, *is* it ? I do hope so ! It often is, when you begin like that," cried Queenie, ingenuously, " with : ' I once knew a girl.' But if it's you, won't you tell us ? "

But Loraine simply flashed her a smile, and went on, jongleuse squatting in a bracelet of sunshine, romancing to the group on the loggia :

—" So while he was away, she tried and tried and tried and failed, and tried again, and was tempted by her old habit, and had to start anew from the beginning . . . but she did succeed at last, and just in time for his return. How she longed to show them to him—ten little oval shields of pale pink pearl guarding her soft finger-tips. . . . But he found her lying in bed, with her wrists in bandages, her hands amputated——"

" Oh, *Loraine !* "

Loraine's voice had grown harsh : " A child fallen in the way of a motor-car—— The girl, saving it, had her fingers mangled in the wheels—— They had to operate quickly. Well . . . you wouldn't have desired her to hold back, would you, because her hands were beautiful now, and she had so wanted to show them to her lover ? At first he could not understand her distress that he had not come a day sooner ;— only one day *sooner*, she kept on repeating. He had been away a year and two months ; and just a year and two months it had taken her laboriously to allow her nails to grow for his fastidious pleasure. Ah now, but you needn't look downcast, Queenie, my dear, for I've a happy ending all ready and waitin' for you, to be served with shrimp sauce an' parsley : for when she told him, crying from weakness and disappointment, poor maid !—he loved her all the more passionately—an' what man wouldn't ?—for the beautiful hands that she had sacrificed to keep a human child unhurt, before she had ever been able to show them to him at all. They remained his dearest treasures, those ghost hands with their ten little oval shields of pale pink pearl. . . . An' there are, indeed, two jokes to this story I've told you ! One of them being that it illuminates your side of our quarrel, Val, instead of mine ; which I knew before I'd even begun but, being noble, I was not letting that stop me ! "

" It's humiliating to be backed by one's opponent," said Val. " What's the other joke ? "

" The other joke is hidden in the story itself, not in its moral ; clenched tight in the two hot palms of the girl I once knew, who lost her hands and won a happy martyrdom. For listen again : she had been in such a wild state of nerves, during the night before her lover turned up, that she had bitten away every one of her pretty new nails . . ."

" Oh, *Loraine !* But that spoils it ! "

—With a laugh for Queenie's shocked exclamation, and declaring that she was tired of high society, Loraine flitted away indoors, to the kitchen, where, through the window, she could be heard entertaining the infant school and Luigi . . .

But, " I *did* think at first, didn't you, Giles ? didn't you, Miss Power ?—that Loveliest was going to tell us a story about herself. Something mysterious in the way she twinkled at me, when she said ' A girl I knew ' ! "

" The heroine quite certainly *was* going to work out at herself," Giles delivered a verdict rather unusually caustic, for him. " And that was the third joke. . . . She remembered only just in time that it would be difficult to account for the fact that she still had her two hands. I saw her . . . realising this. It isn't likely, otherwise, that Loraine would let such a chance slip ! "

. . . And Val silently sent Toni a reassuring message. Giles was not in the very least in love with Loraine any more, whatever he had been last February. Giles saw right through Loraine. . . . " After all," said Val aloud, " she does hang our empty hours with tapestries ! "

" You've caught that florid style from Loraine," he teased her.

" My dear Giles, we're a florid family ! "

" A torrid family ! A *horrid* family ! Richard's the only austere member of it ! "

Aunt Elsa cried : " Vot is that about the family ? "

And Richard looked up, at sound of his name : " I was wondering about that accident with the car," he said. " I don't see, honestly I don't, *how* she could have had her hands mangled, and nothing else, while the child escaped unhurt. Where, exactly, was the child, while the wheels of the car went over her hands——? "

—" And what make of car was it ? " remarked Giles, very seriously ; " that's the really essential question. . . ."

CHAPTER VII

"LORD, how it's pelting down!" Richard remarked. "Didn't know you got these tropical rains here. It looks as though we're going to have a cloud-burst."

Giles, whose foot had almost healed during the last week's skilful treatment and massage, limped across to the window: "There's a whole crowd of people coming up the hill. Wonder if they're coming here, or if they're just taking a walk. They seem a bit wet.—Val," he added, as the door opened, "about twenty people are coming up the hill. You don't happen to know 'em, do you?"

Val smiled at her assembled house-party. "Yes," she said, "I saw them as I dashed down from the studio. It's my Aunt Amélie and my Uncle Nathan——"

"What!" shrieked Aunt Elsa, overturning her work-basket.

"—my cousin Etienne, my cousin Camille, my cousin Jeanne-Marie, two brats—presumably the property of Camille and Etienne—and another four or five whom I don't know. Cousins, too, perhaps!" Her hands in her pockets, and still that odd, ironic smile on her lips, she leant back against the wall, and watched the effect of her announcement.

Loraine cried at once: "Ah, but how thrilling!" and dashed out, bare-headed and practically bare-shouldered, into the rain, to welcome this still unknown portion of beloved family.

"You vill stop here!" cried Aunt Elsa, but it was too late.

—At the same time, Richard ejaculated: "The San Remo lot! Christ! Shall I bolt?"

"Yes! No! At once! Sit where you are!" from Aunt Elsa. "Gott im Himmel! Why didn't Amélie let me know? A little consideration——"

"I shouldn't worry, Richard," said Val, laconically. His

249

episode with Jeanne-Marie had been fierce while it lasted, but it was six years since Richard had been saved—by her, as it happened!—and the older generation—led by Aunt Elsa, as it happened!—had been routed. Little Jeanne-Marie's excuse for her wilful swerve aside from virtue had been, according to Richard, so ardent an admiration for her famous grown-up cousin Val, that she desired to imitate her in everything . . . "Well . . . here we all are!" said Val.

The San Remo family, of course, could have had no notion that Richard was actually, and at this moment, staying with Val. It was too late to do anything: already the clamour of voices was pouring like an inverted waterfall up the garden path. Aunt Elsa suddenly realised that, apart from the unparalleled catastrophe of Richard in the house, she would also have to answer to Amélie for the bewildering presence, countenanced by herself, of Toni's husband with Loraine. Amélie would have heard the scandal—surely Truda and Wanda and Henrietta and all of them in London would have written. A dozen possible lines of action darted through her head; she attempted, giddy with horror, to seize them all and perfect one of them, at the same instant as the front-door opened. . . .

—"Mrs. Rakonitz," the ubiquitous Queenie was saying at her elbow, " I don't think we have chairs enough if they should stop and want to sit down. Shall I——"

Aunt Elsa, unhappy and beset, cried angrily: "You are good for nossing, I tell you, nossing, nossing, nossing!"—And with a guilty soul and reeling brain, and a tongue gallantly babbling affection and welcome, she trotted out into the hall to meet that dear Amélie.

Val, with a humorous shrug of the shoulders, followed her.

At once a clamour of explanation, hospitality, family affection, news and reproaches, introductions and greetings and solicitude, beat and shattered with such overwhelming din against its imprisoning walls and ceilings, that it seemed they must at any moment collapse.

(. . . "This," said Giles to Richard, in the sun-room, " this is the cloud-burst!")

"But Amélie——"

" But Elsa——"

" No, but such a treat, such a surprise——"

" You had my letter ? "

" Ach ! You sent a letter ? "

" But I tell you, three whole days ago ! "

" But it is impossible ! And Camille's children,—how fine they look, how pretty ! What, only eight, the youngest ? Ach, and so wet——"

" Shall I get dry shoes, Mrs. Rakonitz ? What size——? "

" If you would be so kind, *ma chère.* . . . But what a surprise, Elsa, to have been met, outside, by a new sweet little cousin ! And she tells me she is a daughter of our Uncle Andreas. *Pas possible !* Na—*eh bien*—and *what* do you think we have come to tell you ? "

A shrill scream from Aunt Elsa ! . . . " No ! *Engaged ?* The little Jeanne-Marie ? Your baby ? And this is her fiancé ? You must let me—yes, an old Aunt—she always kisses ! So . . . and again . . ."

" At once I said : ' Nathan, we must take him over to see Elsa. It is our duty, and a pleasure. San Remo is only three hours away ; *ce n'est rien !* "

" But what a day to come ! What bad fortune ! So soaked, and no road up here. . . . You had to walk."

" And this, let me present you, is Orlo's father, Count Vassiloff ; and his uncle ; his sister ; his sister's husband. My dear cousin, Madame Rakonitz. . . ." Then, in an aside : " I could not leave them behind, you understand ? "

" Such a real pleasure. . . . But dying of hunger and thirst you must be, yes ? "

" My dear Elsa, what room have you for such a party ?— From all you wrote me, I thought the house was much, but much larger."

" Sorry," came in Val's voice, unexpected, cool and clear, amidst the froth and tumult. " But of course we can manage quite easily."

. . . " Oui, oui, oui, from Moscow . . . that terrible revolution has driven us here as *émigrés*, Madame Rakonitz ; just poor *émigrés* now——"

—" Why do you say that, when you know that you are one of the best and oldest families——? "

" My dear Amélie, but how enchanted they will be in England! You have written to the family? They have heard? But why has nobody told me before? Only two days ago?—no, three?—And a dinner-service. . . . Yes, yes, *yes*, your mother will tell you that old Aunt Elsa always gives a dinner-service! And you who have lived with me like a daughter, wiz my own daughters—— But all in white, Jeanne-Marie!—and on a day like this! As trotzig as ever with your extravagant ideas! Even a bride! For after all, only three days engaged—— Why do you allow it, Amélie? And ze nurse, she can speak Italian? She can go in ze kitchen with our Italian servants? "

" But she *is* Italian! I have told you three times! "

" But you have *not* told me that Camille's children's nurse is Italian! But Nathan will surely have rheumatism if we stand here! Val, why do you not take them where there is a fire? And you, Orlo—I may call you Orlo? Of course. And your uncle and father and sister and brozzer, too? "

" They are not all called Orlo," Jeanne-Marie explained, sedately cheeky. And the torrent poured into the sun-room.

Three out of the four Russians had fastened themselves on to Val; and with bright, light, mad eyes, and with that ghastly fluency which is characteristic of their race, were telling her just how their souls behaved when toppled from riches and high estate, and thrust into positions of beggared humility in San Remo. She saw, from her confinement within these barriers of unrestrained soul, that Aunt Elsa's reckoning had come, and that she could not assist her. . . .

Loraine, in her childish joy at meeting another branch of the Rakonitz family, had quite forgotten that there was any reason whatever for embarrassment on her behalf; and was fully occupied, as well, in charming Uncle Nathan, Etienne, and Camille, the relatives nearest to hand, and in making friends with the two children, while stripping them of their soaked shoes and socks. Queenie presently reappeared with a whole armful of assorted dry garments; rivulets and pools of water

were dripping from the visitors' clothing all over the tiled floor ;
Terry and Mac were barking furiously ; the Russians had got
well away with the story of their spiritual life . . .

—And here were Aunt Amélie and Richard suddenly brought
face to face, as two who meet across an open grave. Last time
they had met had been at Aunt Elsa's house, late on the eve of
Richard's enforced marriage with Jeanne-Marie. And then
Richard, incited at the eleventh hour by that rebellious traitor,
Val, had firmly, heavily, desperately, and quite obstinately,
refused to atone for his villainy. . . . Last time they had
met !

"How do you do, Aunt Amélie?" said Richard . . . and
suddenly he caught a comic look from Giles, and became in-
fected by the prancing spirit of gay lunacy rampant in Val's
cottage. He saw, too, that Aunt Elsa was about to have
hysterics ; and that Madame de Yong's bosom, corsetted and
controlled and usually implacable, was now heaving slightly
from the tempest within. . . . Richard's gloom lifted, and his
deep-set eyes twinkled. "I say, I must congratulate you. I
hear Jeanne-Marie has just got engaged. Topping ! You
must be awfully bucked, you and Uncle Nathan."

"And such a wonderful match !" quavered Aunt Elsa.
"Not a penny, you say, but noble, and an old title, and zere
may be anozzer revolution the ozzer way round, in Russia.
And, till then, if the dear Nathan's business is going so well as
you boast——?" And then, with a quick twitch of the understanding, Aunt Elsa realised, amazed but with exquisite relief,
that Amélie must be, logically, just as frightened as she was
herself; and that this encounter with Richard was—to say
the least of it—decidedly inconvenient. Here was she with her
young daughter, Jeanne-Marie, tall, slim, golden, a *jeune fille*
in white, with cast-down eyelids, and a heart presumably
cherished and unsophisticated ; here *cette pauvre* Amélie was,
so proud to have a daughter newly engaged, bringing her
daughter's fiancé to San Goffredo, knowing that dear Elsa was
there ; partly to boast, over Val, that Jeanne-Marie was now
rangée ; partly in genuine affection, because the de Yongs, not
anglicised like the London branch of Rakonitz, still held close

to the family tradition that neither birth, death, nor marriage should rightfully take place among them, unless all the other available members of the family were called in to triumph or to mourn. . . .

—" And the first thing we meet is that dreadful Richard ! " wailed Aunt Amélie, in silent consternation. The one episode in Jeanne-Marie's career that must at all costs be buried and forgotten, concealed from Jeanne-Marie's prospective husband and the prospective husband's father, uncle, brother and sister ! If only she had not brought them all along ! But how could she know ? How *could* she have known ? How like Elsa not to have informed her ! And now, what was Richard going to tell ? Would he be discreet ? How would Jeanne-Marie behave ? Would she be discreet ?

. . . " How are you, Jeanne-Marie ? " spoke Richard's slow, English voice, like an ominous thudding accompaniment of drums to Aunt Amélie's mounting panic.

Val, rising above her enthusiastic Russians like Aphrodite from the waves, just caught a glimpse of the meeting between the hero and heroine of an old story, before she was once more submerged.

. . . " How do you do, mon cousin ? " Jeanne-Marie was sublime—a snow-maiden, virginal, without a tremor. " It's a surprise that you should be out here visiting Val. Maman, will you present to him my fiancé ? "

Richard wondered if she knew that he was married ; that he had two sons. He exulted, thinking of Jim and Tommy ; of Molly's seat on a horse ; of the long stiff furrows of freshly-turned earth, on his farm. He exulted in his escape from all this—this foreign mess. Good old Val ! Oh, good Val ! Not all Jeanne-Marie's fairness could lure him into even a passing spasm of regret. His lot had fallen into pleasante rplaces. He had sown his seed in English soil. He shook Count Orlo Vassiloff heartily by the hand, thinking, with no rancour, what a fine-looking fellow he was, and wondering why Aunt Amélie looked so scared and yet so indignant ; and why Aunt Elsa hustled their little group away from what she thought a dangerous moment . . . thus landing herself, plumply and

neatly, out of the frying-pan that was Richard, into the fire
that was Giles:

"But vait, Amélie. . . . So many people, so much family,
and half of you don't know ze ozzers; and now see, we have
left Giles out, and there he is standing with no one to talk to.
Come here a minute, Giles—yes, he has hurt his foot, poor
boy—and meet your Aunt Amélie."

"Giles?" said the formidable Amélie, enquiringly.
"*Giles ?*"

Aunt Elsa remembered, then, with a sinking at the knees.
She remembered that in the eyes of Amélie and Nathan, Giles
ought not to be here; and if he were here, Toni should be
here too; or, if Giles were here without Toni, then Loraine
should not be here with Giles; and that, finally, if Loraine and
Giles were here together, (even if, as Val had said, there was
nossing . . .) then, most undoubtedly, she, Aunt Elsa, should
not be here, countenancing this terrible situation, lending
Rakonitz sanction to it, presumably in acquiescence with such
flamboyant immorality.

Giles came forward, smiling pleasantly. Like Loraine, he
seemed to feel no shame whatever.

"Giles?" repeated Aunt Amélie. "Not——? *Mon Dieu*,
Elsa!"

Aunt Elsa, in a last frenzied attempt to redeem her own
character in the eyes of Amélie and Nathan, who were contemporaries, and had the severe standards of their generation,
tumbled into a hectic improvisation of a Mr. Joddard who was
staying with Val on a visit. She trusted that the link between
him and Loraine might not have been revealed as yet; and
that in this haphazard confusion of strangers and relatives, it
would remain concealed until the end of the disastrous afternoon. But almost immediately she had to reject this idea;
for alas! she had already mentioned Giles, to Amélie, as being
one of the family, and Amélie's cousin-by-marriage. Alternatively, it occurred to her that she might locate Giles (as far as
Amélie was concerned) in the villa at the foot of the hill; and
that it should be Loraine who was staying up here with them,
the sweet little new cousin, Andreas' great-granddaughter.

" But naturally, Amélie, I am chaperoning her ! " How would that do ? . . .

And then all these evasions and subterfuges collapsed, as Amélie repeated :

" Joddard ? Giles Joddard ? Is that the one who was the husband of *cette pauvre* Antoinette ? " Her beady eyes flashed ; the little hairs above her lips bristled ominously.

" That's the low fellow," Giles assented, seeing that Aunt Elsa had gone all to bits. . . . " But *is* the husband, not *was*. I suppose, in a sort of way, I'm your nephew."

" He lives alone at the bottom of the hill," whispered Aunt Elsa, feebly. " But he has hurt his foot, poor boy." She had a sudden, magnificent, half-crazy inspiration that if she could get Amélie up to her own room, now, and then take her into the spare bedroom next door, and say that was where Loraine slept, it would effectually free her from suspicion of sanctioning the Giles-Loraine entanglement. It made, after all, so much difference where people slept. . . . But this idea was destroyed anew, when she recalled that the little spare-room would be full of Richard's razors and other masculine evidence. She had made her worst blunder in stating that Giles lived at the foot of the hill. If she had said that Loraine lived there, where would have been the harm in Giles sharing a room with Richard ? With a heavy sigh, Aunt Elsa resigned herself a victim to circumstantial evidence ; and feeling no better, as she afterwards told Val, than a *procureuse*, she led zat dear Amélie upstairs to take off her hat, and change her soaked shoes and stockings. She tried very hard to lead the talk round to rheumatism, sciatica, lumbago, and other perfectly harmless manifestations of nature.

But Aunt Amélie realised that she had only one defence against Aunt Elsa's spiked reminders that Jeanne-Marie was a *jeune fille* with a past—and a past, moreover, perilously in the vicinity !—and that was to raise a still greater storm of indignation against Aunt Elsa's own vulnerable spot ; so she refused to let her moral sternness be propitiated nor hoodwinked on the subject of Giles and Loraine. Elsa had no right to allow it ! Elsa had no right to call Giles " that dear boy," when *cette pauvre petite* Toni was *desolée*, fretting her heart out, an abandoned wife, over in London ! Elsa had no right to call Loraine a " dear girl." They were sinners . . .

Brushing back her oily black hair ferociously from her plump and pasty face, Aunt Amélie went a little too far. She told Elsa that not only would Elsa's own four good girls have their chances of marriage imperilled by their mother's slackness of outlook and tolerance *si outré ;* but she said, furthermore, that she did not like her own daughters to meet . . .

" You speak to me *not* of your own daughter ! " cried Aunt Elsa, " who was no better than a charlotte in a broth-house before she was eighteen, yes, and still I kept her in my house so that you and Nathan can marry her quickly to hide her shame ; and a good sing, too, that Richard turned his back on her, for he has got a much, much better vife now, who vos a good girl before she vos married, which vos more, Amélie, than your Russian Count will be able to say if he knew, which I suppose you have not told him ; no, but *I* will, unless you are polite in zis house, remembering where you too must shame yourself and not trying to teach me, isn't it ? " . . . And then Aunt Elsa wound up with a sentiment which demolished in a few stupendous words her own virtuous, stern and autocratic principles, and those of the whole Rakonitz family of the past seventy-three years ; and swept her right across, a rebel, a deserter, a flaming deserter, into the ranks of the young generation : " As for Toni in London, what you reproach me with, she knows how to manage her own affairs better than you and I can manage them for her, yes, even if we don't know what she is doing and vy !—And if you have now finished brushing your hair, Amélie, and it is not at all becoming at your age, the way you do it ; it should be softer round the face, for it is not as though your nose turned up, no !—we will go downstairs."

. . . Aunt Amélie was very subdued when they joined the others. Aunt Elsa, on the contrary, was flushed, and her bright sloe eyes gleamed triumphantly. In the full sight of Amélie, she gave Loraine, in passing her, a warm kiss, quickly and spontaneously returned by Loraine, always ready for demonstrations of affection from her darling Auntie. And then Aunt Elsa, with a slightly piratical roll in her walk, crossed the sun-room to where Richard and Giles, Jeanne-Marie and her fiancé, stood in a little knot; and cracked one or two hilarious jokes with Giles on the subject of betrothals—jokes distinctly Viennese in flavour, which surprised even Jeanne-Marie; then she pinched them all heartily by the ear, yes, even Count Orlo . . . and felt much better. Her knees had ceased to quake, and she would never fear Amélie again !

But the amazing behaviour of Aunt Elsa was only one item that contributed to the making of the rest of the day into a sort of jocund nightmare. Not one of Val's original house-party was behaving normally, except Loraine, to whom a fitful and freakish atmosphere was, indeed, normal. Nobody appeared to sit still for long. Clumps of them rushed from room to room, in varying and often surprising assortments of two and three and four; sat down to eat and drink, stood up again to dance to the gramophone; scampered through the rain up to Val's studio to see her pictures; scampered down again, single file, like supers in a cinema : Aunt Elsa, Uncle Nathan, Aunt Amélie, Val and the Russians, nurse and the children, Loraine, Camille and Etienne, Richard and Jeanne-Marie, Giles last of all, limping.

In Uncle Nathan, a mild little man with the upturned, twisted moustaches falsely attributed to villains, had sprung up a fervent admiration for Queenie. He had never before seen anything so beautiful as Queenie; not even his own daughter, Jeanne-Marie, was as beautiful as Queenie. Queenie's job, for the afternoon and evening, was mostly an attempt to collect chairs together—as many chairs as there were people— in whichever room the visitors happened to be congregated. And as Uncle Nathan belonged to a chivalrous age, and could not bear to see so lovely a girl performing low, menial offices like carrying chairs, he spent his hours rushing along in front of her to open doors, wrestling with her in an attempt to snatch a chair from her hands ; or, if he were too late, rushing breathlessly along behind her : " Mais je vous en prie, je vous en prie—pardon—laissez-moi—it is not right—dear child, I am almost old enough to be your father "—and indeed, Uncle

Nathan, whose eldest child, Camille, was at this time thirty-seven, was really quite old enough to be Queenie's father !

Val quite simply could not free herself from her attendant Russians ; wherever she moved, the Russians came too. They said they had discovered in Val a precious sympathy for their sufferings, and a frankness and courage in the agonising art of living, which reminded them entirely of their own lost country. Val was helpless : whatever she did, whatever she said, roused them to ecstasies—it was so Russian ! Finally, she resigned herself to being a Dostoievsky heroine in spite of herself ; resigned herself to their confidences, which streamed limpidly on and around her, pouring down upon her head, winding in coils about her ears, a limpid, ceaseless flow, stark and shameless. . . .

Giles, whose innate spirit of harlequin perversity flourished amazingly in surroundings like these, devoted himself to Aunt Amélie. Even better than confiding in Queenie, was the bizarre sensation of confiding in Aunt Amélie. As blandly and as childishly, almost, as one of the Russians, only with a look in his eyes that betrayed his intent to those who knew him well, he confided in Aunt Amélie the entire inner history of his marriage, involving a long sequence of events which had never taken place ; quoting scraps of letters which Toni had never written him ; reviling Loraine, whom he declared had been the evil genius of his life—Loraine's flicker of a wink at long-distance range, tested his gravity for an instant ! And, in a grand peroration, he begged Aunt Amélie to act as his ambassador, and start off instantly for London at his expense, if she didn't mind travelling third-class in a good cause, and see his poor wife, and say that if it had not been for that *sale chien* of a Montenegrin mackerel, Giles would never have deserted her. . . Giles was perhaps going a little too far in his revelations when he thus implicated Toni, but it was so difficult to remember that Toni was not actually there, to be amused by his performance. In the medley of fantastic events which had made to-day so grotesque, it would hardly have been surprising to him if he had suddenly caught Toni's eye, instead of Loraine's, across the room, and solemnly winked at

her. Letting Toni down? Absurd! Of course Toni was
laughing too. Distance was nothing, to-day; and actions which
had gone before, were lying severed from the present moment,
impotent to control it. Cause and effect were a senseless jingle.
Time was a farce, and could be dealt with and demolished, as
disrespectfully as whacking a bald head with a bladder. It was
the world's mistake, hitherto, to treat time solemnly. . . . He
had not yet married Toni—— He had just seen her in her
yellow dress, beside the duck-pond, sun in her eyes, laughing!
. . . Leap four-and-a-half years!—What a good time they
had enjoyed! . . . Babs, Paul, and Antony. . . . An unreal
scene about some fool of a fellow called Belworthy, remotely
connected with a firm of dressmakers in Hanover Street. . . .
All dissolved at a touch of the imagination. Nothing was true
except this mad assembly of mad people, cardboard puppets
dressed in tinsel. . . . Presently, they too would dissolve.
What could be more ridiculous than these persons from the
Russian stage?—the sort of play only highbrows went to,
special performances—— Well, and here *was* a special performance; only they were related to him, yes, soberly, link by
link, like this—like this, see?—He had met Toni and married
her; and Toni's cousin was Jeanne-Marie, and Jeanne-Marie
was soon to be married to Count Orlo, and Count Orlo had
brought along his father, his uncle, his sister, and his sister's
husband—— Query: how was the husband of the sister of
Count Orlo related to Jimmy? . . . Just another link or two,
and there you are! And who was that girl singing French
nursery chansonnettes, acting them so drolly and with such
spirit, to divert the two children—foreign brats!—Who *was*
the dancing girl? She had Toni's face, only . . . That was
Loraine, Loraine Rakonitz. Why, he had done a bolt with
Loraine, eight months ago; left Toni for this girl; and yet
his Aunt-by-marriage Amélie was still his Aunt-by-elopement
Amélie! . . . What a silly game! What a damn-fool game!
How cracked we all are! "I must tell Queenie about that!
Queenie'll be shocked": "Oh, Giles!'" . . . Hullo! and here
was Val in her Chinese coat—in Loraine's Chinese coat. She
had gone and put it on to show the Russians, perhaps; or

because Queenie had been telling Camille, mother of the brats, how lovely it was ; or because Val herself felt crazy and many-coloured, and found in her coat the symbol of her mood, as a musician would find it in a burst of what is called modern music.

The San Remo party were to take the eight-twenty train home again. Queenie, still in the rôle of " the only practical one," had suggested to Val, in a low discreet voice, that there should be no sit-down early dinner—she had had enough of carrying chairs about, even with the assistance of infatuated Uncle Nathan !—but a sort of stand-up supper with drinks and refreshments, whatever she and Marietta could improvise.

So everybody roamed about, and took what they liked. Two carriages had been ordered to wait for the party, at the foot of the mule-track by Villa Bel Respiro, to drive them to the station. It was now well after seven o'clock ; some of the party were still eating and drinking ; some were dancing ; the gramophone was playing the " Julian " tango.

" Ah, these new French tangos, they're no good," cried Loraine, impatiently ; " stiff as pokers, and correct as a Church Meeting ! Put on an old Argentine tango, and we'll show them, Giles. No, I forgot your foot ; but Etienne said he knew the Argentine tango." So Loraine snatched off " Julian," and put on " Cup of Sorrow," instead ; and she and Etienne swayed and glided and dipped, their bodies free and pliant, her hip pressed sinuously against his ; while the Russians thoroughly enjoyed the performance ; and Richard thought : " Good Lord ! If I ever saw Molly do that—— ! "

. . . Val seemed disturbed about something. Released for a moment from her troupe of attendant Russians, she had walked across to Aunt Elsa, asked her advice, showed her . . .

Aunt Elsa gave a shriek.

—" Loraine ! " called Aunt Elsa. " Loraine, stop for a moment zat nonsense, isn't it, and come and look at zis, and tell us a little how we had better take it out, quickly. It was you who rubbed that stain for me—egg and tomato—from my mauve satin, quite vonderfully. And Val has spilt somesing—wine, I think—on to her coat."

Aunt Elsa had forgotten, in her agitation, that there had ever been a certain question of ownership.

Loraine had stopped tangoing at Aunt Elsa's first summons. She was always ready to help on a question of practical efficiency, rather proud of her leadership in such incongruous matters. Val showed her the blemish on the coat—a dark splash on the cyclamen brocade, and spreading over a plaque of the embroidery.

" Isn't it a shame ? My hand shook. It's that Barolo wine, I think. I only just noticed it. What am I to do ? "

. . . But Loraine, seeing the stain, had suddenly stiffened. " You fool ! " she accused Val, hoarsely. " You aren't fit to wear it, spoiling it like this. You big, clumsy fool ! "

. . . A hush fell on the noisy chattering groups round the room. Unconsciously they fell into a semicircle, their faces turned towards Loraine and Val, watching the development of this swift, inexplicable drama. Too late, Aunt Elsa remembered that she should not have consulted Loraine about the damage to the coat. With a sinking heart, she waited for the revelation that must come, now. Loraine was shaking with temper ; she would not be likely to control her tongue, after her coat, her precious coat, had been violated while worn by another.

Richard, too, expected that now Loraine must surely divulge the secret they had all been keeping from Val. He drew nearer. So did Giles. . . .

" It'll never be perfect again," half sobbed Loraine ; and, with what seemed to Val an absurdly passionate gesture, put her lips down on the embroidery where the splash of wine had darkened it, as though she would have protected it, had she been able, with a barrier of her own flesh. " It was perfect ; it'll never be perfect again."

Val pulled herself away. " A trifle over-excited, aren't you ? " she said, pleasantly. " You'd better run home to bed."

Loraine lifted her head ; she could have wept over her coat, but she enjoyed insulting Val ; it was rather a relief from her pent-up desire, ever since Richard's arrival, to be herself handling, stroking, wearing that gorgeous creation which Val had so casually spoilt. " You are the school-girl type," she said, uttering every word scornfully and distastefully ; " you believe you are an artist, but no artist could have injured such a work of art. Oh, you'd be all right in tweeds or a ' gym-dress,' or a nice, simple, white evening frock that you can ' send to the cleaners ' ; those are your style. And then you have the cheek to flaunt about the whole evening wearing my——"

Richard crashed in, just in time. He said anything that came into his head, however discourteous, which he thought might divert her fury less perilously from Val to himself : " Your manners are barbaric, Loraine. Just keep them in check, or else you needn't bother to come up here again."

He had achieved his purpose.

Loraine flung savagely round on him : " This house was Heaven before you came into it. I was always happy up here. You've brought in a dry-rot. Ever since you came, everyone has turned against me : Val and Aunt Elsa and Stefania and Terry. . . . You kept Giles up here, so that he shouldn't be with me ! You've got him over on to your side. Treachery ! Do you think I haven't seen it ? I'm *not* coming here again, not while you're here."

And with a cry that was partly another sob and partly an animal choking in rage, she hurled herself over the low window-sill, and vaulted, arms outstretched in front of her, as though pushing something away, from terrace to terrace of the garden, until she disappeared, running through the rain, under the olives that met over the mule-track.

. . . Val sighed. " How like Loraine not to have gone through the door," she murmured.

" Mon Dieu ! " exclaimed Aunt Amélie. " Quelle colère ! C'est épouvantable ! "

The Russians were all smiling, with animated, childish eyes. . . . They felt quite at home and comfortable.

" Please, Miss Power, I think I ought to go after Loraine, and sleep with her to-night. I do, really. She'll make herself ill over this. She's terribly upset. I think I'll go down, even if you forbid it," finished Queenie, very bravely.

More melodrama !—" All right, my child ; why on earth

should I forbid it? Aunt Amélie, I'm afraid it's time you all made a move, if you're going to catch that train. Queenie and Richard will go down, and show you the way. The carriages ought to be waiting by now."

But Queenie had already started. " Take down some brandy," Val called after her, " if you think Loraine is likely to have a heart-attack. She never has any brandy in the house. And by the way——" she raised her voice, for Loraine's votary was already half-way down the path, " you might ask Loraine, when she feels a bit better, what I'm to use to get those stains out of my coat? "

CHAPTER VIII

QUEENIE came up to breakfast the next morning, big with importance and secrecy; obviously she was complacent with the knowledge of being now aware of something hidden from Val. She patronised Val a little, at breakfast.

" Loraine's been very ill indeed, all night. I sat up with her."

Val refused to take any but a flippant view of the severe illness : " Is she coming to lunch to-day, to help eat up yesterday's supper ? "

" No, indeed she isn't." A touch of indignation was audible. " I'm not sure whether she will ever come to this house again ; not unless—— But I was wondering, Miss Power—I don't know whether I ought to say it ?—but I do believe Loraine might be brought round, if you were to apologise to her. She's awfully fond of you, you know."

" My dear Queenie, why should I apologise ? Because Loraine kicked up the devil of a scene in front of a crowd of relations, over a spot I'd made on my coat ? "

" Oh, but——" Queenie began . . . and very perceptibly checked herself.

Aunt Elsa came down to breakfast, just then ; and Richard and Giles strolled in from the garden a minute or two later.

Giles said : " You've put up with me for a long time, Val. My foot's almost well, so I'd better get down the hill to-day."

" I shouldn't, if I were you," said Val, significantly. " Loraine's ill."

Giles whistled. " Body of Bacchus ! Then I'll stop where I am for a bit ! Anyway, I'm going back to England soon." Heedless of the sensation he had just caused, he turned to Queenie : " How's the Martyr of Bel Respiro ? Pale, but forgiving us all with her last breath ? "

Queenie lifted her chin to a reproving slant. " I don't think

Val has any right to keep you away from Loraine, just now." It was the first time she had ever called Val by her Christian name, but she was a little shaken out of her usual sedate discretion.

" You shall not mix yourself into it, yes ? " cried Aunt Elsa.

Richard, who, like Giles and Aunt Elsa, had already guessed from Queenie's demeanour that now the secret of the coat had been unleashed for her benefit as well as theirs, and was consequently in a panic that she might let it re-escape upon Val at any instant, tried the same tactics with her, as last night with Loraine : he sought to divert her girlish indignation upon himself : " Loraine always kicks up ten times more fuss than anyone else, with fifty times less reason for it," he growled.

" Mr. Marcus, I thought you were abominably rude to Loraine last night. After all," Queenie went on, very temperamental and defiant, after her night spent in Loraine's company, " she was a guest in your cousin's house."

" It would be awfully jolly, Queenie," suggested Val, " if you were to teach us a few manners. Richard and I are terrible barbarians, you know ; we haven't even learnt the rudiments of good behaviour."

Queenie subsided for the nonce ; she could never cope deftly with sarcasm. And Aunt Elsa said :

"Mean you zat she is really ill, or zat she is only putting it on ? "

" Both," answered Val. " It *does* make her really ill when she's unpopular. I know Loraine ! She needs popularity as other people need oxygen ; and if she doesn't get it, she'll slowly lose her strength and sink. It's a queer phenomenon."

Queenie entered the lists again. " Oh, I don't think that's generous of you, Miss Power, and I don't believe you understand Loraine at all ; really I don't. She's not a bit easy to understand, but I promised her I would do my best. You see——"

" Thank you, Queenie. I don't need you to explain Loraine to me."

Queenie flushed a dull, resentful red ; she was of the type that takes offence slowly but thoroughly. " Loraine is being very kind to you, really," she began.

Richard got up abruptly and walked away to the window. He realised that he could not push back the secret any longer, now that it was fairly leaping from Queenie's tongue. Aunt Elsa looked at Giles. He shrugged his shoulders. It had better come now.

"Loraine's often been kind to me," replied Val. "Really, Queenie, Loraine and I agree excellently, and that's why I so hate this gaudy, picturesque, wounded-animal-at-bay business."

But Queenie, still smarting under the public snub she had received, said : "You never give Loraine credit for anything. She *can* do—noble things."

"Ach! Richard!" gasped Aunt Elsa.

Richard drummed with his knuckles on the window-ledge. "Go on, Queenie, spit it out and get it over!"

"Get what over?" asked Val, surprised at the nervous edge on his voice.

"All right, I will. You all sit on me because you think I'm a fool, and you are all beastly to Loraine. You even try to get Giles away from her, and the whole time it's *her* coat!" Queenie sprang up from her seat and turned her face, with its facile pink-and-white, full in Val's direction, so as not to miss anything of her expression. "The Chinese coat that you're so proud of—it's Loraine's. Mr. Greenways meant it for Loraine. He sent it out to her and not to you, because he was secretly in love with her. It was ' a message painted in silk.' Loraine knew at once that your cousin had made a mistake when he handed it to you, only she was too fine to say anything. She wouldn't say anything now, even though you have turned her out of the house. . . . I expect you'll be furious with me, but I don't care. I like justice!" finished Queenie.

And waited for the skies to burst.

"Well, and so do I, of course," said Val, very cheerfully. And the two men silently applauded. "And if the present is meant for Loraine, she must have it, though still I don't see what all the wow-wowing was about. I'll run down with it after lunch, but I must get some work done first." And she sauntered out into the garden, and up the path towards her studio.

Queenie looked disappointed. "She didn't seem to mind a bit!"

"You expected her to start spitting and fuming like your pal, the Queen of the Tiger-cats, didn't you?" queried Richard, to whom championship of Val had lent sudden and quite effective eloquence. Deeply troubled, he followed Val out of the dining-room.

"Now you, Queenie, go and do some work perhaps, yes?" Aunt Elsa was nearly weeping, but still vituperative; "and not be always running down and up, down and up, down and up the hill, making mischief."

Queenie was nearly crying, too. She suddenly felt very young, and wanted England and Potley Green and her mother and her nice friends at Potley Green Tennis Club. Her moral digestion, having been fed almost entirely on cold mutton and rice pudding, was not equal to all this *pâté-de-foie-gras* and truffles. And she had thought it would be so lovely to see "abroad." "I promised Loraine I'd come down again this morning," she blubbered.

"Then you have nemis promised her." Aunt Elsa dropped into a land of idiom whither Queenie could not follow. "You sink yourself very clever and pretty, isn't it? And you are nossing, nossing but a stupid goose and a fressack and a meesnick-in-Prague, and I am sorry, terribly sorry for the man who marries you, if he ever does which I sink he von't. And now go to your room, and do, for Heaven's sake, try and be a little bit useful with all zat appetite you have; for I see myself, wiz my own eyes, that even zis morning you eat more bacon than anyvon; and I should sink not your first breakfast either; I should sink from vot I know of you zat you take good care you have one before you come up the hill. And all ze curtains and ze bed-covers can be taken down and vashed, and ze rings put back. I have said it for ze last fortnight. To-day I mean it shall be done, if I have to trot after you and tell you all ze time. Du Himmel! One would sink you were an ornament and a princess, teaching us all our vays and manners! Now you stop looking at me like a sack of macaroni! Once you have let ze poker out of ze pig, you cannot put it back!"

—"*Per piacere*, Signorina," said Stefania, coming in at that opportune moment for Queenie, who was too stunned by Aunt

Elsa's outburst to have escaped of her own accord. "*Per piacere*, Signorina, Marietta does not know what to say to the *stiratrice* who has spoilt one of the Signore's English shirts when ironing it. She is here just now."

"Let her off lightly," Giles called after the departing Queenie. "As I was the signore who owned the shirts, I don't feel inclined to prosecute!" He turned to Aunt Elsa, now crying briskly and with immense gusto. "I say, you did let fly! It was great! I wish I could have taken it down!" Then, as Aunt Elsa's hysterical grief did not abate—grief compounded of sorrow for Val, wrath at Queenie, and reaction after yesterday's valorous combat with Aunt Amélie—Giles came and sat beside her, on the arm of the big chair; and without embarrassment, or any other of the usual soul-hindrances of young ex-officers brought up in the atmosphere of English public-school and country-house, he set himself to the task of comforting her. Most amazingly did he comfort her . . .

. . . .

Richard stood at the door of the studio. "Good old Val!" he said, finding her coolly occupied with the finishing touches to a characteristic portrait of Ettore and Vanna—a simple couple who kept a comestibile shop down in San Goffredo. She had been at work on this, off and on, before the inspiration of the Chinese coat had caused her to fling it aside. "Good old Val!"

She gave him the ghost of her own ironic smile. "How long have you known, Richard?"

"About ten days."

"Loraine told you?"

"Yes."

"Has she told Aunt Elsa too?"

"Yes."

"And Giles?"

"Yes."

"Anyone else?"

"A lot of Italian riff-raff!"

"You all let me make a pretty fool of myself, didn't you, swanking about in Loraine's Chinese coat? Why, I refused to let her wear it to be painted in—her own coat! Loraine was really rather generous—she spared me, then."

"Sorry, dear"; he was too inarticulate to express that thickness in his throat, which rose at sight of her cynical gallantry; "it was I who was the fool, making such a blunder. I don't quite know how to get it right again without hurting you. As for Queenie——"

"Oh, Queenie doesn't count," said Val contemptuously; "but I'm afraid there will be a reckoning with Loraine."

It was with the full consciousness of such a reckoning impending, that she sauntered down the mule-track, a few hours later, with the coat over her arm. The front door was opened by Manuela. The servant's hard, intelligent eyes gleamed at the coat, and then gleamed oddly at Val.

"My poor little Signorina is ill," she said. "I do not know what happened at your *festa* last night, but she came home very ill; all night I sat up with her, *la povera bambina*. It was not necessary that that other one, that young Signorina with the fair hair, should come down to nurse her; I alone would have been enough; I who am practical for illnesses of the heart. But what you have brought there will do her good; it is better than medicine for one who has a temperament like my Signorina, whom I love as if she were my own child."

"Damn the woman!" thought Val; "then *she* knows all about it, too. How Loraine must have let her emotions rip, in the night!" And in spite of the ache that shook her almost unbearably every time she thought of Stephen Greenways, she could not refrain from a little mischievous smile, imagining what her cousin's star night must have been like, with Manuela and Queenie as combined audience, ministering angels, and chorus.

Loraine was lying as Val had anticipated, remembering previous minor collapses : a still, white little figure in a white nightgown in a white bed; her mournful, uneven eyes, and the flat, wooden line of light brown hair, the only touches of colour. Her face was like a sorrowful goblin's.

"Here's your coat, Loraine," said Val, very gently.

CHAPTER IX

SHE did not look at the coat for quite a long time after Val had gone, but kept her head turned towards the window, where the dim softness of a rainy day blurred the silvery foliage of the olives, and the sea beyond. Thus she lay, tantalising herself. It was good to know that behind her in the room, broadly spread over two pegs in the wall where Val had hung it, was all that richness of colour ; good to know that when she arose from her bed, now that she felt the strength rushing back in her veins, she could feast upon it at her leisure, as she had always wanted to do ; learn to know apart the tiny brilliant butterflies ; learn to know her coat . . . *her* coat, now. Slowly, luxuriously, she dragged her eyes away from the world outside, turned on her back, hands clasped behind her head, and looked at the garment. Yes, it was even more of a miracle than she had imagined. Loraine stretched her limbs, and uttered a low sound that might have been a purr of content. How happy she was going to be, onwards into the next day, and the next, for ever after. Val had been such a darling ! No need to quarrel with Val, in the future ; between them was that subtle and elastic understanding that could be stretched and stretched, but never snapped ; for always it sprang back again to perfection. Val had behaved so beautifully over the coat, and everyone up at the cottage would begin loving Loraine once more. . . . Now that her nervous, flamboyant mood had been smoothed down again to restfulness and charm, she already loved them all. . . . Aunt Elsa and Richard—oh, she could easily make it up with Richard ; he had said brutal things, but she liked men to be frank. . . . And Queenie ? Queenie had made mischief, of course Queenie must learn not to be a mischief-maker, but at least she had been very loyal to Loraine. . . . Stefania and Terry. . . . All loving her again. . . .

A fold of the coat was turned back, showing the vivid green silk with which it was lined. It lay so boldly against the wonderful anemone pink, that Loraine's heart shivered with the poignancy of her appreciation. How glorious it was to love her friends, and be loved still more in return, and to own such a coat. . . .

Oh indeed, she felt very much stronger. She had been so ill this morning; the blood seemed to drag through her veins reluctantly; now they were filling like a stream into which the rain has poured; and like the stream, it sang little songs through her body . . . lilting, dancing along. Presently she would get up, and dress, and put on the coat, and go out, so that people should see her in it, and be glad because of it, as she was glad. .

Presently. There was no hurry.

And then, quite suddenly, as though some elusive influence passing outside had given her memory a sharp tug, she let herself think of Stephen Greenways. . . .

The coat was, after all, only a symbol of the richness and rareness of the romance which had inspired the sending. She was tired of the dull hues of ordinary love-making. Stephen would be different. He would transfuse into her life the same exotic tints as that coat, by simply hanging there, had showered into the room. Far away, where little yellow men worked with coloured silks, love was like that all the time, and Stephen was bringing it to her, this brilliant enchantment. He had sent her a message painted in silk. Soon, perhaps, he would send her a letter, written in words that were a further spell to illuminate the commonplace day. And after that . . . he would come himself.

So real for the moment was the expectation she had conjured up, that she actually started forward, sure of seeing Stephen, when the door was cautiously opened. . . .

But it was Manuela, with a glass of hot milk. The servant scrutinised her mistress closely; then she looked at the coat; then back at Loraine—and her smile was satisfied.

" E bella, n'é ? "

Manuela nodded, raising her hands to express in gesture the

admiration for which her tongue was inadequate; then she sat down on the end of the bed. She told Loraine over and over again how like an angel the signorina would look in that coat; how the citizens of San Goffredo would run and stare, and afterwards for many years tell each other about the beautiful English signorina in the Chinese coat; and above all, how the cavalieri would all become infatuated and fall at her feet, and die, and stab themselves. . . . "It is the English signore who sent it to you because he is mad for love, is it not so, my signorina? The Signorina Val, she stole it from you; she was wicked, but now she repents and brings it back."

Loraine corrected her, carelessly: "You must not speak so of the Signorina Val, Manuela. She did not willingly steal it. It was a mistake."

"I once knew of a mistake; it was *così:* two women there were, and one man . . ." She sat for a long time beside Loraine, gossiping, softly, maliciously, happily, about the enemies of the signorina; or, with just that typical lewdness in her manner, of the lovers of the signorina, and all the gaieties of intrigue.

Finally, Manuela said: "An English signore arrived here at San Goffredo, not two hours ago. I think it must be the same. . . . Luigi saw him at the station, and heard him speak to the station-master; and then he passed here on his way up the hill."

The swift association of ideas sent Loraine's eyes flying to the coat. Stephen! . . . It must be Stephen!

"You should have told me before, Manuela."

"*Mà!*" The servant was delighted; "it is he! I can see it by the Signorina's smile and the softness of her eyes; but how could I know? He went up the hill. If a man desires hotly, he comes straight to the house of the beloved one, and tells her of his desire."

"But Manuela, see, the lover's road is not always straight; sometimes it seems to lead away, and it curves, and it returns again. For the sake of courtesy he must make pretence that his visit is to the Signorina Val, in whose house he enjoyed hospitality last time he was here. Presently, later on . . ." Loraine's

voice grew dreamy . . . "later on, he will come down here to
visit me. . . . So I will rest first, and then I will feel stronger,
and rise and dress and wear his gift. But . . . hush, Manuela !
You will remember ? " She put her fingers to her lips, enjoin-
ing silence, and Manuela nodded several times ; while her
discreet and yet jocund look was a dig in the ribs and at the
same time a blessing. Still in the atmosphere of conspiracy,
she tiptoed from the room.

. . . Stephen had come. Yielding herself to the hypnotic
sway of the coat that hung on her wall opposite the bed,
Loraine lay luxuriously planning the future as though she
were in no hurry to savour reality.

. . . Still with those indolent, englamoured movements, she
presently rose, and made her toilet ; the drizzle of rain had
stopped, and she could see, by the reflection over the water,
that the westerly clouds had split and were barring a sky of
tender green and primrose.

She put on the coat, for the first time.

Then she went to the window, and looked out. She looked
up the terraced hill, to where, on the left from Val's cottage,
the olives parted and made a gap against the sky. There, the
sun had just dipped . . .

CHAPTER X

OUTSIDE the gate of Bel Respiro, Val met Lola with
the afternoon post, and Terry. Terry was plainly
meditating a visit to Loraine; and Val, once his idol,
politely held open the gate for him to pass through. Then she
took the letters and a few journals from England out of Lola's
hand, and went slowly up the hill towards her home.

She felt depleted.

When she had first heard from Queenie that Stephen had
sent the coat to Loraine, and not to her, her first thought was
at all costs to prevent a scene; to handle the affair lightly;
not to let Loraine see that it mattered to her, beyond the
material loss of a charming and expensive present. She had
succeeded in these aims, but the effort had left her emotionally
ruined and bankrupt. She was quite certain, she had been
certain all along, that Stephen's present was significant only as
a herald is significant, because he announces his master. If
Stephen had sent her the coat, it had meant, viewed straightforwardly and without false diffidence, that Stephen cared for
her, and that Stephen himself would be following soon. Stephen
had sent Loraine the coat; well, it meant the same thing;
only the direction was altered. She did not hate Loraine; she
hated herself, the unconscious buffoon of this episode. . . .
For naturally she had written to Stephen to thank him; and
—this is where shame stole in and burnt her cheeks and scalded
her throat—she had, in her frank manner, detesting veiled
allusions and mystery and pretended modesty, let him read in
this letter that she expected him to arrive soon, and would be
glad for him to come. She had gone on to say, in typical Val-
fashion, rather emphasised because of her recoil from all the
Loraine tricks of intrigue and delicate complication: "I'd
rather like you to know this, Stephen; it might save us a

difficult interview if I say it now : I've led the sort of life which I consider more or less all right, but which, according to Puritanical standards, would be considered all wrong. I'm not the sort of woman who debates, in a perpetual agony of indecision, through four hundred pages of a novel, and three acts of a drama, whether she should tell or should not tell, and goes on nagging the problem for years ; because I don't think it's a problem that matters, not to that extent, anyway ! I've never wanted to flap my private life, like a red flag, in people's faces ; it's undignified, and not worth while. But I might as well be telling you now, because you might have strong views on that subject. To some men, I know, it makes all the difference in the world—in fact, the difference has astonished me. I simply can't guess whether *their* sense of proportion has gone to pot, or mine ? . . . I feel perfectly sane and happy, but this may be a delusion. I may be utterly miserable and hopeless ; I may be wrung, tormented with the desire to atone ; I may be, but it doesn't feel like it : the sun shines out here more often than not, and I'm keen on my work—both good things ! Don't imagine I'm doing anything so Sardou-ish and overwrought as Confessing my Past ; I'm just mentioning it, so there you are !——"

She had written all this to Stephen . . . and there had been absolutely no need for it. He simply did not care a tinker's curse whether she were good or bad ; pure, or steeped in cherry-coloured sin ! Val had to clench her fists hard while she imagined Stephen's amazement on reading that letter ; imagined him wondering how chivalrously—for he was a decent type of man—he could cover up her blunder without too deeply humiliating her. There had hardly been time, as yet, for her to receive his answer. Probably he would ask Loraine's permission to pretend that he had all along meant the coat for Val ; probably he and Loraine would be able to afford this kindness to a beggar. . . . " And I can't even work ! " cried Val to the unresponsive olives. That had been mere bravado, this morning, using paint and brushes on an old portrait of Vanna and Ettore. The picture she had wanted to paint, the one in which Loraine had pleaded in vain to sit as model—

that could never be finished now, lacking the Chinese coat.
Finished? It was hardly begun. "Oh Lord!" said Val,
slowly, "what the hell am I to do?"... And here was home,
full of people who were sorry for her. Reluctantly she pushed
open the dining-room door; only Giles was there, sunk in
one of the big arm-chairs in front of the fire.

"Where's everybody?" asked Val, listlessly. "Here, do
you want to see the papers?" She handed him the rolled-up
copies of the *Onlooker*, and one or two others.

"Aunt Elsa has gone to bed," said Giles, "overcome by the
too-powerful violet rays that were in the air yesterday and
to-day! Queenie, I think, is writing a long, long letter to her
mother—I'll see if I can steam it open before it goes to the
post; it ought to be worth reading! And Richard, with a
strong man's oath, has taken Mac out for a good long tramp
over the hills—the kind of tramp that you're so keen on, Val!"
He eyed her keenly. "Up to the neck, aren't we, Val, you and
I? You're putting up a good show, though. I take off my
hat to you."

Val's acknowledging smile was a little weary; but she was
too raw to stop and discuss what had happened, even with
Giles; so she left him, and went out to the solitude of the
studio.

Giles had nothing else handy to read, so he opened the
Onlooker; but he knew already, more or less, what he was
going to find in it. Such daily papers as came through to San
Goffredo had already told him that; and all the exuberant
letters from exuberant theatre-goers, which Val and Queenie
had been receiving from England this past week. Colin on the
front page, Colin on the back page; interviews with Colin and
special articles on Colin; photographs in every conceivable
position; in every conceivable scene of his new play; Colin
Martial with the Vauxhall racing model he bought yesterday,
and the Rolls-Royce he meant to buy to-morrow. Colin
Martial, London's Idol, Darling of the Gods, Our New
Dramatist, Not-Yet-Twenty-Five; seen at the Fifty-Fifty,
seen at the Embassy, seen at the Kit-Cat, at Ciro's . . . in
fact, there hardly seemed to be a moment of the day or night

when Colin was not seen ! Already, cigarettes and restaurant
dishes were being named after Colin. He had made such a
splash as a whole Heavenly Host might have made, falling into
the middle of the Pacific Ocean. Every thirty or forty years,
it happens that young ambition achieves a dramatic success
of this nature; once it begins, it cannot stop; as at a
unanimous touch, all the fame-bells are set ringing; all
the paper lying about catches fire; all tongues chatter the
same name; all the sheep of fashion run hustling, pattering,
crowding into one narrow alley, hardly knowing why they
run.

Colin Martial was twenty-four and eleven months when his
comedy " She Burnt Her Boats " was tentatively put on in
London, with himself and Lucilla Danby in the two leading
parts. He had explained in an engaging interview, the day
after, that the title had actually been " She Burnt Her Boots "
. . . but that he and Miss Danby had decided that it would be
unlucky to correct the misprint in the preliminary announcements. This radiant sort of fooling with the Gentlemen of
the Press, was typically Colin. Stuffed away in a drawer,
awaiting their propitious hour, Colin had four or five other
plays as yet unproduced. Now, managers were, so the papers
reported, " fighting " for them. . . . Giles had a fantastic
vision of several middle-aged and glossy gentlemen with silk
hats, their foreheads spangled with sweat, lungeing violently
at each other with umbrellas, while Colin stood by, with that
faun-like smile which Giles knew so well—it was much more a
matter of the eye-brows than mouth. He and Colin Martial
had been good friends in London, during the protracted
carnival years which followed their meeting in the last month
of the War. They had both been at the high tip of popularity
in their set; both amazingly good dancers; both in possession
of unflagging high spirits. Giles was no less witty than Colin,
though his style was lazier; and Colin never allowed any of
his own numerous adversities to act as an extinguisher. Giles
remembered, now, looking at the frontispiece of this week's
Onlooker, headed " The Most Talked of Young Man in
London," how Colin used to solace himself over any set-back,

by rushing round to the studio, to plan, with a chubby relish that destroyed any sort of ghoul-like effect, how he was going to " do in " such and such an enemy ; and eventually reduce the whole lot, by his staggering triumphs, to a state of abject and imploring pulp !

. . . But it was incredibly like the simplest fairy-tale that it should actually have happened like that. Giles could imagine, knowing his friend so well, just how gloriously Colin was enjoying himself, and with what appreciation of detail ; no jargon of dust-and-ashes, no affectation of " dead-sea-fruit " and the hollowness of success, for Colin ; grapes tasted like grapes to him ; and cheers were cheers, not empty plaudits. He had been recalled fourteen times, that first night of " She Burnt Her Boats " ; and when he had at least expected the critics to be sour or caustic on the subject of too-easy success, the majority of these, too, were enthusiastic. As for gold, it must have been pouring in like the spring tides, from north, south, east, and west ; showering down with the surprising bounty of tropical rains ; thrown up as from hidden springs and fountains. Lucky Colin ! Prince of Luck ! Fortunatus ! Holder of the magic end of the wish-bone ! Dreamer whose dreams came true. . . . Giles murmured Kipling's lines, finding in them that queer solace which comes to the indolent man when a poet has fitted his mood with a perfect phrase :

> " Drawbridge let fall, it's the Lord of us all,
> The Dreamer, whose dreams came true."

. . . They singled out Colin, now, like a flash of summer lightning. Colin had never longed for more than this which had just been given him. His present success encircled the whole space of his dreams as with a ring of rubies.

And yet—" Dreamer whose dreams came true "—Giles had always imagined him older, more battered than Colin ; and without Colin's confident, springing impudence . . . The long, burnished slope led straight to the castle now, after it had looped and led away again for so many maddening years. All the malicious elfin host were pressed in panic against the walls

and battlements. . . . Here was the real dreamer at last, and
they had to yield :

> " I'll not fight with the herald of God!
> I know what his master can do . . ."

But he was tired, tired ; he walked slowly, and his eyes were
dazed and incredulous.   There was neither pomp nor arrogance
about this lonely figure on the long burnished slope till now
untrodden.   Surely he could hardly have realised that he was
a conqueror ?

> " . . . Open the gate, he must enter in state . . ."

Reluctantly the great doors were rolled back. . . . Giles leant
forward to peer at the face of the dreamer.   Breathless, half
terrified, and in awe, he recognised it.   His own face, as he had
always known it must be !   Though not yet his own face ; this
Giles was much, much older ;   more exhausted ;   so worn-out
by the fight that he trailed nearer and still nearer to the dancing
glitter of the castle walls in front of him, without ever seeing
that he had arrived. . . .

But what damned silliness !   His own face ?   And when had
man ever been further from dreams-come-true ?   It was Colin,
Colin, Colin Martial for whom the drawbridge had been
lowered ;   for him the gates were opened.   Giles railed scornfully at his own despicable, fatuous, self-deluded vanity, which
made him, even now, confronted with the unimportance of
his existence, yet try to drag himself, harnessed to a tawdry
allegory like a chariot borrowed from the Lord Mayor's Show,
into the lit streets where the cheering was.

He slowly turned the pages of the *Onlooker*, seeking for dis-
traction, and knowing he would not find it.   Colin was ubiquitous ;   Colin was everywhere.   The editor of the *Onlooker*,
like, probably, every other editor in London, had got Colin on
the brain . . .

In Venice, in a gondola, Giles had said to Toni : " I'd love
to stand in front of a cheering, raving, hectically applauding
crowd, all because of me ;   just for a moment focussing the sensation I'd won ; drinking it in.   I don't know for what, though ;

and it doesn't really matter . . ." Toni had been amazed, almost shocked ; she had called his ambition " cheap "—and, laughing, he had admitted it. So, with the thought of Toni, and idly turning over another page, he came to " Rosalie's " weekly article on " Fashions of the Hour "—and learnt that the firm of " Toni's," of Hanover Street, had designed Lucilla Danby's truly marvellous toilettes in " She Burnt Her Boats." Lucilla Danby had a reputation for smartness. And " Toni's " —or Toni, if you like !—had certainly created a sensation by the originality and daring of their designs.

In fact, " Toni's "—or Toni, if you like !—was sharing in the fun, too. Toni was on the pinnacle, hand in hand with Colin ; not quite so dizzy a pinnacle, perhaps, but good enough. Toni also would be sought after, congratulated, in the thick of it. . . .

Giles closed the *Onlooker*, and let it slide from his knees. He knew now that he was jealous ; jealous of Colin, of Toni, of both, over in London. He was sorry . . . for he despised jealousy ; he could mock at himself for being jealous, but he could not deny it. Here he was, in Italy, rather sick and out-in-the-cold—a very futile sort of man, with nothing to do and nothing done.

And his foot ached. . . . This additional trifle aggravated the sense of failure. Colin Martial had *all* the glory and the fun and the riches—and two feet that, presumably, did not hurt him with a single twinge. It was only when you were down-and-out, reflected Giles, unreasonably, that you sprained your ankle. Colin could dance . . . with Toni. They would be pointed out, excitedly : " Look—that's them ! Look ! " . . . " If I'd been in London, they might, perhaps, have allowed me to help shift a bit of scenery, now and then ! " . . . For what else could he do ? Out of it all, yes—but Colin and Toni had each their special job. You can't manufacture glory with hot air and gas as the sole ingredients.

He had made a mistake. He had been a fool. Of his own accord he had left it all. He was down among the dead men . . . there were no lights, no saxophones, down among the dead men !

What sort of new steps were they dancing now ? Would he

be able to do them, again? He would have to submit humbly
to be taught . . . and by that time they would have swung on
to something else. Colin composed music, too, and songs;
Colin's fox-trots would be played and danced to, now, wherever
you went in London. . . . "Varasdin" was a pretty useful
fox-trot—yes! Giles was still ahead of them all, with that; it
would not yet have reached there; he had seen in the papers
no mention of "Gräfin Maritza" coming to England. The
rhythm of "Varasdin" jerked its way through his brain again,
less and less jauntily . . . dragging along at the place of a funeral
march. . . .

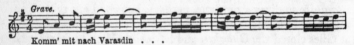

Komm' mit nach Varasdin . . .

. . . Toni was quite complete without him, since this had
happened. He had meant to go back, but he would only be
in the way. She had her success. People were anxious to
catch Toni as she passed, and make her join them—gay, careless
Toni, screwing up her deep blue eyes with laughter. He could
not go back now; he might have gone back before; but now
it would look as though he were the sort of rotter who kept
away only until it were worth his while to repent.

. . . Giles lay there in the arm-chair in front of the fire, in
Val's cottage in Italy. Italy was a beautiful, warm country;
and the sun was fading the flames, as it sank softly towards the
line of hills along the west. He lay there, with the *Onlooker* at
his feet; and he was home-sick . . . he was drenched in his
sickness for home, and the taste in his mouth was salt with it. . . .

—Suddenly he heard the front door flung violently open.
Then the door of the dining-room. A man in a heavy overcoat
entered impetuously, dumped down a suit-case, looked round
the room, his eyes dismissing Giles as an object of very minor
importance.

"Hullo, Greenways! You?"

"Where's Val?" demanded Stephen Greenways.

"Up in the studio, at the back. You know your way, don't
you?"

" Yes. See you presently." Greenways strode across the room towards the door which led into the garden.

" It doesn't much matter if you don't," murmured Giles. Then he roused himself : " Look here, Greenways——"—the other man stopped impatiently—" that Chinese coat you sent out here——"

" Well ? "

" Did you mean it for Val ? "

" Whom the hell else should I mean it for ? " said Stephen Greenways, simply. And he disappeared up the garden path.

" And so Val's all right, too," murmured Giles, but not bitterly now. Kindness was reasserting itself. Rather Colin to have leapt the moon and caught the sun between his palms, than some greedy and unhumorous bloke, with no quicksilver in his veins nor generosity in his spirit. Colin, at least, would never grow inflated with the contemplation of Colin ! And as Colin was all right, that young Mercury, and . . . Toni was all right, and Val was all right, and Stephen !—Well, Giles wasn't going to be a growling, surly, misanthropic sort of bear. It was not a bad proportion of people, any old way, to be all right, even if he did not happen himself to figure among them. He rose, and stretched his limbs, smiling at the thought of the scene that was certainly going on, at present, up in the studio —scene dabbled all over with silver and vermilion, like some glowing page of illumination. He was damned glad for Val. Val had been awfully decent to him and Loraine. . . .

And as he thought of Loraine, Queenie came tripping into the room, carrying a letter.

Queenie had washed her pretty face, and bathed the red rims of her pretty eyes, and done her pretty smooth hair very becomingly, and had chosen to put on a pretty white frock ; all of which had, somehow, a demurely reproachful air about it. She was feeling much better.

" Has Lola gone to the post, yet, with the afternoon letters, do you know ? " she asked of Giles. And he answered, mendaciously :

" Yes, I'm sure she has ; I heard her going down." For he saw that Queenie was holding a bulging, fat envelope in her hand ; and he still hoped for a chance of relishing some of its contents.

" I've been writing to Mother," said Queenie. " It does do one good, you know, when one has a fit of the mopes, to pour it out to someone who understands. I expect it's quite likely that Mummie will send me a telegram to come straight home, after she has read my letter ; because, though I didn't want to upset her, I had to tell her a little bit how I had been treated : for I do think, don't you, Giles, that Mrs. Rakonitz was very unfair in all she said this morning—in fact, she was more than unfair ; I think she was a little bit vulgar ; and nothing would worry Mother more than thinking I was with vulgar people."

" What makes you think our Aunt Elsa vulgar ? " Giles asked, sympathetically. Truth to tell, he *had* thought that Queenie had been made to suffer rather unnecessarily from Aunt Elsa's overwrought nerves and fluent oratory.

" Well, I mean all that she said about my appetite. One doesn't talk about people's appetites, in front of other people, and making it seem as though I ate more than my help was worth to Val !—It made me terribly uncomfortable. Besides, I'm not fatter ; I think I'm thinner lately. And—oh, lots of things she said. Of course, she's foreign—one has to make allowances for that !—but it doesn't follow at all that foreigners need be vulgar *because* they're foreign. I've known most awfully sweet foreigners. In fact, when they *are* refined and polite, they're sometimes better than us."

Suddenly and earnestly, she delivered herself of a load of perplexity : " Sometimes, you know, I don't understand them a bit in this house. Do you ? *Don't* you think them rather— odd, sometimes ? Even rather loose ? "

" It depends what you mean by loose."

Queenie could not explain. She just knew her neat little code of right and wrong : " There's no harm in flirting." " Of course God sees us." " As long as one remains really good." " One is only young once, that's what I say." But morals, here, were juggled so skilfully ; so criticised and man- handled ; made to stand on their heads ; pulled to pieces and put in a corner. Queenie was laughed at when she had said nothing funny. Her ethics were rejected, found wanting, by a code that seemed, according to Potley Green, to have no sense in it. Finally, she had to take refuge in the notion that she alone had any steady ideas at all of virtue, humour, or politeness. It was to Queenie's credit that she had tried very hard to remain polite and patient; not to answer back; to be helpful and deferential to the aged; she had strongly impressed the new English chaplain when he called for the first time at Val's cottage, by her undoubted influence for good, in this abode of the heathen and infidel. It was the easier for Queenie to keep on trying, because she was unwaveringly sure that she would have her reward elsewhere.

—" But I do think she's a bad-tempered old beast ! " cried Queenie, reverting to Aunt Elsa, and the scene of the morning. " She's jealous of me because I'm young."—Giles raised one eyebrow, quizzically; he didn't agree that Aunt Elsa was jealous of Queenie—— " She's always trying to get me out of the house; always rubbing it into Val that I'm no good at housekeeping. It's rather insulting to Mummie, in a way; because, although she wasn't brought up in a Viennese *kitchen*, she's a very clever manager indeed. They all say so, in Potley Green. And we keep our servants almost longer than anyone. And I expect *hers* were always giving notice—spiteful old cat ! I'm awfully silly, of course, to let her depress me by anything she says; and I'll take a cup of tea up to her room presently, because I think one ought to rise above things, don't you? But somehow I felt that this morning was just the last straw, especially after the night we had had—Manuela and I—sitting up with Loveliest."

" I've had a fit of the hump, too," said Giles, in that state of genial intimacy which both Val and Loraine had so sternly forbidden him, on the ground that it was bad for Queenie.

She eyed him with concern. " Oh, why ? " she asked. " I do wish you wouldn't. It does bother me so."

" It's awfully nice of you to care, Queenie." . . . He resisted the temptation to state pathetically that his own mother was dead as a sentimentality too lush even for Queenie's consumption. Instead, he said : "Did you know that Stephen Greenways had come ? "

" What ! " cried Queenie. " Oh, where ? Oh, he hasn't, has he ? Oh, when ? Have you seen him ? What did he say ? Where is he now ? Down the hill with Loveliest ? " This, of course, accounted for Giles' despondency, if Greenways were down with Loveliest !

" On the contrary, up the hill with Val."

" With *Val* ? "

Giles nodded. " Loraine's story was a fantasy, Queenie. I don't suppose she meant to make it all up. But Greenways' romance with her never existed except in her own brain. It was a piece of gorgeous, ornate embroidery, like the coat itself. . . . And all that we've been hiding and whispering about and worrying over ; and the taking sides, evidence and clues and secrets, the sacrifices and the revelations and the rest of it—those were equivalent to the silk butterflies, the birds with scarlet beaks, the rainbows, and the silvery herons, and the thousand tiny stitches in the petals of a Chinese blossom." He took some joy in elaborating his metaphor, seeing that Queenie had paid it the compliment of her Church-and-the-Best-Poetry face of attention. " Well——" he dismissed it, " a feverish dream of Loraine's, and we were drawn in . . . every one of us. Now it's just shrivelled to nothing. Greenways sent the coat to Val ; he'd get a bit of a shock if he knew what had been going on about it."

" Then," gasped Queenie, " you must go straight down to Loveliest, of course. How lucky that your foot is well enough!"

" Ain't it ? " said Giles, without emotion. " Must I go down just now, Queenie ? Why ? Won't you do, instead ? I don't like being a messenger of evil tidings. They always killed them, in ancient history, you know."

" Sometimes," Queenie said, very puzzled and intent, " sometimes I can't understand you—I mean, not so well as at other times."

" Ah ! " said Giles. " Is this sometimes, or one of the other times ? "

Queenie went on : " You must see that you would be more

good than I—me, I mean—to Loveliest, just now, when she's
having to give up Stephen."

Giles wanted to contend, fractiously, that Loraine could not
give up that which had never been in her possession; but
it was not his habit to argue logically with Queenie. He
preferred to shake her into manifestations of " pricelessness " !
" Well, it's rather a pity," he said, with that unworthy object
in view, " that you think I ought to stay with Loraine,
because I was just thinking of taking the next train back to
England."

" What ! " cried Queenie. " What ! To England ? Oh, but
you're not ! You mustn't ! You weren't ! How callous of
you ! "

" I've got a wife in England, and three children. You've
been taught morals, Queenie. Isn't it right that a penitent
man should return to his wife ? "

Queenie wriggled. . . . She was flattered that Giles should
have set her up as the angel at his cross-roads; but what a
responsibility ! A girl can do so much. . . . She fenced for
time before giving the decision which would settle him one
way or another. " What made you want to go back, so suddenly ? Is she ill ? "

" She's quite too flamboyantly well, I should think." He
picked up the *Onlooker*, and flicked the pages rapidly.

" Oh ! " cried Queenie, over his shoulder, two or three times.
" Isn't that Colin Martial ? Oh, there's one of Colin ! That's
Colin Martial, too, isn't it ? Isn't he fascinating and attrac-
tive ? I do so love his smile."

" Here ! " Giles pointed out to her " Rosalie's " Fashion
Article.

Queenie read it, much impressed by Toni's share in London's
theatrical sensation of the hour. She could not quite make up
her mind whether it were etiquette or not, to congratulate
Giles. " But I don't think," said Queenie, clinging to the
special line on which she hung out her ethical washing, " I
don't think you ought to go back; not yet, anyhow; not till
you yourself have done something rather Big to bring to your
wife; something to justify yourself."

" That's a difficult measurement," Giles contended. " Just how Big will something have to be, before it justifies myself ? "

" *You* must judge of that," Queenie said, looking at him with clear, straight eyes. " No one can live another man's life for him, you know ! ' One by one we must all file on through the narrow aisles of pain '—I don't really like Ella Wheeler Wilcox, though I used to once—I feel I've rather grown beyond her ; but it does seem to me that she has got hold of a deep truth in that, don't you think ? But you must be tremendously glad, Giles, that your wife has done so well."

Giles forgot that he was talking to Queenie, and lapsed into honesty. " I'd be a hell of a lot gladder if I'd done it, and she were being glad that I'd done so well."

" Oh, Giles ! " with a reproving flutter of the eyelids.

He felt curiously tired and near breaking-point, although he could not have told what had so gnawed his vitality. Even ragging Queenie wasn't as much fun as it had been in the past ; rather a poor game, in fact ; and he had lost all desire to read what was in the letter she had written to her mother. " So you think I ought to go down to Loraine, and see her through this Greenways reverse, do you ? Righto ! I'm going ! I intended to, all along, as a matter of fact ; knew I should have to. You might see that my things are bunged into a suit-case, Queenie, and that one of the infant school brings it down."

" Are you sure that your foot——? "

" Oh yes, my foot will carry me. So long ! I'd keep away from the olive terraces, if I were you, Queenie. I've just heard the studio door open. They're probably going to stroll out into the sunset . . ."

He limped away.

Queenie reflected. " There's really a lot of good in Giles . . ."

CHAPTER XI

. . . L ORAINE went to the window, and looked out.
She looked up the terraced hill to where, on the
left from Val's cottage, the olives parted and made
a gap against the sky. The sun had just dipped.

She saw, for her sight was wonderfully keen, two figures
standing in black silhouette against the clear, pale colours of
the opening. She saw that it was Stephen Greenways and Val.
And then she saw them embrace ; and from the curve of their
bodies, she knew with unfailing sureness that he had just told
her of his love, that he had come out to San Goffredo especially
to tell her. And for the very reason that he loved Val, he had
sent Val the Chinese coat, the Chinese coat that Loraine was
wearing.

Loraine turned, leant with her back against the window,
and stared with menacing eyes at the hateful emptiness of the
room. Why wasn't there something that she could tear and
tatter ? something tangible, yet something of no account ?

And at that moment she heard footsteps limping through
the hall. The door opened, and Giles came in.

. . . Something for her to tear and tatter ; something that
was of no account.

Giles saw at once that there was no need for him to be
messenger. Loraine knew. " Am I of any use ? " he said, and
his heart was hammering unevenly, foreboding a row. He was
unafraid of most things. But quarrels with Loraine, who
reminded him so of Toni—another row with Toni !—it was
more than he could bear. If only it had been a quite different
woman of a different race . . .

And Loraine began to trample and to tear :

" You ? You've never been of any use ! You're the sort
who comes in whenever we are wanting something else. Do

you think that *any* man'll do for me? That if I can't have one, I'll have another? Is it a cheap vampire you're thinking me? Have I ever sucked blood for the sake of blood? You're smiling because a man, out there yonder, has jilted me. But I'm a man myself, and a man who jilts women . . . carelessly, callously, when the fun's over. It's fun that I'm after, and beauty and magnificence and courage. You've got none of these to give me. Why, I ran through you in a week;—less than a week; a day, an hour. I've been bored with you, ever since. You of any use? You, who let yourself be won in an evening? Toni and Val and I snap our fingers at such slippery spoils. The Rakonitz women aren't easily satisfied."

"So it seems," said Giles. "But I didn't know you'd been bored as long as that, Loraine. Why didn't you tell me before?"

"Haven't we been telling each other? Haven't we——"

"Oh!" he exclaimed, irritated by her trick of phrasing, "don't turn everything I say into a question!"

"Haven't we told each other," she stormed again, "when we roamed in discontent from island to island, in Greece? Weren't we telling each other, then? Weren't we escaping from each other, and doing it together in the hopeless way that people do when the woman won't hurt the man because he's poor stuff and can't bear the hurting? When we ran away from solitude, and rushed up to Vienna, where the streets were animated, and the cafés crowded—wasn't I telling you then, that I was bored and bored and *bored?* And when we left Vienna, and rushed down here again, where there was Val of my own family, and Aunt Elsa, the darling—wasn't I telling you then? Wasn't I?"

"You may have been! Rather a long-winded way, when you might have put it into four words: 'I'm bored with you.' Why chase half over the map, first?"

"I can't stop in one place for ever, unless I'm in paradise. I have to go on and on. It's the gipsy in me. Because you were there, because you had left your wife, I had to drag you with me! I'll have to go on dragging you with me, I suppose."

"I shouldn't worry!" said Giles. His temper, too, was

sliding over the edge of control. "You're forcing me into being crude, Loraine; but you might as well know that I've been, for weeks, for months, just as bored and sick with the whole affair as you. More, perhaps—because I chucked up something that'll be hard to get back . . . on that night when you were so up against it and begged me to get you away from it all——"

Loraine began to laugh: "Dear me!" she scoffed. "And what could I have been meaning by that?"

"Don't pretend!" sharply. "You can't have forgotten! I own that I was fairly fed-up that evening, too, at the Hambone. Toni had let me down pretty badly, and I'd just found it out."

And again Loraine laughed.

"And there were other reasons too, why I wanted to leave England." He was not going to tell Loraine, who already held him too cheaply, that one of these had been terror that he was clinging too close to popularity, too elated by it, too dependent on it; and that he recoiled from the vision of the man he might become quite soon, unless he broke away. For Loraine had wanted to rely on him, on his strength and his protection, and his quick, practical, masculine sense of action; and she had appealed to him for all this just at the critical hour, when Toni, Toni who was Loraine's cousin, and so like her, had fatally humiliated his manhood; shown him that she had no need of him; that, indeed, she had been chivalrous in protecting him; and that she was capable of sudden decisions without support from the weaker male. That strange night when he and Loraine had met at the Hambone, and had danced and danced together. . . . And then, in Loraine's mad, impetuous way, they had left behind the dancing, and the drinking, clinking crowd, and had walked and walked through empty, dawn-grey streets, further and further north; he believed it was Hendon where they had finished their fantastic truancy, And Loraine, in the mood of a panic-stricken child who can no longer bear its fears alone, but must beg for succour from ghosts and goblins, had confessed to him how her sense of herself, of her own personality, had gone astray, because she was never alone, and almost never with her own kin, who did not want her, but always and always among strangers, who only cared for her to amuse them : " But my will has grown flabby and flattered, that it has. I used to be able to rule it with : ' I'll go ' or ' I'll stay,' and be glad of my own strength to go when I was sick of the cymbals, the hollow, hollow cymbals. But what has changed me an' what has weakened me, Giles ? For I stay on and on, and I sink in deeper and deeper, and I'll die—I'll die—for want of a hand to lift me away. Giles, I can't live in the shrill clamour of this town any more ! I daren't tell anyone else ; I had to tell you, to-night ; I felt you could help me, and no one else but you. You *can* help me. It's like being stifled slowly in black velvet, folds and folds of black velvet. If you could take me away, right away, a clean cut—ah now, can't you ? Won't you ? Have you ever dreamt of an octopus, Giles ? It's a dream of horror, and it comes to me every night. . . . Giles, it's only you who won't condemn me for fuss over nothing ! You feel strong and so sane ; you'll pick me up, and not let me struggle ; you'll carry me away, even if I try to get back ! . . ."

And now, eight months later, Loraine was laughing : " And you deserted Toni, for a reason as poor as that ! My faith ! "

" Leave Toni out of this, please."

" Ah—the stern Englishman ! I was waiting for that, I was indeed ! ' Leave my wife out of this vulgar quarrel with a low baggage.' . . . But I'll speak of my little cousin how and where I want, to the husband who has let her down and left her to fend for herself, with three children and a mass of debts and a business that had gone to pot . . ."

" I offered her my help in the business. She laughed at the notion."

" She knew you were just no good except as a sort of hired mountebank, to liven up a dud party ! You had a reputation for that, I hear."

Giles flushed, but went on, ignoring her gibe : " And I left a note to Jimmy that three-quarters of our income was to be paid direct to her."

" Fine of you ! " cried Loraine, in mock admiration ; " I'm struck all of a heap ! Four lines on a sheet of paper, telling the man who's drawing the money he never worked for, that he needn't give you more than a quarter of the money that you've never worked for. Renunciation can do no more. And that absolved you from *all* further responsibility. Ah, it's a gallant rescuer you were to me, and a hero to the tip of your tongue : ' Don't be afraid, Loraine—I'll take you away out of it all ! ' You'd no *right* to take me away ! What was I to you? How dared you leave Toni, for me or anyone else ? I'll never forgive you for leaving Toni, who's a thousand million times too good for you ! "

Sadly enough, Giles answered : " I'll grant you that. Yet if you felt this, need you have asked me, of all the world, to rush you away from London, and from all that was terrifying you ? "

" Need you have come ? Need you have come ? I had no man belonging to me—— We who are the lone pirates, dash in anywhere to make a capture. Why need I have spared you, or pitied your weakness ? Can't you resist a temptation ? Am *I* trustee of your faithfulness ? Had there been never a promise to Toni, my Toni, that you might have remembered ? Frightened, was I ? and pleading for help ? . . . Well, then, you— you knight in armour, tell me, another time, that I'm to go and get a man of my own, and not hang round besetting you with a whining tale ! Another time, say : ' I'm married ! '—No, men haven't the guts to say it ! They think it's *infra dig.*, not dashing enough. . . . They're ashamed of it, bless their sweet eyes ! Ah, but I'd have respected the Giles Goddard, my cousin's husband, who'd have turned on me, savage, and whipped me off, that night, that night you were so kind, so considerate—— How dared you humiliate Toni Rakonitz, by deserting her ? She who ought to have had the pick of a husband from end to end of the long world ! "

Giles bowed his head, silently, to his bludgeoning, on Toni's behalf, from this surprising quarter. . . . He admitted that most of it was just and deserved ; but wished, nevertheless, that Loraine could contrive to be as inarticulate as so many times she had stated she was; and a little less picturesque in her rhetoric . . .

. . . " And if it's true what you say, that she was impudent and would have none of your help, and tilted back her head, laughing and behaving badly—for I know Toni, and I know Val, and the cool indifference of them that makes you so angry you could choke them!—But if I'd been you, I *would* have choked her, sooner than left her, to follow another not so good! I'd have choked manners into her, and humble ways——"

" The cave-man stunt? Oh, I think not, Loraine. It really *isn't* done, you know. And as for Val——" He drove attack over the border, from his country into hers—" As for Val, if you loved her so much, why the devil had you got to interfere? Push your claims between her and her man? You're simply an insatiable dramatist. . . . You lied, when you gave us all to understand that Greenways must have meant the coat for you, because of things that went before, and that only you and he knew about: things he had said to you—' A message painted in silk. . . .' He can never have said it. He doesn't remember you exist. If you had seen his face, just now, when he asked me where Val was . . .''

" Ah . . . don't!" With hands flung out, she warded off his revelations. But she had not really cared about Stephen; only about being the centre of Stephen's romance. And she felt it was he, not she, who had blundered, in the destination of his gift. A gift to the beloved should be so surely appropriate that no doubt could be raised. And the Chinese coat was not inevitably Val's; it was Loraine's. Exotic, brilliant, artificial, Loraine wore it as though the thousand tiny yellow men with pigtails and large spectacles, who had patiently laboured on it with a million stitches, had all the while thought of her and seen her before them. And Val? Loraine's one-time criticism had been just: Val looked marvellous . . . in riding kit.

" You can't blame me," Loraine proudly defended herself, to Giles: " I gave the man credit for an imagination he hadn't got. He had had the privilege of knowing *me*. . . . And then he sent out that coat, without the owner's name on it, to San

Goffredo. Look at it—look at it well, now—look at it on me !
Was I wrong, to *feel* it mine ? *He* was wrong—not I. And if
he hadn't the subtlety and the vision to have prepared me
beforehand with the one perfect phrase : ' I'm sending you a
message painted in silk. . . .' I had to do it, for him ; and
pretend, as hard as I could, that he *must* have sent it ! And
you, with a skull as dense as his, call that ' lying.' A lie ?—Ah,
what's the difference ? What's the difference between God's
lies and my own ? If life is just tame for the moment ; if it's
flat and insipid ; if it's like a bath that isn't cold enough, and
isn't hot enough to make the blood tingle ;—am I to get no
praise at all for what I did to put the colour in ? To cram it to
bursting with excitement ? When I told you I needed your
help, and you gave up everything to take me away, oughtn't
you to be grateful to me ? "—Skilfully, she pushed the war back
again over the border and into his territory—" I provided you
with the test, didn't I ? I provided you with the chance to
make a sacrifice ? I tuned up the fiddle. . . . And then, afterwards, when you've had all that richness you didn't deserve—
that Heaven couldn't bother to give you, but which *I* gave you
—then you draw yourself up, and talk stiffly about telling a lie ;
and it's thanking me on your knees you should have been, for
inspiring an occasion to be loyal to Toni, against odds, and when
you were angry with her into the bargain. You could have
been proud of yourself then ! But weren't you just the chivalrous rescuer ! " she mocked, " and couldn't I see your passion
drinking me up like dry blotting-paper drinks up ink ? And
didn't you just feel well with yourself over our scamper out
into the blackness, the sensation we caused, and the gaping
and talking we left behind ? And yet, if you're not feeling quite
so well with yourself now, at least thank me, Giles, thank me,
you fool, for setting you free from your ordinary, humdrum,
everyday complacency ! ' Am I of any use ? ' you say, courteously. Divil a bit of use, to me or to anyone else. You've
made me bad friends with Toni, an' that's all you've done. I
could have mastered terror alone and without you, last February.
I appealed to you, for the evening was strange and grey, and I
wanted to light it with battle and resistance. I wanted to fight

for you—and lose. I wanted to hear the flames of your loyalty go roaring up to illuminate the dingy skies——"

"In fact," Giles interrupted, "you were dull that evening, and wanted something to do." He strode over to the table, scribbled on a block of writing-paper, and tore off a sheet; while with his other hand he never ceased ringing the china bell that stood near.

"*Dio!*" cried Manuela, rushing in. "*Dio!* But what is it? What has happened?"

"Here," said Giles, curtly. "A telegram. Here's money," he plunged his hand into his pocket. "Take it down to the post now, at once, immediately, *subito*, you understand? It's for England, and it's to go '*urgente*.' Go, Manuela!" And directly she had clattered away, her wonted insolence intimidated by his manner, he turned, smiling, to Loraine. "Thanks, Loraine; not for then, but for now. I was afraid you'd need me to look after you, still. As you've no use for me, and never had; as you're not afraid, and never were, I needn't wait any longer." He limped into his bedroom. Loraine followed him, a thin ornate little creature, proudly sheathed in the warm gleam and glitter of colour from Val's coat. She followed him, mimicking him, mimicking the way he had spoken to Manuela, the way he had spoken to her . . . He was trying to get down his suit-case from where it stuck out from under a pile of other boxes and bags and blankets, on top of the tall cupboard; but it was not easy, with his lame foot, to climb on to a chair; and the suit-case was just out of his reach. He turned round and swore at Loraine; she swore back, mimicking him . . there might have been twice Giles in the room, and no Loraine at all! Then, furiously, he pulled down the whole pile of lumber, that clattered and thumped to the floor round about him, raising clouds of dust, so that he began to cough. . . . And still Loraine, as though wound up and prompted by a demon, stood there watching whatever he vainly attempted to do and burlesquing it. . . . Maddening him, with her flitting resemblances to Toni. . . .

"Take off that coat!" he shouted at her, between coughing, and tearing open the straps of his suit-case. "Take it off, damn you ! It's Val's coat, not yours ! You nearly did her in, pretending it was yours ! You look horrible in it ! " . . . But that was not true : Loraine looked like the lovely little goddess of an Oriental temple, in the coat.

. . . The suit-case was locked. Giles turned out drawer after drawer, throwing the contents on to the stone floor. He had lost control of his temper, now. He only knew that he had been cheated and tricked and laughed at ; that he had been Loraine's fool ; that he had left Toni behind, and now he was going back to Toni ; that he was wildly glad of his freedom to go back ; wildly glad to be released from the thrall whence all the glamour had faded long ago, before even the summer came ; wildly suspicious of yet another trick which might serve to keep him here. . . . His key ! What had Loraine done with his key ? But he wasn't going to let that hold him back, when London and Toni lay at the end of his journey—— Not a trifle like that. He found other odd keys ; drove them into the lock ; could neither turn it, nor shake it free. In his frenzy, he broke the key in half ; glared at Loraine as though she were responsible for this, too . . .

" I'm not going to let that stop me," he muttered. Another suit-case, hers, would do ; what did it matter ? . . . Just chuck his things in ; there was time to catch the 6.15, if he hurried. Let her pack for him ! Let her help him, as women should, instead of standing there like a bloody little Chink idol. . . . He told her so !—His breathing was short and quick, as it still was, sometimes, from that weak spot on his lung, that was the result of being gassed eight years ago.

—" Go back to Toni ? " scoffed Loraine. " How *pleased* she'll be ! Was that a loving telegram you sent her ? ' Rejoice, darling ! Put out my slippers, and let it be grilled kidneys for breakfast, because I've actually decided to come home again ! ' . . . She won't take you back, Giles. Don't you fret about catching that train. An odd day or two won't make much difference, it's I can tell you that ; not in the eternity that'll have to pass before Toni Rakonitz takes you back. Don't I know her better than you ? Aren't we one blood, she and I ? "

" Stop asking me questions, I tell you ! " Giles thundered at her. That blasted drawer had stuck, now ! Rotten Italian furniture ! Rotten everything ! He tore at it . . . and blandly and suddenly it gave way under his hand, so that he staggered backwards.

—" Toni's proud," Loraine went on. " I'm too close to Toni not to be understanding how she feels over things. She has no use for a man who lets her down. Ah ! I could have told you that at the very moment you were doing yourself in. Toni's a man—she's got her job."

Giles took no notice : shirts, suits, socks—he aimed them •towards the open suit-case from every part of the room, as he ransacked drawer and cupboard. They lay in heaps on the floor. Then he rammed them all in, indiscriminately, boots on top— what did it matter ? And all the while, Loraine's gibes pattered and fell around him like hailstones, like poisoned arrows flung by a deft hand. He didn't know why he stayed to pack ; and yet it seemed to his obstinate fancy, that he could not leave anything of his property behind with Loraine ; that there must be no scrap of substance for her to hold him by, nor to show that he had ever belonged to her.

That was all, now, thank the Lord. He pulled down the lid ; it wouldn't nearly close. He thrust his knee on to it, pressing with all his strength. . . . It wasn't true, that Toni had done with him ! It couldn't be true that he had sacrificed all that he cared for, for the sake of a delusion, a fairy-tale, a witch's shamming. He wanted, during these last moments at Villa Bel Respiro, to be able to tell Loraine all that he thought of her. . . . To compress his rage and contempt into a few biting words that would sear and scorch—— But he couldn't find the words, and there was no time. . . . And this damned suit-case still wouldn't close . . .

He began to cough again. He couldn't stop coughing. Through the sound of it, Loraine's voice still beat on. . . . He wanted to laugh at the nonsense she was spouting : a lot of eye-wash about having taken Toni's husband, because, loving Toni, she was so enjoying the act of send-ing him back again . . . Sending him back ?—But he was going back; of his own accord he was going. If only this cough . . .

Suddenly Giles collapsed, exhausted, his arm thrown out across the suit-case, his head buried on his arm. When he looked up again, some fifty seconds later, the sleeve of his coat was dabbled and stained with blood, and blood was pouring from between his lips.

PART IV

POWER OF APPOINTMENT

CHAPTER I

COLIN MARTIAL'S Rolls-Royce, Toni driving it, drew up, with that expensive silence characteristic of its kind, in front of the house in Regent's Park.

"You did that very nicely, my little one," said Colin, emerging from the glowing cave within, and helping her to alight. "Did you have a pleasant afternoon? Did you enjoy the nice play?"

"I did *not*," said Toni firmly, hunting for her latch-key; "and I'm not going to see your piffling play again, Colin. This is final! Seven times, and one Saturday matinée—— You wouldn't enjoy it yourself, you know. Coming in? Oh, by the way, lest you should think me rude, I *did* enjoy my lunch!"

"How do you like 'Sole Colin Martial,' pronounced in the French way, please?" asked the sole's proud godfather, leaning up against the body of his car. "I haven't tasted it yet, myself. You know that sort of levée that we successful dramatists are compelled to hold, during our hurried lunches; it's always worst during the fish course: 'Thunk you, thahnk you, *so* kind of you!' . . . all the time, while you hogs are guzzling. Darling, you *don't* think I'm spoilt by my tremendous triumph? I think it's simply marvellous that it hasn't mounted to the boy's head, so young too, and all!"

"I haven't looked at your head," said Toni. "I've been too busy with my own. Who was the large gentleman in the corner with his back to us, who said all through lunch that 'She Burnt Her Boats' is the most degraded play in London?"

"Do you mean that fat-bellied rudeness with the white

walrus whiskers and the querulous crest of silver hair? My dear, that's the editor of *Wise Words to the Wee*, and he's upset with me, because he put in his Weekly Wow-wow to the Wee, that they are to tell all their Duddees and Mummees to be sure to take them to see ' She Burnt Her Boats ' in the Christmas holidays. . . . And that was before he saw it himself. No, I'm not coming in, Toni, my love. I'm going to drive my own car—that celebrated actor-dramatist, Colin Martial, at the wheel—through several shop-windows—they won't mind, it's such an advertisement !—partly because I can't control her yet, and partly because I want to buy some stockings for mother, without getting out ; silk stockings, a long way past the knee ; twenty-one pairs, so that she can continue for three weeks, and then I'll get her some more."

Toni allowed her speculation to rest for a moment, sympathetically, on Mrs. Martial . . . who was a comfortable, staid little soul, who would probably suffer much secret perturbation at thus having to renounce her habit of warm woollen stockings, just now, at the beginning of November, with the cold weather coming on. And then Colin pursued, flushed and radiant : " I'm going home ; and there will be nine little interviewers sitting on the fence, and they'll all tumble off at my approach ; and they'll ask me, first, if my fortunate parents are alive? So inquisitive, dear ! To which I reply : ' But yes ; one of each kind ; making two in all ! ' . . . And next, they'll want to know if I've written a new play since yesterday, and what it's about ? I did tell one of the last batch that I'd just written, between dawn and daybreak, a charming little comedy called ' The Gizzard of a Ptarmigan ! ' And he said : ' Ah ! I see, a naval play ! ' . . . Toni, what *could* he have meant ? "

" Try spelling ' naval ' the other way. . . . No, sorry, Colin, I didn't mean that ! Anyway, it doesn't quite meet the case ! "

. . . They were very happy in each other's company, Toni and Colin, at the present period of their good fortune ; and loth to separate. So much was happening. Colin's success, to which Toni had contributed with her excellent " creations " for Lucilla Danby, was as yet fresh and succulent. It was

success of a kind to amuse their sophistication, and to thrill
what was left of the child in them both. So now they lingered
on, with nonsense for their shuttlecock—Toni held her latch-
key in her hand, Colin had one foot already on the low step to
the driver's seat. And then a telegraph boy came smartly
round the corner, and was about to run up the steps to the
front door of Toni's house, when she stopped him :

" For me ? Goddard ? "

" Yes'm." He delivered an envelope, lighter than the usual
orange.

Toni opened it, and read.

. . . She lifted her head a trifle higher than usual, as though
she were welcoming someone, but a mocking welcome, frosted
with anger. Her smile tantalised . . . it was like the taste of
almonds.

Colin was watching her intently : " Who is it from, Toni ? "
Telegrams were a commonplace in his life, of course ; but he
could see from Toni's expression that this one had a special
significance.

" Oh, nothing—no one ! " And Toni quoted : " ' A man of
no importance.' "

" Darling, Oscar Wilde's a leetle out of date. I suppose it's
from Giles, to say he's coming back to you ? Isn't that too, too
sweet of him ? "

" You're a quick guesser, Colin." She handed him the telegram :

" Coming home at once. Giles."

Colin tore it up, and threw the pieces into the mud, under a
passing motor-lorry. " There ! " he exclaimed. " That'll save
you doing it ! The cow ! Does he think you're waiting about
for his convenience ? Give him delicate *hell*, Toni ! "

" I'm going to," asid Toni, briefly. " I'm sorry you tore it
up, though, Colin. It was a noble and romantic gesture, full
of friendship and all that ; but I wanted to see when it was
sent off, and from where. I've no idea, thanks to you, when to
expect my lord and hero."

" Look here," cried Colin, impetuously. " Don't bother
about Giles. Why should you ? Come back home with me,

now. We'll have some dinner together somewhere; and then, if you don't mind seeing the show again——"

" I do," was Toni's heartfelt interruption.

" Oh well, drop in opposite, and see ' Who's From Hu-la-hu ? ' instead. And after that we'll zip off in the car down to Market St. Dunstan's, over Sunday. Mummie loves having you about, you know. We'll have a perfectly innocent day of frolic, romping and picking buttercups and tossing each other cowslip-balls, all in the green October country ! . . . *Come* along, Toni ! " suddenly serious. " Don't wait for Giles ! Don't be soft about it ! " Colin had bottled up his sentiments until now, on the subject of Giles' desertion ; but he had felt very hotly about it ; being a perfectly moral man. But Toni shook her head, and laughed.

" Thanks, Colin. You're a darling. Here, kiss me tenderly upon the brow. . . . But I'd rather stay and cope with my husband. I'm in a temper, you see—the very devil of a temper, and I want to get rid of it. I've been wanting to get rid of it ever since last February. It would be a pity to waste all that good bad-temper. So long ! You won't get your stockings—it's Saturday."

Colin departed, with a few last injunctions as to the harsh treatment of a defaulting husband—injunctions given not wholly in the wise and tolerant spirit with which Mother Marjorie, for instance, advised girls and young matrons, in the pages of *The Weekly Muffin.* And Toni let herself into the house. The sitting-room was empty. Susie was probably upstairs in the nursery with the children ; she was a devoted and happy grandmother.

. . . Toni slipped off her furs, and stood looking down into the fire, still with that mutinous smile twisting up the corners of her mouth, that bitterness of anger in her blue eyes. It had been unprofitable work, being wrathful with a husband at the other end of nowhere ; and Toni, as far as she had been able, had shelved her emotions last February, until she should once again meet Giles face to face. She had needed all her energies to devote to the business ; to haul it back again into prosperity from the perilous condition into which it had sunk. If she had then and at once given way to the pitiable rôle of a broken-hearted wife, she could certainly not have been in Paris the next day, as she urgently required to be, to collect her new spring models. So she had said nothing all that day; nothing even to Helen; but had absorbed herself in "Toni's." That evening, however, she had allowed herself the luxury of thinking about Giles and about Loraine . . . but principally Giles; and all she would like to say to him went raging through her brain. . . . She must tell someone! She must storm at someone! Whom could she implicate in the responsibility? It was not a friend she required; certainly she dreaded, most of all, her own family knowing. . . . "This, you see, is what comes of marrying a stranger and a Goy!"—If they did not actually say as much, she would perceive it in their silence, in their hints and their sympathy. . . . (But they had said a good deal more!) Besides, even such remnants as were left to the family's older generation would assemble and take counsel, and their tongues would clack: "But vot is she going to *do?* Surely, she vill do something about it? One cannot do *nossing!* What is that poor Toni going to *do?*" . . . They would be too vehemently interested, too curious, steaming with good counsel; firmly identifying their horror and their grief with Toni's; Toni's with theirs. How different from the Goddards, with their nonchalant, athletic existence; each unit self-contained, absorbed in some impersonal sport; not unsociable, but not bothering about the others except in an off-hand, good-humoured sort of way, when, by hazard, they met!

—Damn the Goddard point of view! Suddenly Toni had felt goaded to draw them into this; not to suffer their indifference for another instant; to damage their taboo on tribal participation, by forcing them to listen to all she had to say about Giles and what he had done to her . . . all the intimate, wounding things that they would shrink from hearing! Why should they be guarded? If she had married into Giles' family —why, hadn't Giles also married into hers? If her family must go through the shame and sorrow of seeing a Rakonitz coolly abandoned, the Goddards should hear what a Rakonitz had to say on the subject! Damn and damn and *damn!* They

had got to help her! They had got to stand by! They had
got to be warm and human, if she chose that they should!
And if she chose to revert to type, to be the orthodox young
Israelite bride and wife and mother, wailing aloud for her lost
bridegroom, the husband who had forsaken her, the callous
father; if, in the time-hallowed fashion, she had retired to her
opulent bedroom, and, yielding up any effort of reticence, had
lain with dishevelled hair upon the bed, and wept; her mother
and aunts surrounding her, her babies tumbled picturesquely
upon the (rather too thick) carpet—all except the last babe,
whom she would, of course, clasp close to her (rather too
exposed) bosom; if she chose to call in the Goddards, the male
Goddards, the Gentiles, to play their parts in such a scene as
this, natural to her instincts—or to half of them: the Rakonitz,
not the Lake, half!—well, damn it again, only Giles would be to
blame! Let his relations slang *him* if they liked!

—Toni imperiously rang up Jimmy Goddard at his club;
sent a message down to the card-room that Major Goddard was
to come at once to his daughter-in-law, in Regent's Park.

But when, less than twenty minutes later, Jimmy did walk
in, Toni's resolve suddenly stiffened into pride . . . and then
doubled up into silent chuckling. Poor little Jimmy was so
obviously apprehensive!

Pride!—after all, she was not going to give way in front of a
Goddard; she could use their code as well as any of them. " It
simply isn't done, Toni." . . . She could hear Giles' voice
saying it, in his semi-mocking, indolent way, so that you could
never tell how much he meant, or how much he was laughing
at you. It simply wasn't done, to flop into helplessness, to
clamour shrilly for solace, unless your last vitality were brought
so low that surrender had no alternative. As for the Goddards,
if they preferred to remain exclusive and outside human
tragedy, let them remain there, for all Toni cared! So she
welcomed Jimmy charmingly, and gave him a whisky-and-soda
—as she had done on their first meeting in 1921 on Richard's
lawn; and she told him that there were a few points in her
business that were perplexing her, in connection with the
enlargement of the premises, and—er—certain rights connected

with drainage and frontal repairs; she had wanted to consult Jimmy . . .

And James Goddard played up. The hurried note he had received from Giles, explaining about the future disposal of the income his father allowed him, had told him more or less what was happening; nor was he quite as unconcerned as Toni believed him. He would have left her alone, thinking she might prefer it; but directly he had received her message, he had hastened along to her, prepared, if necessary, to supply any natural demands for comfort, or to meet any natural storm of indignation. Toni's manner of meeting catastrophe both relieved him, and with a jump, aroused his appreciation. He played up to her, remaining there for an hour or two; the business blind did not occupy either of them for more than five minutes. Thereafter, Jimmy displayed the wildest high spirits—he insisted on being taught the new French tango; pleaded for the gramophone to be turned on; called for a bottle of champagne. . . . He and Toni would crack it between them! He treated her as though she were a party; himself like a mountebank at the party; but a startlingly witty mountebank, with a fastidious taste in the quality of his audience. Only Toni was the right companion to his hilarious mood, he conveyed . . . Helping her?—oh, certainly a Goddard was helping her through her bad hour, but in how different a way from what she had anticipated. Yet she had felt, instantly, on his entrance, instead of the layers and layers of unresponsive good form that she had expected from him, a shock of warm contact and affection; his funny, wistful, light brown eyes flickered over her slimness and the valorous carriage of her small head, with an expression almost maternal in its tenderness. . . . Yes, she was glad she had chosen not to " behave badly," where Jimmy was concerned. She too, although she had always liked Jimmy, had never felt quite so near to him as on this evening, when Giles was not mentioned.

—Later on they talked of Giles, of course; but not that night. Later on, when Toni came back from Paris. Jimmy had found out from Hanover Street when she was expected, and met her at the station. It was pleasant to see him there.

They discussed it all, then, over an epicurean dinner at the
Maison Basque, and a curiously close friendship between them
dated from then.   Jimmy was, as a matter of solid fact,
genuinely upset and disapproving over his son's defalcation.
A rampant hedonist himself, deplorably waste ground in his
moral acreage, he yet, oddly enough, believed tenaciously in
the rules that he broke.   Giles should not have left Toni—and
this judgment was not passed in relation to the neighbours or
to the world :   "Don't care a tinker's curse what people
think !" said Jimmy.   "People?   Good Lord !   But the boy
was wrong."   And Toni was right, moreover, to lift her chin,
and shake back her hair, and tell him to go to hell, and not
come back till morning. . . . No better way of treating Giles.
He told her so, and she was glad of his support.   "They say
I'm mad—and heartless.   And that I ought to *do* something ! "
"*Do ?*   What can you do ?   Go after him with a halter and
bells on it ?   Sprinkle salt on his tail ?   You go ahead and take
no notice, Toni, you impudent baggage ! "   He shook her
gently by the shoulder—she was the stuff, his little daughter-
in-law !—wrenched up her face towards him and towards the
light :   "Don't fret, m'dear ! " he added.   "But you are
fretting, of course you are.   *I'm* no good, I never am.   Come
to ' No, No, Nanette ' with me, to-night."   He would hum
" I want to *be* happy, and I can't *be* happy . . ." for weeks,
after that, nearly driving Toni out of her senses.   And then
he took her to " No, No, Nanette " again, because he said he
felt so awfully in touch with that fellow in it—the silly-ass one,
the Joe Coyne part . . . good-tempered chap, but always in
hot water . . . " —till I've made you happy too-oo ! "

So, since last February, she had seen a lot of Jimmy.   He
had been in London most of the time, until July, when he had
taken his three grandchildren and their nurse back to Gloucestershire with him, and Toni had managed to dash down for a
couple of long week-ends, and then for a whole ten days.
Jimmy, like Giles, was startlingly frank on the subject of himself ; the crust of conventionality which surrounded his confidences was so thin that, as Toni had put it—" You could walk
right through, and make yourself at home inside."   He was a

queer little chap, Jimmy. . . . You thought of him as a
" little chap," and talked of him as a " funny little man," for
all his six foot of height, because when he wasn't there, it was in
those terms that you inevitably thought of him. Gradually,
from observance of his ways and from what he told her, and
from odd memories drawn at random here and there from her
own life with Giles, she found herself reconstructing Nancy's
life with Jimmy, as though it were still capable of fascinating
her as a spectacle. In fact, Toni became fond of Nancy, as of
one who had inevitably gone through much the same sort of
trial as herself.

For Jimmy was, mainly, a hilarious clown. Had Nancy
realised that, when she married him ? If not, it must have
been a disconcerting discovery, and not what you expected,
when you allied yourself to the only son of a line of Gloucestershire squires. Besides, Jimmy was in the Army—a subaltern in
the Field Artillery, when she married him ; major, by the time
he retired.

—Well, and were they all made to measure, even in the
Army ? She might have noticed the incipient clown in his
face, had she scrutinised it more than lovingly : wide, thin-
lipped, laughing mouth, that broke deep creases at either end
of it, and left them there ; his eyes—not in the least like Giles'
eyes, but light brown and trustful ; they flitted uneasily from
face to face, as though pleading for something withheld or
forgotten—sad eyes ; and again a clown's freakish twist to the
thin, light brows that lay so high above them ; and Jimmy's
thick hair began to grow a long way back from his forehead,
and Jimmy's wiry body and limbs were a perpetual jumping
betrayal of his nervous system, screwed too tightly for his own
ease or anyone else's. And yet Jimmy's audacities were uttered
in the perfectly orthodox gun-room-and-country-house voice ;
and Jimmy wore completely orthodox gun-room-and-country-
house clothes—except when he was in London, when he again
succumbed, as though by second nature, to convention and the
best tailors. So that it was really quite a little time before you
could observe what a droll little man he was. . . . Toni reflected that it must have been a shock to Nance, when she first

woke up to it. She suspected that Nance preferred men who were not oddities ; but that, having a brave spirit, she championed Jimmy, with all his behaviour thrown in, unweariedly, as far as the outside world was concerned—the hunting set, and the gentleman-farmer set, and the Army set ; and that she went on championing him until the day of her death ; she went on championing him, even to Jimmy himself, so that he was never sure how much he had maddened her. Toni was only sure of this : that the more unhappily he suspected it, the more surely he did himself in. Terrified of losing Nance, he set about the job of alienating her and irritating her, so deliberately as to suggest either that there was indeed an insane streak in his composition, or that he felt so unsafe in his power to keep her, that he had to keep on and on testing the slender silver cord, testing it with weight and unexpected strain : " There, will it stand *that* ? . . . will it stand that much ? " . . . So that was how Jimmy had acquired his anxious look, pleading to be reassured.

If he had only given up philandering ! Toni would have been able to tell him that, had she been a friend of theirs : friend to him, and friend to Nance. For of course she knew all that Nance didn't tell Jimmy, about it ; they were precisely the things that she didn't tell Giles. . . . But Jimmy was worse than Giles ; more blatant, noisier, less philosophic. His philandering meant even less ; but oh ! the hurly-burly, the bustle, the terrifically over-elaborated illusions that he created all about and around them ! " He doesn't mean a word of it," Toni told Nance ; the Nance who had so mysteriously become alive, and her contemporary. " Nancy dear, don't you see ? He's hopeless, of course, and he makes one's head ache and I wish to heaven he'd stop being the-life-and-soul-of-the-party. But—oh, you must understand, Nance, a noisy man is often terrifically inarticulate——"

And Nance was no fool : she *did* understand ; but she couldn't be bothered to keep on understanding ; she became tired ; and this, to her, was synonymous with defiance : she pretended not to care a kick of a horse's hoof for him, any longer ; pretended to laugh at his shout and whirlwind of infidelity; pretended, even, to believe in it. Toni could have sworn that Nance did not really believe in it, not for a moment —you couldn't, if you were as intelligent as Giles' mother must have been! It was all a part of the buffoon Jimmy, the popular Jimmy, the ninety-times-forgiven-by-his-wife Jimmy . . . who didn't exist at all, but was terrified of vacancy or uncertainty about himself. The clown and the philanderer at least he knew well, and could fill in the outlines, and create a huge uproar about it all. . . . And Toni saw all this, scene after scene : the breakfast-table; dressing for a party; after the party, on the way home. . . . She saw it as a plot, which develops from mist into pictures, and then slowly dissolves again, in a fade-out at the cinema, when they want the audience to know what had happened twenty and thirty years before the modern story. She supposed that she and Giles were the story, Jimmy and Nance the fade-out. Jimmy, during the last eight months, had talked to her about Nance for hours, as though every time he had just come away from a row with her; or from her amused, but wholly detached, silences. He could talk about his love for Nance to Toni; but she had no illusion that it was only to her, because they had become such good friends, that he could talk about it; and only because it had all happened so long ago. . . . She was quite convinced that during Nance's lifetime, and to every casual stranger who had passed half an hour in their house, Jimmy had equally unburdened himself, in his queer, trustful sort of fashion, about his love for his wife, and his own many faults, and so forth. . . . And there was Nancy, out in the garden with the other visitors, knowing quite well what Jimmy was doing; and he, gabbling on and on, would know equally well that she knew what he was doing, and despairingly recognise her disdain. But he was wound up to it, and had to go on. . . . " Oh, Jimmy, you're *dreadful !* " cried Toni, wringing her hands helplessly, for she could do nothing any more; Jimmy was such a darling, she would so gladly have helped him; but she was his daughter-in-law; and Nancy had died when she was thirty-two, Toni's own age——

It was all twenty years ago !

Nance had been worn out by the hopeless, needless burlesque

of an uncontrollable passion-for-Nancy which Jimmy had
kicked up at the wrong times, with an exaggerated frenzy;
again to conceal, for some peculiar Jimmyish reason, his real
but different love for Nance.—" Yes, but look here," Toni
argued, exasperated—for how could you throw up a shield in
front of this foolish man, when every time he seized it and
flung it away, exposing himself anew—" even the things that
you could have impressed her with—you do them as though
you were in a circus ring, with a sort of pretence clumsiness.
And lots of people wouldn't even know that you have to do a
thing frightfully well, before you can even begin to pretend
that you are doing it like a clown. What's it all *for*, Jimmy?
In Heaven's name, what's it all for? What's the sense in it? "
And Jimmy grinned, and answered : " Oh, it raises a laugh,
you know; it raises a laugh!" . . .

Well, thank goodness she had not been their contemporary,
and a friend to both. She could hardly have borne to watch it.
She could hardly bear to watch it, even now, when one of the
couple was below grass and beyond caring, and the other in his
middle fifties; she could hardly bear to watch it as it came
through in fragments from the broken past, fragments that
Jimmy told her, and what her imagination told her, and what
her memories of Giles told her. Perhaps, after all, if she had
had the chance to speak all these wisdoms her fancy dictated,
separately, to Nancy and to Jimmy, no help would have come
of it. Perhaps, after all, she had better keep to her own job
with her own man. Had she not married the son of Jimmy
and Nance, and herself made an unholy mess of it? Had she
not Giles to cope with, who was coming back, perhaps to-night,
perhaps to-morrow? Giles, who was at once easier and more
difficult than Jimmy; not so boisterous; not so transparent;
the Great War in his system, and the more indolent code of the
generation after Jimmy's; Giles, who had kissed Aimée instead
of a barmaid, because barmaids were out-of-date; and who told
his wife more than ever Jimmy had told his, maybe because
marriage mattered less. . . . "And I don't believe," murmured
Toni, finding it difficult to abandon the parallel, and to think
of her parents-in-law with the usual bored respect of a daughter-

in-law, " I don't believe that Jimmy would have left Nance in the lurch."

The clock chimed seven. . . . Colin was a nuisance—— Why had he torn up the telegram, and chucked the pieces into the road? Thanks to his loyal impetuosity, she did not even know from where Giles had sent it off; he might have been already at Calais; he might walk in, now, at any moment. What would she say to a husband who thought he could come back whenever he pleased, just by announcing himself? It was rather brave of him, Toni thought, to risk it; in his place, having done what he had done, and knowing Toni, she would most assuredly have stopped away, out of range. For this was no meek and sorrowing wife whom he had abandoned!—But she was glad, all the same, how glad! that she was going to see him again—— Glad, glad. . . . She could hardly hear what was going on in the outside world, for the heavy thumping of her heart, and for her exultant gladness, and for her anger with the man who so coolly and so kindly had announced that he was coming home. . . . Damn his condescension! And if you were not of the class that could heave half a brick when emotion failed to express itself convincingly in words, what was the alternative welcome? . . . Toni could no longer sit still, nor stand gazing into the fire. She tramped up and down the room, her head bent, her light, graceful, swinging walk a comical and unconscious burlesque of what a man's heavier tramp would have been under the same circumstances. There had hardly been time, last February, for her to give way to all the fierce, hot resentment that was now bursting up from within her. She had been due in Paris, the next day; and then an overwhelming amount of work; and—in that perverse way that fortune sometimes twitches at your sleeve—a record season. All through March, April, and May, the reputation of " Toni's " had leapt, like a chamois, up the steep slopes from humiliation to renewed successes. Fresh premises, fresh capital, fresh blood, the combination of these only needed good luck, and—" By God, we had it too! " Toni recollected, still amazed at the way the business had responded, after its years of slow growth, and its further years of slow disintegration, to the strong team-work of herself and Miss Thompson and Helen Czelovar. Old clients came blandly back again, as though, indeed, they had never bought their clothes elsewhere; new clients, considerably impressed by Toni's designs, spread abroad the tidings that this was *the* place at which to order—say, half a dozen afternoon and evening dresses. In July, Toni was able to slacken her efforts a little, and recuperate in Gloucestershire; and she snatched another long week-end in the middle of September, after the International Dress Exhibition which had kept her frantically busy. Now and then she had heard from Giles, and carelessly had scribbled a few lines in answer, telling him how the children were. . . .

She made no comment when she heard that they had gone to Vienna, Giles and Loraine. Vienna !—and Toni had longed to go there, more than to any other city in the world ! Toni's own Vienna, though she had never yet set foot in it. She had desired all the intoxication of starting out for it, at last, with a man whom she loved; and on that night of their party in the studio, the night of the torches flaming through the snow —and the night, incidentally, when she had first met Loraine —it had flitted through her mind that she would go with Giles . . . that she would prefer to go with Giles, had she the choice of all other men. . . . Strange, for she had not married him for love ! . . . But they would go soon, quite soon. . . . So Toni had thought, in the midst of her good time. Yet somehow it had been put off and put off : Paul, and then Antony, were born; her freedom was cramped with engagements; Toni was so popular, and Giles was so popular; and they had taken the new house—oh, all sorts of things ! Presently, and quite soon, they would go to Vienna. And now he had gone with Loraine. . . . Toni saved that up, too, for and if ever she met Giles face to face again . . .

Giles might be here at any moment.

Val's wire, with its amazing news, arrived early in September, tossed into the bustle and hurly-burly of preparations for the Dress Exhibition : " Giles and Loraine turned up here last night—calmly propose to stay—what do you want me to do about it ? " And Toni, still wearing her debonair attitude, like a cap with a feather jauntily stuck in it, had swaggered back her telegram in reply : " God bless the happy couple—Toni."

Toni thought no more about them. Or—very nearly she thought no more about them. The order to dress Lucilla Danby for Colin's play had rushed in on her, next, crowding out everything else. Lucilla Danby had always liked Toni, and admired her ; now she was able to give the firm its chance. She let her have a free hand in building the costumes. Great fun, those weeks before the production of " She Burnt Her Boats." In a way, Toni enjoyed them more than she had relished anything during the years of her good time. For she was using her creative power, her organising ability ; and a good time was thrown in gratis, as a mere extra. She and Colin and Lucilla were a triumvirate ; as it turned out, a triumphant triumvirate : for—damn Giles !—here was the first night of " She Burnt Her Boats " ; and along her own line, Toni and " Toni's " had arrived, as surely as Colin. Lucilla, of course, had arrived years ago ; success was nothing new to her ; but she was very proud of the children, as she nicknamed Colin and Toni. Her remarks to Colin on Loraine's habits of kidnapping were caustic to a degree ; and Colin had rep⹁ed with his own unflattering opinion of Giles' desertion. Toni had guessed at their loyal attitude. . . . But what did Giles and Loraine matter ? " She Burnt Her Boats " was good for a year's run, at least ; and she had been given orders to dress three other important productions for the autumn and winter.

—And now, to-night or to-morrow, Giles was coming back. Quarrelled with Loraine ? Perhaps. Quarrelled with Loraine, so coming back to Toni ! Or perhaps Loraine was fed up with him, and Toni can't be fed up with him because she's his wife ! Right ! Let him come quickly, while Toni's blood is at its present heat, while Toni's eyes are gleaming, scornful blue under level brows. Let him come now !

—And, as though she had been overheard, a sharp ring pealed through the hall, followed by a heavy knock. Toni stood rigid and motionless. She could not remember if Giles had ever knocked and rung like this ; of course, he had always had his key. If this were Giles—God ! would Quimper never answer the door ?—then Giles was in an imperious mood. All the better for the teaching! She always preferred to attack where she found resistance.

The front door was opened; she listened tensely, but still she could only hear the drumming in her own ears . . .

Then the clamour and confusion of her senses were stilled as though by a miracle; and everything seen, everything heard, took on clear, distinct edges. Quimper brought in a telegram. Not Giles himself—yet; but this would have been sent off from a nearer stage on his journey home. Would she have to endure another night's waiting? She had waited for eight months, to let loose her anger. But she felt she could not endure another night.

" There will be no answer, Quimper," said Toni, before she even opened the envelope. She did not want Quimper there, watching her; she was afraid she might look too glad . . . Although, of course, she was not glad, unless you could be glad and angry at the same time. But Quimper had gone now, and Toni could read the message. It had arrived only just one hour after the last one. He could not have journeyed much further in an hour.

But he had journeyed a great deal further. . . . She read: " Come at once—Giles had hæmorrhage—dangerously ill— Loraine."

CHAPTER II

—" **M**UMMIE ! " cried Babs, flying into the room. " Here's a ninkpot for you. I made it ! " She thrust the object into Toni's unresisting hands. It was cardboard and plasticine and tin-tacks and burnt-out matches ; it wouldn't hold ink ; and it was, moreover, the fourteenth inkpot of its kind that Babs had presented her with, during the last three days ! Susie had also received a great many inkpots, and so had all the servants. Babs ran them up in five minutes ; and expected, each time, the same outburst of gratitude, surprise and enthusiasm as when the first inkpot had been bestowed upon the first recipient. Even Quimper was growing weary of inkpots.

—" It's a ninkpot, Mummie ! " Babs cried again, quivering with excitement. " I made it myself, and now I'll make you another ! "

Toni stared at the gift. A plasticine and cardboard inkpot happened to be among the last things she could desire or use, considering the circumstances.

. . . Not a moment to spare, now, for her children. But in Toni's swimming, twilit mind, in which all thought seemed dim and submerged, glided slowly this conviction : that as she had neglected her family and her business, for a " good time " ; and neglected Giles, for her family and the business, so one day she would have to pay for neglecting the children ; even as now, in the peril of losing Giles ; even as last year, in the collapse of " Toni's " ; and before that, in the reproach of Aunt Eugène's death. You were not let off from payment, ever. And while you were busy catching up with one bill, another was presented, with destiny's most ironic bow. . . . The thought gaped at her blindly, like a fish from its aqueous depths . . . then vanished again.

316

—Suddenly the numbness passed. Toni regained command of her energies. She sent Babs dashing away to fetch Susie; she rang for Quimper; she told Quimper to look up trains and boats; she scribbled a telegram to San Goffredo, to be telephoned through to the Post Office, saying that she was starting at once. Briefly, and without cadging for comfort—no time for that!—she related to Susie what had happened; begged her to superintend the packing of whatever emergency hand-luggage might be necessary for her to take out with her, to Italy. She wrote a few lines to Helen, handing over the direction of " Toni's," indefinitely. Then, the telephone being free again, she rang up Jimmy's Club, and succeeded in getting hold of him. Had it not been for the outbreak of foot-and-mouth disease in Gloucestershire, Jimmy would have been down there, hunting.

It was impossible to tell the effect of her tidings upon him; but he promised to come round at once.

" Your train is from Victoria—nine-ten, Madam," said Quimper, in melting accents, the only sympathy his sense of good form permitted. " You will be wanting something strengthening to eat at once, Madam. I will tell Mrs. Quimper."

Toni nodded. Then she looked at the clock again. Last time she had looked it was to wonder when Giles might be expected to appear over there, in the doorway. Her mind fretted over the space between Regent's Park and Villa Bel Respiro on the Mediterranean. . . . She saw the strip of land that was still England; then the strip of sea; then the great slab of France that must be crossed; then delay in Paris—her impatience struggled vainly against the idea of that three hours in Paris!—and then more France; and a long, torturing journey in and out of tunnels, beside the sea, stopping at every sun-scorched Riviera resort; Ventimiglia—more waiting!—no, she could get a car there—would it be any quicker, though? You can't fight space, you can't fight it! You just have to conquer it, inch by inch. And others of her family were out there with Giles: Loraine and Val and Aunt Elsa; and she, to whom it mattered most—she *did* care so desperately!—must

cross all that land and sea before she could get to him. . . .
" And I haven't seen him for eight months," thought Toni. It
occurred to her that she might fly to him—fly as far as Paris, at
all events—but she dismissed that again : the wind was high ;
she could hear the hurl of it against the windows ; she could
not risk an accident ; Giles might be wanting her. . . . And
that, while it lasted, was soothing as some cool and precious
ointment,—the idea that Giles might be wanting her. She
did not know if people talked after a hæmorrhage, or were
unconscious. Would he have been able to say : " Send for
Toni ! " ? Or was she merely sent for as a formality, because
she was the wife ? Again she went to the telephone, gave the
number of the doctor who usually attended them. Funny,
how she was able to remember his 'phone number, and all the
other numbers she had needed ! Usually she was obliged to
look them up ; usually her memory refused to retain 'phone
numbers. But to-night they jumped into her mind just when
she wanted them, sharply, in black and white, like little crotchets
and quavers. The Doctor was in, too ; trivial things were
going right ; it must mean, then, mustn't it, that the big things
would go right, as well ? She asked him about hæmorrhage, and
he gave her all the information she desired. Susie, at her elbow,
prompted her to ask, furthermore : " And ought I to take out
anything, any sort of drugs, or whatever might be wanted for
nursing, that they wouldn't be likely to have in a small, Italian
village ? " Again, the Doctor was helpful ; and the nurse
from St. Olaf's was sent flying round to the nearest chemist's.
Toni went upstairs, and changed into her warm travelling
things. It seemed to her that she was doing everything too
quickly. . . . She wanted to cram time full to bursting, with
none left over, before the nine-ten left Victoria. She went
down again to the sitting-room ; she could not bear to stop
with the children ; and, anyhow, Susie was putting them to
bed. She began to pace the room again, as she had done while
waiting for Giles to give him his dose of " delicate hell," as
Colin had put it. Supper was brought in, and she nibbled
some food, absently, while still on the move. She was too
feverish to sit down. Her foot struck some obstacle on the

carpet. It was the inkpot Babs had made for her. Toni picked
it up and fondled it, laughing tenderly. . . . How absurdly
things happened: "Hæmorrhage, dangerously ill"—"Mummie,
here's a ninkpot. I made it for you . . ." Her laughter began
to shake nearer to tears. . . . " I won't cry ! " muttered Toni.
" I'm—I'm damned if I will ! Look here, I'll tell myself this :
if I cry, it's a sign that I won't get there—in time. . . . That'll
keep me from it ! " And indeed, she did not dare cry, having
once fixed this penalty in her mind, as a deterrent—— For
this was Toni's funny way of managing herself.

. . . Giles, Giles !—Ah, here was Jimmy ! " He might have
come before ; he couldn't have hurried," she thought, resentfully. " Those Goddards don't care what happens to each
other. . . . I suppose he had to finish his billiards or his bridge,
or whatever it was ! " And then realised it was still not yet
eight o'clock. She had ordered the car for eight-forty, to drive
to the station. She opened the front door, herself, to Jimmy.
It was too painful to wait in the sitting-room, while he was
admitted by Quimper. " These Goddards don't care—— "
But to-night, at least, they would not be likely to turn on the
gramophone and drink Lanson 1914, as in February, last time
she had urgently sent for her father-in-law.

. . . " *Jimmy !* " The first sight of his face was a shock,
even in the wan and blowy light of the porch. Bridge ?—
Billiards ?—Why—but Jimmy had grown old ; his skin was dry
like parchment ; the lines on his face were drawn deep and
tight. Gun-room-and-country-house ? Gentiles indifferent to
each other ?—Toni was suddenly ashamed. Would she never
come to the end of realising her arrogant mistakes ? It was
plain to her, in that one moment of revelation at the open front
door, that Goddard cared for this son of his, as agonisingly as
any parent of Israel could have cared ; fatherhood was not a
Jewish monopoly. . . . And here, once again, was David
mourning for Absalom.

Toni, who had rather wanted to be supported, braced herself
again to support the male in trouble.

. . . " He'll die ! " exclaimed Jimmy, to comfort her. " Of
course he'll die ! The other two are no good—Reg, Freddie.

Blasted prig Reginald always was; and Freddie simply a waster like his father. A damned healthy fellow like I am, goes on living all right. Toni, darling! My dear child! . . . But Giles was the only decent one. Hæmorrhage—it's always fatal, always!"

Toni had had enough. She spun round on him, and: "Go to hell!" she snapped: "and stop making an exhibition of yourself! It won't do, Jimmy! I won't have it!"

Her father-in-law floundered for a moment; then, among his incoherent emotions, regained some sort of a footing. "Sorry, old girl!" he said. "That's what I wanted—a slosh between the eyes. You've got fifty times my pluck; most women have, nowadays," he finished, ruefully. But Toni knew that his Army record, though brief, had held a recommendation for the D.S.O. for service during the Boer War; his first campaign, and, he thought, his last, for he retired almost directly afterwards. But 1914 fetched him out again.

In silence, she mixed him a stiff whisky-and-soda. All her outstanding associations with Jimmy were connected with mixing him whiskies-and-sodas! . . .

"That's better! When does our train leave, Toni?"

So he *was* coming along, too? Well, of course, it was obvious, now, how he loved Giles. . . . Toni wondered whether Giles had concealed, in the same idiotic way, an equally fervent affection for his father. Probably; she seemed to remember now. . . .

"Nine-ten. Can you come off like this, just as you are, Jimmy?"

"Why not?" he queried, simply. "I say, Toni, we're not exactly going to enjoy that journey, you know."

"I know, Jimmy. I know."

"You're not fed up with the boy, still?"

It occurred to her that Jimmy knew nothing of the first telegram she had received, and was still ignorant that Giles had announced his home-coming, and that Toni had been preparing a reception for him. Oh well, what did it matter? It was not worth the telling. "No, Jimmy, not an atom fed

up. Of course I'm not. We'll have it out together, Giles and
I," she continued, steadily, "when he's better."

"You think he'll pull round, eh?"

Heavens! How dependent he was; his eyes more than
ever like some sad little clown's. "Oh, he'll pull round——"
But then she rejected that . . . After all, Jimmy was no baby.
"Loraine said: 'Dangerously ill,' in her telegram. We
might as well stop giving each other syrup, Jimmy."

Jimmy declared, cantankerously: "That gassing may be
at the bottom of it—that gassing he had in '17. It left a
weak spot. You never know, you never know! People ought
to die in order, one after the other. I don't want to see my
son die. Why should I? I'm twenty-six years older than he
is. I don't want to go on living!"

"Rot!" said Toni, relapsing into the schoolgirl. "You
love life, Jimmy, you know you do!" And it was true:
Goddard was fond of horses and hunting; fond of wine and
food; fond of laughing, and the sound of his own voice; fond
of vapid, pretty, tantalising little ladies—girlie-girlies would
have been the term for them while he was still a young man;
fond of reading—an unexpected trait, this; fond of the town
and the country—yes, Jimmy loved life; even his fits of rue
and remorse had a queer relish to them; but above all things,
he was fond of company: he would leave an empty paradise
for a convivial purgatory, any day of the week!

"Oh, I know I'm keen on things," admitted poor Jimmy,
woefully, "and they're not big, noble things, either. I just
like to enjoy myself—why, I'd got three little Bits out of
'Who's from Hu-la-hu?' having supper with me to-night.
Sumptuous little Bits!"—he began to wax enthusiastic . . .
and then suddenly remembered—— "And there you are,
you see! I oughtn't to be supping with Bits, at my age. I
ought to be thinking of Heaven, or working for the Empire.
I can't help it. I wanted to die when Nance died. And if
Giles dies——"

Toni groped round despairingly for something to divert
Jimmy from his obstinate partiality for the word "die"; she
simply could not endure listening to it for another ticking

twenty minutes.—Babs' inkpot!—"Your eldest grandchild
made this"; with rather a shaky laugh, she held it out to him.
"We've been deluged with them lately; Babs' latest craze.
I wonder what put it into her head? She's not an author's
daughter, so it can't be hereditary."

"Babs isn't my eldest grandchild, confound it!" grumbled
Goddard. "Reggie's brats——" he came to a dead halt. "*Oh
God!*" he exclaimed; and if he had been broken before, he
was now appalled, horror-stricken.

"What is it, Jimmy? What is it?" Was he seeing ghosts?
Could it be that Giles——? . . . Toni cast one shuddering
look over her shoulder in the direction where Jimmy was
blankly staring. Nothing—nothing there.

"That Will," groaned Jimmy Goddard; "that infernal
Will!"

Toni could not understand. "We ought to be starting in a
minute or two," she reminded him. "What Will?"

Her father-in-law's face had inexplicably hardened; there
was an irritated rasp in his voice as he explained to her—for-
getting "Toni's"—in the way that men of his type explain
business to women of inferior mental capacity: "If anything
happens to Giles now," he said, briefly, "I can't leave a brass
halfpenny to you and your children; it'll have to go, every
penny of it, to Reggie or Fred, or both. The Lord knows I
don't *want* to leave them anything," he added, getting more
and more irascible at the look of wonder in Toni's eyes—for
she had thought Jimmy disliked his eldest son pretty thoroughly
—"Giles was to have had it all—you know that, and he knows
it—the whole bag-of-tricks—it's close on a hundred-and-twenty-
thousand pounds. I can't touch the capital. I've only got
Power of Appointment to leave it among my children—that's
where Hell comes in.—Oh, confound it, Toni, don't *gape* at
me! It's as clear as anything."

"I know," said Toni, coldly, "but I'm rather stupid this
evening, so——"

"Oh, I'm sorry, I'm sorry, little girl. But Giles' kids, you
know. . . . I'm fond of 'em; cheery little beggars! I don't
like Reggie's two, and if Fred had any, they'd be worse: he's

a bad hat, Fred; and crooked into the bargain. I'm a long way from being a saint myself, but I won't stand for any of Fred's transactions; I'm ashamed of them, and that's a fact. No, it'll have to be Reggie. You see, Toni," much more gently, " all the income we're living on now, I and Giles and you and the kids, it was all settled on Nance by her people; the old man was infernally rich, and Nance was the only child. By the terms of the settlement, if she died before I did, I could use the income, and bequeath the capital among her children and mine; but not away from them; not to *their* children."

" Oh, but surely——" Toni began, " that wouldn't be leaving it away from Giles, if it were to Babs and Paul and Antony ? " She couldn't fight for herself, when it was a question of inheritance; but she could, for Babs and Paul and Antony; she had always believed that they, at least, would be secure. This was panic of a new kind creeping in. . . .

" I *know* it's the same thing ! I know it's the same thing ! But you can't alter legal provisions. I can lump the money as I like, provided it doesn't go away from Reggie and Giles and Fred. I can divide it equally, or leave it all to one, or cut it up between two of them, leaving out the third. Well, Reggie's got plenty, more than he wants; he's an acute business man, Reggie; never parts from a penny if he can help it. Fred's done himself in, long ago. It was all going to Giles; of course it was; we're—we're good friends, Giles and I, though we don't make a song and dance about it; but if Giles dies like this, before me, I'm helpless; if the children were starving in the future, I'd be helpless."

" It isn't fair ! " Toni cried wildly. She was fast held in the grip of her bitterest dread. . . . Toni had known poverty; it was no vague outline to her; she had dragged through it for years; she could recite its dingiest details : being poor and ill ; being poor and envious; being poor and tired; being poor and having to stick to uncongenial work; being poor in ugly surroundings; being poor and frightened. . . . Oh, Toni knew ! being poor and bitter; poor and out of it—yes, even down to the last line of the chant : poor and hungry. Toni knew ! Well, that was all long ago; no need to rake it all up in her mind. But—not for Babs! She couldn't bear it for Babs, and the other two; she had thought them safe; she had thought, by marrying into Goddard territory, she had struck gold, unearned increment. . . . However hard-up they would be temporarily, there was *money behind;* that was the glorious feeling: you leant up against it, like a bulwark; it kept the cold winds off, like a mountain; all that bulk of their grandfather's money, it was bound to come to them some day: not money that was being earned, bit by bit; and which depended precariously on toil or hazard; but money *there*, there and waiting!—The children were all right!

And now. . . . But Jimmy was scrutinising her, a queer gleam under his lids that were like wrinkled leather. . . . He was even smiling a little. . . . Toni was aware that she had betrayed herself to him, as she had not done when Giles had left her; nor even when she heard that Giles was dangerously ill. She was scared, and for a moment she let Jimmy see it; dead scared. . . . "Oh, Jimmy! I didn't mean—it was just —I've been horribly hard-up, you know. It isn't much fun, but I shouldn't mind it again for me alone," she gasped, incoherently. "Oh, Jimmy, please, please—*do* something!" She had flung out her hands, in the first realisation of what her father-in-law had been explaining to her; and he had seized them. His grasp was warm and kind; firm, too. Goddard had changed in the last few minutes. If Toni had been free to notice it, she might have said that he had acquired dignity.

"The car's there," he said. "We ought to be starting, Toni dear; and free your mind of all this Will business. Giles may recover, you know. That woman, your cousin—what's her name?—Loraine—she's probably a scaremonger; and anyway, nobody's poor and starving yet. Your income goes on just the same, you see—what you and Giles have always had, the two thousand per annum. I wish to God I could make it more, or lay by a thousand or two every year—I'm probably good for another twenty years yet—but I'm so damnably in debt myself. I don't know how I do it, but I always am. There's an overdraft of more than seven thousand pounds at my Bank, on guarantees of income; so that I'm tied up everywhere, don't you see? But never mind, don't worry, Toni, don't worry. . . . Come along now!"

Susie had appeared, and Quimper; and the next few moments were sucked under in the vortex of urgent departure —Susie's last comforting words, whispered with Toni in her arms—— Quimper's heartfelt: "And we do hope, Mrs. Quimper and me, Madam, that you will find the master better; and please send for me if you want help in bringing him back here from Those Places Abroad."

All this had given Toni no time for reflection; and even during the twenty minutes when she and Jimmy sat silent in the car, driven by a chauffeur from the garage, between Regent's Park and Victoria, the immediate urgency of getting along, getting along, passing that lorry, getting along, cutting through that jam of traffic before the policeman stopped them, getting along, was all that really mattered. . . . Getting along! Suppose they missed their train! Suppose she did not catch the boat to-night! What a fool she had been, wasting time; actually talking to Jimmy placidly, as though they had not got to cross half London—or so it seemed to her—in twenty flying minutes!

But the chances of traffic were kind, for once. They drew up at the portals of Victoria Continental platform as the clock boomed nine; and she had no luggage to fuss about, only the one suitcase. It was after Jimmy had been to buy the tickets, and met her again at the entrance to the platform itself, that he dealt her yet another shock:

"Toni, my dear, I hope you don't mind, but I won't see you further than this. I was coming down as far as Dover, you know, to put you on the boat; but really, I don't see what good I could do. I'm a depressing sort of fellow, and when I think of poor Giles . . . You'll be all right, won't you?"

"But weren't you——?" Toni began, blankly. They found a first-class carriage, fortunately nearly empty, and Jimmy helped her into it, settled her rug over her knees, placed the suit-case in the rack, and gave her her little book of tickets.

. . . She had been absolutely sure that he had intended to

travel right out to San Goffredo with her. Why, he had taken it for granted, and so had she. His favourite son was dangerously ill. Surely there had been no question of just seeing her off, whether from Victoria or from Dover?—or had she misunderstood, when he talked of " starting soon " and " when does our train go ? "

" I'd be no good out there," repeated Jimmy, guessing her thoughts. Perhaps she had looked at him reproachfully ; Toni hoped not, for she could see he was suffering, under his bravado of making this into quite an ordinary parting for an ordinary journey. " Not a bit of good ; I'd get in the way ; men always do, you know, over illness. Nance used to say I was hopeless if anyone was ill. Keep me posted about the boy, won't you ? " And then he added, as though to insist that he had never contemplated accompanying her further than Dover : " You'll get a porter all right, you know, who will put you on the boat. Used to travelling, aren't you ? I shouldn't have been much good. We'd have only sat staring at each other for the next two hours. By Jove ! I could do with a whisky-and-soda. Shall I get you one, Toni ?—No time, though ; they're going to blow the whistle. Oh, you've got your brandy-flask well filled. I'd take a good pull if I were you. Good-bye, my dear little girl ! Buck up ! " And Jimmy added, earnestly : " Take a *good* pull at the brandy ! . . ." as he jumped off the step, and the train moved slowly forward and away from him . . .

CHAPTER III

TONI tried hard, as the train gathered speed and pulled her out into the dark fields and through light-pricked villages, not to think about Giles—at least, not about Giles ill, dangerously ill; but to think about Giles well. But —was it any better?—Dangerously well, that was how she kept on remembering him; dancing; how marvellously Giles had danced! Ragging her; and she had relished his manner of teasing; it was witty and never crude; ready to recoil, as though at the nervous end of a spring, if it were near hurting her; Giles exchanging swift, racy nonsense with Colin; Giles sunnily shelving his " business " responsibilities, to play in a Rugger match :—" You take on the blooming clients to-day, Murray ! " Giles giving way to extravagance in the ordering of a dinner, totally unrepentant over the bills.

And then, their last scene together : Giles angry, and— dangerously well : " Thank you for sparing me, Toni . . ."

She moved restlessly in her seat. Still, she was nearer to Giles than she had been—was it a quarter of an hour ago? Yes, it must be at least a quarter of an hour or twenty minutes. She looked at her watch ; nearer to Giles? Yes, she had won a victory over three minutes, no more.

" I wish Jimmy could have come with me," sighed Toni, feeling small and thin and desolate.

But had Giles been so desperately well as she had always confidently supposed him? Jimmy had talked of poison gas ; yes, she knew he had been gassed some time back, in the War ; but he had said he was cured; that it never bothered him, and was not likely ever to bother him again. She dwelt on the bare facts of the telegram : " Hæmorrhage "; but that sounded like lungs, tuberculosis. She struggled to recall, for minute inspection, that period of years which she had let slip by so carelessly. Sifting them through the mind, she became less and less sure that Giles had been altogether fit ; surely he had been over-excited, restless, never still ? Was that not in itself a sign of illness ? " Toni mustn't be over-excited "— the old phrase ! But she was so much stronger now ; she had been well looked after ; even the last strenuous eight months had not robbed her of the health she had acquired during her four years of being married to Giles ; but, of course, like all people who were materially well looked after, she had lapsed into callous inattention over others. Perhaps it ought to have been " Giles mustn't be over-excited " ? She had neglected him, in her conceited determination not to be a hopeless sort of wife—the eternally vigilant gaoler ; she had neglected him. What did she remember of Giles, during the last year or two ? Nothing, except that he had been rather going the pace : late hours, dancing, drinking, hot rooms, all the usual paraphernalia. Occasionally she had laughed : " I think you're mad, Giles ! " —at one of his hectic, unreasonable moods in which he would talk and talk . . . " Entertaining bloke, young Goddard ! " their pals had said. Ill ? Of course he had been ill ! But now he was dangerously ill. And as for loafing ?—the conviction struggled up, through layers of self-imposed plausibilities, that she must have *liked* a husband who loafed, who merely played at business ; she must have encouraged it, in order to keep him subordinate. The young matriarch had been taking no risks. . . . Otherwise, how easy it would have been, for a woman of her irresistible energy, to have insisted on some sort of persistent achievement from her husband. For four years she had countenanced his loafing ; why ? Was it wholly normal for her to have refrained from at least suggesting that he should work ? . . . The subterranean instinct, inherited from her grand-mother, Anastasia Rakonitz, and from Anastasia's grandmother —yes, Toni owned it now !—this instinct had enjoyed Giles' manifest inferiority, his lack of leadership. . . . " Keep him there !—it's safer. . . ." It was her fault—Toni added remorse to her load of anxiety ; and having thus considerably increased the weight, she looked again at her watch. . . . Another seven minutes gone ; that was better ! They were licking up time, now. Perhaps if she could manage to attach her thoughts on to a wheel that did not bring Giles round with every rotation, they would lick it up faster still.

So she began to think of Jimmy—Jimmy's face as she had first seen it in the porch: Why—he loves Giles! Jimmy explaining to her impatiently about Power of Appointment, that fatal restraint on the disposition of his wealth: " If Giles should die, I'm helpless; if the children were starving, I'd be helpless." Toni shuddered. . . . Oh please, God, was there nothing nice to think of? Nothing in the future, or the present, or the past? . . . Jimmy saying: " I'm not coming any further with you, Toni." Toni frowned. . . . That *was* queer, you know; she could have sworn that he had meant to come out to San Goffredo, at first, and then had suddenly changed his mind. But why? Because Jimmy loves Giles. . . . And there the wheel began to turn again, clicking at three points, round and round and round: " Jimmy loves Giles "— " If Giles should die, I'd be helpless "—" I'm not coming any further with you, Toni." . . . And so, following each other automatically, in this sequence and to this rhythm, so that she could not tell any more which was the first and which was the last of the revolving three, they began to connect: " I'm not coming any further with you, Toni "—" Jimmy loves Giles " —" If Giles should die, I'd be helpless."

. . . But was there indeed any connection? Was it because Goddard loved his son—for if Toni had been persuaded of anything, she had been persuaded of that !—that he refused to go out to him when he was dangerously ill at San Goffredo? That did not make sense, surely? Things *had* to make sense . . .

The wheels galloped on and on, and time was passing quicker than ever now, for Toni actually, and at last, had forgotten to hunt down the minutes, and had let them fly by of themselves.

. . . It didn't make sense—unless—unless that third point that was bothering her, eluding her, helped her in some way to give it sense.

. . . Power of Appointment among his children only. Toni was a business woman, and she had taken in the legal import of this, better than Jimmy, in his overwrought state, had imagined. The practical side of her brain, cool and competent, and used to technicalities connected with money, had fully assimilated the position Jimmy was in ; and it was still with the practical side of her brain—her emotions for a little while mercifully in abeyance—that she began to consider whether indeed there existed no way out of it ? Whether Goddard, who had loved only Giles among his three sons, would be forced to leave every penny of the capital from which he drew his income, away from Giles' children, to the two remaining sons for whom he cared rather less than nothing ?

The terms of the settlement laid no restrictions, apparently, on the money, once it had passed from James Goddard, to Reginald or Giles or Fred. Reginald, Giles or Fred could bequeath it as they pleased. If Jimmy had died before Giles, and Giles had inherited the money, the children would be all right, whatever happened. A hundred and twenty thousand pounds : Giles could leave it to them, but Jimmy could not. Jimmy loved Giles. So if only Jimmy had died first . . .

The wheel in Toni's brain revolved once—and stopped. It had clicked and bitten on the third cog at last ! With a cry, she sprang up, swaying, from her seat. The two other passengers in the carriage stared at her in dumb surprise. " I've got to go back for something," Toni stammered. Still they stared. She sank down again . . .

Jimmy was going to kill himself. Her intuition had leapt to it, at exactly the same second as her business faculties had told her that there was absolutely nothing else for him to do, if he wanted to make the future secure for Babs and Paul and Antony, Giles' children. He had probably always looked on it as a matter of course that he should die before his son; naturally, being twenty-six years older. . . . Fathers, surely, died before their sons ! But now, Giles was dangerously ill; and if Jimmy wanted to die first, so that, anticipating him, he could, by a few hours, leave his money to a living Giles, then he would have to take the matter out of God's hands and see to it himself. . . .
" I won't go any further with you, Toni. I'd be no good, you

know ! "—Yes, no doubt but that he had meant to come out to San Goffredo ; he had changed his mind . . .

Toni was trembling : " I'll have to go back," she told herself. " I'll have to go back. " How was she to bear sitting still, the train carrying her further and further from Jimmy, standing there on the platform, as she had last seen him. When she had jumped up in the rocking carriage, it had been with the crazy idea that if she jumped through the door flung open, he might still be there, just outside, with that funny grin twisting his mouth, and the kind look in his eyes. It was strange, but between that moment, and when, half an hour before, she had given way to fear, and Jimmy had looked at her and taken her hands, and had said : " It'll be all right, Toni "—she had felt, as never before, protected ; an encounter with warmth and reassurance, as though at last she had encountered, not a pretty illusion of strength, but strength itself : a man who would see to things, and get things done for her.

How funny !—Jimmy.

Jimmy !—But he was not there any more. . . . She was half-way to Dover now ; more than half-way. Jimmy would not just stand there on the platform, after the train had departed. He would have gone . . . to see to things.

" I can't go back, I can't ! " Toni pleaded. " I *must* go on to Giles ! "—Supposing Giles were hammering out time, minute by minute, just as she was doing ; longing for her, asking all time when Toni might be expected, if Toni were not here yet ?

With every atom of her will, and keeping her muscles tense as though she were actually using physical force, she pushed the train forward. No question about it, she must go on to Giles. He was her husband.

And—no question about it, she would have to go back to Jimmy. She would have to prevent this suicide, if she could. Had she not betrayed cowardice when he had told her about Power of Appointment, had she not shown him her deadly fear that her children might have to go through the poverty she had tasted herself . . . But you had to pay for being a coward, even for a few minutes ! She would have to pay, now, bv getting out at Dover, and going straight back to London, instead of crossing the Channel and travelling on and on, until she reached Giles at the other end of her quest.

Jimmy loved Giles; well then, Giles loved Jimmy—that was simple enough!—so anyhow, even if she reached San Goffredo in time, she would not dare confront Giles with that news to tell him: " Jimmy's dead; he's shot himself " . . . for, of course, that was how he meant to do it. Army men always thought of a revolver first; it seemed more friendly to them. " Yes, Giles, I knew; I guessed. No, I didn't do my best to stop him; I had to come on to you. I wanted to be with you, Giles. They told me you were dangerously ill, so I couldn't stop and turn back, not after I'd started, could I ? " Giles would not see the force of that pleading. It was powerful, but not powerful enough. She would have to go back. You see, Giles was surrounded by people, nursing him, knowing his peril, doing their best: Aunt Elsa, Val, Loraine. . . . A swiftly remembered picture, here, of Loraine taking a fish-bone out of Babs' throat. . . . Loraine could be trusted in an emergency; she was at her best when people were ill; and though that made it, in a way, almost unbearable to Toni, the knowledge that, from the practical point of view, Loraine could do as much as she could do herself for Giles, and was doing it, doing it all the time—yet nobody was fighting death for Jimmy, because nobody knew how close to his shoulder death stood; nobody except Toni, who had guessed.

The train was pounding towards Dover fast enough, now, thundering along, swallowing time, swallowing space—oh yes, now, when it was no good, when every yard covered she would have to cover again, when she reached the harbour where the steamer waited, and took the next train back to London.

If only she might become unconscious, and be carried on to the boat and come round again to find herself just drawing up to the French shore. " Oh, don't be an ass, Toni ! " wearily; " even then, you'd have to take the next boat back from Calais, and what good would that do you ? " . . . " *Why* need I ? I want to get to Giles. He's ill, dangerously ill. He may be

wanting me. I can't fail Giles." . . . "You've got to stop
Jimmy; at least you've got to try. Giles will understand."
. . . "But he doesn't *know*; he'll think it's because he left
me, that I've refused to come out to him now!"—And that
was a new thought, and the sharpest pang of all. Surely,
having thought of that, she might now be allowed to go on?
Jimmy was a darling; she was awfully fond of old Jimmy;
but he wasn't her husband, and—after all, she was only guessing.
. . . What a fool she would look, had it never entered Jimmy's
head to perform any such quixotic and heroic act as was being
put to his credit by Toni's inflated imagination!

Toni was still fighting it out, when the train drew up at
Dover quay. She sat silent, while a porter, presupposing her
orders, seized the suit-case and the rug, and carried them off
towards the gangway. She saw the dark shape of the Channel
steamer lurching slightly against the sky. People who were in
a hurry to secure their deck-chairs, jostled and scampered past
her. . . .

"See you on the boat, Miss; my number's forty-eight."
And Toni let him go.

"Show your passports! Passport, please!" . . . It was her
turn now.

"I'm not crossing to-night," said Toni. And disengaging
herself from the block of passengers, she walked back towards
the train platforms, and enquired of an official when the next
train went to Victoria. He pointed:

"Starting almost at once, Miss. You'd better hurry! Got
any luggage?"

Toni's lips were sternly set, but she smiled, then: "No,
no luggage!"—and sprang into the last carriage of the express, just as the whistle sounded and the guard dropped his
flag.

She supposed that her suit-case, labelled carefully with Val's
address at San Goffredo, would reach there before her.

.   .   .   .

Victoria again. And just after half-past twelve.

"Drive to Berkeley Mansions, Mount Street," said Toni, to

the driver of the first taxi on the rank; " as fast as you can."
But she did not really fear that she would be too late to hold
Jimmy back from the purpose she had divined in him. She
did not believe that she would be a second too early, either.
The nightmare journey of the last two hours, by so much more
nightmare than her parallel journey in the nine-ten from
Victoria to Dover, in that it was rushing her relentlessly away
from Giles instead of towards him, had all the same not tortured
her with that worst nightmare of all: apprehension lest her
sacrifice should prove futile; lest for nothing she should be
robbing Giles of the hours that ought to have been claimed by
him alone : Jimmy dead at one end, Giles at the other. . . .
Toni oscillating, fruitlessly, between the two. . . . Too late
for Jimmy, and then too late for Giles. . . . No, it could not
be as bad as that. Jimmy would have needed time, time to—
what was that cliché that men always used at this juncture ?—
to wind up his affairs. Probably, being a light-hearted man,
he would never have bothered, until now, to make the will in
which Giles was to figure as his sole legatee. As the taxi rushed
through the emptying streets, Toni pictured herself walking
straight into Jimmy's library. . . . He is standing with his
back towards her ; near the desk ; absorbed . . . too absorbed
to look round. . . . But here she is, at the eleventh hour and
the fifty-ninth minute ! Here she is, thank God, with presence
of mind enough to dash across the room and jerk up his arm
as he lifts it, so that the bullet flies harmlessly over their
heads.

. . . Toni was oddly obsessed by the certainty that it must
happen like that, and in no other way ; the traditions of film
melodrama had hypnotically fixed her tired imagination : " To
the Rescue of a Suicide ! " . . . Thus the captions flickered,
black on a pallid screen : " Toni Arrives in the Nick of Time ! "
. . . Nick ? They always said " nick "—— *What* was time's
nick ? . . . *Neck*, you silly !—that's the phrase !—" A Neck-
to-neck Race with Time " . . . " She got it in the neck " . . .
nick ? . . . neck ? Oh, I don't know, I'm nearly done . . .
Got it in the neck. . . . It doesn't matter, though. . . . Only
don't let me be too late for Jimmy. . . . Don't let me be too

late for Giles. . . . " God, God," prayed Toni, " give me a hand ! . . . help me to be in time at both ends . . ."

And then the taxi stopped with a jolt and a jarring of brakes, in front of the block of flats. Toni leapt out, handed the driver a crumpled note, and swung up the outer steps. The sleepy night-porter asked her if she wanted the lift. She shook her head ; it was easier to run ; supposing the lift broke down ? Her legs could not break down ; easier to run ; she could run quicker than almost any other girl she knew ; she could run like a boy. . . . And here she was on the third floor, her fingers thrust on to the bell—— That wasn't a revolver shot, was it ? —that ominous crash inside ? . . . Not as cruelly near as that ! And it didn't sound like a revolver shot. Where was Robson, Jimmy's man ? Why didn't Robson open to her ? Another ghastly thought : it was quite likely that Jimmy, on some pretext, had sent Robson out, not wanting to be interrupted, while he—— And then nobody would admit her, ever, for Jimmy couldn't do it, after . . . In a crumpled heap across the desk, and then rolling backwards on to the floor . . .

She would stand here for ever, clamouring.

Again Toni jabbed a frantic finger on to the bell. At the same instant the door was opened :

—" Good Heavens ! " exclaimed Robson, his round, rosy face for once aghast at the sight of Toni. " It's Mrs. Giles ! " But Toni went past him as though he were not there ; she was intent ; blind and deaf to all except the little pictures snapshotted on to her brain : Jimmy's set white face as he raised his arm, the revolver in his hand, pointing towards him—Toni arriving . . . inevitably . . . just in the nick of time——

She threw open the door of the dining-room, which led into the library . . .

Shrieks of laughter poured out, stunning her like a blow ; floods of light ; three girls and Jimmy round a littered supper-table ; laughter and bon-bons whizzing ; and the thin smash of splintered glass. One of the girls, the one in gold and green, was lying with her head on Jimmy's shoulder, weeping happy, hysterical tears of champagne and eye-black ! Jimmy's tie was dishevelled, his head was flung back, his eyes half-closed; his mouth—on the contrary—was wide open; that was because his other two guests were trying to aim *marron-glacés* into the cavity, and noisily betting on points.

—" Oi ! My stars ! Who's this ? " cried the shrill and friendly voice belonging to the girl tightly sheathed in purple. She had caught sight of Toni in the open doorway.

And then Jimmy, too, saw her.

CHAPTER IV

WHEN Jimmy Goddard turned away from sight of
Toni's departing train at Victoria, and strolled
back towards the barrier, he was feeling extraordinarily cheerful, and eased of his former burden of misery
regarding Giles. Funny, he reflected, how little the thought
mattered, that your son was going to die, if you were going to
nip along, too, and, with a bit of luck, get there before him
. . . if " there " existed. That showed, didn't it, that mourning for the dead and all that sort of thing was just perishing
selfishness, because you, yourself, on earth, couldn't bear to do
without 'em ? He found himself whistling as he hailed a taxi—
interrupted his tune for a moment to give the address of his
flat in Mount Street—then sprawled back easily into the seat,
and tried to think solemn thoughts about death.

. . . No good ! It couldn't be done ! Somehow the right
sort of thinking dangled, in a glazed and inaccessible frame,
just out of reach of his brain. But he hoped to be able to get
off some rather hefty stuff in the mental line while he was
actually loading his revolver. For the present—he felt so
absolutely ordinary ! It had always been the same, even during
the War : however close to the guns, he could never get away
from that everyday sort of feeling—not exactly unconcern, not
braver than anyone else, or fearing death less, or anything in
that line ; but he had always imagined that there must exist a
state of spiritual calm or spiritual flame or—or—transcendental
exaltation, that visited other fellows when death was imminent,
and, Jimmy would have tried to explain, made a difference !
He never felt different ; not even now, when, of his own
allowance of life, another three hours was all he had, quite
definitely and without escape.

Jimmy knew exactly what he had to do. He could, on occasions, put in some thoroughly efficient staff-work ; and this

was An Occasion—certainly it was ! . . . He grinned cheerfully at Robson, his man, as he passed him in the hall :

" I've got some important 'phone calls. Don't want to be interrupted," and then went on into the library.

Carrington first ; Sir William Carrington, of Harley Street. Carrington was a well-known brain specialist. That was all to the good, because he happened to be quite a close personal friend of Goddard's, and belonged to the same club—in fact, they had been playing bridge at the same table, to-night, when Toni's 'phone call had come through . . . Lord ! It wasn't much more than two hours ago ! Carrington would probably be there still.

And presently Jimmy was speaking to him :

" Do you get what I want, old man ? . . . Yes, you'd be doing me an immense favour. . . . You see my point, don't you ? . . . I've been called away ; got to leave for the Continent to-morrow morning, latest. I want to make my Will first ; ought to have done it years ago. If you and my own G.P. will witness it for me. . . . Buzz along here as quickly as you can, won't you ? . . . Only I'm rather anxious that both my witnesses should be doctors, because there may be a question, do you see, if anything should happen to me, of the Will being contested. My youngest son is a bad hat. . . . No, of course I never told you ! Why should I ? A man doesn't walk about his club saying : ' My youngest son is a bad hat ! ' They'd sling him out as a first-class bore if he did. . . . What I mean to say is, he'll be pretty sick at being cut out of it, disinherited and all that . . . Yes, by proving me insane when I made it ; most of my family find it damned easy to believe me insane, any old time ! But if you were to put me through an examination first, before witnessing my signature : test my mental balance. . . . Yes—' How many fingers am I holding up ? '—that sort of thing ! . . . Yes. . . . Yes. . . . You've hit it in one ! . . . Well, look here, I won't stop. Don't let me down, now you see how the land lies, will you ? . . . I must try and get hold of my solicitor now. . . . I'm most infernally grateful to you, Carrington ; frightfully dud show for you, toddling round to witness Wills at this time of night, but I don't want to leave it until I come back from abroad. . . . Cheerio! See you presently."

His solicitor, he found at home. To him, too, he explained the situation, more or less as he had explained it to Carrington; with this slight advantage, that old Thurloe-Dale had attended to the affairs of the Goddard family for a good many years. He had, in fact, begun his career down at Walsbury, the nearest town to Jimmy's place in Gloucestershire; so that there was no need to tell him that young Fred Goddard was a bad hat—Thurloe-Dale knew it well!—or how he, Jimmy, was placed with regard to the disposal of his capital:

"Power of Appointment among your children only? Yes, yes, yes, I remember. . . . You're going abroad to-morrow morning, eh? . . . Well, it's short notice for a Will, you know; but it's just like you, Goddard," he grumbled; "you want it all drawn up, signed, and witnessed in about five minutes, and then a whisky-and-soda and that's the end of it! I don't approve of this hustling age! . . . Come now, Goddard, be reasonable: give me your instructions quietly, to-night; and when you come back, next month, you can sign your Will, then. I'll have it ready."

"Ah, but I mayn't be coming back next month. And I won't be bullied into being leisurely and dignified, when I'm trying to hustle like a perishing Yank!"

"But you're not a Yank," protested Thurloe-Dale, from the other end. "Still, I suppose you young chaps have got to be humoured." For James Goddard was a full three years his junior. "And there were, certainly, too many train accidents in France this last summer! You'll be travelling through France, I suppose?"

"I suppose so," echoed Goddard, without revealing more of his destination. "And I don't intend to give Fred a loophole to upset the Will, if anything should happen to me. . . . Thanks, old man. You're a sport. I believe I've still got a bottle of Kressman's '65 in the cellar, to reward you . . . You old devil! I can hear you melting like a torrent in the spring!" . . . And he just heard Thurloe-Dale's answering chuckle, before he hung up the receiver.

Dr. Lang, the general practitioner who had attended the Goddard family whenever they had been in London, for the last twenty years or so, proved also available for that evening's consultation.

Then Jimmy rang for Robson, and gave orders for the '65 Cognac to be brought up. With some vague connection with Wills floating about in his mind, he asked, furthermore, if there were plenty of sealing-wax in the house.

" Sealing-wax, Sir ? " doubtfully. " Red sealing-wax ? "

" Yes—no—I don't know. Fine old mulberry red is what I want, I expect, but we'd better wait until Mr. Thurloe-Dale turns up. I'm expecting Mr. Thurloe-Dale and two other gentlemen almost at once, Robson. When they arrive, bring them straight in here."

. . . And now there was nothing much more to do, except wait. His service revolver was in the drawer of his desk. " I suppose the best way is to put it into my mouth and bite on it," muttered Jimmy. . . . Hm—he didn't like that idea much, now it came to detail. Well, it couldn't be helped . . . Poor little Toni !—she always looked such a scrap—a beautifully dressed scrap—he had appreciated Toni's clothes, the trim and jaunty cut of her, whenever he had taken her out ; and their outings had been pretty plentiful since last February. No follow-my-leader about Toni ; she led the fashion, and other women meekly accepted her innovations. Plucky kid, Toni ! Giles ought not to have left her like that. Still, she had acted in the only possible way, taking no notice, and seeming not to care, however much her family had screamed at her. But then, families always screamed. He could understand Giles, too. . . . There had been times in his own married life, when Nance had conveyed to him, in that detached way so typical of her, that he was really nothing much except a buffoon, and that she could, if necessary, get on perfectly well without him —why not ? And it was true too, damn it ! She could. If that was how Toni had treated Giles—disdainful, careless, and a little weary, too—no wonder his son had bunked.

His son ! . . . but he had never been in the least like a father ; he had never believed he could be a father ; it had always remained a matter for polite incredulity : fatherhood was ridiculous, not for other men, but for himself ; or was it that he was too ridiculous for fatherhood ? Perhaps ! But still, Giles meant more to him than all the rest of the world, even if not from a paternal angle. And when that rather neat dodge for circumventing the Power of Appointment clause had shot into his brain, the relief, afterwards, had been as though Giles were a friend, the closest of his friends, who had stood in need of a tenner ; and he, most luckily, had found one in his pocket, and had been able to fork it out.

Giles' children would be all right, now ; or at least, if not now, in a couple of hours or so, if only Giles could hold out that long and a bit longer, at the other end. That had got to be risked. He had seen the telegram : " Hæmorrhage—dangerously ill," sent off from San Goffredo at 5.32 p.m. If Giles could hang on for another six hours, after that had been sent off—they didn't say " dying," they said " dangerously ill "—Jimmy thought he ought to get the whole business over by half-past eleven, providing the two doctors and old Thurloe-Dale didn't keep him waiting too long. . . . Damn it ! Surely Giles could do his share, and manage to keep alive till midnight, considering his children's whole future and a hundred-and-twenty thousand pounds depended on Jimmy getting into Heaven first.

Lord ! How scared Toni had looked when he had let out about the disposal of the money. He had never seen Toni looking scared, before ; that was one of the things he had admired her for, her grit. She could have had no idea of course, until then, that losing Giles, also lost her children their chance of inheriting from their grandfather. A fantastic business, like something out of a Gilbert and Sullivan opera ! Poor kid, she said she had known what it was to be hard up. . . . He had never realised that ; bless her, she had splashed money about as though she had had it all her life ! Still there *was* something to be scared about ; for, of course, she was not really making any sort of an income that counted, out of selling pretty clothes ; women never paid for their clothes, so where were the profits ?

No hope, not an earthly, that whenever he pegged out, Reggie would do anything for her, or for Babs, Paul and Antony. Hard and avaricious and pleased with himself, that was Reggie. His father remembered how, years ago, when Fred had been on the very brink of making a disastrous marriage, Reginald had stated then that Fred need never hope for the slightest support from him, for he didn't consider himself responsible for shoddy relations acquired through his brother's follies.

. . . Jimmy sighed, fidgeted, lit another cigar. . . . Yes, it was the only way, the way he had suddenly thought of, when Toni had begged him so piteously to *do* something. The only way . . . he had forgotten that Sydney Carton had ever spoken these words ; and certainly he still felt far from any heroic tableau : sacrifice on the scaffold. His mood was still confoundedly ordinary ; regretful of all the good wine he was leaving behind . . . why the hell hadn't he drunk that Château Lafite '75, before now ? Toni could appreciate good wine ; he'd leave his cellar to Toni. Poor little girl, with that foul journey to do alone !—" Wish I could have gone with her. Hope to God she'll find him still alive ! " . . .

Giles, his son.

—Where the devil were Thurloe-Dale and Carrington and Lang ? He had asked them to hurry. . . . Jimmy went over to the desk ; took his revolver out of the drawer, just to make sure. . . . He couldn't risk any more delay, afterwards. Yes, nothing wrong with it ; plenty of ammunition. . . . But he was rather pale, as he closed the drawer and walked back to the fire again. Not much fun, after all, in cold blood. . . . " Shall I get drunk ? " thought Jimmy ; then rejected the notion. " I'm not going out of it, drunk ! "—The front door bell rang. Carrington and Dr. Lang ; they had met on the stairs. A few minutes later, Thurloe-Dale arrived.

" Can you make yourselves comfortable, here in the dining-room, for a few moments ? " asked Goddard, apologetically, of the two Harley Street men. For Thurloe-Dale had said he would want him alone for a short conference, in the library ; to indicate what he wanted set down in his last Will and Testament. It was perfectly simple, really : everything to his son

Giles, and the date. But still, lawyers!—"Whisky for these gentlemen, Robson; cigars; and see to the fire."

By eleven o'clock, the required medical tests had been applied, Jimmy's sanity duly established, and the document was drawn up, sealed, and witnessed by the two doctors. Goddard heaved a sigh of relief. He hoped fervently that they would not protract their visit much longer, forcing him to hospitality over the '65 Grande Champagne. You couldn't turn 'em out, of course, after they had bothered to come round. And besides . . . Jimmy chid himself, severely, for a funk! . . . he could not help hoping, even while he chafed at the delay, that they might stay with him—well, say for another ten minutes yet.

"Well," grunted Thurloe-Dale, heaving himself out of his chair, with a reluctant sigh, a little later, "that's good stuff you've given us, Goddard; but then I always say you keep good brandy and bad port! I've got to be going; late hours don't suit me. No, no," shaking his head, "they leave out a palate for port, nowadays, when they create a gentleman."

His host laughed. "Now what am I to answer to that? You've praised my brandy; you've insulted the port I suppose I brought out last time you came to dinner; you've put me down as one of the younger generation just left the Shop; and, on top of all that, you call me a gentleman!"

Dr. Carrington and Dr. Lang had also risen to go, murmuring something about special cases, and operations the next day. Still laughing and arguing, mellow with the evening's proceedings—an evening pleasantly connected with safe and durable things like property, legal testaments and good old wine—the four men sauntered out into the hall. Goddard, with a queer, dream-like feeling upon him, tried to realise that in another few moments he would voluntarily have exchanged all these comfortable voices, cordial handshakes, future dinner and bridge appointments, for chill silences . . .

As he rang for Robson to help them into their coats, another door bell rang simultaneously; the front door bell.

"Late visitors!" chuckled Carrington. "Ah, Goddard, you should have got rid of us sooner, you know, you ruffian!"

" Lord ! " exclaimed Jimmy, aghast, at this waggish jolt to his memory. " I'd clean forgotten ! " Yes, there they were, the three sumptuous little Bits out of " Who's from Hu-la-hu ? " . . . crowding past Robson into the hall ; chattering, giggling, enveloping the elderly men with wisps and whiffs of perfume, tickling furs, floating trails of scarf . . . the whole atmosphere of Revue.

—" Oh well, give us a kiss, now you *are* here," spoke a resigned Jimmy. " Give us three kisses ! "

" Well, I'm damned ! " exclaimed Thurloe-Dale.

—Peals of protest from the Bits : " I like that ! ' Now you *are* here,' indeed ! And who invited us ? Who swanked about champagne ? Perhaps you think we've no other boys ?— You're a low swindler, Jimmy ! Give me back that diamond ring you gave me ! Shouldn't be surprised if he hadn't got any fizz ! " . . . The Bits had shed their cloaks, by now, and slashed the sombre hall with their vivid colours : green-and-gold, flame-and-gold, dull purple wound about by a Spanish shawl.

" Don't rag him, girls ! " piped the flame-and-gold Bit. " He's not so bad ; don't you see he's got in some of his pals to meet us ? Jimmy knows there's not enough of him to go round !—Girls are hungry, these days ! Introduce us to our supper partners, Jimmy, won't you ? What are you standing there pulling faces for ? I like the one you began with best, the one you call your own ! "

Goddard was wondering what to do, and how best to get rid of them. Should he ask Carrington and Lang and Thurloe-Dale to take them along to the Watering-Pot, or somewhere like that, promising to follow himself, shortly ? It would do that old dug-out Thurloe-Dale a lot of good, to be seen with a Bit at the Watering-Pot ! . . . And then, suddenly, at a chance touch from a soft childish white arm against his cheek—that was the green-and-gold Bit !—he yielded. After all, why not have supper and a spot of fun, for the last time ? An hour or two wouldn't make much difference. The last supper-party— he'd always enjoyed parties ; and these three darlings were specially sumptuous ! No, let Thurloe-Dale and Carrington find their own Bits and take them to a night club! Why should they have Jimmy's? If he couldn't, as he had hoped, experience spiritual uplift during the half-hour before his death, that sensation of light bursting through thin glass—then he might as well have champagne and caviare, with three of the chorus out of " Who's from Hu-la-hu? " as an informal wind-up! Another hour or two—Giles could hang out for another hour or two! Giles had always been a considerate bloke, where his father's pleasures were concerned!

So Jimmy gave a few orders to Robson, with regard to the catering department.

Meanwhile Carrington, with mock propriety, was explaining to the lovely trio how, in point of fact, though there was nothing he and his two companions would have appreciated better than to be their supper partners, yet, alas!—they had not been invited! " Nor does it look as though there were any hope of it. The truth is, my dears, that when Goddard has got some dull, prosy work on hand—for instance, having his Will drawn up and witnessed—he sends for the dull, prosy professional men who do it; but when the real entertainment starts—obviously, we left five minutes too late, or you arrived five minutes too early! "

Thurloe-Dale favoured Jimmy with one mute but eloquent glance, but his graceless client had no excuses to make. " You're a sad dog, I'm afraid," Thurloe-Dale grunted, in the vernacular of his day.

Carrington offered him a lift in his car; and with a few more drolleries, rather too heavy for the occasion, the three professional men took their leave.

" Well," twanged the violet Bit, with the Spanish shawl and the scarlet poinsettias, " these old dug-outs do rather overload the *soufflé*, don't they? "

.   .   .   .

. . . And it was the same Bit in violet with the poinsettias, who exclaimed, after the fifth champagne cork had been drawn and added to the stereotyped litter on the supper-table: " Oi! My stars! Who's this? "

" She looks as though she'd come to the wrong flat ! " the flame-and-gold Bit commented, hilariously.

Jimmy turned his head with difficulty, for he was rather tightly strangled by the sleepy, gurgling embraces of the third and last Bit, flung across his shoulder like a decoration ; and, moreover, a *marron-glacé*, flung by one of the others, had just slipped, whole, down his throat !

He turned his head towards the doorway.

—Toni stood there, wrapped in her long fawn and brown check travelling-coat, her face ghost-white above the dark fur collar ; her eyes heavy, and shadowed underneath. She was looking straight at Jimmy . . .

CHAPTER V

—" **D**AUGHTER-IN-LAW ? " chirped the liveliest of
the Bits, when Jimmy had made it tolerably
clear to them that Toni need not be regarded
as a rival in the Bit profession. " Well, we *are* full of domes-
ticity and what-not, to-night ! Would you believe it, dear,
that when we turned up, the hall was a seething mass of old
family lawyers and well-preserved doctors . . . every one of
them past the age of consent ! "

" And fairly dripping with red seals and documents and
hearty good advice to our Jimmy ! " chimed in the flame-and-
gold Bit.

. . . Old family lawyers? Doctors? Red seals and documents?

Toni turned and looked at Jimmy. He slid back an uneasy,
sideways glance, before he recklessly plunged anew into a
babble of jokes and amorous patter, suitable to the entertain-
ments of his guests.

But Toni understood, now. The shock of finding the
incredible supper-party in progress had at first driven all the
blood away from her heart. And when her father-in-law had
spun her into a chair, insisting that she should join them,
drink champagne, eat fragments of *mousse au jambon* and salmon
pie and what was left of the *pâté-de-foie-gras*, it had appeared
to her a cruelty surpassing all callous treatment she had ever
yet encountered or even dreamt of. Could he really have forgotten Giles ? Or really have supposed that she could forget ?

Jimmy's slightly tumbled wits took a few seconds to recover
from Toni's entrance, and from her dazed and faltering
explanation of having " missed the train "—(" But I saw her
go off in it—or didn't I ? ")—But almost at once he realised
that whatever he had seen or not seen, she was nearly done,
done and dropping, and must be made to drink and eat. He
seized hilarity as a pretext. . . . Toni could hardly contain

347

herself for shame of him; but she swallowed the champagne, in sips, and then greedily; and hating Jimmy, resenting his noisy fatuous hospitality, she ate some of what he was so lavishly and untidily piling upon her plate, and gradually felt better.

. . . But that one look which passed between them, was enlightenment enough. It left very little for either to guess. All that mattered now, was speedily getting rid of the Bits. Speedily ?—It took Jimmy nearly two hours.

.   .   .   .

When he came back from the hall, he found Toni standing up, literally with her back to the wall. She had often given battle in her life, but she knew that this was likely to be her hardest.

" Now ! " said Jimmy.

Toni was glad of the champagne he had forced her to drink. . . . " No ! " she replied. " Not now, nor at any other time. I won't have it, Jimmy ! "

" Look here—why did you come back? You'd no right to come back. You ought to be on your way out to Giles."

" I guessed what you were going to do," said Toni, simply.

" Well, you should have gone on all the quicker, then. *I* don't want anyone to sew the shroud."

" There ain't goin' to be no shroud," said a very grim Toni. " I've told you I won't have it, Jimmy ! "

" My dear kid, be sensible ! There really is no other way. I'm no good alive, am I, except to myself? I give myself a rattling good time, certainly I do, but nobody will be the worse for it when I'm dead, except me, and I shan't know; and you and Giles and the children will be a damned sight better for it. You say you're a business woman, Toni. Be sensible ! "

" My children," said Toni, with slow emphasis, " are not going to live on suicide's money. It'll do them no good. The idea's horrible ! "

" Rank sentimentalism ! " argued Goddard, lighting a cigar. " In a few years, by the time they're old enough to understand anything, they'll know they've got a hundred-and-twenty-thousand quid between them and the world, and it'll take a lot of suicide to blot out the rosiness of a hundred-and-twenty thousand pounds! Take it from me, little girl, the kids won't mind. 'Dear old Grandpa!' That's what they'll say: '*Dear* old Grandpa!'"

"Perhaps the kids won't mind, Jimmy. The point is, that I mind for them."

"Sentimentalism!" said Jimmy again. "All women are sentimentalists, bless 'em!"

Toni's temper blew up and scattered: "Damn you, Jimmy!—don't throw *all women* at me! And damn you for giving me trouble and bringing me back like this, when I wanted to go on! And damn you for making me argue when I'm tired! Supposing I'd found you dead?"

"You'd have fainted."

"I shouldn't."

"All right. We'll see. At least, *you'll* see. . . . I won't. But I trust you to play fair and tell me if you did or didn't, if there's an after-life or any ethereal gadgets of that sort. Though I must say——"

"Theological discussion is frightfully fascinating, of course. But I didn't travel the whole way back from Dover, to discuss whether there's an after-life. Truly I didn't."

"I've still to hear why you did?"

"Guilt. You wouldn't have—— It was because I'd been a coward for a minute or two, wasn't it? And you hadn't the sense to see it *was* only for a minute? Don't talk to me about being a sentimentalist! Just because I said I was afraid for the children, that they might be poor. . . . Of course I was afraid; every mother worth her salt would be, especially knowing the hell of being poor. But I'd have pulled myself together—— Good Lord! Can't I work? Haven't I worked before? My business is doing well; I can develop it; it'll do better. Can't I work? You're just being officious, thrusting in with your great lump of capital that nobody wants. I tell you, Jimmy," said Toni, steadying down, "I can manage, even if Giles dies," —and she was able to say this now, aloud, without flinching, as she had said it so often in her thoughts—"even if Giles dies, I can manage."

Goddard, in his turn, began to get angry. No man, however unsensationally he may have contemplated a sacrifice, enjoys hearing it alluded to as an officious piece of meddling. "You'd better understand that I wasn't thinking of you at all, Toni. Only of the three youngsters. So it's no good being bombastic and blowing up like this, and saying what you'll accept, and what you won't accept."

"They're my youngsters."

"And my son's."

"He left them . . ." whispered Toni.

"And *I'm* leaving them—all I've got. As for being officious —I didn't invite you to my party to-night, did I? You just walked in. That's officious!"

Toni began to laugh. "Darling Jimmy, *why* were you giving a party to-night? Do tell me! Were those the three sumptuous little Bits? Do you know, it didn't seem to me a good night for a party!"

"They were very nice girls indeed," contended Jimmy, still at boiling-point. "But I didn't really ring 'em up and ask 'em to supper, you know; this being one of my busy nights, without 'em! As a matter of fact, I'd invited them ages ago, and it had clean gone out of my head, what with one thing and another."

"Quite . . . what with one thing and another! So they just walked in? But still——"

"Oh well, as they were there, I thought I might give them a bite and a glass; and besides," Jimmy gave his daughter-in-law a wary glance—they had been extraordinarily good pals, he and she—but could she be trusted to understand this much?— "besides, I rather felt I'd enjoy a party, y' know!—sort of cheery send-off. They give a murderer a good breakfast before he gets hanged, don't they? Of course, in a way, it took up more time than I—than I——"

"Speaking as a business woman," Toni remarked, quite unable to believe that these were stark matters of love and death that she and Jimmy could be discussing, "I should say that scooping an extra hour from—what you wanted to do, was a bit of a risk."

"Oh, it was a risk," Jimmy agreed. "I just gambled on that, don't you see? Always was a gambler!" But it was incredibly stupid, and childish, and preposterous, and Jimmy all over; Jimmy, and his son, Giles . . . Giles would have been equally a lunatic, Toni felt. For this one speck of Jimmy's selfishness, his stubborn selfishness, might so easily have crept into the works of his colossal renunciation, and stopped them! If Giles had died first, by as much as five minutes—by as long as it took Jimmy to empty a glass of champagne—then Jimmy would have died for nothing, and might as well not have died at all. He could renounce all life that he loved, but not his little supper-party into the bargain! . . . Yet Toni, at intervals a reckless gambler herself, could not restrain a pang of sympathy. She smiled at him. Queer old Jimmy! Just for the fun of it! . . . Just for champagne and oysters with the Bits!

And she wondered how long she was still to be kept here; whether the conflict were nearly over, or had but barely begun?

. . . "Well, Jimmy?"

"Well, Toni?" . . .

—No, it was not over yet.

. . . "I wish you weren't in the flat," he said, bursting forth after the lull. "I don't know what to do with you. You're in my way. And if I wasted time before—— Good God! aren't we wasting it now? We don't know what may be happening, out there. I ought to be in the Kingdom Come by now!" He pleaded with her—as a man who pleads for his life. And:

"I'm not going to have it," Toni reiterated, doggedly. "I stand here for Giles, as well as for myself. Do you think he'd allow it? Look here, Jimmy, you've got to see this: if Giles and I are in a mess—oh, it's no good talking of Giles as though he were a saint, simply because he's so ill—he's done nothing but loaf and philander. And I've been a loafer too, and extravagant and careless and callous. . . . We can't shirk our penalties; and this mess is one of them. Pay your own forfeits—that's the law. *You* can't wipe it out for us, and put us right again, by one shot of the revolver. You simply can't; it's not —not mathematics. What do you imagine I'd have felt like, ever afterwards? A life of sick green horror—that's what you were going to lay on me. I'd rather work and work and work. . . . If Giles dies—and don't make me have to say this again, Jimmy, you beast!—I've told you already I can provide for the children; I'm not afraid, any more; and meanwhile, you'll go on allowing us the same income. So stop fussing; we're not nearly destitute; not nearly up against it."

"And stop making speeches," Jimmy retaliated. "These are all air-bubbles. Prick 'em, and—wooff! We're human, you and I. Money isn't; it's a fact. Facts are safer than human beings. Work?—Supposing you die? You can't work for 'em when you're dead. Supposing I die, presently, in a year or two? There goes your two thousand a year, as well!"

"But, my dear old Jimmy, we're not *all* going to die. This isn't an epidemic! You're morbid and unreasonable."

"I wasn't saying a thing about epidemics, not a thing! You can't tell. I'm not a young man any more. If I die at once, this minute, as soon as I can get rid of you, it's some use. If I die in a year or two—it's no bloody use at all!" He banged himself down into an arm-chair.

"Are you ailing?" his daughter-in-law enquired, with polite interest. "I'm sorry. Gout? What's the mortal complaint that's going to carry you off in a year or two?"

"Men of my age are liable to get all sorts of things. Livers. . . . Why, old Carrington, the doctor I saw to-night, he said to me: 'Gosh! Goddard. I wouldn't have your liver!'"

"Is he an American?" asked Toni, coolly.

"American? Carrington—Amerrington?" said Jimmy, getting muddled. "Why should he be?"

"Why does he say 'Gosh!' if he isn't an American?"

"Look here, Toni . . . it's all very well to be flippant, but these are rather serious matters, you know."

"Much too serious not to be flippant about them. But if Giles dies, Jimmy, and you die, and I die—even then, Babs and Paul and Antony have got to take that much risk. You call me a sentimentalist?—I'm not so sentimental as to believe my children ought to be as immune as small gods, and at any price. They won't be destitute, either; I've got a brother who's quite a good sort, and he'll earn more one day than he's earning now. I've got friends, too"—she thought of Lucilla Danby and Colin Martial—"and cousins"—yes, Maxine, Helen, Val; but even as they passed in single file through her mind, Toni knew, she was certain, that the cousin who would look after her children with the utmost fidelity, if she were dead, would be, not Maxine nor Val nor Helen, but Loraine ; Loraine, who was nursing Giles even now, now, while she stood here and talked—" Oh God ! " thought Toni, " I can't bear it any longer. I've got to put an end to this ! " . . . Smash his resolution !—And as she braced herself for the final tussle, she heard, from very far away, Jimmy's voice, gun-room-and-country-house-voice, voice that was the essence of a whole world of Goddards before ever she separated them into individuals . . . she heard it hectoring her ; sheltering behind the customs of a breed of men that do not consult their women ; putting her in her place. . . . For he was not sure, either, how much longer his determination could remain braced against persistent attack :

" Now look here, Toni, I've had about enough. I've made up my mind, and you can't alter it. My son is dangerously ill, and his children have got to be provided for. Adequately. It's my business to do so. And women are better left outside all this."

" Are they ? " Toni's sadness was cayenned with scorn. . . . " That stale old tag !—Life and death aren't male prerogatives, Jimmy. We can't be left outside ! Jimmy, I want to go to my husband. He may be dying, and another woman is with him. . . . I want to go to him ; I'd started to go to him. You can understand, can't you, just how much I'm longing not to keep him waiting ? Besides—I may not be in time."

" Then you'd better not have turned back," Jimmy rapped out.

Toni delivered her ultimatum : " I'm not going to move from here. I'm not going to leave this room until you promise me, swear to me, that you won't do yourself in. I'll just stay here . . . You wouldn't—in front of me, I imagine ? "

" No."

" Giles has sent for me. May I go, Jimmy ? "

If this failed—but it couldn't fail. She saw that, from Jimmy's face. He was not a cruel man, and he had imagination. . . . Enough to realise that this delay was monotonous torture to her nerves.

" You're holding a pistol at my head with a vengeance, Toni ! "

Her mouth curved into a faint smile. . . . " A substitute for the other pistol," she murmured. " Well, Jimmy ? "

" Toni, dear—— "

" I mean it, Jimmy."

Silence.

Then she broke down. . . . " Oh, Jimmy, I *do* so want to go ! "

Jimmy shrugged his shoulders . . . and surrendered. " There's no boat any more to-night," he said. " To-morrow morning. I'll go with you." And Toni knew his promise had been given.

But though she acknowledged this with a casual : " You're a sport, Jimmy ! " she could not tell him, then or afterwards, just how much of a sport she had thought him for his idea of —what she had stopped him from doing.

. . . The room wavered, rose and fell in a blur. . . . Not yet, though—she mustn't allow herself to collapse yet, before she reached San Goffredo. " You're a sport, Jimmy ! "—that was all right, wasn't it ? Perfectly cool and decent and so forth ?—She had married a stranger, of a strange race and code, but she did not want to let down Giles, especially now. . . . But what a comical race they were !—Look at Jimmy, for instance . . . " Oh, I must laugh—I—I can't help it . . . Oh, Jimmy, Jimmy, your B-b-bits—— And your face when you looked up and saw me !—The one who dripped eye-black all over your shoulder—— Jimmy, if you could have had a looking-glass in front of you—— Oh, how silly ! How funny and silly . . . and what fun to be a Bit, a sumptuous little Bit in gold-and-green. . . . To be three Bits !—Could I be a Bit if I wanted to, Jimmy ?—Oh, it was all so funny—so f-f-f-funny—— "

Goddard did not try to stop her incoherent mixture of laughing and sobs. Better not. He stood looking down at this—valiant scrap of defiance ! She had slithered into the big arm-chair, limply huddled with her face hidden, all the fight gone out of her . . .

—Jimmy's features rumpled into an expression of acute tenderness. . . . Giles' wife ! And she *had* understood, too, about his supper-party for the Bits.

CHAPTER VI

TONI spent what was left of the night, in Jimmy's flat. He vacated his bedroom for her. She was too exhausted to return to Regent's Park; and also she shrank from the inevitable questioning of Susie and Quimper and the children, who were supposing her by now half across France. She did not sleep. Her will felt boneless and inert, sapped by her late struggle with Jimmy; but her physical nerves had not yet been able to relax. It seemed as though they had forgotten the trick of relaxing. They were stretched tighter than the strings of a violin, and sleep could draw no lullaby from them. Perhaps, her old nurse would have said, perhaps Toni had been over-excited. . . . And yet, oddly enough, she was not fretting any more over the possibility that Giles might die, or might, indeed, already be dead before she could even start on her journey to him. She had been in time to save Jimmy, she reflected, with childish logic, and so they would let her be in time to save Giles, too. And if not . . . You had to bow your head, sometimes. All her capacity for fighting had been expended, and what possessed Toni now was humility—a dazed recognition that she had been wrong all the time; wrong about men. She had thought they were inferior and no good. She had built up her whole outlook and philosophy, confidently using this as its basis: men were no good, no good. The Rakonitz men had been no good; Danny had been no good; Giles had been no good . . . he had let her down. This certainty had been her shield and her talisman She had gloried in it—the indestructible truth which she had rescued from the midst of destruction. Who could hurt her, while she held on to this talisman?

And now it was gone. Her hand was clutching emptiness. The map which had been drawn to scale was false in its first measurement, and, therefore, worthless. Jimmy had done that to her. She had cried out to Jimmy for help, begged him to "do something," as you instinctively cry out without the faintest hope that the appeal will be met and answered. And Jimmy—here was the miracle !—Jimmy actually had not failed her. He had been ready to do something ; had planned to die, quietly and without a fuss, not even thinking himself sublime. . . . Jimmy had been going to shoot himself, so that she and the children—Giles' children—might be secure in the future. That she had guessed his intention and been able to wrest a victory over it was beside the point. Jimmy had meant to do it, and he would not have bungled. Well, yes—if Giles had died during the hour of Jimmy's supper-party with the Bits— that might have been the flaw in his efficiency. That might have proved fatal. Yet it was so human, too. . . . Toni smiled in the darkness—— Then frowned hard at the mental image of her own arrogance, her swaggering, brilliant arrogance, in the past. Had anyone come to her and told her, as a story of someone else, about Jimmy's plan for circumventing the difficulty of his limited Power of Appointment, how she would have scoffed ! "Men don't do these things ! Why, I've tested men again and again. They're rotten ; they break ; lean on them, and they crumple ; ask for something, and they have nothing to give, unless by giving they would not rob themselves !" . . . That had been the only thing she had known for certain. Now she knew nothing at all for certain. She was adrift ; dazed as a blind man who has had a staff knocked from his hand.

And if Jimmy were not wholly futile, what about Giles ? What about Jimmy's son ? The case of Giles had long ago been tried and dismissed, but here was fresh evidence. If she had been wrong about men, wrong about Jimmy, then perhaps Giles, too, was a man a little nearer than stars away, from her her first illusion of men ? "I don't know," Toni confessed into the darkness ; "I don't know anything . . ." It was so bewildering, now, to know nothing ; so unlike Toni Rakonitz. Her immutable world wobbled, shivered into atoms. Humpty Dumpty had a great fall . . . She was very tired, and she could not sleep. "I don't know," repeated this new and diffident Toni. And yet, on the whole, she was glad that the old bitter obsession had been snapped. It was as though something within her which had been bound in steel, was now loosely slung in velvet. Not so safe; less invulnerable; but she felt warmer, happier, more serene. Men were no good— but sometimes men were; some men. Her belief had not swung to the other extreme; she had finished with extremes. " Sometimes, some men "—that was enough; and " perhaps " —that was good enough, too. For even James Goddard, re- deemer of her faith, had not been able to resist, at the eleventh hour, three Bits from a revue chorus.

. . . The hours drummed on towards morning. Toni did not sleep. But even when seven o'clock struck, and eight o'clock and nine, she did not stir, nor take any initiative for their journey to San Goffredo. Jimmy was doing it all. She had yielded her leadership to Jimmy. At twenty minutes past nine, he came in, fully dressed, with her breakfast, and the largest assortment of every sort of toilet, washing, and dressing implement that a chemist's shop could possibly yield. " I got 'em to open, round the corner, ten minutes before the time," said Jimmy, with pride. " It's the only shop open on a Sunday. And I can lend you a dressing-bag. You let your own things go on to Italy last night, I suppose? I noticed you hadn't got any. Didn't know what size sponge-bag you took, so I bought three." He displayed the three. He had, indeed, solved perplexity by buying three of everything, in varying sizes: tooth-brushes, sponges, hot-water bottles . . . Toni accepted the multiplicity of her unexpected trousseau, and thanked Jimmy for his thoughtfulness, in the same spirit as she now accepted everything, spiritual and material, in the grotesque disarray of earth and heaven reborn.

" Our train leaves at eleven," Jimmy explained further. " And—look here, my dear, I've just 'phoned through to Regent's Park to find out if by any chance another telegram might have come after you left. There wasn't anything, though. I knew you wouldn't want them to know you hadn't left, so I pretended I was me."

" And weren't you? " asked Toni.

" You don't respect your father-in-law as you should, you mocking little devil ! "

" Don't I ? " She held his hand very tightly for a moment —such a solid Jimmy to cling to, where previously there had been space only, and her own proud independence.

" Did you sleep ? No, of course you didn't. Eat some breakfast, and then get up, child. We mustn't risk being late at Victoria. With a bit of luck I'll be able to get you a *wagon-lit*, in Paris, to-night. You'll be ready to sleep by then. I've wired to San Goffredo that we'll both be there by to-morrow evening."

The prophesied bit of luck came to pass, though it may be that it was less fortunate than Jimmy, in his exultation, had supposed. For Toni, who throughout the day of train and boat and train again, had remained in her docile, quiescent condition of a weary child, leaving all that was to be done to Jimmy, and still too supine even for fear on behalf of Giles, Toni really did sleep in her swaying bunk ; slept heavily from Paris to Marseilles ; from Sunday night to Monday morning ; slept without dreams and without terrors. . . . And woke, strong enough again to care, and to be desperately afraid. Jimmy could not pacify her feverish impatience, now. All through the day, and all along the Riviera coast, she sat fretting ; fretting at the little white towns, cleanly glittering in the sunshine ; fretting at the endlessly recurring tunnels ; at the unendurable halts at every station. In her awakened panic, Giles died every moment, and time was a sack of lead, too heavy for her lifting. . . . Till at last the sun sank, and they had crossed the frontier into Italy. Another three hours, two hours. . . . By the time they actually jogged into the small dimly-lit station of San Goffredo, Toni was beyond speech and beyond sight. . . . She stumbled down from her carriage on to the p atform. . . . If here were a face familiar to her, she could not see it.

Then, through the blackness that wheeled and jigged in front of her eyes, she heard the voice of her cousin, Richard Marcus—" Giles is better ; out of danger. Come along."

. . . They were jolting along in a rickety carriage ; palms

and the sea on one side, houses on the other. . . . Which house was it? Toni dared not ask. Soon she would be seeing Giles. . . . How big the stars were, and how they flashed in this dark blue sky of the South! Richard and Jimmy, opposite her, were talking about hunting, and Gloucestershire, and foot-and-mouth disease. How funny men were! Didn't they care?— But Toni pulled herself up with a jerk, away from the old intolerance. Of course they cared. She must remember her lesson. . . . And, remembering, she smiled to hear Jimmy say, in the old gun-room-and-country-house voice: "The Berkeley's hardly been out at all, this season. Damned shame! Couldn't have been at a worse time of year. I'd one or two good runs with the Duke's, but most of the time I've been in town."

"Then you haven't seen my wife, I suppose?" said Richard, rather wistfully.

"No. Your farm hasn't suffered, has it?"

"Not touched us yet, thank goodness. Here's the house," said Richard. And Jimmy leaned forward suddenly in his seat . . .

. . . Figures on the steps, at the front door. . . . Aunt Elsa, Val . . . Toni was hardly aware of them, nor of Aunt Elsa's tearful kisses. And then her cousin Loraine came through a door at the far end of the stone hall; and Toni quickly went up to her, as though it were the most natural thing in the world that it should all happen like this, at the end of a journey; and that Loraine, who had been nursing Giles, should hail her, now, with that quick dependence on the strange, subtle fellowship that held between them, and say at once: "In there, my dear. . . . I'll keep the others off."

. . . "Decent of you to have come, Toni," said Giles.

PART V

"... HIS HOUSE IN PEACE"

CHAPTER I

VAL sprang up eagerly, as Toni entered the studio.
"Well, what did he say?" Then she added:
"You're looking fagged, Toni. Here, make yourself
comfortable on the divan. It wasn't bad news, was it?"

"Oh no; he corroborated what the other doctors said.
Specialists usually do. Tubercular lesion of the left lung, the
one that was weak from being gassed. He said that Giles must
live entirely in Switzerland or in a climate like this, and be very
careful, and never be agitated, and not work hard, nor shout at
the dogs, nor dance, nor drink . . . And he might live another
twenty years, or he might not. Giles asked him—you know
Giles' sunny off-hand way, when anything serious is in question——"

"Gun-room-and-country-house voice?" asked Val, with a
smile.

"Well, yes. He asked: 'What odds that I die, at any
moment, Sir?' . . ." Toni came to an abrupt stop.

"Well?" from Val, impatiently. She did not wish to force
Toni, but she felt she had to know this exact answer of the
specialist who had just been summoned from Cannes, a fortnight after the hæmorrhage had occurred. The great man had
only yesterday arrived on the Riviera, from England. They
had lost no time in calling him in for a consultation.

Toni answered, slowly: "'About three to one' was what
he said. And then apologised for the unprofessional verdict.
A thirty per cent chance of life. . . . It isn't very much, is it,
Val?"

After a long pause, she went on, " You thought he was ill, didn't you, when first he and Loraine turned up here? He had T.B. then already, you know. Ffolliot says that he must have had it in him for over a year."

" Yes, he struck me as being not so much ill as overwrought, in a sort of spiritually unreasonable state ; that *is* a T.B. symptom, of course. Otherwise I shouldn't have dreamt of keeping them here ; I'd have booted them out, at once. *Your* husband and Loraine, indeed! " Val spoke with belated indignation . . . but then she softened again, for she had grown fond of Toni's husband. " Toni, I believe his infatuation for Loraine was, again, only a symptom. It's not much of an excuse, but it might make you feel rather more comfortable about it all." She wondered if she could explain, more coherently, that unreal quality of tremble and glitter that she had suspected in Giles' infatuation ; though she had only seen it when very much on the wane. She and Toni had not talked about this, yet. The actual fact of the illness, and the turmoil it created, combined with Val's own engagement at this time, and the perpetual come-and-go in the group between her cottage on the top of the hill, and the Villa Bel Respiro at the foot of it, had not allowed much leisure for quiet conversation, during the past fortnight. Toni and Loraine and Giles and Aunt Elsa were down at the villa, with Manuela to look after them : Val herself, who, in Manuela's words, was " not practical for the illness," remained up at the cottage, still, with Queenie and Richard ; Jimmy Goddard and Stephen Greenways stayed at the San Goffredo hotel. . . . Loraine had been the only member of this motley collection who, with astonishing tact and gentleness, had somehow been able to control the atmospheric delirium. So angelic had she been, and withal so competent and helpful, that Val could hardly believe her the same Loraine who had brewed such a pot of mischief in their midst, over such a smoke and flame and sputter, in the weeks that went before Giles' collapse. How strangely they had all been relying on Loraine! Aunt Elsa, ever most unsparing of herself during periods of trouble, was yet too old to stand much of the wear and tear of it, this time. She had stood by so many bedsides. . . . And Toni herself had suffered a natural reaction of intense relief, after her arrival, and had been too broken in body and nerves to be able to captain this emergency. Without any blatant display of tactfulness in her action, Loraine had arranged to slip off from Bel Respiro, and stay up at the cottage with Val, from the time that Toni had arrived to look after Giles ; but she was, after all, compelled to remain where she was. They could not do without her. " Queer, queer creature, Loraine ! " Val reflected. . . . She wondered if she should continue the subject of Loraine and Giles, with Toni. There was one view of it, her own, in fact, that Toni ought to hear. She was looking more rested, now that Dr. Ffolliot had actually been, and pronounced his verdict, and gone again ; lying prone, face downwards, on the couch, her chin propped on her hands, gazing into the log-fire.

" Toni, d'you know—I'm not sure if Giles—— Toni, I don't believe there ever was anything . . . It's difficult to put it delicately ! "

" Darling, you haven't. You're as bad as Aunt Elsa ! She's been at me, too, very upset and incoherent, trying to tell me that ' Val says zere vos nossing . . .' The rest of her conversation was hardly decent, so I won't repeat it to you, Val, as you're not married yet. Come back to me in a year's time, and I'll tell you what Aunt Elsa and myself, two mellow matrons, said to each other three days ago. No, I haven't had it out yet with Giles. I haven't talked to him at all."

" Don't be an ass, Toni ! "

" Well, talked—— We've had a little polite conversation, of course. We're quite terribly shy of each other, tiptoeing about on broken egg-shells. After all, eight months' separation on top of a hell of a row—— And I suppose he can't forget that he ran away from me with another woman ; and I can't forget how ill he is ; and there you are ! The diffident courtesy of our mutual approaches and retreatings must be quite amusing to a looker-on."

" That means," said Val, " that there's a beautiful reconciliation scene somewhere on the horizon ; but you haven't got to it yet."

" No, we haven't got to it yet. There'll be plenty of time.
I shan't have so much to do out here for the next twenty years
or so."

Something odd in Toni's inflection, regret which had pushed
its way in without her meaning it, caused Val to glance at her
keenly :

" So you're going to settle out here, too ? "

" What did you think ? "

" I can't imagine you away from London," Val rejoined,
honestly. " You're such a little cosmopolitan, Toni."

" I've had my good time . . . And if I hadn't, can you
imagine me away from Giles—now ? "

" And then there's the business."

" I'll sell my share of it to Helen. Capable young woman,
our cousin Helen ! She'll run it just as well as I, and love
doing it, especially on top of our success with ' She Burnt Her
Boats.' "

" And the children ? "

" Have them out here ; Mummie too ; good for them."

Val's eyes wandered to the window. Three ascending ranges
of hills lay in soft curves across the valley, their terraces misty
with foliage of the olive, splashed here and there by the
autumn flame of wild cherry, or parted by the dark up-
pointing sword of a cypress. On the lower slopes, some last
shrivelled leaves of yellow and mottled purple hung on in the
small crooked vineyards. . . . Were these to be Toni's surroundings for all Toni's future days ? Her gay little cousin
who wore such exquisite clothes, and who danced with such
exquisite joy ? . . .

" Shut up, Val ! Don't sentimentalise ! " Toni had interpreted her musings.

" I didn't say a word."

" You were just going to, though."

" I can sentimentalise on general lines if I want to, I suppose?
I was thinking how strange it was that a Rakonitz should come
back to live on the land. It's the first time for several generations, you know. It's always been big cities and big business,
art and luxury and culture. The feet of our family have always

been set on beautiful drawing-room carpets, never on the soil; never, at least, since—let me see—how long ago?"

Toni began to reckon back the generations: "Grandmère and Aunt Simone—your grandmother, they lived in London, Paris, and Budapest; and then their father, that was Sigismund, our great-grandfather—he and all his family lived in Vienna. . . . Fourteen brothers and sisters, wasn't it? At least, some of them settled in Constantinople and Madrid. Andreas, Loraine's great-grandfather, started the Spanish branch. And *their* parents, Babette and Simon—oh, we're right back among our ancestors, now; they begin to be ancestors when they're beyond great-grandfatherdom!—Babette and Simon travelled up to Vienna, from the city of Pressburg; though only after they were married. Before that——"

Val reminded her: "We've reached the original soil at last, Toni. Babette's mother—— Don't you remember her vineyards in Hungary? Old Weinberg was a wine merchant growing his own grapes, and she superintended them. Seven generations and nearly two centuries, counting backwards from your Babs. . . . Are *you* going to grow grapes, Toni?"

Toni shrugged her shoulders.

"Perhaps. But from a practical point of view they don't pay as well as artichokes, in this neighbourhood. I've been making enquiries. Vines are more picturesque, of course. But artichokes and peaches are the paying lines."

"Do you want this cottage of mine?"

"'Do you want my studio?'" Toni quoted, from five years ago. And Val laughed:

"I'm sorry to be such a house-agent. But I shan't be here much longer, you know, so you can have it. Stephen wants me to marry him soon after Christmas. He's got to go to China and Turkestan, to find a seed about the size of a pea. . . . It's needed for some new drug or other—I don't know; I haven't quite got the hang of his profession, yet. I'll bequeath you my cottage and my staff and my dogs and Aunt-Elsa-in-the-winter, complete, if you care to take them on?"

"I'll take your staff—I like the infant school!—and I'll take Terry and Mac too, and, of course, Aunt-Elsa-in-the-winter.

But it's really disgraceful, Val, the way that giddy old lady is spending longer and longer on the Riviera, and less and less time in London with her own family. Last summer she was only home for four months—no, less. Of course her favourites, Melanie and Pearl, are frantically busy with their jobs ; and Gisela is a wash-out ; and I think, between ourselves, that Freda's going to get married to a nice old-fashioned American who wants a nice womanly woman to take out to the Middle West with him. Still, it's jolly to have Aunt Elsa aunting about the place. No, thanks, I won't have this cottage. It isn't big enough to hold the three brats and the nurse and Giles and me and the staff and Mother and Aunt Elsa."

Val began to reckon out just how Toni might crowd them all in, by some close and clever arrangement of space ; but Toni shook her head with some determination.

" No, that won't do. I want spare-rooms as well, quite a lot of spare-rooms. You see, Val——" And suddenly she turned shy. She could not quite confess, even to Val, the cousin with whom she was most intimate, how her secret longing—now that it seemed to her that she had failed at everything else—was to have room for any members of the Rakonitz tribe who might at any time need to be sheltered and fed. Bed and food were, after all, simple things to provide. And Toni, who was still feeling humble, thought that here, at least, she could be of use, tangible use, without once again making a mess of her ambitions. The idea of bounteous hospitality brought her a glow of comfortable satisfaction. It was, though she did not define it thus, the matriarchal instinct . . . Always the wanderers of the tribe had returned to the tents, knowing they would find there shelter and bread and meat, not grudgingly given . . .

Val's next remark unconsciously chimed in with the trend of Toni's thoughts. " Perhaps, on the whole, you had better have a spare-room or two. I shan't feel so hopelessly astray and homeless if I can always find permanent headquarters with you when I come back from China and Central Asia and South America, and all the other really accessible and convenient spots that Stephen proposes to take me to."

" What about your painting ? " Toni asked of Val, just as, a few minutes ago, Val had asked of Toni : " What about your business ? "

" Oh, I can paint anywhere if I want to ; and if I don't, it doesn't matter. I'd like to have finished *that*, though " ; and she indicated a canvas on an easel in a shadowy corner of the studio. It was the unfinished picture of the Chinese coat, and Queenie in the kimono jacket from Regent Street. Toni had hardly noticed it before, in the rush of happenings ; but she scrutinised it now with interest :

" It's good."

" It would have been good, yes."

" And corrosive as a splash of iodine. You *are* a cynic in paint, Val ! Can't you finish it, after all ? Why not ? The coat *is* yours, isn't it ? I heard a sort of wild epic, a jumble of battle and misunderstanding and the wickedness of Queenie, from Aunt Elsa ; and I wrung some disgruntled fragments from Richard, too. What became of the coat ? You haven't shown it to me."

But it was Val's turn to be reticent. She did not think, on the whole, that she would tell Toni what had become of the coat. . . . It was rather too vivid and painful a memory : how she and Stephen, that Saturday evening of his sudden arrival, had wandered, in a dense and silvery dream of happiness, down the mule-track—only to find what looked like tragedy at the foot of it. It was after they had become engaged —yes, with delightful and old-fashioned formality, actually plighted their troth, up among the olives at sunset ; and Val had suggested, in that spirit of careless bounty, that desire to give away what is of no value, which comes when you are happiest, that Stephen should pretend that Richard had made no error, and that he had indeed meant his present of the Chinese coat for Loraine and not for Val.

" Yes, but look here," Stephen had protested, " I meant *you* to have it. It's too good for anyone else. Not good enough for you, but much too good for your cousin ! "

But Val had wanted to spare Loraine as much as possible. After all, in glorious possession of what counted, she had little need of a Chinese coat into the bargain. But, to Loraine's pride, it would be Death by a Thousand Slices to surrender the coat, and thus acknowledge in front of them all that she had only imagined it to have been sent to her, and by a lover. So Val had pleaded anew with Stephen, and eventually persuaded him. Prompted by Val, Stephen was going to say that he had sent the coat out to Loraine because it struck him, seeing it, that it would suit her so marvellously, that it was predestined for one of her type, and he hoped she agreed with him ?—He was going to say this quite casually, in order that Loraine might not suspect Val's generosity behind the gift. . . . " Oh, Stephen, we can afford that much ! "

" It isn't the price," Stephen had begun, typically masculine . . . and Val had laughed softly, for it had not been the price in hard cash that she had meant, either. . . . And here they were, outside Bel Respiro, and the front door open, so they walked straight in without having to summon Manuela.

The central room was empty ; but Loraine, hearing their voices and footsteps, called out from an inner room . . .

And there Val had found her, kneeling on the floor, supporting Giles ; heedless that the coat she wore, the Chinese coat, was dabbled and clotted and rigid with blood. . . . Spoilt.

No time then, of course, to care about anything except to succour Giles. But later on, when he was out of danger, it occurred to Val, with a certain ironic amusement, how Loraine had raised a very tempest when she had thought that it was her coat which Val had inadvertently stained with wine ; but when it proved to be Val's coat, which Loraine had totally ruined, nobody minded ; least of all, Loraine. When blood happened, something real, then an artificial work of beauty was just trumpery . . . and Loraine as human, as compassionate, as the rest of them !

Still, being Giles' blood, Val did not think she would assent to Toni's request to be shown the coat ; so she made a clever swerve aside from the direct question :

" I might have been able to finish the picture, if Queenie hadn't gone off to England. Queenie, as a model, was essential, and nobody else would do. I wish her mother hadn't just then taken it into her head that we were a vulgar household, and that the Belle of Potley Green must come home at once ! "

"Well, but Queenie wrote home, you know, and told her mother that you were all not-quite-nice about things."

"Did she? *Did* she? How do you know?"

"Giles told me; he was frightfully amused over the whole show. Apparently Queenie confided in Giles."

"Worse than that," Val said. "Giles confided in Queenie. They were a comic pair. He was fascinated by the tom-fool things she said on every occasion."

"It *was* hard luck on Richard, to have to escort her home to England!" For he had fixed his own date of departure and already taken his ticket, when the telegram came from Queenie's mother. So that it seemed most natural they should travel together.

"Poor Richard! He did splash into the sort of soup he most detested, when he came to stay with me out here. He hates scenes and theatricals, can't stand foreigners, isn't comfortable abroad anyway, disapproves of moral irregularities, is terrified of illness . . . and got landed with all that, and a day with the San Remo lot and Jeanne-Marie into the bargain. And a journey home with Queenie, to put the lid on it all. Can you imagine, Toni, when he gets back to his farm, what he'll say when Molly meets him with: 'Well, old thing, what sort of a time did you have?' 'Bloody awful!'" Val excellently mimicked his gruff and reticent manner; "'*Bloody* awful!' . . . And he'll never speak of it again. I adore Richard!"

"Richard got on well with Giles, didn't he, in spite of disapproval of moral irregularities?"

"We all liked Giles. We *do* like him, in spite of—no, not our disapproval of moral irregularities! But you'd think, wouldn't you, that our loyalty to you would have done Giles in? But even Aunt Elsa is fond of him, against her judgment, bless her!"

Toni raised her eyebrows, in whimsical protest: "Traitors, all of you, to talk of loyalty. . . . Was there no one to fight for my cause, with Giles?"

"Only Loraine," said Val, coolly. "Only Loraine. She was slanging him like hell, you know, for deserting you, when he had that hæmorrhage. Queer, isn't it?" . . .

CHAPTER II

HELEN CZELOVAR bought the goodwill of " Toni's " for a thousand pounds. She was paying rather highly for it, as she had already put in two thousand pounds nearly a year before, to pay for her partnership ; and also Toni's original backer, Mr. Caley, had not yet had his capital returned to him, though he was receiving the agreed percentage. But the firm's success in dressing Lucilla Danby for " She Burnt Her Boats " had sent up the value tremendously. They had as many stage orders, now, as even an enlarged staff, working in enlarged premises, could cope with ; and they could ask practically what prices they pleased, and get them. " Toni's " in Hanover Street was the fashion, and Helen had never been so happy in her life before. Helen was of the same Rakonitz fabric as her cousin, and therefore, though she regretted the cause of Toni's withdrawal from the business, she was glad to be in solitary control. " You young women nowadays ! " ejaculated Raoul Czelovar, helpless in her hands, and quite unable to conceal his adoration for his ugly, smart, independent little daughter. . . . He paid the thousand pounds with hardly a struggle. It was Helen, not Toni, who suggested the sum. Toni would have made it less.

" And now," said Toni, to Giles and Jimmy and Val and Loraine and Aunt Elsa, " now I can buy a house out here."

Scattered among the semicircle of hills, which rise in tiers that recall a Roman theatre, round the arena on which San Goffredo is built, are occasional single houses, large low buildings, cream or pink or lemon-coloured, with vaulted ceilings and stone floors, curiously solid and ancient within, compared with the effect of gimcrack charm that you get from the outside walls of coloured plaster. These houses may once have been inhabited by rich Ligurians, but they have fallen into disrepair; and now peasants own them, huddled untidily into one portion with very little light or air, sharing the rest of the house with their goats or mongrel dogs. They pound a living from cultivation of the olives which cover whatever terraces are roughly marked out as their property; and perhaps they have each a crooked vineyard, a vine pergola on pink-washed pillars, a pig or two, and some incompetent-looking fowls. The sudden brilliance of a tree stuck all over with oranges will take your breath away, as you round a corner of the tumble-down loggia; and you hear the scattering feet of dark shy children flying from your approach; for there are children everywhere—you would not be much surprised if one of them suddenly lifted a head over the stone edge of the well, and then savagely ducked it down again to be free from strangers' scrutiny.

You imagine, of course, that these peasants are so affectionately entwined with their own piece of land that no enticement and no price will persuade them to leave the house in which, presumably, they and their parents and their grandparents were born, and they and their children and their grandchildren will eventually die. You will be wrong. The very first thing that the owner will do, if you should wander that way, and look too long at the view from the doorway down between the lacing olive branches to the sea, will be to try and sell it to you. He will follow you about, dropping in graceful stages from his first preposterous price, intimating that since you are you . . . He will point out the " bella vista "; all of them, in fact; he will wave his hand with a flourish towards the spaciousness of the rooms; and he will amaze you by his reckoning of the rich profits you could extract from selling the olives that are on the land belonging to the house. He will suppress such minor matters as no light, no road, no water . . . Eventually, with an air of humorous deprecation and extreme honesty, he will draw your attention to the fact that perhaps the house is a little dilapidated; he is a poor man; he cannot afford to spend money on repairs; but you, of course . . . Well, you, of course, have the wealth of the Incas at your command !

Toni discovered, with diminishing surprise, at least a dozen

such houses on the surrounding hills, in the neighbourhood of
Val's cottage ; and each one was a treasure and a gem until
Loraine gently led her to perceive the insuperable objection,
whatever it was. As it became known that the Signora from
England actually wanted to purchase a nice sun-baked house
with some ground for cultivation around it, she was followed
and besieged by wooing Italians, all of them lyrically chanting
the beauties of their properties, and the still greater beauties
of Toni installed within their properties. Again and again,
Val and Loraine with harsh words packed them off. They
merely went politely round the hill, and returned by another
looping mule-track.

Jimmy Goddard had gone to Monte Carlo. He said that his
nerves were giving way under the strain of being shown a
succession of dank stables, rat-infested dungeons, and lightless
cellars ; and of being assured in dulcet tones that these were
the ideal dining-rooms, drawing-rooms, and bedrooms for an
English lady of high degree.

Eventually, however, and just about Christmas-time, Toni
found her house. She declared enthusiastically that it was a
peach ; and the description was not so far from the truth as it
usually is, for the dwelling was the warm bloomy yellow that
only ripens after long basking in the sun. It was on the spur
of the opposite hill from Val's cottage, and at exactly the same
height. " If I'd stayed," remarked Val, " we could have run
up a suspension bridge over the abyss, and run lightly to and
fro . . ."

The garden fell away, not too steeply, south and south-west.
Some of it was open to the sea ; some was sheltered by old
strong olives, bent but never broken. The rest of the hill-side,
amounting roughly by English measure to about thirty acres,
went in with the house.

" Artichokes, peaches, and perhaps vines," said Giles briefly,
when he inspected it. He had been talking with a friendly
landowner of adjoining terraces, who had given him useful
information as to the best sources of profit in that part of the
country. Toni, for the time being, left that aspect of the
future to him ; she hoped it would amuse him and keep him

from brooding, though she had noticed no signs of brooding, as yet, in Giles. But Giles had become to her an enigma, as difficult to describe as the shape of an oak. She knew, now, only how little she knew of what was going on behind his nonchalant habit of saying things the reverse of what he meant. And still they had not talked together ! . . . What Val called their " beautiful reconciliation scene " remained on the horizon, and drew no nearer. It was so impossible to begin. . . .

Meanwhile, having bought the house, she occupied herself with its interior. She wanted to send for the children and for her mother as soon as possible, and they could not move in until at least their home was comfortable. The road which wound along the coast to Porto Filippo, looped conveniently at the point nearest Casa Vecchio, to meet their private *salita :* a rather more formal and decorative mule-track than was usually found ; almost, indeed, a succession of broad steps laid in even cobble-stones. This was a lucky accident ; she need not spend money on the approach. All the more for lights, hot water, bathrooms, thick rugs everywhere, big open fireplaces built into the deep stone walls. " Stables and dungeons, indeed ! " scoffed Toni, at the absent Jimmy, after she and Loraine, with tribes of laughing, willing Italian workmen for ever coming to them for orders, had concentrated for a couple of happy weeks on their future residence. " Why, look at it ! " Toni was really enjoying herself. They dispensed, in regal fashion, with architects and plans ; and merely went from room to room, saying, with an imperious gesture : " Here a window ! Here a door ! Here a flight of steps ! " By dint of saying " Here a window ! " very often indeed, she soon succeeded in flooding every room with warm golden light. On Loraine's advice they caused wooden floors to be put down, as they were so much warmer than the familiar red and white tiles of Italy ; and in spite of the fact that their foreman or impresario exclaimed several times a minute : " Body of Bacchus ! " whenever he realised the madness of the order given, they ordered two bathrooms ; and hot and cold water to be installed in every bedroom. As for the system of drainage and other aids to cleanliness on which she insisted :—" Body of

Bacchus! *Mammà Mia!* " exclaimed the foreman, reeling.
. . . But he was a splendid workman, when the initiative was
not his. All Italian workmen, in spite of the prejudice against
the lazy South, could give points, in this respect of sheer
energy, to almost any other race in Europe. But Toni soon
discovered that they must not be left to their own devices for
more than ten minutes at a time. Otherwise they would paint
more shutters on the walls than there were rooms behind the
shutters; and they would run up little, sham, curly towers and
balconies and castellated improvisations in plaster, in order to
get a genial and rococo effect like a bad joke.

Toni often wondered how she could have managed without
Loraine, during this period. Loraine was indefatigable, burning with zeal; a stern glint in her eye for almost hidden
defects, which reminded Toni curiously of her own methods of
supervision in her workrooms in Hanover Street. Val, of
course, was sweetly useless. Val strolled over, occasionally, and
laughed at them · but she atoned for her indolence by handing
over all the furniture of her cottage to Toni : " Though what
you want with seventeen bedrooms, my child, I really *don't*
quite know! There are seventeen, aren't there ? The house
reminds me of one of those rambling old vicarages in the wilds
of the West of England, built in the days when every vicar had
seventeen children. You've only got three. I'd shut up some
of it, if I were you. It will cost a fortune to furnish, even with
my goods and chattels to begin on."

But Toni was obstinate. She wanted all her bedrooms. She
loved Casa Vecchia already; it had a kindly and protective
unity, in spite of its insane, baroque architecture; the different
levels on which different portions of it were built; the stone
archways sunk into the walls; and the unexpected flashes of
bright blue sea wherever Toni's haphazard windows had snared
them.

" It's awfully generous of you, Val, to hand over all that
stuff. Won't you want it yourself ? "

" I can't take it to China," argued Val. " Stephen would
hate travelling even with a divan and three arm-chairs, to say
nothing of ancient rosewood and mahogany bureaus and chests

and cupboards. I don't really mind . . . I'm a nomad, as Loraine would say ! "

Toni laughed. " I've never met anyone less of a nomad by nature, than Loraine ! Why . . . she stays put ! If you set her down in the middle of a desert, she'd run up a tent and call it home, and say how convenient it was, and never want to leave it. I wonder why she thinks she's a gipsy ? "

" Oh, she's got scores of pretty lines about herself," said Val. " And, by the way, Toni, as I'm off the day after to-morrow, I'd rather like to hear first what you're going to do about Loraine ? "

" About Loraine ? " Toni was wilfully dense.

" Yes ; how are you going to get rid of her ? You're quite right, she *does* stay put. She's also divinely unaware that she's ever responsible for any trouble that ever springs up around her. She said to me, simply and sincerely, the other day, wide eyes gazing into mine and all that sort of thing : ' I'd do anything in the world, you know, for the family. Ah, if only people had chattered a little less, lately, and minded their own business more, none of this silly, *silly* fuss need ever have happened.' I didn't quite know, of course, whether taking away your man, and trying to take away mine, came under the heading of doing anything she could for the family, or of minding her own business and not chattering ? "

" It's not put on," Toni interrupted. " Loraine's plausible, but she's quite sincere. She really is fond of us all, you know."

" I've noticed it," said Val, drily. " When is she going ? "

" Going where ? "

" Toni, I'll shake you in a minute ! "

" Going where ? " Toni repeated. " She's not going. Why should she ? "

Val looked at her curiously. " Well, I'm damned," she said. . . . " Then is Loraine going to live with you at Casa Vecchia, Toni ? "

" Of course," replied Toni, taking it for granted. " Where else should she live ? " The surprised lift in her voice was not quite genuine, though it challenged Val to produce any objection whatsoever.

"Loraine!" murmured Val. "Loraine at Casa Vecchia! In the best bedroom, naturally. Well, well!—I always will say, Toni, that you've got a lovely disposition. . . . What about calling it Casa Hanwell?"

"It's you who are the lunatic!" Toni ceased to pretend that she did not know what Val meant. "There isn't a best bedroom, by the way. There are bigger and smaller bedrooms, and south, east, and west bedrooms, but all the seventeen are heavenly. Val, didn't you know that there's no safer siren one can choose out of all the world to live in the same house with one's husband, than the siren who has once ensirened him? Directly it's over, she's helpless—you must see that!—Dead as mutton! Do you imagine that the knight in Keats' poem, the 'alone and palely loitering' one,—do you suppose he'd even look at 'La Belle Dame Sans Merci,' now? Why, if they met face to face on the towing-path——"

"*What* towing-path?" asked Val. "Your scenery's so mixed."

"—He'd brush past her with merely a brusque 'Pardon me,' not noticing her outstretched arms. He might even topple her into the river."

"*What* river?" asked Val.

"Oh, any old river . . ."

Val was not in the least convinced by these psychological deductions of security; but as she was returning in a couple of days to England, to be married, she did not want to quarrel with Toni. Perhaps Toni knew what she was doing! . . . It seemed to Val a very curious arrangement, even though it might be based on the strong claims of family affection.

"Well, bless you, my child; and bless Loraine, and Aunt Elsa, and your mother, and Babs, Paul, and Antony—and Giles . . . he'll need it. I hope my dogs will be happy with all of you; under the circumstances, I wouldn't be Terry and Mac for a kingdom. . . . However—we'll be returning in two years, so Stephen says, and I'll come out here and give you all decent burial, and put up a few crosses."

"Aren't you going to back a survivor?" Toni laughed.

"When two matriarchs get into one generation—no . . ."

But Val added this last reflection to the vast heap that she had the wisdom not to say aloud.

.　　.　　.　　.　　.　　.　　.

Toni was standing on the loggia of Val's cottage, facing west. From here, she could look across to Casa Vecchia. They were moving in the next morning; and a week later she expected Susie and the children and the nurse to arrive from England. She had been up here all the afternoon, superintending the transport of the last pieces of furniture. The cottage behind her was empty. It was over a month, now, since Val had left Italy. Jimmy Goddard had returned to England at the same time. Aunt Elsa and the dogs had moved down to Villa Bel Respiro. To-morrow they were all moving to the new house— the old house—on the spur of seaward-facing hill across the valley. Red tiles, golden walls, green shutters . . . and at the back, a small grove of orange trees, glowing with their fruit. . . . " My home in Italy ! " she said to herself, trying the sound of it : " My villa in the South. Yes, we grow oranges. Would you like to pick one ? Or a passion-fruit ? " . . . How funny ! And how funny, again, looking at it from here, to think that to-morrow she was actually going there to live, with her husband and her children and her mother and her aunt . . . She noticed that the shoulder of the hill behind the house cut off the sun ten minutes earlier every evening, than from Val's cottage ; this was rather annoying ; she was greedy of sunshine, for Giles' sake, and wanted to scoop in all there was. Still, ten minutes was not much !—and all this dozing warmth was jolly, at four o'clock on a January afternoon . . .

—" Is that you, Loraine ? " she called out, hearing someone open the door that led on to the loggia from the dining-room. The others had let her come up here alone, this afternoon, while they packed their private belongings.

But it was Giles, not Loraine.

—" Giles ! But you oughtn't to climb the hill, when you needn't. I'm sure you came up too fast."

" I came up like a snail," said Giles. " I sat down and rested for half an hour on every cobble. In fact, though you didn't

notice it, I began to come up yesterday. . . . I say, our residence looks well from here, doe n't it ? Rather imposing.
Let's call it ' The Towers.' "

" If you make another suggestion like that," Toni threatened,
" you *shall* have towers, ever so many of them ; these
workmen can run them up in no time. It isn't that they've
got no taste—they've got bad taste ; I mean, they destroy
something good to construct something bad in its place. I
only just saved a most gorgeous sort of natural alcove, vaulted,
with a little window punched into the arch at the far end, in
Loraine's room ; they wanted to pull it down ! "

. . . Then she became aware of Giles leaning against a pillar,
and scrutinising her with an odd smile :

" Loraine's room, eh ? Did you really think Loraine was
going to live with us over there, Toni ? "

Somehow, Toni was frightened. This really was the first
time, since her arrival in Italy, that they seemed on the brink
of really talking together, instead of nervously skimming over
a polite surface. She tried the same method with him, as
previously with Val, on this same question :

" Yes, of course she is. That's all settled."

" It's all settled," Giles agreed ; " but not the way you
mean. How is it you haven't mentioned this before, Toni ? "

" I took it for granted," lied Toni.

" Oh no, you didn't, my child. Otherwise you *would* have
mentioned it before, in the natural course of things."

" Yes, well——" Toni hesitated. Once, she would have
been imperious about her wishes in the matter ; and later, she
would have acted pretty persuasion, knowing all the while that
she could coax her own way. But this was a more honest Toni,
who said : " Yes, you're right, Giles. I did take special care
not to mention it. You see, I thought that in the hurly-burly
of actually moving, and so many things to see to, and the
furniture and the dogs and Marietta and everything, that she
would sort of slip in with the rest, without your scenting it out
till it was too late ; and that then you'd just accept it."

" —You hoped, in fact, that I'd take her for a dresser or an
oak chest or a tea-service, did you, in the confusion of the

moment? You are an ass, Toni! The idea is purely preposterous, of course, that Loraine should live with us—after what's happened."

"She's one of my family," chanted Toni, reverting to ritual. "And she's tremendously fond of me, and of Aunt Elsa, and the children,—especially Babs, and all of us."

"And willing to put up with me, d'you think? Cheers!"

"Loraine's miserable, away from the family. Of course, conventionally, I know I ought to owe her an undying grudge because she's the woman you ran away with——"

. . . It was easier to speak about it, now, in the heat of what looked like a quarrel between her and Giles, than it had been during the past few weeks of mutual courtesy and deferential shyness.

"But I'm not jealous of Loraine, and she knows I'm not. The blood tie can be very strong——"

"Blood your grandmother!" exclaimed Giles, rudely. "Good God, Toni, has it never occurred to you what I'd feel like, having Loraine always about the place, to remind me of the blazing fool I made of myself?"

"I suppose . . . from an ordinary point of view—— But Giles, we're *not* the ordinary eternal-triangle: man, wife, and Other Woman! You can't pretend we are! It might be difficult, living with Loraine, but for a different reason; she's got a temperament like an African savage, I know; I'm prepared to cope with that; and I think, too, in time, if she lives with us, that I can get on top of it."

"Or she can, on top of yours," said Giles. "Thanks, I don't want my house turned into a sort of War of the Rakonitz Succession. What about a little peace, for a change? And then there's Babs. Our small daughter, I gather, has got a wild rave on Loraine. Not very good for her, to encourage it, is it?"

"Where Babs is concerned," said obstinate Toni, "I want to win a victory over Loraine's actual presence; a positive, not a negative victory. Babs is going to learn to love me best *with* Loraine in the house *and* in the room. . . . You do see, don't you?"

"I might, if I were thinking about you at all," Giles answered.

" But all this silliness would be frightfully bad for Babs ; and I'm simply not going to risk it."

. . . Toni wondered, in a dazed sort of fashion, if it could be actually true that Giles was winning the mastery over her in this belated tussle of their wills, and after four years of marriage ? If so, it had to be attended to at once, and firmly ; because, after all, however decent it was the rule to be about these things, she was in the magnanimous position of being the one who had to forgive. If she were prepared to forgive both Giles and Loraine, it surely was not for Giles to say that Loraine must not be forgiven ? What she had secretly desired, of course, in the unreasonable state of nerves which had overpowered her after the intense forty-eight hours preceding Richard's " Giles is better," was that Giles should feebly plead Loraine's cause, instead of strongly combating it. Then, and in that case, she might herself have been natural and sensible : she might herself have sent Loraine packing. For she did not really want Loraine as a permanence at Casa Vecchia, upsetting everything. She, like Giles, wanted peace in the house. But they had irritated her, all of them—Richard first, by a piece of advice, characteristically delivered ; then Val ; now Giles . . . all of them assuming that she was Loraine's enemy ; or that if she wasn't, she ought to be. . . . " Yes, I *know* . . ." But Toni was animated by a last perverse flicker of one of her old moods. . . . Was Loraine alone ? Was there no one to stand up for her, as she, by Val's report, had stood up for her cousin Toni, while Giles had packed his suit-case ? No one ? . . . Well, then—— Still half-laughing, half-angry, quite convinced that ultimately and whatever she said, luck would rid her of Loraine, Toni was impelled to talk more and more nonsense, calling it loyalty :

" Loraine's my cousin," she said. " There are some things you can't understand, Giles. In our family, we don't disown our relations or turn them away from us. Loraine would be utterly forlorn, left hanging about in the cold. I believe it really is the deepest passion of her life, this desire to be near her own people ; to settle down with them, and be counted in. Do, for a moment, get above the—oh, the personal aspect of this business, and try to realise how awfully cruel it would be to rebuff her and thrust her beyond the tents."

Giles remained totally unmoved. In fact, Toni's slight lapse into picturesque statement had the opposite effect on him than she intended. He hated picturesque statement; it reminded him of Loraine. . . .

"It's all very tragic," he assented, nonchalantly; "but it's not my business. My business is concerned with you and the kids and our daily life."

. . . The sun had set behind the hills; and a chill had blown in, as always, with the quick-falling dusk along the Mediterranean. Giles ought not to have been out-of-doors, but they were both too preoccupied to notice this.

"If it were one of your people——" Toni began . . . and then she stopped. No, she could not, of course she could not tell Giles how, at a crisis, she had sacrificed everything she most cared for, a little while ago, in order to plunge to the rescue of Jimmy, Giles' father. Not one of her own family, but Giles' father. An unspoken agreement, or so it seemed to Toni, existed between her and Jimmy, that this affair should never be spoken of to anyone. Anyhow, she could not have flaunted it in front of Giles, now. It was too like exacting an exchange of generosity. But still . . . she compromised by putting it in general terms—"If it were one of your family whom you wanted me to help, Giles, I'd do it, whatever it cost."

"You're thinking of that time when you stopped Jimmy from shooting himself," said Giles, at once, and startling her.

"You know—about that?"

"Yes, of course I do. Jimmy told me. . . . Darling, it's no good expecting Jimmy to keep secrets. He never does. He doesn't see the use of them. Nor do I, as a matter of fact. Yes, that was pretty fine of you, Toni. Decent of you, too, not to chuck it at me, just now. But all the same, the eye-for-an-eye-and-tooth-for-a-tooth business doesn't apply, here. I'm not going to have Loraine in my house, in our house. I know Loraine. There'd be no end of trouble. Oh, she'll be all right; she'll drift about from one branch of the family to another. You'll get a postcard from Stockholm, or from Trieste, or Seville, saying how Great-aunt Sarah, or Jezebel, or whoever it is, adores her, and how happy she's going to be for the rest of her life. . . . And about six months later, another postcard will turn up with a different postmark, telling us that she's a nomad and can't settle down, although old Cousin Naphtali Eleazor is simply *begging* her to make a home with them at Geneva !—And we'll know by that, that there's been mischief in Stockholm or Trieste or Seville. . . . Toni dear, I'm not ungrateful over Jimmy. You can simply stuff our house with your family, aunts and uncles and grandmothers bulging and flapping out of every room and window, Rakonitzes and Czelovars by the dozen, if you like, and I'll be a noble and splendid host to all of them. But not Loraine, my dear, not Loraine."

"It's Loraine I want," said Toni, dangerously. She was stung in her most sensitive region, that her husband should make a comic picture out of her family fanaticism ; yet she would have been ready to do so herself, at a more normal moment. The pace of their quarrel quickened ; though Giles remained, as usual, outwardly imperturbable.

"Then you can't have her. She's leaving this evening on the Vienna express. I ordered the carriage to be at the villa at ten past five."

Queer that their long-expected reconciliation should have blazed out, instead, into this violent dispute. Queerer still, that both should be enjoying it.

Toni repeated, incredulously : "You—told—Loraine—to leave—my—house ? "

"I expect she's packing now," murmured Giles.

Toni did not heed the airy interruption : "Without consulting me ? "

"Unless you call this, consulting ? "

"When ? "

"Actually, in so many words, this morning. She's been expecting it for a long time, though. Loraine's no fool. Besides, we know each other rather well. I might have given her longer notice, but I'm a considerate bloke, and I know that Loraine prefers it this way. More melodramatic. She can always get a thrill from the fact that she's been brutally slung out."

" It's a thrill I'm not keen about. It violates hospitality——
Good Lord, there's nothing worse ! And my own cousin, too !
And Loraine might even say it's jealousy—that I'm still
jealous of her."

" Which you are ! And at the same time, frightfully bucked
with yourself for being original enough to want her to live
with us. Which you don't ! . . . Where are you going ?"
He intercepted her as she pushed past him, towards the path
that led down the hill—" Lord, I wish these perishing doctors
would let me have a pipe, now and then. Blighters !—Toni,
where are you going ? "

" To cancel your orders," said Toni. " Loraine stays." She
twinkled jauntily up at him. . . . How tall he was !

" Loraine goes." But he was still smiling. How blue
her eyes were !

" You'd no right to sling her out without my permission.
When people act high-handedly——"

" You'd no right to arrange for her to live with us without
my permission. And when people act as though they had bats
in the belfry—I'm sorry, Toni, but I win over this. You can't
fight me. You've gone further than it's safe, already. You
can't fight a husband who might die at any moment, Toni, if he
gets over-excited. . . . Or had you forgotten ? The odds are
one to three that I'll live, anyway ; a second hæmorrhage
might be fatal . . ."

Toni stared at him, incredulously. Surely he could not be
using this weapon against her ? It was unbelievable, from
Giles. She continued to stare at him. . . .

" Dirty trick, isn't it ? " he said, serenely aware that he had
dealt final destruction to her guileless conception of a very
special gun-room-and-country-house code. . . . " Well below
the belt, and not what you'd expect from an English gentleman."

. . . But, with a burst of horror, Toni realised—brushing
aside the point whether he should have used this or that
weapon—that it was true, deadly true. She had no right ever
to fight with Giles, or to allow him to fight with her. She had
failed in vigilance, and it was bitter that he should have had to
remind her of it. If, in consequence, anything should have

happened to him !—already she might have done him harm, with her silly wrangling, her prate about family and pride and hospitality. . . . As though anything mattered besides keeping Giles alive and with her, guarding instead of exposing him ! As though Loraine's going away could possibly matter ! All happening shrunk to a pin-point, and she saw only Giles. If he were to cough now——

If he were to cough, Toni felt she could not bear it.

" Giles ! " she cried out, in panic. " You're not—going to cough ? "

And at that, his teasing half-smile broke into the laugh so typical of him at all times of stress.

" Cough ? No, of course I'm not going to cough ! You're a brick, Toni, not to hate me for having said that ! But I really thought we'd been quarrelling long enough, and that I'd better end it . . ." He had her in his arms now, and she was clinging to him as though already she might have let him slide too far into the waiting danger. " Toni dear, it's no good, you know !—we shall have a hell of a life unless we can face it and talk about it quite naturally, this possibility that I may peg out at any moment. The odds are rather too big to ignore it, you see. If I'd even a fifty-fifty chance. . . . Well, but we don't want to walk about on tiptoe, do we ? Laboriously avoiding egg-shells all the time ; being heavily bright and tactful ? And I simply refuse to lean back, sky-blue and precious, against a stained-glass window, for the rest of my life. Stained-glass doesn't suit me. Starting and jumping and looking self-conscious if anyone happens to mention illness or death—it's too damned uncomfortable, Toni, hushing things up ! Let's take it in our stride. We'll have a good time in spite of it, while the good time lasts."

" I can't bluff it out, like you can, Giles," she whispered.

" Only don't call my bluff ! I couldn't want to live with any single person in the world, Toni, except you, under these circumstances. . . . As it is, don't worry, child. It won't be so bad. And now—look here, it's getting cold. We ought to go down. Besides——" his eyes quizzed her again—" it's nearly time for the Vienna express."

CHAPTER III

. . . LORAINE, from the lower step of the villa, looked up
at Toni and Giles. Aunt Elsa was standing at
the front door, too; and Manuela; and Luigi,
the wine-merchant's son; and Stefania, but not Marietta;
and, by an unfortunate chance for Loraine, Mac, who was
indifferent to her departure, but not Terry. Manuela was
weeping stormily, and protesting eternal fidelity to her
beautiful little signorina, who was going away because there
were some who were cruel and jealous and forgetful of benefits;
but she, Manuela, would serve no other mistress while the sun
shone and the mimosa bloomed . . . Under cover of this
shrill and embarrassing volubility, Toni and Loraine said good-
bye to each other:

. . . "Yes, Toni darling, it *is* sudden, but that's the only
way I can leave, when I love people and a place. Any other way,
I couldn't bear it. But I'm too restless to settle down. I think
I want to—and then, when I see it looming so close in front of
me, a home, and regular meals, and the same bed noight after
noight, then my blood begins to tramp up and down in my
veins like a sailor tramping the deck in a tempest. You do
understand, Toni darling, that it isn't that I want to be
leaving you? But that I'm a nomad . . ."

Yes, Toni understood all right. Pretence was necessary,
here; and so she, too, picked up her end of it, and helped her
cousin Loraine to pull it taut:

"I'm so terribly sorry, Loraine; but I do agree with you,
that if one must go, it's the best thing to rush off and not hang
about over it. You've been a brick about helping me move
into the house."

"Ah, but I enjoyed that," quickly from Loraine. "Confess
now, Toni, you couldn't have managed it without me? Not in

384

that time? Not with the babies coming out next week? Ah,
and kiss my lovely Babs for me, and tell her that her Loraine
will be passing this way again, sometime . . ." Their eyes
encountered steadily.

"Whenever you do," said Toni, "you know that Casa
Vecchia has got a room for you, don't you?"

—"You'll be missing your train, Loraine," called out Giles,
from his obscure position behind the mourning group on the
top step; and the driver of the carriage called out a jovial
warning in Italian, at the same instant. Loraine plunged once
more up the steps, flung her arms around Aunt Elsa, drawing
that warm-hearted old lady's tears, by a last impetuous kiss;
hugged Mac—it ought to have been Terry, but Terry had gone
after a bone!—patted Manuela consolingly on the shoulder;
flung out a genial "Take care of yourself, Giles!"—a farewell
which nevertheless was laced with mockery; ran down the
steps, and sprang lightly into the carriage. She had begged
that no one should see her off at the station—she could not
bear formal partings, she said.

"Vienna, Prague, Budapest, Warsaw, Bucharest,"—exul-
tantly she reeled the names off her tongue. "Ah, I've stopped
in one place too long! . . . Good-bye, Toni!"

"Good-bye, Loraine!"

The very jingle of the harness and the crack of the driver's
whip, as the carriage drove off, seemed to assist in the pantomime of an eager traveller, of fresh gipsyings, and of Loraine's
impatient pity for those beloved but stupid creatures who
remained heavily behind.

It was a gallant exit. . . . But her last glance was for Casa
Vecchia, visible on the spur of the hill, through a gap in the
olives.

CHAPTER IV

BABS was the first to tumble from the high carriage of
the train, on to the platform, at the frontier station
between France and Italy. How like Babs! Toni,
rushing frenziedly along in search of her party, picked her up
from where she had fallen, and hugged her delightedly. Babs
was not crying. She was trying to explain something to Toni ;
something quite irrelevant about a toy which Quimper had
given her on parting, and which, when wound up and placed
on the deck of the Channel steamer, the day before, had run
between the rails and into the sea, and—and they wouldn't
stop the boat ! She became incoherent and stammering in the
attempt to express her indignation against the captain and the
crew who would not stop, when she, Babette, daughter of
Antoinette Goddard, *née* Rakonitz, had ordered them to do
so. . . . But meanwhile, here was Toni's mother, encumbered
with Paul and with much luggage, slowly clambering down ;
and bulging just behind her, in the dim sickly light, Nurse and
Antony and more luggage ; and they all stood, bewildered in
the centre of jabber and gesture from the three porters whom
Toni had previously commandeered, and who had followed
her from end to end of the train ; while some people who did
not belong to the party at all, wanted one of Toni's porters,
and feverishly expressed an altogether wrong-headed notion
that Susie's travelling-rug was theirs. Toni, throttled by Paul
and then again by Babs, was unable for the moment to cope
with pandemonium. . . . She suddenly was aware of a queer
sensation, as though she were back in the nursery of the house
in Holland Park, the nursery where she had passed her own
childhood. She could not tell whence such an impression had
drifted, like a few bars of an old waltz. . . . It could not be
just seeing her mother ?

" . . . And so I thought I'd better bring him along," Susie briskly finished her explanation.

" What ? " cried Toni, as the trucks clattered past. " *Who* along ? "

" There," Susie pointed through the racing crowd of travellers. " He's just got out of a smoker. You *can't* have forgotten him, Toni ? Don't tell him you have. He'd be so hurt. And I don't think, and nor did Truda, that he's changed much, except for his American accent, and you haven't heard that yet. Oh dear, hadn't we better get along to the Customs, or those other people will all get there first ? "

. . . Toni rubbed her eyes. And here again was the face she must have seen, half-consciously, just now, accounting for that vagrant memory ; only now it kissed her, and said—Susie was right, with a strong American accent : " Gee, Toni, you've grown ! Not going to give your old Uncle Ludo the frozen mitt, are you ? Susie told me you'd be tickled to death to see me . . ."

He had been one of those uncles who had suddenly whisked her up, all lacy frills and curls, and had held her screaming above his head, much nearer the ceiling than she liked, so that she remembered him clearest as seen from upside down. Uncle Ludo, Ludovic Rakonitz, Anastasia's second son, the one who had done something not altogether satisfactory and had been sent abroad, the cause hushed up. . . . A letter stamped Nicaragua. . . . And another fleeting recollection, now, of her head and Danny's bent close together over a large map : —" Oh, and Toni, just listen to the exports—rosewood, tortoiseshell, indigo, hides, and gold chains . . ."

She wondered, still a little bit dazed, how many of these Uncle Ludo might have brought back with him, from Nicaragua.

—No time for questions now. " Nine small pieces, Madam," said the nurse, " and eight big. That's what made it easy to remember. Of course, coming out here for good, like this, there'd be a lot of luggage as well as what you had sent by sea. And I do hope the master's better."

. . . " *And*," Babs went on, for she was truculent in sticking to a subject that interested her until it had been given its full meed of attention, "it wasn't as though they couldn't have stopped the boat and gone to fetch it, Mummy, because there were *lots* of little boats all round the edge of the big boat, on strings, and they'd only got to cut the strings——" . . .

"And when I heard mother was dead, Lord, I got the shock of my life! And it was funny, that, because in a sort of way I'd expected it. I'd reckoned up how old she must be; and yet, when it come to hearing it from Truda—I dunno—the Rakonitzes were centenarians, most of 'em. Susie tells me she used to talk about me a lot," added Uncle Ludo, sentimentally, "but that she didn't hand me out anything in her Will . . . Who got those Bokhara rugs, Toni? They were worth something. I had a pal who'd have given me a good price for them. He was a millionaire."

Toni smiled. This was the authentic Uncle Ludo, brimming with family solicitude, and acquisitive with the very next breath. They had long ago given up all idea of ever seeing him again. It was over fifteen years since any of them had had a line from him, telling of his flittings or whereabouts.

Separated from him for a little while, while they were being hustled and pressed against the counters in the *Dogána*, and before their luggage was wheeled in, she asked Susie a few rapid questions. There were more important subjects to tell and to be told about, than Uncle Ludo, of course: Giles, the children, their new home; but the reappearance of a lost uncle was undoubtedly a startling thing to have happened. Besides— why had he come out here with Susie and the children and the nurse from St. Olaf's?

"My darling, he just drifted along. The old lady was dead, you see; and in Truda's flat, the one she took last year, there isn't an inch to cram anyone. It seemed, after all, the most natural thing to bring him. There wasn't time to let you know, but I supposed you'd want him out here. I don't believe the poor boy has got a penny, even though he's been making his fortune all these years.—Oh dear, Toni!" Susie broke off in distress, "do ask them not to open just *that* trunk of mine. It's the one with all the things in it I didn't mean them to see!"

Susie, having only married into the family, was not a cosmopolitan, and could never make herself understood by foreigners, nor yet quite rest in their ways. She had lived for sixteen years an alien in the house of the Matriarch, and remained an alert sweet-natured, cosy little Englishwoman, with nothing in her composition that was in the least eccentric nor richly-flavoured.

" *Of course* you had to bring him," Toni cried, heartily, " if there was no home for him anywhere else. You were absolutely right, Mummy darling—and won't Aunt Elsa be excited ! . . . I'm sorry, but I'm afraid you'll have to pay on those. You shouldn't have brought them, you know. You can buy them here."

" *Can* you ? " said Susan Lake, mistrustfully.

Nurse had managed to sweep off Babs and Antony, out of the hectic mob, into the waiting-room ; but Paul clung obstinately to Toni, giving short, spasmodic squeezes to her hand. An odd, self-reliant little chap, Paul, and so plain. She had always bothered least about him of all her children ; and yet, according to Nurse's accounts, it was he who had missed her most. The Customs-house at Ventimiglia was hardly a suitable place for a remorseful Toni to yield herself up, at last, to a scene of adoring her children, so she controlled the impulse ; but she felt a quick thrill warming her when she thought of having Babs and Paul and Antony permanently with her, now, at Casa Vecchia, that big old house with a garden for them to play in, and the hills behind the garden, and the sea at the foot of the hills ; and lots and lots of time, an unfettered wind and wash of time, to devote to them,—yes, she herself, without gaiety claiming her at one swing of the pendulum, or the urgency of business in Hanover Street at the other. How tremulously glad she was that her racial instinct had been strong enough to call her to bear children, even while—*gamine de son siècle !*—she had rather petulantly thought it a nuisance, and a hold-up to all her pleasures. If she had waited . . . She and Giles would never dare have any more children in the future, even if he lived. Never mind, here were three ; life need not be meagre. . . . But then her thankfulness quivered to a sudden fear : supposing Antony, who had been born last of all——? She would have to look after Antony very specially and carefully. Was it hereditary? She could not remember. Some said it wasn't; but the specialist from Cannes had said that Giles must have had the germ of his illness in him, unrecognised, for at least a year . . .

Uncle Ludo elbowed his way to her side. " I guess this young fellow must be tired of being used as a football," and he lifted up Paul from among the close press of legs, and set him on his shoulder. Paul clutched anxiously, again, for Toni's hand.

" So the Uncles came a crash over sapphires? " Ludo Rakonitz went on, determined to engage Toni in cheerful reminiscences, even though her luggage—nine small pieces and eight big, according to Nurse—was in the process of being vindictively examined. " In nineteen-ten, they tell me. Poor Uncle Max! If I'd been there! . . . It seemed queer, when I landed, not being able to go round to him to borrow a dollar or two. Queer not to find anyone much to go round to. What's become of 'em all? It's not that I mind, either, having money refused to me," he explained, ingenuously. " The Uncles often said no, after the first few times. It was not finding anyone—d'you get me?—who *will* refuse me money. . . . That's what gives me the lonesome chill. But I can put up at your shack for a bit, Toni, while I look around, if your husband don't mind? What sort of a city d'you live in? Will it stand developing, d'you think? Good climate? I tried my hand at developing a burg, once. I reckon we'll have to see about it! "

. . . Toni smiled again. Yes, this *was* Uncle Ludo, in spite of the twang. It was also, in varying shades and tints of the same temperament, her father, Bertrand; and her cousin Derek; and her grandmother, Anastasia, to the life; and, so they said, her great-uncles Andreas and Eugène and Isidor, dandies of Vienna. In Uncle Ludo was comically personified their tribal gathering; sanguine, swaggering, affectionate. Extravagant as Maxine; bragging and voluble as Loraine; imperious as her own little daughter, Babs; physically indolent as Val; handsome as Val's grandmother, lovely Simone . . .

She wondered how her English husband would welcome the derelict Rakonitz?

CHAPTER V

"MUMMY," said Babs, "is this how you dressed when you were young?"

Toni, looking at the photograph, was conscious of shock. "This" was her own mother, Susie; pretty Susan Lake, at the age of twenty, and in the costume of the eighteen-nineties: wasp-waisted; voluminous skirts lifted coquettishly from the ground by a hand deftly trained to this trick; balloon sleeves with long tight cuffs; high stiff collars, white boater hat, tennis racquet and balustrade: a fresh and simple girl, complete in every detail of her period; sentimentally cherished by Susie, no doubt, as a reminder to herself of what Toni's father had seen in her, to love. Thirty years earlier or thirty years later—it was all the same to Babs; yet it struck Toni, feeling modern as she did, as utterly grotesque that the child should be a whole generation out. "Is this how you dressed when you were young?" . . . Why then, was she already among the aunts, among the old ones?—"Yes, darling," said Toni, answering Babs, "more or less." And presently Babs ran off again. She was helping Grannie to unpack and arrange her room.

But Toni stood by the window, alone, and looked out over what was, for once, a quiet grey landscape; a cloudy sky hung over a dull sea; frogs threw up a monotonous croaking from unseen patches of water. Italy might have been rural England. It was between tea and supper-time, and the house was very still. Giles, who had been talking about artichokes, all day, enthusiastically as a man with a long life before him, had gone off with his friend, the Italian landowner, who would tell him more about the cultivation of artichokes, and show him several thousands of that fascinating vegetable in very early bearing. Uncle Ludo, settled down now at Casa Vecchia, with the air

of one conferring a benefit upon his poor relations, and conferring it heartily and generously, was probably in the little town,
ruminating on his plans for developing it : on getting capitalists
interested, and on running up a casino and a golf-course and a
tennis club, and two or three swell hotels. Aunt Elsa and Susie,
with Babs to help them, formed a corner of warmth and hubbub
and busyness establishing themselves in that part of the house
where Toni had lovingly allotted them bedrooms.   The
nurseries formed another such cheerful area ; and probably
there the dogs were congregated too, and Stefania and Marietta,
in adoration of Paul and Baby Antony ; and laughing in their
pretty friendly fashion at the good-natured attempts of the
nurse from St. Olaf's at making herself understood by them.
The severe nurse from St. Olaf's had amazed Toni by stating,
firmly : " This, Madam, is the life that suits me," after twelve
hours spent in an Italian home. She, who had rejected their
studio in Kensington as a too indecorous and unconventional
abode, said that San Goffredo, and its happy semi-barbaric
multiplicity of mules and peasants, cafés and carabinieri, its
dark little shops cowering away from the blaze of sunlight, and
stocked with alien wares, its motto of " Never do to-day what
you can put off until after midday next week," its line of
oranges in full fruit down the principal street—she said that
this was the life that suited her !

"And is this the life that suits me ? " Toni wondered . . .
for to-day there was no glow of the South, in compensation
for her exile.

Yes, Babs' question had upset her ; and though Toni knew
she was a fool to be upset about such a childish mistake, yet
that sense of outrage persisted. She did not mind the inevitable
yielding to old age—— Well, she need not bother about that
yet ! Even Babs could hardly say she was old. But yielding up
modernity, that was quite another thing ; that piqued Toni,
of " Toni's " in Hanover Street ; Toni, who had led the
fashion ; whose pride it was ever to be more than up-to-date ;
Toni, of whom the throng had said : " And so young still ! "
when she had recently scored success by designing the costumes
for " She Burnt Her Boats."

Would she have to sacrifice all this, now she had left the cities?

She saw herself, with all her contemporaries in the family, Val and Maxine, Deb, Eileen and Sylvia, but mostly herself and Loraine, as the children were just beginning to view them as a matter of course: the Old Ones; mothers and aunts and things . . . stodgy, but representative of inescapable yesterdays. She saw herself and Loraine, from this younger standpoint, growing gradually eccentric, full of character, easy to label. . . . Loraine would be known as the aunt, presently the great-aunt, who travelled a lot, and never said beforehand when she was arriving, and wore funny clothes. And she, Toni, a more static figure, was the one who had the big house, and invited them all to stay sometimes, and who could be—yes, a little bit frightening, even to twentieth-century babydom. You always took on more distinguishing characteristics when you were placed back among the mothers and aunts and the old ones, than while you were just the usual age, dancing and wearing modern clothes. " Oh damn! " cried Toni, in sudden revolt, " and I'm not ready for it yet ! "

Suddenly, and still goaded by pique, by that careless needle-thrust from her little daughter, she ran up to her bedroom, and put on the very latest and most exquisite creation that she had had built for her just before leaving London. She was ahead of the season, then. Her two-and-a-half months in Italy would have brought it just abreast of her. Toni flitted about the room, humming in her queer, happy way, out of key, but giving herself an intense pleasure in a way that no other person singing to her *in* key could ever have done. She was strangely fastidious about her toilet this evening; merely dressing would not suffice; she revelled in the sybaritic preliminaries, as well: first a hot bath, with a profusion of "subtilité" salts in it; then her apricot georgette underclothing, never worn, hitherto; her hair carefully waved, and fiercely brushed to the right shape of shingle; her nails manicured. Her arms and neck and shoulders, when she was eventually satisfied with them, though still too slender, were smooth and creamy as the lining of an old Satsuma bowl. Toni adored the sensuous *feel* of things, even more than the sight of them. . . . She cuddled her cheek down to meet a hunched-up shoulder, now, and slowly rubbed her flesh against her flesh. Hyper-civilisation. . . . —Where could Toni be going, to-night, out here in San Goffredo? Yet she was critical as an artist, whose painting would presently be on exhibition to the whole world.

And the dress she chose to wear was " Sauve Qui Peut."

It was a very special dress. Toni had designed the original model for herself, against Helen's judgment. " Sherry and vermilion are impossible colours together," Helen had argued ; but she had made amends, later on, by her inspired christening of the frock, the moment she saw it on Toni. " Sauve Qui Peut " was a dress of the cities. Its tint was drawn, less from the petals of flowers than, subtly, out of the heart of wine—mellow, sophisticated wine, that you drank slowly, while the most modern music was being played. She had worn it only twice in London, in November, before she had been summoned away ; and people had turned their heads to look, as she passed. Sherry-coloured georgette clung like an embrace straight down the supple shimmer of her body, pointed by arrow embroideries, in sequins of the same shade, into the scalloped edges, just below the knees. So far, good Toni ! . . . moderately good ! But on either side—and here was the challenge—three vermilion godets swaggered in between the scallops. They were much shorter than the rest of the short little frock. They appeared and vanished unevenly, as Toni moved. They were—an impertinence, if you like ; she meant them to be a bright red impertinence . . . tongue in the cheek ! Helen had said vermilion and sherry-colour were not possible together . . .

Sauve qui peut !

And cosmopolitan Toni was looking her best. Rebellion always touched her with a flush and sparkle that her looks needed, to transform what was usually sedate, into that quality of fascination most attractive, because it is so evanescent. Toni *was* in rebellion ! She wanted to prove to herself that she need not become old-fashioned, even though she had left the cities behind her. . . .

She ran downstairs, a living silhouette cut out of the next-number-but-one of *Vogue*.

The big central sitting-room of the house was empty, save for its logwood fire that creaked and shifted; save for Val's little West-Highland terrier, who wagged a welcoming stump of tail at the sight of Toni, and showed every disposition to dance. He liked his mistress to be gay.

—" This is no good," exclaimed Toni, with angry petulance. . . . And then she laughed at herself. What had she expected to find ? Colin, and all his night-club gang ? The latest saxophone band ? What had she dressed up for ? She had come to live on the land, she and her family. She flung herself into the big arm-chair. Content had fled for the moment. She wanted the cities again. The Rakonitz family had always lived in big cities. Always ?—well, for nearly two hundred years. You could not expect Toni, the gayest of them all, to become directly, at the call of necessity, like the mother of her great-great-grandmother : Babette's mother, who had had vineyards in Hungary. Not all at once; little by little, perhaps. She would have to do it, because Giles was ill, and could not live in the cities. She must say good-bye to them; those that she knew, like London and Paris and Rome ; and those she knew vicariously, like Vienna and Budapest. She had never been to Vienna or Budapest, but she knew them through legend, through snatches of song, fragments of vivid description from those who had been there; and she knew them racially, because they were in her blood, the tradition and the song of the cities of Central Europe . . . She did not know that she was crooning the " Caprice Viennois," to a crooked rhythm that Kreisler himself would not have recognised ; for she was seeing Vienna, and at the same time Paris. . . . She had heard it that night last March, when, following an intangible mood, she had gone alone to the Chauve-Souris, at the Théâtre—where was it ? Somewhere down the Champs-Elysées, for she had dined at Laurent's, first. She savoured again the perfect sophistication of the French restaurant. Such a hot room !— But she sat near the door, and just beyond was the cool drumming of the fountain in the outside court ; and an oblong of

scarlet came into that vision : the brocade hand-bag that had
cost her six guineas . . . but it was worth it, for the intense
satisfaction she derived from knowing it hers, this symbol of
expensive luxury with its tiny jewelled clasp. . . . But she
had bought that, daring poverty, before she was married ! It
had tumbled into the wrong picture. . . . What does time
matter ? Paris. . . . The Chauve-Souris. . . . "It's the
' Caprice Viennois ' ! What luck ! " . . . Nothing could have
led her to expect it, as the curtain had gone up, showing starkly
a window set in the wall of a house, heavy snow on the sill,
heavy snow loading down the branch of the tree across it ;
leaded panes, and behind them a glimpse of a drawing-room,
a lamp, a piano . . . and, dimly seen, two graceful women
wearing that sort of square-necked and puff-sleeved costume
that went with hair that might almost have seemed bobbed, in
its square cut round the cheek and neck. And Toni knew that
cultured drawing-room behind the sharp wintry weather. . . .
Her neighbour remarked afterwards, amiably, that Madame was
seeing the performance for the second time ? yes, surely, for
she had murmured ' Caprice Viennois,' before even the first
bars had been played, and before those tall ladies, unreal in the
lamplight behind the window, had begun to sing her favourite
melody. . . . Still dreaming it right, humming it wrong, she
had come out of the theatre, into the mad pattern of the
whizzing taxis, zig-zagging down a thousand spokes from a
shifting centre ; the grand up-curve of the lamps, as though
swung on air, as far as the Arc de Triomphe. . . . Paris ! . . .
" Caprice Viennois ! " . . . Vienna !—Funny, how it all blended !
Grandmère had told her about Vienna ; and Danny, who had
had the luck to stay there in the later and more cynical era of
Franz Rakonitz, imperturbable hero of the 'eighties, Danny,
too, had told Toni. . . . But that was a different Vienna. . . .
And Val's had been different again : the artist's Vienna. Her
swift sketch—Toni had it still—or no, she hadn't, she had
lost it, probably, but she had kept it for quite a long time !—
sketch of those two cabaret artistes, Rudi and Nadine, standing
for a moment in the pallid early morning of the Karntner-
Ring, just outside the " Kleiner Heisser Hund." . . . A

deserted corner in the rain; a garish advertisement of lights
set in a triangle of red glass on top of a pole, claimed attention
for the café; underneath it, Rudi stood, bending a lithe cane
between his hands, his eyes slanting to Nadine, cloaked, patient;
waiting, with her pretty stupid smile of eternal acceptance,
till he should be done with his pose . . . for he was showing
off to Val: " *Moi, je suis très sadiste!* " . . . The cane
pinged! He hoped he was sinister, instead of merely cheap,
cheap and sad. . . . Poor little Magyar dancer!—Val had
thrown an astounding air of dissipation into her few impressionistic pencil lines. . . .

Toni's humming changed from the aching defiance of the
Caprice, to an unexpected Tango: " Mangia, mangia, Papirusa ! " . . . That had been their tune, Rudi's and Nadine's.
What was Papirusa? . . . paprika?—flower of the vermilion
pepper, perhaps?

—A different Vienna. Anastasia had never been taken to
the Kleiner Heisser Hund. Franz must have gone, certainly;
and Uncle Louis, and Anatol; *roués* of the last generation.
But Toni *must* have seen Vienna! Of course she had! Breakfast in the Prater—— No, that had been in " Lilac-Time ";
and she had seen " Lilac-Time " in London . . . Again her
light, tuneless humming ran an accompaniment to her crowding
thoughts. . . . Schubert, Schubert's birthplace . . . she had
an etching on a post-card, showing that. Had Danny sent it?
Or just one of the " Vienna lot," when she was a child, to
encourage her to play the piano nicely? It was the Stephanskirche that Danny had sent on his post-card, with the arrogant
boast, scrawled right across its tall Gothic tower, that he and
Franz had been " bummelling " the night before . . . and he
had a headache, this morning!

. . . But that " set " of a drawing-room behind the snowy
window-sill might have been the Matriarch's drawing-room in
Holland Park, where Toni had lived as a child. . . . Paris,
Vienna, London—of course she knew the cities; and when
she did not know, she could piece together in sheer conviction:
Vienna and gaiety, officers in light blue uniforms, and all the
musical comedies that had ever come to Daly's: " Shall we

try, just we two?" . . . Danny had taken her to the "Count
of Luxembourg" straight after her father had died, because
she was fifteen, and could not bear the atmosphere of black
crêpe and woe and wailing any longer. . . . Perhaps Babs would
be younger when *her* father died? What tune would it set
itself to, in Babs' mind? What were the tunes now? Fox-
trots and fox-trots: "I'm a little bit fonder of you, than of
myself . . ." but next year, next month already, would be a
string of others to choose from. Fashions ran so quickly,
nowadays . . . Too hard to keep up. . . . She would have
to let go soon, quite soon, as soon as this dress should be out-of-
date. . . . What tunes?—But of course Giles was not going
to die, so she need not bother to say it with music. . . . "Say
it with Music"—that had been the same time as "Kalua"
. . . Colin and Betty coming down the lane in the snow. . . .
The snow *motif* again—— Inconsequent, that "Kalua"
should have been so essentially the right tune, with Elizabethan
costumes! That had been a good night . . . she and Giles
had danced together nearly all the time. Good? Well . . .
they had first met Loraine that night, and Loraine had gone
to Vienna with Giles. . . . And now Loraine had gone to
Vienna alone. . . . That tune which Giles was always whistling:
"Varasdin" he called it, but it had not come to London yet,
he had heard it in Vienna with Loraine. . . . Not a bad fox-trot;
but after "Kalua," she had liked "Parisian Pierrot" best of
them all. . . . And Toni crooned:

> "The Rue de la Paix
> Is under your sway . . ."

Toni of "Toni's"—it might have been Toni of the Rue de la
Paix to-night, where she sat, smoking one cigarette after another,
disconsolate and beautifully dressed. . . . Sauve Qui Peut!—
and no one to see her; Toni, singing alone in the big arm-chair
in her house in Italy.

Drifts of smoke . . . drifts of tune, and of old gay days. . . .
She thought of wine; of that dinner with Uncle Max, when he
had opened a special bottle of vintage Château Margaux for
her sole pleasure; and had promised her one day a glass of

Imperial Tokay. How she had thrilled when he had said she
had a palate! A royal compliment from Uncle Max, and a
glass of Imperial Tokay . . . but she had never had the two
together, as she had so longed to have. . . . She saw herself
sitting on a balcony overhanging the Danube, the sun flicking
sequins on the river; and opposite, the shining green domes
and spires of a royal palace. This must be Budapest. . . . Yet
she had never been to Budapest!—Never mind, someone had
been there, someone who belonged to Toni, wherever the
Danube touched . . . She was a child of the Danube's cities,
and she knew well how they would look.

—The Matriarch had played the "Blue Danube" . . .
while she and Maxine were trying to get Grandmère's debts
added up and squared; and they had not been able to resist;
they had danced; and Anastasia had been pleased to see them
dancing. You couldn't dance to the "Blue Danube" now, of
course; the rhythm was out-of-date. . . . Out-of-date, out-of-
date, how that word kept on coming round! "Mummy, is this
how you dressed when you were young?" And some future
day, no doubt: "Mummy, I suppose you waltzed to that old
'Blue Danube' thing, when you were young?" Eighteen-
ninety and nineteen-twenty would be all the same, to young
nineteen-forty. Then, and now!—they looked so much alike
when you came to balance them. This was "now," but it
would soon be "then." . . . And when, in London, she had
danced to "Parisian Pierrot," it had been "now." . . . And
before that, too: "I'm Runnin' Wild"; and before that:
"Limehouse Blues"; and earlier still: "Dardanella" and
"Whispering" and "Jicky" . . . but they had all seemed
like "now"—— The "Blue Danube" must have seemed
like "now," to Anastasia Rakonitz, telling the story of great
balls and banquets and lavish hospitality, to her grandchildren,
to whom it was all just a curious kaleidoscope of the past, more
attractive than history, because Grandmère, whom they could
see and touch, came into it.

. . . Always the great cities, and always hospitality; a
bounty of food and drink, open doors, and a genial clamour of
welcome to greet you at the very threshold. These came into

all the stories. These marched in triumphant beat from generation to generation, linking them. They were in the very spirit
of the Rakonitz tradition; not a passing fashion, not a thing
you could not keep up with, but a custom that went back and
back. But if Rakonitz hospitality in the capitals of Europe
meant entertaining, meant all the splendour of glass and china
and silver, all the profusion of rare food and mellow wine, yet
hospitality when brought down to its rock foundation, when
carried into the country and on to the land, meant not so much
entertainment, as sanctuary. You came to be " entertained "
by Rakonitz when you were at the top of your fortunes; you
would come to sanctuary when it was shelter you needed, a place
to sleep in, and the plain nourishment of everyday food. Perhaps
this was a truer and more ancient meaning of the word. Toni was
only partly able to define thus her sense of a personal fulfilment,
after all, which lay, instead of the expected hollowness, beneath
her disappointment at having to drop out from the cities.

She had a fanciful vision of a figure standing in the flap
doorway of a tent, and holding out hands in greeting.

The development of splendour within rooms, loaded tables,
glittering candelabra, strange expensive savours, had only
happened later. Yet all these, too, she had loved. . . . It was
only because chance had taken her away from them, that she
would unconsciously be forced to complete the wide sweep of
the circle. Good-bye, then, to dancing beautifully and dressing
beautifully and being " in the movement "; the movement of
London and Paris and Vienna and Budapest; Rome, perhaps,
but not so much, because Rome, like Madrid, was in a kingdom
which kicked exuberantly into the sea from the very edge of
Europe; they were not Central Europe, where Toni felt at
home. But she would have to learn to be at home here; to
keep open house, as her ancestors had done. At least there was
room enough, at Casa Vecchia; and a vineyard to recall the
mother of her great-great-grandmother, who had lived in the
country too, in Hungary. Lavish hospitality and good manners
under stress—these were simple things, she could not bungle
them. For she had brought nothing, or so it seemed to her,
no gain of experience or wisdom that was of any use to anybody,

out of more than thirty years of life in the cities . . . She had
been tenacious where she should have let go, she had laughed
where she should have been serious, she had only looked ahead
to see what never happened ; her love, whenever it came, was
always too late to shield away harm ; her loyalties had been
those of a fool ; her betrayals . . . ah, Toni dared not think
of them ! And her values were now rattling about loosely as
dice in a box—she could not tell, if she turned them out, what
would lie uppermost.

. . . " Giles," whispered Toni, answering fear and boredom
and self-reproach.

What would Toni find in Italy, to replace her textures and
sheens ? Homey, sun-hot things : the breadiness of bread ;
the rasp and happy-go-lucky treatment of daily wine in its
flask, compared with the rare and distinguished wines that the
Uncles used to collect in their cellars ; the hot midday beams
slipping over firm satiny cheeks of huge onions, mauve and
silver and gold, that dangled in bunches above the olive-wood
pile ; small sweet figs on the trees, free for the gathering ; the
three Italian children, Val's servants, singing while they stood
round the open-air wash-tub under its lattice of vine ; the
pungently delicious, aromatic scent of a lemon leaf, snatched
from the tree in passing, and crushed between your fingers ;
and tangerines that were still on their leafy stems when brought
in for dessert ; the warm silkiness of Mac's coat, after he had
been bathed and dried in the sun ; Aunt Elsa's spicy cooking,
a treat for festivals ; Babs' arms, deepening through all the
shades of golden-brown, as the summer went on. . . . Mentally
Toni held this sun-baked collection against her memories of
Uncle Felix's famous collection of little objects of crystal,
amber, and jade. Anastasia had inherited it, after his death ;
and so it had gradually disintegrated. She had sold some of the
things, and some she had given away, and a good many had
been lost. But Toni could recall especially how an enthralled
child, herself at eight, had been allowed to touch with careful
finger-tips an ivory ball, an *ojimé*, as used by the Chinese to
slip above their belts, at one end of a strip of silk, to balance
the pouch at the other end. An exquisite picture encrusted

the ivory; a marvel, to have been wrought in so many rare fabrics and metals on its tiny diameter: mother-of-pearl, ebony, green coral, silk and painting and lacquer.—To hang a mere onion beside this? And though she had always recoiled with a queer horror from Uncle Felix's most valued snuff-box, with coarse hairs shut in its very crystal, yet she had loved that other snuff-box of scarlet enamel and gems, with a tiny feathered bird that sprang through the lid and sang a song; and his lump of carved red amber that felt sticky to your lips, instead of polished, as a child might have expected. She had not thought of Uncle Felix's curios for years, but they belonged to the cities of merchants and connoisseurs and artists . . . so she remembered them now, these miniature perfect adjuncts of culture and civilisation, and of a family who could discriminate; who thought nothing fine enough but the best and finest. But the treasure-house was shuttered, and the treasures had rolled away into dim corners, and into the keeping of strangers. . . . " I wish I knew what had happened to that ivory *ojimé*," thought Toni, meaning, in a momentary lapse from grace, that she wished she had it here, for Babs to play with. . . . For Toni to play with.

The remnants of the family, one by one obliged to give up their big houses, had since had unwelcome experiences of what was second-rate and dingy; they had scattered and rebelled, intermarried with aliens, broken the rules, and forgotten the glory . . . And they were beginning to feel the need again, of a big house; one, at least, where they could meet, hear news of each other, return after journeyings, recuperate after a time of bad luck; a house to be ill in, if necessary; or a house in which to grow old. Even, most wanted of all, a house where you could first rush to proclaim good fortune, and find someone who cared to hear of it. Oh, nothing symbolical! Not a spiritual refuge, or any such portentous significance—but just solidly a house, a big house, Toni's house . . .

—Uncle Ludo's voice was heard outside in the hall: "Toni!" He came in, rubbing his hands. "Gee!" he exclaimed. "You've got the glad rags on to-night! I've been looking round," he continued. " Not much hustle about this little one-horse burg of yours ! We must really get a move on. I brought up a bottle of that Italian stuff, Vermouth, from the Bar San Goffredo. They've put it down to your account. Is that all right ? For to tell you the truth, Toni," said prodigal Uncle Ludo, " I haven't got more than five lire on me at the moment."

. . . Rosewood, tortoiseshell, indigo, hides, and gold chains ?
—No, certainly he had brought none of these back with him.

But for the next half-hour he was discussing with terrific gusto as to whether he should erect tennis-courts first, at San Goffredo ; eight to begin with ; or whether a golf course would be more attractive to the Riviera visitors whom he meant to hypnotise in large swarms to this prospective super-Monte Carlo of his creation.

Every now and then he referred back to the big towns of South America : Rio de Janeiro, Santiago, Buenos Aires, dwelling lovingly on the syllables as though they had meant much to him. " You, too ? " thought Toni. . . . For he did not describe the plains nor the mountains ; Uncle Ludo was no child of Nature. San Goffredo, it seemed, by the time he had done with it, and by the time all the millionaires had done with it, whose capital he was confidently flourishing as though it were his own, was to be architecturally and socially a sort of blend of Buenos Aires, Rio de Janeiro, and Monte Carlo. Why not ?

. . . " You've gotta have a drink with me, Toni," concluded Uncle Ludo, feeling generous, and thirsty after his long mono-logue ; " Yep, and out of this very bottle. I like standing my pretty niece a drink ; betcherlife I do ! "

He rang a bell for Stefania, and told her to bring glasses, and lemons, and soda-water, and a bottle of Angostura, if that were in the house. " Make her understand, will you, Toni ? It's a Lima Lifter I wanta mix.

—" And now," a ter he had enjoyed himself thorough y over the ingredients of a Lima Lifter, " we'll drink to the success of—San Goffredo in Ten Years' Time ! For mind you, young Toni, *you're* coming in on the ground-floor, you and your husband. *You're* going to have preference shares."

But just then, interrupting him, Babs ran crying into the room, followed by Aunt Elsa, vociferously protesting . . .

" I want Loraine," wept Babs. " She hasn't gone away. I won't have her gone away. *She's* a hateful ! " with a frantic kick in the direction of Aunt Elsa. " She's an old hateful ! I want Loraine."

" But quite quite suddenly she seem to remember," Aunt Elsa explained, in great distress, but indignant too. " Not a vord about Loraine until now, and she as happy as anysing helping Susie to unpack ; and zen suddenly, but suddenly, all zis ! One of ze servants must have said that Loraine had been here, and she hears ze name, forgets again, remembers again. She was just marching out of ze room, as trotzig as she can be, to find her, when I call her back, and tell her Loraine has gone away—— And you see ? "

Toni, surveying her prostrate child, was not far from tears herself. " Babs, darling——" But was there no end to reminder of how she had neglected these beloved three of hers, in past days ? She saw, stretching in front of her, a long slow era of patience ; yet, if the child now banging desperate heels upon the unyielding floor, had grown up normally, know-ing her mother first and before anyone else, a word from Toni would have held the requisite magic to quell trouble. She felt shamed, in front of Aunt Elsa, mother of four obedient and worshipping girls, by her own lack of power : " Babs, darling——"

Uncle Ludo put down his untouched glass, and tried the time-worn, avuncular method of calming a frenzied child by picking her up and swinging her high above his head. " There ! Gosh ! Who's going up to the ceiling ? My word ! " Babs lunged out, more furiously than ever, for his face. She managed to get hold of a portion of it, and squeeze it. Hastily he dumped her on the floor again. Babs' imitation of an enraged centipede, in her downward flight, caught his Lima Lifter, swept it over, and smashed the glass.

" Loraine ! " she wailed, subsiding from sheer noise into

pathos. And " Damn ! " exclaimed Uncle Ludo. " Now I'll
have to mix it all over again ! "

" You vill do no such thing, not while I am here," cried Aunt
Elsa, catching sight of the festive preparations of bottle, syphon,
and glasses. Ludovic still belonged to the generation whom she
had bossed. The generation directly after hers, Wanda and
Truda and Haidée and Melanie, had all been partially intimidated by the tyrant side of Aunt Elsa. Toni and Toni's contemporaries, she had learnt to leave alone ; but Babs again—
she would stand no naughtiness from Babs . . . or so she had
thought hitherto ! But now Ludovic was fair prey for her
rusted little needle-claws ; and Aunt Elsa, who had cried with
hysterical ecstasy at his reappearance among the living, and
cried with grief that the miracle had happened too late for
" zat poor Anastasia " to clasp him in her arms, Aunt Elsa now
began to enjoy herself in the good old way :

" But I must beg of you, Ludo, not here to bring your bad
habits. Goodness knows where you have been, and what you
have learnt, and ze first sing zat happens when I am not
zere—— And you with such a yellow face ! But it is poison,
I tell you, that stuff ; poison for the liver ! A little wine at
table now and then, I allow it. But zis drinking in between
meals, no ! "

—" Want Loraine ! " wailed Babs.

" Say, Aunt," Ludo began, his patience obviously on a very
short tether, " you jes' do'know what you're talking about.
You're talking through your hat. No one in their senses could
call a simple Lima Lifter, strong drink. Have one yourself ? "
He made an attempt to recover geniality.

" I am not talking through my hat, no ! " Aunt Elsa's
nerves had been upset by her rough-and-tumble with Babs ;
and also she felt the power of dominion returning with every
second. " And you will be polite to me, Ludo, while you are
a guest in this house, you who could not bozzer even to write a
letter, not once, for your poor mother's birthday though you
could not forget it as it vos the same day as your own, and zat
you would take good care to remember ! "

" Oh, sakes alive, yes, I'll be polite ! I *am* polite. I was being polite to Toni. I can't ask a lady to have a drink on me, and then pour it away."

"And whose drink vos it? That is vot I want to know. And you playing so grand the host, while I expect poor Toni has to pay for the bottle, isn't it?"

"Mind your own business!" shouted Uncle Ludo, who, if he had been yellow before, was certainly purple now.

Toni had forgotten the disconcerting Rakonitz habit of being incredibly rude from an affectionate heart. Bewildered by the hubbub—"Want Loraine!" wailed Babs—she could not see any means of restoring peace. Giles, strolling in at that moment, seemed to her an aggravation of disaster. He could not be of any possible use; and she hated him to see and to hear her family in the full hullabulloo of strife and enjoyment. . . . For, to her surprise, she found herself classifying Babs with Aunt Elsa and Uncle Ludo . . . They were all just Rakonitzes, stubborn and obstreperous.

Giles had overheard Aunt Elsa's last remark. It was an easy scene to understand, even for one who had walked from outside into the middle of it; the properties were so obvious: Toni's distress; the various bottles and cocktail glasses on the table; Babs, a squirming blot of red stockinette on the floor, sobbing for Loraine . . .

—"So I've been caught, have I?" he remarked, with a nod towards the bottle of Angostura. "Thought I'd hidden it away safely. Well, I'm glad you're in for it too, Rakonitz! If you weren't here, I'd have to face Aunt Elsa alone."

And that restored Uncle Ludo from isolation and irritable discomfort, to the pleasant security of one who confers a boon upon the house by his presence. Goddard seemed genuinely glad to have another man at his back; and no wonder, with all these women fussing! Men must have their drinks—— Men stood together—— Two of us—— Well . . . gotta remain good-humoured, of course!—He winked at Giles; and, with a sideways nod at Aunt Elsa, indicated that the old lady, bless her, was a bit upset, and needed placating. They could have their drinks afterwards . . .

" Oh, I've been getting it in the neck, all right," he remarked.
" Toni and I were just sitting down to our cocktails. Funny
thing, you know, I remember Aunt Elsa in old days, began to
get lively directly she heard a bottle of fizz being carried up the
road, before it was even in sight."

" But shame yourself, Ludo ! " cried Aunt Elsa. . . . The
tiniest dimple began to show, just under her left eye.

" Right ! " said Giles. " I *thought* she was a good fellow.
We'll all have cocktails, and Aunt Elsa shall have two. . . .
We'll drink health to the house. We haven't done it yet, and
it's rather an important ceremony. Babs, being our eldest
daughter, shall join us, representing the other two," he added.
. . . And the portentous roll of his voice caught Babs' ear, as
he had meant it should . . . so that she stopped crying, and
sat up, and looked, first at him and then at the preparations for
cocktails, with the beginnings of an awed and fearful joy ; for
Babs, like Toni, adored the combination of ritual and festivity ;
and in her small soul, the words " Drink health to the house,"
started a tremble of excitement ; although she did not quite
know what they meant, yet she gathered she was to take part
in something important. . . .

Babs forgot Loraine !

Loraine ! . . . Giles could not bear to see the hurt in Toni's
eyes, when her own baby had cried for Loraine. He did not
think that a cocktail would agree with Babs ; but he did think
that the continuation of passion and woe would agree with her
still less.

The hiss of soda, the clinking of ice, the swish of lemon
round the squeezer, the gurgle of liquid through the neck of
its bottle . . . Toni was reminded of the many times she had
heard the tuning-up of such an orchestra in London, during
her good time. The cut and distinction of the dress she wore,
helped the illusion. But Giles was puzzling her. . . . Was it
just luck that Giles had hit on the right things to say and do,
to subdue the wrangling ?

" But Giles," cried Aunt Elsa, " it is not right for you eizer,
no, zis drinking ! The doctor said a little good wine with meals,
not too much ; but drinks, no ! "

" I know he did, and I know it isn't. But we'll throw what's left in the bottles out of the window, after this one bout. No, we won't, we'll chuck 'em up on the roof and hear them smash, like on the prow of a boat that's going to be launched ! "

Babs began to jig up and down. This was the sort of reckless spirit that she approved of. Her father appeared to her as a most excellent man, who actually of his own accord suggested breaking things, instead of telling her to be careful not to do so.

—" And then, you see," Giles continued, handing Aunt Elsa a very full glass, and kissing her directly afterwards, so that she nearly spilt it—but Aunt Elsa loved being kissed by handsome young men ; she melted, and sparkled, and called him a " nottee boy "—" we'll be out of temptation ! . . . You won't mind chucking away the rest of the stuff, will you, Rakonitz ? " Giles asked, in an undertone.

Uncle Ludo was hypnotically convinced, now, that he was one of the hosts of the occasion ; that the Vermouth was provided by his generosity ; and that his further generosity would be willing to associate itself with Giles, and " humour the women " in their silliness.

Uncle Ludo was in a very good temper. So was Aunt Elsa. So was Babs . . .

CHAPTER VI

IT was two years later, and Val had returned from China. Leaving her husband and very small son behind in London, she came out to San Goffredo to see how Toni and Giles were faring, and Aunt Elsa, and Susie, and the three children, and Uncle Ludo. She found Little Klaus there, too, recuperating after nervous, financial, and matrimonial break-downs; but she just missed Wanda, who had stayed four months, and then been reconciled again to Aunt Berthe, with whom she was living in Paris. Next week, Toni expected Moya Moss; and then Little Klaus would have to go home, because Moya was his wife, and they could not get on together. It was unfortunate that when, in an explosive scene, they each threatened to leave the other, they both determined to rush out to Casa Vecchia . . .

"Isn't Toni ever coming? What on earth is she doing?" demanded Val, impatiently. It was their first burst of hot sunshine since her arrival, three days ago; and Giles was eager to show her his cultivated domain, now a beautiful, blue-green nightmare of artichokes. But Toni had kept them waiting for several minutes. "What *is* she doing?" Val said again, hold-ing Toni's husband responsible; "and who's she talking to? He looks like a huckster of Turkish Delight."

"Carpets, I believe," said Giles; "you're not far wrong, Val. He's an old Armenian on his beam-ends; been tramping for three days now, as far as I can gather. I've given him a lot of shoes and socks and macaroni and letters of introduction to the English consul at Genoa, and other really useful things. I thought he'd started, but it seems that Toni's doing the social act. Toni!" he called out. "We're waiting!"

"I'm just this minute coming," floated back a plausible answer from the terrace . . . and Giles and Val continued to fret at the foot of the garden path. Toni's voice sounded so confident that she was indeed just that moment coming !

Val remarked : " She grows more like her blooming grand-mother every day. Yes—— Listen ! " . . . For Toni, with her undoubtedly inherited gift of seductive geniality, which acknowledged no barriers of time, space, nor class, could be heard telling the Armenian beggar how Eugène, the brother of Sigismund, who was the father of Anastasia, who was the mother of Bertrand, who was the father of Toni, had left Vienna and gone out to Constantinople, in his youth, and had traded in mother-of-pearl and semi-precious stones ; and had settled there, and married Chryse Stefanopoulos. . . . " I wonder if you ever met him, if you were a merchant too ? In the bazaars, perhaps ? " . . . And here followed one or two confidential family anecdotes ; to which the Armenian politely responded with some rather more gruesome and less engaging family anecdotes of his own : " Turkish officer him wanta my wife, and so . . ." The talk rippled on.

Val swore softly. " Toni ! " she called out again.

" Coming," replied Toni.

Giles laughed.

" We needn't wait," he said. " She'll follow on presently, when she and her pal have had their pow-wow."

The sun had shouldered the heaviest rain-clouds to the right and left, and was spattering the sea with silver. Down all the hills the water was pouring and pouring itself away. The leaves of the olive trees stirred into a soft shine ; and from terrace to terrace and over the ranges, light ran with swift heels. Val wanted to enjoy the drenched colours and broken scents that the sun had released all about her : mimosa in the garden ; hyacinths and narcissi growing wild in the grass beyond the encircling wall. But Giles, striding along by her side, disdained her facile artistry, and talked of vines, peaches, and principally artichokes, with the expert knowledge of a professional horticulturist ; and a proud enthusiasm that it was difficult to believe could be aroused by these monotonous slopes of spiky plants, with their folded purplish buds. He amazed Val by telling her that he had cleared three hundred pounds last year, in sheer profit; and, unless a bad frost came along, expected to double it this year. As for his future plans, they might have been made by a man with a leisurely thirty or forty years of life stretching in front of him, in which to watch them slowly grow to maturity. He was going to plant young lemon trees along a south wall; and, next autumn, row upon row of early peas: " —In a space over there—d'you see? I'm going to have the rough ground cleared and prepared for them ";—also groves of asparagus fern, and more mimosa, for all of which there were ready sales in the flower, fruit and vegetable market at Genoa:

" Agriculture's easy out here, you know, from the business point of view, although the climate's the devil—about five months of drought, and then a week of tropical rains that wash the whole hill to nix, with a mad wind through the mountain gap in the north, to finish off what might be left. But as for the actual trading, you join a Society, get a number, and bung whatever you've got into your own numbered baskets on the train every day; then you wait for the cheque to come back. The Society does the rest."

Val suggested: " You lose some of the actual excitement of competition in trading, don't you, that way? "—But she remembered, as she spoke, that for Giles such a loss would be an advantage. She was suddenly conscious of an immense respect for Toni's husband, who was contriving to live as keenly as though every day were his first; a job far more difficult than to follow the philosopher's precept, and live as meritoriously as though every day were his last.

" The vines are really just for fun. There's not much profit to be made out of them in this part of the country; but we enjoy our yearly vintage; and in about 1940 it ought to be quite drinkable. Italians, you know, tell you their wine is ' very old!—it has been nearly six months in bottle ! ' "

. . . Val was thinking of that episode which had become legendary in their family; how the mother of their great-great-grandmother, Babette Weinberg, whose very name meant " wine on a hill," had invited all the peasants who sold her grapes at the fair in Pressburg, to dine and sleep in her house,

saving them the expense of going to an inn ; and how, entertaining them to dinner, she had carelessly spilt a glassful of wine
in a red stain across the cloth, so that they might not feel uncomfortable if they should clumsily spill anything on the cloth,
afterwards. It was a memory which might naturally spring to
her mind, looking at Toni's Italian vineyards, but she wondered
if she were dreaming, when Giles remarked, interrupting her
musings : " Toni does so enjoy being mistress of the vintage,
every year ; and she carries it off well, too. I like watching her
at it. In a way it seems as much her job to entertain and make
people feel cheery and bucked with themselves, as designing
dresses. D'you know what I mean, Val ? " Val nodded. " For
instance, when we gave a big dinner to all the peasants who'd
been picking our grapes, Toni began by chucking over a glass of
wine herself, right across the table-cloth, as if by accident, of
course, so that none of them should feel uncomfortable if they
spilt anything afterwards—which they did, buckets of it ! But
I thought it rather specially charming of her."

Val's eyes narrowed. She looked at Giles questioningly. . . .
Then she suppressed a chuckle. " *Very* charming," she assented,
as seriously as she could. She would not give Toni away ! . . .
Toni was wonderful, really wonderful !

" She's looking radiantly well and happy. I was rather
surprised, in a way, that all this mixed crowd always in the
house, doesn't worry her to a shadow."

Giles was examining with some intentness an alien tribe
that had infested a branch of one of his peach trees.

" Oh, I expect they all just get on well together," he said,
casually.

" Quite ! " . . . there was a hint of dryness in Val's tone.
" But I happen to know my family Rakonitz, and I've been
shut up in the house for three days already . . . They all
come to you, don't they, over everything? And Toni hasn't
noticed ? "

Giles laughed, and yielded the point :

" I think they do prefer to come to a man, you know, when
there's one handy."

" Tribal instinct. Don't you—hate it ? "

He contemplated the question, grave for a moment :

" Not too much. It's what you—no, you're a heathen !—but it's what your ancestors would have called my Day of Atonement, I suppose. . . . Did you see any decent shows while you were in London, Val? Anything that wasn't Colin's, I mean? It must be infernally difficult to find a West-End play that isn't Colin's, since ' She Burnt Her Boats.' "

—And Val found herself talking away very fast about revues, and popular names in the theatrical world, and even answering his lead about Colin's fantastic successes. It struck her, through all her vivid and racy descriptions, that she did not in the least know what Giles was thinking about? . . . Was it that his own dreams of valiant and glittering achievement had fallen and got lost in the crevice between " having a good time," and " being very careful " ?

. . . Presently she, too, dropped into silence. The blaze of the sun, beating down on to the rain-soaked hill, had induced a sort of drowsiness. . . . Was Giles really keen on growing endless and eternal rows of artichokes, and on playing patriarch to the Rakonitz family?

—" Glorious career, isn't it? " he said, as though she had spoken aloud. She glanced at him quickly, but his face was quite expressionless, and she could not tell whether he meant his own or Colin's.

But she felt a curious desire to cry . . . and cry . . .

In a whirl of blue-black hair, Terry came flopping from terrace to terrace, subsiding with a grunt at Giles' feet.

" Eternal fidelity of a dog," murmured Val. " He was *mine*, once. On the whole, he was more pleased to see the Armenian carpet-pedlar, than me. I expect the fancy kit reminded him of Loraine. . . . She always dressed to represent Trouble-in-the-Balkans. Do you ever hear from Loraine? "

" We get a temperamental post card, now and then. The last was from Prague."

" Ah—' I'm a nomad ! ' " . . . But Val could not help a pang for stay-at-home Loraine, so tired of her picturesque gipsy disguise.

"Did you know that Toni wanted her to come and live with us? I had to scotch that, of course."

"How?" curiously. "I've often wondered."

"Oh, I told her I mustn't be overexcited, or I'd get a hæmorrhage and die, and then she'd be responsible. Taking a mean advantage, wasn't it? But I had to do something drastic. . . . Toni's a bit mad on this idea of family loyalty."

Val said, reminiscently: "Yes, she always was. It was over a romantic family debt that she did in her affair with the one man she's ever loved."

"Isn't that an amazing coincidence?" mocked another man . . . and gave himself up to hearty enjoyment of Val's confusion. When he thought she had suffered enough, he said: "But you should have seen Toni's face when she realised that I'd hit below the belt! Toni's got a marvellous illusion about public-school Englishmen, and the things they don't do, and all that. . . . Wonder where she's picked it up? That sort of fellow must be no end of a tick!"

"If he exists at all," said Val.

"He doesn't, of course. . . . Toni's much more of a decent Englishman, than I am. It really is *not* done, Val, to exploit a hæmorrhage to get your own way, is it?"

"How are you, on the whole, Giles, now?"

"It's so nice of you to ask," he replied, lightly; "I believe I'm a shade better, on an average. I've got a bet with Jimmy, that I'll manage to survive his natural death, after all. If I *can* manage to hang on, loudly creaking, the kids will come into all the money, you know; but it's only about one chance in a hundred that I live longest. Dear old Jimmy is so infernally wiry! And it's in the terms of the bet that he doesn't undermine his constitution by hard drinking or anything of that sort."

Val stopped squarely in her walk: "Look here, Giles, you're not telling me that you and Jimmy have really got a bet on, over this?"

"An even tenner. An artichoke tenner, on my side! It's not got to come out of the income that Jimmy allows us."

And Val, failing for once to catch from him a responsive

gleam of irony, realised, as she had done over and over again with Richard and with her own husband, that men will not joke, cannot joke, about their drinks and smokes, nor about a bet . . .

Giles went on : " It does give a crack of excitement to every day, when you don't know whether you're going to survive or not : ' The kidney beans are cooked too hard ! Will Giles lose his temper and die of it ? '—that sort of thing ! Oh, I'll win out on old Jimmy, yet.—Hell ! " he broke off. " Look at those blasted fools walking over there ! Can't they see it's planted ? " He went off in the direction of " those blasted fools " ; but even though they had to be hastily prevented from trampling down his beans, Val noticed that he did not run, nor shout out angry directions. . . . It might mean a hundred-and-twenty-thousand pounds to his children—and to himself a tenner, not to get excited.

And while she was watching him, Little Klaus came up and joined her.

" I've been taking Terry for a walk, but he ran away. I c-called him, but he didn't come. Terry isn't very obedient. I don't think he's been well trained. I'm n-not sure, really, if I ought to take the dogs for walks. Last week, Mac k-killed a hen, while he was with me."

" It *would* be," thought Val ; but omitted to say it. And yet Little Klaus had received the Croix-de-Guerre, for efficient organisation of a town under heavy firing, during the War.

" Where's Goddard ? Oh, d-down there ! I like Goddard, don't you, Val ? He's an awfully decent fellow. He's been f-frightfully understanding when I talked to him about M-Moya and me. I'm not at all sure, Val, that cousins ought to marry. There was Aunt Anastasia, you know, she m-married her first cousin, and look at all the trouble there's been."

" But Moya isn't your *first* cousin," Val reminded him, consolingly. " About your sixteenth, nine times removed. There—may have been other things ? "

" There were lots of other things. I've t-told Giles all about them. . . . But I'm glad T-Toni didn't marry her cousin ; and I'm glad you didn't, Val."

" There weren't any I'd have married with a pitchfork——"
Val began, and then checked herself hastily.

Little Klaus rambled on, in his usual punctilious fashion :
" And b-by the way, Val, I haven't congratulated you yet on
having a son. You m-must have thought it terribly rude of
me. It *is* a son, isn't it ? What is his name ? "

" Giles," said Val, rather to Little Klaus's surprise. Though
he was too polite to say so, he seemed to find a slight irregu-
larity in Val thus naming her son after Toni's husband. " But
we always call him Hong-Kong Bill," Val went on.

" That s-sounds like a champion breed, or a prize-fighter ! "

" I hope he'll be both. Has Toni's visitor gone yet ? "

" Do you mean that queer old Armenian, who came up to
b-beg in the rain this morning ? No, Toni's still entertaining
him. I think they're talking about mutual friends . . ."
Little Klaus's soft apologetic voice betrayed no wonder as he
stated this fact. " But it *does* seem funny, doesn't it, that a
c-civilised creature like Toni should have m-married a farmer ? "

. . . Val was hardly attending to him. She repeated,
absently : " Yes, it does seem funny that Toni should have
married a soldier. . . ." Her eyes were still on Giles, walking
towards them again, across his field, and not too quickly up
the slopes.

VIRAGO MODERN CLASSICS

The first Virago Modern Classic, *Frost in May* by Antonia White, was published in 1978. It launched a list dedicated to the celebration of women writers and to the rediscovery and reprinting of their works. Its aim was, and is, to demonstrate the existence of a female tradition in fiction which is both enriching and enjoyable. The Leavisite notion of the 'Great Tradition', and the narrow, academic definition of a 'classic', has meant the neglect of a large number of interesting secondary works of fiction. In calling the series 'Modern Classics' we do not necessarily mean 'great' — although this is often the case. Published with new critical and biographical introductions, books are chosen for many reasons: sometimes for their importance in literary history; sometimes because they illuminate particular aspects of womens' lives, both personal and public. They may be classics of comedy or storytelling; their interest can be historical, feminist, political or literary.

Initially the Virago Modern Classics concentrated on English novels and short stories published in the early decades of this century. As the series has grown it has broadened to include works of fiction from different centuries, different countries, cultures and literary traditions. In 1984 the Victorian Classics were launched; there are separate lists of Irish, Scottish, European, American, Australian and other English-speaking countries; there are books written by Black women, by Catholic and Jewish women, and a few relevant novels by men. There is, too, a companion series of Non-Fiction Classics constituting biography, autobiography, travel, journalism, essays, poetry, letters and diaries.

By the end of 1988 over 300 titles will have been published in these two series, many of which have been suggested by our readers.